ROCKETS' RED GLARE

Gregory S. Dinallo

ST. MARTIN'S PRESS / NEW YORK

ROCKETS' RED GLARE

Copyright © 1988 by Greg Dinallo.

Library of Congress Catalog Card Number: 87-27949

ISBN: 0-312-91288-9   Can. ISBN: 0-312-91289-7

Printed in the United States of America

St. Martin's Press hardcover edition published 1988
First St. Martin's Press mass market edition/December 1988

10 9 8 7 6 5 4 3 2 1

For my parents who never knew—who by word and deed taught me to believe in human potential and hard work. And for my wife and son whose tolerance and love keep those beliefs alive.

Prologue

It had almost come undone once—almost. The documents declared 124,000 tons of offshore crude shipped on the *VLCC Kira* and pumped off at Puerto Sandino, Nicaragua. But neither the cargo nor the destination was important. The numbers were what caught Dick Nugent's eye that June day in 1981. Dick had a habit of making associations to remember them. He had once seen the *Kira*'s capacity listed at 125,000 tons, and it stuck—$125 per hour was what he paid his analyst.

Why hadn't the supertanker been fully emptied? he wondered. Was the *Kira*'s captain running a little side business? Or hadn't her compartments been filled to capacity in the first place? Why the one-thousand-ton discrepancy? Why 124 and not 125?

As cost effectiveness coordinator for Churchco Industries, a mega-conglomerate based in Houston, Texas, Dick was well-paid to notice such things. He had been putting in long days to finish a comprehensive evaluation of Churchco's Petroleum Division. The tonnage discrepancy on the *Kira* was one of many items he had uncovered, and he attached no special significance to it.

The next day, Dick filed a detailed thirty-six-page report of his findings, and took the late morning flight to Miami, where he would begin a similar evaluation of Churchco's Medical Products Division.

The following morning, Churchco's founder and board chairman, Theodor Churcher, in his ongoing role as a consultant to the Soviet Union's Industrial Ministry, departed for Moscow on a CC-10-60, the long-range jetliner manufactured by Churchco Aero-Space.

At fifty-seven, Churcher still had the lean physique of a long-distance runner. His soft graying hair complimented his chiseled profile. He appeared to be moving forward even in repose.

Four hours into the flight, thirty-nine thousand feet above the southern tip of Lake Erie, his incisive, green-speckled eyes darted across Nugent's report. Churcher paused to down the last swallow of a Gibson, then resumed reading and nearly gagged in disbelief when he got to the item on page twenty-three—the item concerning the *Kira*.

That evening in Moscow, Churcher dined with an old friend in an apartment on Proyezd Serova Street, just off Dzerzhinsky Square at the hub of the capital city's central ring. The antique-filled duplex had a dark, gloomy feeling, and lacked a woman's touch.

Its occupant, Soviet Minister of Culture Aleksei Deschin, was a large, solid man with dark eyes set deep behind high Slavic cheekbones. He had the look of the Bolsheviks flanking Lenin in the Socialist realism murals that decorate government buildings—one who had aged well, handsomely. And, indeed, women were attracted to him, and he to them; but long ago *the* woman had slipped away, and he'd since lived alone with the emptiness.

Churcher eased the cork from a bottle of '61 Margaux he'd brought his host, and solemnly filled two goblets with the premier cru.

"I have an internal problem, Aleksei," Churcher said somewhat suddenly.

Deschin swirled the bordeaux to the rim of his glass, inhaled the rising bouquet, and smiled. "If this doesn't settle your stomach, Theo," he said, "nothing can." Though heavily accented, Deschin's English was very fluent.

Churcher smiled despite his concern. Then he removed page twenty-three of Nugent's report from his pocket, and handed it to Deschin. The key passages concerning the *Kira* and the tonnage discrepancy had been bracketed in red.

Deschin slipped on his glasses and began reading.

Churcher stood and, taking his wine with him, crossed the

room that had once known grandeur. He stopped at the large bay window, and looked out at the rain pelting the Square.

The intimidating statue of Felix Dzerzhinsky—the Polish expatriate who founded the Cheka Secret Police, forerunner of the KGB—stood at its center, the rain-slicked bronze glistening in the darkness.

Deschin finished reading, and quietly joined Churcher at the window. The cultural minister's eyes had taken on the spooky nervousness of electroshock patients.

For a few moments, neither spoke.

Finally, Deschin said, "You have a very bright person in your employ, Theodor." He breathed deeply and added, "Very, very perceptive."

"The best," Churcher said, still looking out the window. "Harvard MBA. Top of his class. Smart as a whip. I have big plans for him."

Deschin nodded and set his glass on the sill. He carefully refolded the red-bracketed page on the original crease lines, then pinched a corner between thumb and forefinger, as if the square of paper was contaminated, and held it up to Churcher.

"Who else has seen this?" Deschin asked softly.

Churcher shook no slowly. "No one," he said. "He reports directly to me."

Deschin thought for a moment, then lifted his glass and drained it. He swallowed hard—forebodingly. He said nothing.

Churcher stared at him in silent appeal.

Still, Deschin said nothing.

A profound sadness came over Churcher as he lowered his eyes, acquiescing.

The two men turned to the window and looked across Dzerzhinsky Square at the rain-darkened granite monolith that housed KGB Headquarters.

The following evening, Dick Nugent returned to his room in the Americana Hotel in Miami.

Nugent was tiny and precise, with thinning hair above black-framed glasses. He knew he personified the nitpicker he was, and kept an off-center view of life's minutiae to himself. Dick was a loner and had no need to be liked, but craved professional esteem. As corporate whistle-blower, he enjoyed enviable autonomy, and had spent the day wielding it ruthlessly.

He entered the room carrying a bulging attaché and a bag containing a pint of Häagen-Dazs. Odd name for an ice cream, he always thought. The *sound* of it was pure concentration camp—Auschwitz, Bergen-Belsen, Häagen-Dazs. He envisioned Mel Brooks screaming, "No! No, help!! They're sending me to Häagen-Dazs!"

He chuckled, tossed the bag and the attaché on the bed, and emptied the contents of his pockets onto a table. It held an assortment of file folders, Churchco letterheads, and the portable Olivetti that traveled with him. He stripped to his shorts to shower, and heard the door to the balcony sliding open behind him.

A square, calm man—who, he thought, bore a remarkable resemblance to his Uncle Elliott—slipped into the room and leveled a 9mm Kalishnikov at Nugent's forehead when he turned.

"Do as you're told," the man said in perfect English tinged with a slight Russian accent. "Do you understand?"

Nugent nodded emphatically. His hands trembled as he raised them.

"Wallet, traveler's checks over there," he stammered, pointing to the table.

The man shook his head. He gestured for Nugent to lower his hands, then slipped a sheet of Churchco stationery from the stack onto the table. Richard D. Nugent, Cost Effectiveness Coordinator, was imprinted beneath the corporate logotype on the letterhead.

"Sign your name, please," the man said calmly.

"My name?" Nugent asked puzzled, his voice cracking. "I—I don't get it. I mean—"

"Near the bottom," the man interrupted gently. "Like a letter."

Nugent was paralyzed by fear and confusion, the words sticking in his throat. "One of my—my reports get you canned or something?" he finally asked.

The man nodded, picking up on Nugent's lead. "Haven't worked in six months," he replied. "This will change that."

He pressed the Kalishnikov close to Nugent's ear, and flicked a ballpoint pen across the table with the forefinger of his other hand.

"Please," he urged gently.

Nugent's fingers scratched at the table, unable to capture the elusive pen. Finally, he got hold of it and scrawled his signature across the sheet of stationery near the bottom.

The man flipped open Nugent's wallet and thumbed one of the credit cards onto the table. His eyes darted from plastic to paper and back. Satisfied the signatures matched, he holstered the Kalishnikov, fumbling briefly with the leather tie-down, which refused to fasten over its brass pip.

"Sorry," Nugent blurted, relieved. "I mean, nothing personal. I was only doing my job. I mean—"

Weapon secured, the man stiffened his hand—fingers aligned, thumb crooked back, palm parallel to the floor—and straightened the bend in his elbow with a sudden snap. The hand exploded from within his sport jacket, covering the short distance from the shoulder holster to Nugent's head in an eyeblink. The hardened edge drove upward, connected solidly across the width of Nugent's lower brow, and silenced him. The force of the blow shattered the bones that form the eye sockets and frontal section of the cranium and lifted him off the floor.

Before unleashing the expertly delivered smash, the man stepped to his right—adjusting his angle to insure the momentum would propel Nugent toward the bed, where he landed with a barely audible thud and lay motionless.

The man took a pair of surgeon's gloves from his pocket, pulling them on as he returned to the table. Then he rolled the sheet of Churchco stationery into the Olivetti and typed a suicide note above Nugent's signature, copying from a draft he brought with him. When finished, he removed it from the typewriter and slipped it beneath Nugent's wallet.

Then, he crossed to the bed, hefted Nugent's limp body over a shoulder, walked out the sliding glass door onto the balcony, and eased him over the railing.

Early the next morning, a pool maintenance crew found Nugent's broken body on the concrete decking, below a line of balconies.

The caption in the *Herald*'s late morning edition read: "EX-ECUTIVE LEAPS TO DEATH."

The subsequent police and coroner's investigations concluded that Richard Nugent had taken his own life. They found no evidence of foul play nor witnesses thereto. The suicide note presented a familiar profile: depression, a failed marriage, business pressure, diminishing confidence, debt, thoughts of embezzlement, a meaningless existence.

Reactions of friends and business associates were contradictory, ranging from "Not Dick, no way, not a chance," to "He was sending out a lot of signals, I just missed them."

Those in Churchco's Petroleum Division whose professional shortcomings were revealed by the posthumous publication of Nugent's report snidely attributed his suicide to guilt. But none of them were reprimanded for the oil tonnage discrepancy. Dick Nugent had caught it for the *Kira,* and all references to it had been deleted from his report.

BOOK ONE

HOUSTON

"Zealous to aid mankind, each of three was a saint. Fired by the same wise aim, marked by the same restraint. Though each took his own individual course, For all roads lead to Rome."

—LA FONTAINE, *Fables*

Chapter One

SIX YEARS LATER—1987

On a cool day in February, Theodor Scoville Churcher rode the grounds of his Chappell Hill estate on horseback, as he did every morning. His reined hands punched the air as he let the black Arabian full-out in a grove of aspen.

Soon, the big horse exploded from the trees.

Churcher leaned back exhilarated.

The hard-breathing animal settled into a slower cadence, and pranced toward an early Napoleonic era mansion that presided over acres of lawns and formal gardens where fountains splashed.

Churcher had purchased the structure years ago from a bankrupt French nobleman. He had it dismantled, crated, shipped, and reassembled here—40 miles northwest of Houston—as a wedding present for his wife, Cordelia. The headstone that marked her grave stood beneath an immense live oak on a line between the mansion and his private museum.

As the pick of the prizewinning Arabians he raised cantered beneath him, Churcher thought about the latest addition to his vast art collection. By the time he returned to the stables, he'd become especially anxious to spend the half hour prior to departing for his corporate headquarters with the masterpiece.

Churcher swung down from the saddle and handed the reins to his son, Andrew.

"Hell of a ride! Hell of an animal!" Churcher enthused. "Double our GNP when he gets to stud. Packs the wallop of a twister."

"Be a good name for his first foal," Andrew said.

Andrew Churcher was slim and rangy, with reddish hair, glint-
ing eyes, and a love of animals and open spaces—a cowboy in
the most noble sense of the word. He was as approachable as his
father was intimidating. His preference for saddle over desk
chair, chaps over business suit, bedroll over four-poster—that he
found the whole of his father's activities an anathema, and told
him so—had once ended communication between Churcher and
his only son for almost a year.

Churcher nodded enthusiastically at the name Andrew suggested. "Yeah, I like that!" he bellowed, slapping Andrew
across the back. "You got it, boy. That's what we'll call him—
GNP."

Andrew scowled.

"What's that mean?"

"I said, *Twister*'d be a good name."

"The hell you did," Churcher said, his expression softening
as he mused, considering it. "Not bad, though."

"Well, that's what I meant," Andrew said, surprised at the
admission. He had no doubt it would be short-lived. It was the
thing that irritated him most about his father. He would keep
coming at you until he found a way to turn things his way. Theodor Churcher was never wrong.

"But, not what you said," Churcher went on. "Word never
came out of your mouth, right?"

Andrew nodded grudgingly.

"You have to articulate, boy. Articulate. Never assume someone's going to read your mind. And to make sure you don't forget it, first foal's going to be named GNP." He snapped his
head, turned, and strode off.

Churcher smiled the instant his back was to Andrew. He was
pleased at the exchange; pleased that once bridged, the chasm
had continued to narrow, thanks to the Arabians. The spirited
animals had provided a common focus, and brought them together. Andrew raised them with the love and dedication he had
neither family nor career to absorb. And Churcher reveled at millions they generated in sales and tax write-offs.

Andrew's eyes had too many lines for his twenty-eight years.
They crinkled with admiration as he watched his father leave the

stables in that aggressive, jut-jawed strut. The old coot *was* right, he thought. He swung an apologetic glance to the horse.

"Sorry about that, old buddy," he whispered.

He polished the glistening coat on the animal's neck with his palm.

"We'll name the second foal Twister, okay?"

The Arabian snorted as if it understood.

Andrew grinned. Despite the friction, the newly burgeoning relationship was important to him, too.

After showering and exchanging riding clothes for a Saville Row three-piece, Theodor Churcher crossed the grounds to the entrance to his private art museum.

The stone entrance kiosk perched atop a rolling hillside, and was the only part of the museum above ground. The twelve galleries and immense storage rooms were buried beneath tons of hard packed earth.

Inside the kiosk, Churcher used an electronic card key to summon the elevator and descend to the sanctum below. Then, for the next thirty minutes, at which time his preprogrammed Rolex would interrupt, he sat in communion with a turbulent work.

The pigments were deposited in broad, impulsive strokes that hurried across the canvas evoking the all too swift passage of time. They delineated the baleful "Portrait of Dr. Felix Rey." The hard-edged figure stood against a frenzied background that was in sharp contrast to the subject's cool, incisive stare. The signature in the lower right corner read simply—"Vincent."

Churcher was awestruck by his newest acquisition. The power of it consumed him, and assured him of his own. Indeed his collecting went beyond appreciation. The act of possession, of exclusivity, of having what no other man would have, had always been the wellspring of his ambition and confidence. He stepped closer, until the edges of the rectangle blurred and the texture of the strokes sharpened.

Suddenly, something disturbing caught his eye. The spell rudely broken, he scrutinized the suspect area, and found it—a single brush stroke on the doctor's large, fleshy mouth out of sync with the others; an overworked splash of alizarin crimson

where a smaller brush with much finer bristles than used else-
where had carefully pushed the thick paint into the proper shape.

Finding it was equivalent to noticing one frame missing from
an entire movie. But details were Churcher's strength. This
unique acuity, combined with imagination, ambition, and hard
work, had redefined the meaning of success in business.

Churcher was deep in concentration when the Rolex beeped,
directing his attention to a round of meetings. He flinched and
clicked it off. An unnerving hollowness came over him, as if a
monumental indiscretion had been threatened with exposure—
and one had. He wasn't concerned someone might discover his
museum was a concrete bunker built to withstand a nuclear holo-
caust. No, it wasn't exposure of his paranoia that frightened him,
but exposure of its genesis.

Churcher felt the strong pull of his business engagements and
knew he had to leave. He glanced once more at the Van Gogh,
lifted it from the wall, zipped it in a leather portfolio, and took it
with him.

He had no doubt it was a fake.

That same afternoon in Dunbarton, New Hampshire, a lakeside
hamlet just south of Concord, a swirling wind blew snow against
the facade of a stone cottage. The modest dwelling stood on a
rise at the end of a long, unplowed drive.

The door hadn't been opened since the doctor, who visited
weekly, closed it when he left five days ago. A glistening drift
curved up the weathered cedar to a knocker that hung from the
mouth of a brass lion's head. The cat's-eyes kept watch over
acres of bare maples and snow-laden evergreens.

In a dormered bedroom on the second floor, Sarah Winslow
lay under an old quilt. Her eyes—once clear blue and sparkling
with mischievous appeal, but now dulled, the whites glazed
yellow—stared out the window into the haze she had come to
associate with February, the month of death.

In the Northeast, people died in February. Sarah's father died
in February; her husband, Zachary; an aunt; and half sister, too.
And Sarah was quite certain when it was her time, it would be in
February. Therefore, every year since the diagnosis, this being
the fourth, the first of March was the most important day of the

year for Sarah Winslow. But today, and every day for the last week, the pain came from deeper inside than ever before, and she knew this February would be her's.

She dreaded it. Not because she was afraid of death—she'd long since come to grips with the idea, lately even welcomed it—but because of a nagging awareness that not all her affairs were in order. One in particular, long ignored but never forgotten, demanded her attention.

Sarah turned her head from the window. Her eyes swept the room, taking in each item: the eyelet lace curtain, blown by warm air that came from a grille in the floor; the delicately flowered wallpaper she'd hung one spring in a redecorating frenzy; the bentwood clothes rack, heavy with coats and sweaters and topped by her collection of hats; and the stained mirror, silent witness to her patient taming of Zachary during the first months of their marriage forty-five years ago.

Finally, as they had many times each day in recent weeks, Sarah's eyes came to rest on a framed black-and-white photograph.

She looked at it sort of sideways, with the annoyed expression she managed to affect whenever the picture beckoned. The very same one she used to level at Zachary whenever he reminded her to do something she had been purposely avoiding.

Sarah rolled onto her right side and pushed up shakily on an elbow. She squinted hard at the picture, staring it down like an old adversary.

"Be sure. Be certain," she told herself. "Got the rest of your life to make up your mind." She managed a sarcastic chuckle and grimaced at the pain it sent through her, then settled back onto the pillows.

She lay there unmoving for a few moments.

Then she slipped a hand between the buttons of her nightgown moving it down across the warmth of her stomach until it touched the softness below.

She left it there until the twilight came over her and the pain went away.

Chapter Two

"Romance her if you have to, Phil," said the President of the United States.

"No way. Not for all the Porsches in Stuttgart," Keating replied in a tone born of their many years together in the military and government.

"For your *country*," the President chided. "I'm your Commander-in-Chief, old buddy, and I just gave you a direct order."

President James Hilliard winked, wrinkling his strong Gallic face, then smoothed his auburn beard. The first President since Benjamin Harrison in 1893 to sport one, he was fastidious about it.

"I can just see Will's column now," he said. "How does the President expect to tame the Russians when he can't tame his own facial hair?"

Keating responded with an obligatory chuckle.

A short time earlier, Philip Taylor Keating, chief U.S. disarmament negotiator, had crossed the snow-dappled grounds of Camp David to the presidential cottage to discuss upcoming talks in Geneva. During the next few days, Keating would be briefing NATO representatives—assuring them the United States could go toe-to-toe with the Russians and come away with a draw, without jeopardizing any member countries.

The two men sat in shirtsleeves across the table in the library. The President leaned back and centered his tie between heavily starched collar points.

"We need her, Phil," he said sternly. "Support from Bonn is the key. Whatever it takes. I don't want Gisela Pomerantz screwing this up. And according to Jake," he went on, referring to

Jake Boulton, director of Central Intelligence, "neither does Premier Kaparov. Despite official denials, his health is deteriorating rapidly, and it's no secret he sees disarmament as his legacy. You with me?"

Keating nodded automatically. He heard the words, but he was thinking about Gisela Pomerantz, West Germany's deputy minister for strategic deployment. They were young diplomats when they first met twelve years ago at the NATO Defense College in Rome. And Keating could still hear the ringing voice of the orientation officer that first day.

"As NATO's most promising diplomatic and military personnel," the instructor intoned, "you'll be called on to manage crises on a global scale—and we're going to teach you how. Now, it's very important you make fast friendships here. These personal alliances will pay off down the line when you contact someone you actually know to get action in a crisis situation. Also important is the need for consensus, which, as you know, is always NATO's biggest problem."

Keating recalled how one afternoon while walking Via Condotti with a group from the college, Gisela had impulsively taken his hand and pulled him to a *gelati* vendor in Piazza de Spagna. She purchased a cone of the rich Italian ice cream and insisted he have some.

Keating was head-turningly handsome, with the black curly hair and ruddy complexion of the Irish seamen who were his ancestors. He looked right into her eyes and licked at the chocolate-flavored gelati.

"I think we should forge *our* alliance gradually—" Gisela said. She noticed the soft gelati was running down the waffled cone onto her fingers, slipped one between her bowed lips, and slowly sucked it clean. "We'll share simple pleasures—first," she went on suggestively, offering Keating an ice-creamed fingertip—which he seriously considered, then declined.

Keating almost smiled at the recollection—the friendship she had suggested was indeed a fast one. But she had blown the consensus; very tempted by her, he was also very married.

When he returned to Washington, Keating told the story of Pomerantz's advance, and his wobbly retreat to his best friend, Jim Hilliard, who was, at that time, the junior senator from Illi-

nois. They had been classmates at the University of Chicago Law
School, and Keating served as best man when Hilliard married
Janet Davidson, his childhood sweetheart. He cried with him at
her funeral.

Now, in the Presidential Library at Camp David, Keating was
meeting with the man whom he had helped win the presidency.
"Never forget, do you?" he asked.

"Not when history's on the line," Hilliard replied.
"Pomerantz is a screaming hawk, Phil; *the* potential stumbling
block to the smooth progression of the talks. And nothing, nothing's going to endanger the capstone of this presidency."

Hilliard stood, circled his chair, and came around the table to
Keating.

"One day, Phil, schoolchildren, when asked who's responsible for nuclear disarmament—for leading the world from the
brink of atomic annihilation to days of peaceful coexistence—are
going to—"

"Are going to answer, President James Hilliard," Keating interjected, completing the President's sentence. "I wrote that
speech. Remember?"

Hilliard smiled and nodded.

"Damn good one, too," he replied.

The President settled for a moment, then leveled a forthright
look at Keating.

"I may have blown the economy, Phil," he said, "and God
knows Central America's far from licked, but I'm going to pull
off arms control. And if it means you shacking up with Gisela
Pomerantz, so be it."

Keating nodded tight-lipped and, with a straight face, said,
"Promise me one thing, Jim—" Despite their long friendship, he
called the President by his first name infrequently, and only when
alone.

"If it's in my power," the President said, equally serious.

"Promise me," Keating went on, "that no classroom full of
kids will ever be asked, 'Who shacked up with Germany's deputy minister for strategic deployment?'"

Hilliard broke into hearty laughter.

Keating laughed along with him, thinking that he'd said it
jokingly but he really meant it.

*   *   *

It was evening in Moscow, and cold. Twenty-five degrees below zero cold.

Three men who shared a very different view of President James Hilliard's place in history were meeting in the office of the Soviet Premier in the green-domed Council of Ministers Building, the eighteenth-century headquarters of the Soviet government inside the walls of the Kremlin.

Premier Dmitri Kaparov, a stooped, wizened man with a puffy face and jaundiced skin, sat at his leather-topped desk, turning the pages of a maroon briefing book. Chief Disarmament Negotiator Mikhail Pykonen and Cultural Minister Aleksei Deschin sat opposite him; Vasily Moskvin, the Premier's longtime aide, off to one side taking notes.

The room was stifling hot, kept that way due to the Soviet Premier's failing health. On a pedestal next to his chair, and centered beneath the vigilant portrait of Lenin, stood a portable dialysis machine. Two blood-filled, clear plastic cannulas snaked from ports on the machine to a shunt that had been surgically implanted in the underside of the Premier's left forearm. The plastic loop protruded through a slit made in the seam of his jacket sleeve.

The highly sophisticated machine that had taken over the work the Premier's shriveled kidneys could no longer perform hissed softly while the three men spoke.

"Well done, Mikhail," Kaparov said, closing the large volume. "Your usual inventiveness and thorough preparation are clearly in evidence."

Pykonen dabbed at the space between his upswept brows with a handkerchief, wondering why the cultural minister had been included in an arms control briefing. "Thank you, sir. I'm confident we'll attain an equitable position by the time the talks in Geneva are completed."

Kaparov shifted the weight of his disease-riddled body, and smiled with a radiance he rarely exhibited since becoming ill. "Good," he replied. "Because Minister Deschin and I have a way to guarantee it will be even more than equitable my friend— much more."

The Premier often made such inflated statements, Pykonen

thought; a device to create the impression an assignment was of vital importance, even when it wasn't. But disarmament was the dying Premier's obsession; so Pykonen knew this wasn't one of those times.

Kaparov placed a hand atop Pykonen's shoulder. "You'd think by now, Mikhail, there'd be nothing about your government you wouldn't know, hmmm?"

Pykonen let a thin smile tighten his lips.

"Even my wife still surprises me once in a while," he said with a mischievous twinkle.

Deschin and Kaparov chuckled heartily.

"Well," Deschin said, taking over, "let's begin with something you *do* know. It's been over twenty years since Comrade Khrushchev placed the highest priority on establishing a missile base in the Western Hemisphere."

"Cuba," Pykonen grunted solemnly. "That I know."

"It was sound thinking, Mikhail," Deschin went on. "We had enormous psychological and strategic pressures created by American missiles in Europe to overcome, as well as the limited accuracy of our own. Our guidance system technology was terribly primitive at the time."

"It still leaves something to be desired," Premier Kaparov added, shaking his head in dismay.

"I recall those days very well," Pykonen replied. "The U-2s were driving the Defense Ministry crazy. The minute we shot that one down over Sverdlovsk in sixty, we knew that our missiles would be detected no matter where we deployed them—*as* we deployed them." He paused, considering the propriety of what he was going to say next. "If I may," Pykonen resumed gently. "We knew deployment in Cuba was doomed from the start. I never could fathom why we went ahead with it."

"Because your Premier came up with a brilliant idea," Deschin replied. "And I happened to know an agent of influence whom we induced to cooperate. With typical Soviet ingenuity, we turned adversity to asset."

Pykonen's eyes were wide with curiosity, now. He leaned forward in his chair, hanging on every word.

"You see, Mikhail," Kaparov explained, "we deployed

knowing goddamn well we were going to get caught. In fact, we counted on it.''

Pykonen looked at them with disbelief. ''You mean, the missiles, the warheads, the launching complexes, the maintenance equipment, they were all—a ploy?'' he asked, amazed by the concept.

Kaparov nodded emphatically. ''The ultimate triumph of disinformation, my friend,'' he replied. ''We fooled the Americans and their U-2s. Fooled them into thinking they had forced the Soviet might to withdraw and promise to never do such naughty things again.''

''And,'' Deschin chimed in, ''that act of contrition kicked off a plan that has gone like clockwork.''

''In other words, that proval the Americans called the Cuban missile crisis was actually a victory?'' Pykonen asked, almost afraid to say it.

''Indeed, the celebration rocked the walls of the Kremlin for days,'' Kaparov replied devilishly. ''Of course, no one outside heard the cheering, and few inside. Premier Khrushchev confided only in those involved directly with its implementation. To this day, many Politburo members and military leaders have never been briefed.''

Pykonen shook his head as if clearing it, and took a moment to collect his thoughts.

The hiss of the dialysis machine filled the silence.

''But what about Penkovskiy?'' he finally asked, referring to Colonel Oleg Penkovskiy, the high-ranking Soviet officer inside the Kremlin who was spying for the West at the time. ''He kept Washington informed of our every move. The Americans knew everything. How could they not know it was a deception?''

A look flicked between Kaparov and Deschin.

''True, my friend. Penkovskiy told them everything,'' Kaparov replied with feigned solemnity, before adding, ''everything Premier Khrushchev wanted them to know.''

''He was part of it?'' Pykonen asked, awestruck.

''The best part,'' the Premier said, adding with a facetious smile, ''Imagine how shocked we were when we found out what that nasty traitor had been up to?''

"But Penkovskiy was shot," Pykonen protested.

"There's an elderly gentleman living quite comfortably in a dacha in Zhukovka who would find it very hard to agree," Kaparov replied puckishly.

Pykonen's jaw dropped. "I had no idea," he said, feeling left out. "This plan—it's nearing completion now?"

"Yes, Mikhasha," the Premier replied, with paternal fondness. "And you are the key to it."

"Incredible," Pykonen muttered.

"More so than you think," Deschin said. "We now have what the world believes the U-2s forever denied us."

The bushy upswept ends of Pykonen's brows twitched as if electrified. "We have a missile base in the Western Hemisphere?" he asked in an amazed whisper.

Deschin nodded slowly. "Far superior to Cuba. Similar strategic advantages of course; but, as you might imagine, much more impervious to detection."

"An astounding scheme," Pykonen said.

"Indeed. We had spirit in the KGB in those days, Mikhail," Kaparov said, laughing at a recollection. "We nicknamed the project—*MEDZHECH*."

Pykonen looked at him puzzled. "An acronym?"

"Precisely," the Premier said. "A combination of *MEDLYENNIY* and *ABZHECH*."

"Ah," Pykonen said, pausing appreciatively at the implication. "A very SLOW BURN, indeed. Slow and most painful to the Americans," he went on, realizing that now he could negotiate for virtual elimination of American and Soviet nuclear arsenals, and still retain a first strike capability which no one knew existed.

"Indeed," Kaparov said. "You see, the defections we've nurtured, the codes we've broken, the double agents we've compromised over the years—they were all merely inconveniences that forced the Americans to work harder. This—*this*, once strategically revealed, will force them to make concessions. We'll be able to lean on them, the way they *think* they leaned on us in Cuba." Kaparov raised his brows speculatively, then swiveled to the green telephone and pushed a button.

A woman doctor with bunned hair, a white lab smock over her dress, immediately entered the office and crossed to the Premier.

"Is there a problem?" she asked anxiously.

"Yes," Kaparov replied. He gestured impatiently to the tubes coming from the shunt in his forearm.

"Untie me from this hissing leech."

The doctor frowned admonishingly. She stepped to the dialysis machine and studied the gauges, checking the levels of blood gasses and toxins, then silenced the air-driven pumps. She took Kaparov's arm and quickly disconnected the red-stained cannulas from the shunt, wiped the connectors clean, and tucked the plastic loop into the opening in his sleeve.

The Premier stood and stretched his atrophied muscles. Then, leaning on Pykonen and Deschin for support, he directed them to a window that overlooked Red Square and Lenin's mausoleum directly below.

"The Kremlin Wall will soon have another resident, my friends," Kaparov said.

Pykonen's eyes protested.

"Within three months, I'm told," the Premier went on. "But when that day comes, because of SLOW BURN I will rest in peace. Come, Mikhail, we'll show you the details. I know you'll appreciate the sheer ingenuity of this installation."

They turned from the window and left the office.

The heavy doors closed slowly, as if exhausted by the centuries of turbulent history. The halves of the latch came together with a metallic clang that echoed in the domed space.

The life-prolonging dialysis machine waited silently to resume its futile task. The label on the stainless steel fascia read, "Churchco Medical Products."

Chapter Three

The men with whom Theodor Churcher did business had names like Boone, Clint, Ross, Bunker, and Tex. And some, despite lengthy separation from public office, were still called congressman, governor, or senator.

The talk was always of oil, natural gas, ranching, real estate, communications, space exploration, and defense, of mergers and takeovers—of investing. Not in dollars, but in what they called units.

In most parts of the country, talk of units conjured up images of real estate deals. In Houston, ever since Churcher coined it some three decades ago, a unit was a measure of wealth. At the time, Churcher wanted a clever phrase to symbolize what he had accumulated and indicate his intention to acquire more. Having estimated his holdings to be worth one hundred million dollars, he promptly declared he had—one unit. At last count, he had well over ten.

The incident with the Van Gogh that morning, not the growth of his billion-dollar empire, had been foremost on his mind, distracting him all that day and into the early evening.

Now, he restlessly prowled his suite of offices atop the sixty-five-story Churchco Tower, evaluating countermoves. He went to the arched window that framed the shimmering Mexican Gulf thirty miles to the south, and gazed at the lights of the drilling platforms twinkling on the horizon.

Those sons-a-bitches! he thought. Then, realizing he was alone, the last to leave, as always, he shouted, "Those dirty sons-a-bitches!"

He turned from the vista and crossed the black carpet to an

immense slab of glass which seemed to float in the center of the room.

There, on the neatly ordered desk lay the leather portfolio, and next to it, taunting him, the Van Gogh.

Churcher returned "Dr. Felix Rey's" penetrating glare for a long moment before two quick thrusts of his forefinger turned on his speakerphone and initiated an automatic dialing sequence.

The East Coast was in the frigid grasp of the worst winter in over half a century. Week after week, the nation's capital had been battered by blizzards, freezing rain, and subzero temperatures.

Churcher imagined what it would be like on the streets of Washington, D.C., that night, and shivered.

A click signaled the phone connection had been made. Two rings followed, but no electronic beep to indicate the call was being taped, though Churcher knew it was. A woman's voice came on the line.

"Good evening," she answered in a proper British accent. "This is the Embassy of the Soviet Socialist Republics. How may I help you?"

About an hour later in Havana, GRU agent Valery Gorodin was in his office in the Soviet Embassy on Calle Guevara doing paperwork. Perspiration rolled down his neck and filled the creases of his brow. The stifling hot room had once been a Castro torture chamber, and Gorodin had no doubt information was literally sweated out of the victims.

Gorodin had been an outstanding foreign language student at the Moscow State Institute of International Relations in the late fifties, before it became an elitist institution. While at MIGMO, Gorodin, the son of a train yard worker from Kazan, fraternized with the privileged offspring of those in *nomenklatura*, and developed a driving ambition to join the elite class, comprised of those who hold important positions in party and government. Indeed, doctors, lawyers, scientists, engineers, and architects are excluded by the Politburo and Central Committee who confer membership. Those so blessed enjoy pampered life-styles: choice apartments, country dachas, chauffeured cars, gourmet foodstuffs, freedom to travel, and VIP accommodations.

Gorodin knew that his gift—rapid fluency in any tongue: Arabic, English, French, German, Spanish, among them—was his entrée. Recruitment by the KGB upon graduation from MIGMO, the first step. He was excited at the prospect of joining the "Service" and about to accept their offer when Colonel Yuri Pashkov, the GRU recruiter, caused him to reconsider.

"GRU is the main intelligence branch of the Soviet General Staff," Pashkov explained as they dined on hearty Russian fare at Lastochka, a restaurant on a barge moored in the Moskva near the Krimsky bridge, opposite Gorky Park. "Our mandate comes from the military. Strategic intelligence, the key to the Supreme Soviet's future, is our focus. You see," Pashkov went on with a quiet confidence that appealed to Gorodin, "despite appearances, KGB are essentially—policemen. Their primary role is internal security, not foreign intelligence. Oh, they get headlines, but the most meaningful global tasks are charged to us, to GRU. And an agent so assigned has international mobility unlike KGB, who, *if* fortunate enough to be posted abroad, is restricted to his assigned country. GRU is a grand tradition, Valery," Pashkov concluded, "an elite coterie of the motherland's best and brightest. Strength of character is our trademark. Pride in anonymity our reward."

Gorodin was eager and conscientious when GRU assigned him to Cuba. It was the cutting edge of Soviet foreign policy, the place where SLOW BURN had just been initiated; and during installation of the "missile base," on-site security—assuring that the grand deception wasn't compromised—was his task. But that was many years ago, and the once promising career path had proved a dead end. Lately, he spent his time forwarding payments from the Kremlin to a SLOW BURN collaborator, and filing sektor memoranda with GRU Headquarters—Military Department 44388.

He was at his desk preparing the monthly report when his *KGB* assistant entered. Aleksandr Beyalev—or the *schpick,* as Gorodin called him, using derogatory terminology for novice—was delivering a cable.

"From Washington, comrade," he announced a little too crisply. "Top secret."

Gorodin read the cable, and winced. "Churcher wants a meeting?" he wondered aloud. "We just *had* a meeting." Then

feigning further confusion, he held the cable out to Beyalev, indicating the paragraph. "What do you make of this part here—
about Deschin?"

Beyalev's narrow face soured as Gorodin knew it would. The
zealous fellow made no effort to hide his contempt. Soon he
would outshine his paunchy burned-out boss, and take charge.
He had no idea he was the key to Gorodin's plan to get out of
Cuba.

Indeed, thoughts of *nomenklatura* had dimmed, but not died.
Though the two agencies were unfriendly rivals, and separate
Embassy *rezidenturas* the rule, facilities and personnel were
often shared in smaller embassies such as Cuba. And Gorodin
had slyly feigned a willingness to collaborate, and petitioned the
KGB *rezident,* the ranking intelligence officer, for an assistant
who would "show him up," and be mercifully ordered to take
over. The ire of his superiors and the harsh Soviet winters were
worth chancing, Gorodin thought. Nothing could be worse than
spending the rest of his career with soaking wet armpits; his ass
stuck to the vinyl cushion of his desk chair.

"I'd say the part about Deschin means exactly what it says,"
Beyalev responded dryly. "Churcher is insisting Comrade Deschin attend the meeting."

Gorodin pulled a crinkled cigar from a box on his desk. He
pushed it between his lips, and lit it, all the while eyeing the
standard issue 9mm Kalishnikov in Beyalev's sweat-stained
shoulder holster. Gorodin inhaled deeply, trying to remember in
which desk drawer was his own. "I can't tell the minister of
culture he must be here in eight hours for a meeting, the reason
for which I haven't the slightest clue," he said.

Smoke came in a steady stream from his nose and mouth as he
spoke, creating a hazy cloud between them.

Beyalev waved it away impatiently. "He couldn't make it in
time, anyway," he said in a tone that implied he was enumerat-
ing the obvious. "It's six fifteen A.M. in Moscow. Next flight
departs at noon. Flight time twelve and one quarter hours. ETA
Havana four thirty P.M. tomorrow afternoon. That means—"

"Forget Aeroflot," Gorodin interrupted. He abhorred the staccato parroting of data at which Beyalev was expert. "The minister of culture doesn't fly Aeroflot. He has all the aircraft of the

Supreme Soviet at his disposal. Supersonic fighters. SSTs! I'd think *I* wouldn't have to remind *you* of that."

Beyalev emitted two scratchy sounds that were intended to be an emphatic rejoinder. He cleared his throat and started over in a stronger voice. "Well, if the minister departed within the next two hours on an SST, he could make it in time—if need be."

"*Well*, perhaps you'd be big enough to let *him* decide that," Gorodin cracked with a wiley smile.

Beyalev nodded blankly, wondering how he had lost the offensive.

"You do think this should be decided in Moscow, comrade?" Gorodin prodded.

Beyalev swallowed in embarrassment; his pronounced Adam's apple was still bobbing when Gorodin fired the coup de grace.

"You do recall how to contact Moscow?"

Beyalev nodded and hurried from the office.

Gorodin's smile broadened and gave birth to a chuckle that ended suddenly. *Deschin—what does Churcher want with him?* he wondered.

* * * * * *

Sarah Winslow had slept through the afternoon, awakening after nightfall. The photograph had come slowly into focus when her eyes opened, and she had been staring at it for a while now.

A group of young men and women, most in U.S. Army fatigues, smiled back at her. They stood in front of a World War II jeep. The Red Cross emblem painted on the side was repeated on their arm bands and on the tents in rows behind them. Sarah, second from the right, appeared to be leaning against a crease where the picture had once been folded, cracking the emulsion. Her sleeves were rolled up to her elbows. A stethoscope hung from her neck. Her face glowed with goodness and clearness of purpose; the face that greeted many wounded GIs whose eyes flickered to life in the field hospital near San Gimignano, an ancient walled city just south of Florence in central Italy.

Next to Sarah, on the other side of the puckered crease, stood a uniquely attractive man. He projected a quiet intelligence and an air of intense pride that made him stand out. Unlike the others, his attire was civilian: a cracked leather vest, plaid shirt, baggy wool pants, and mud-caked rubber boots. One of his hands was bandaged. The other hugged Sarah's waist in a possessive gesture which she clearly welcomed.

The photograph stood at an angle, in a wooden frame, on a dresser across from Sarah's bed.

A few years ago, after Zachary died, Sarah removed the photograph from a trunk in the attic, from beneath the books which concealed it, and put it next to the snapshot of she and Zachary and Melanie on the canopied lawn glider. Zachary was a good husband, a loving one, but a man of rigid discipline and conservative principles who would never have understood.

Sarah's eyes became distant, her concentration so intense she took on the unseeing stare of the blind—a signal to those who knew her that she was making up her mind about something. Then she sat up decisively, and swung her stiffened legs over the side of the bed. Her shawl slipped from her shoulders. She paused briefly to retrieve it, and marshall her strength. The dresser, once a few quick steps away, was an arduous journey now. She struggled to a standing position, and shuffled toward it. The room began whirling around her. Lately, every movement, no matter how measured, made her dizzy, and she despised being so feeble.

"Dammit, Zack," she complained aloud in a dry, little-used voice, "I hadn't planned on dying angry—let alone angry at myself."

Sarah steadied herself against the dresser, grasped the photograph, and turned it facedown. It had a brown paper backing that was glued to the edges of the frame. She pierced it with a nail, and hooked her finger in the opening, ripping a jagged line to a corner. Her fingers slipped between the backing and the photograph, searching for what she had hidden there half a lifetime ago.

Her heart pounded with anticipation and the fear of uncertainty. Maybe it wasn't there? Maybe Zachary had found it and couldn't bring himself to confront her? Maybe she had underestimated him, and he could have handled it? God, the thought of being married to someone all those years and not knowing him terrified her now. Sarah's pulse rate soared. Her face flushed vermilion, warmer than in summer when she sat close to the window, her head thrown back, taking the sun.

She removed the backing completely, revealing an aged white envelope. The flap was sealed. The stamps cancelled and postmarked, Concord, New Hampshire, January 17, 1946. The letter was addressed to:

> Gillette Blue
> Allied Forces Headquarters
> Sector 43-N, Florence, Italy.

Gillette Blue was the code name assigned to an OSS operative by the American Military Command during WWII. And Sarah knew, so addressed, the letter had the best chance of reaching the right person. Surely, Army personnel—who in tribute to his cool, finely honed intelligence had referred to him as "that guy with the mind like a razor" and code-named him accordingly— would see it properly delivered. Yet, stamped in red across Sarah's precise, flowing script were the words:

ADDRESSEE UNKNOWN/RETURN TO SENDER.

At the time Sarah wrote the letter, she and Zachary, a carpenter by trade, had been married almost four years. They'd spent the first in a trailer while Zachary built their house. The second and third they had been apart—he in the Pacific with the Marines, she in Europe with the Red Cross. They had completed their service tours and returned to Dunbarton within weeks of each other, and those days in the spring of 1945 were the happiest of their lives. Shortly before Christmas of that year, Sarah gave birth to Melanie.

One morning, early in the New Year, Sarah sat in her bedroom nursing her month-old daughter. When the infant dozed at her breast, Sarah placed her in a cradle, and went to the desk next to the window. She placed a blank sheet on the blotter and began writing. The pen moved swiftly across the onionskin, for she had written the words in her mind many times.

On this winter evening, over four decades later, Sarah backed to the edge of the bed, clutching the envelope, and sat down. She lifted the phone on the night table, and painfully worked the rotary dial.

The phone rang once.

Sarah heard a recorded voice say, "Hi, this is Melanie. I can't come to the phone right now, but if you'll leave your name and number—"

Sarah sagged against the pillows as her daughter's voice continued. A profound loneliness came over her. She pulled the quilt to her chin and waited for the beep.

Outside, the wind howled.

Sarah's fingers tightened reflexively around the envelope, as if making certain it wouldn't be blown away.

* * * * * *

The polar gusts had pushed south into New York City that night. Manhattan's litter spiraled in the corridors of dark stone. In a top floor apartment on East Twenty-First Street, loose-fitting windows rattled against their frames.

The tiny ad in the *New York Times* had proclaimed:

> GRAMERCY PARK—grt studio, plstr
> mldngs, mble f'plce, circ stair to
> blcny, skylts, view, prk key $1250

Within an hour of spotting it, Melanie Winslow had won a footrace to a taxi; survived the crosstown gridlock; climbed four flights to a decrepit, trash-filled studio apartment; and—without a moment's hesitation—had written a check for $3750, the first and last month's rent and one month's security.

Despite its condition, the apartment was a real find. Gramercy Park, long one of Manhattan's prime areas, was an urban oasis enclosed by a cast-iron fence whose gates were always locked. The circa 1870 buildings on its perimeter stood on a parcel of land controlled by a century-old trusteeship, and only their residents had keys to the well-maintained park.

Now, six months and countless gallons of paint later, Melanie was in her bed on the balcony that was reached by the circular staircase when her telephone rang and the click of the answering machine cut it short. Her momentary reaction caused her muscles to tighten and rhythm to quicken, both to the liking of the young man beneath her, who let out a soft moan.

He caressed her thighs, moving his hands up toward her rolling hips, and pulled her down further onto him.

Melanie whimpered, and segued into a slow rocking motion.
Familiar words began running through her mind.

Funny, she thought, how her mother's favorite saying always
came to her when she was with a lover. She'd never heard her
use it in this context, of course, only in reference to chores or
schoolwork—when Melanie had procrastinated and Sarah had
caught her, and warned, "Either you're on top of it, or it's on
top of you, kiddo." It must have registered, Melanie figured.
She liked being in control.

The young man lifted his blond curls from the pillow. His
moist lips began delicately kissing the points of Melanie's breasts
that quivered in a taunting rhythm above him. He ran his tongue
across them, across their smooth opalescence.

He did it repeatedly, slowly, unendingly.

Melanie began whimpering, "God, oh god, oh god," then
shifted to a patter of anxious squeaks.

Her movements quickened. Her head snapped from side to
side, long brown hair whipping in constant motion. Her hands on
his shoulders, pinning him beneath her, nails cat-scratching
across his chest.

"Ohhhh, yessss," she moaned, drawing the word out,
then repeating it at closer intervals and with increasing volume,
"Yessss, yesss, yess, yes, yes!" The last was an exuberant
shriek that reverberated off the skylights and echoed through the
cavernous space. Then a sudden rush radiated from her center
across her trembling flesh, attending to every pore.

She tumbled onto the pillow satiated, and let out a lusty growl.
"Tom, ohhhh, Tom," she purred.

"Tim," he corrected, a tremor in his voice.

Melanie looked at him out of the corner of her eye and grinned
mischievously, like a child.

He raised a brow and grinned back.

They tangled their glistening bodies like knotted snakes and
laughed out loud.

He first caught Melanie's attention earlier that evening in the
Hotel Dorset Bar, an elegant watering hole on West Fifty-Fourth
Street, a short walk from the City Center Theater where she

worked as a modern dance choreographer. The Dorset catered to a professional clientele, and Melanie often went there on nights she needed to be with someone—preferably someone from out of town.

As it turned out, Tim-Tom was a local brat, and Melanie decided to wait until morning to tell him she wouldn't be seeing him again, and why.

Chapter Four

Ten hours had passed since Churcher's call to the Soviet Embassy in Washington triggered the cable to Gorodin in Cuba. The exchange of coded communications between Havana and Moscow that had followed got the Houston business magnate the meeting he wanted.

In preparation, Churcher had spent most of the night scrutinizing paintings in his underground museum. He moved from Renaissance Masters to Dutch Realists, to French Impressionists, to canvases that spanned the history of great art. He skipped right past some, and went directly to others, knowing which, if any, might bear the same stigma as the Van Gogh. Though not an expert, once alerted, he had enough knowledge to make cogent evaluations. To his anger and disappointment, his efforts confirmed his suspicions rather than eliminating them, as he had hoped.

He left the museum well before the beep of the Rolex. The elevator door hadn't finished opening before he was out of it, and dashing through the kiosk toward a limousine.

A uniformed chauffeur opened the rear door with an economy of movement, and nodded.

"Stand on it, son," Churcher barked.

Without breaking stride, he jackknifed at the waist, and propelled his taut six-foot-three frame into the big car. His attire blended with the gray velvet interior, where tinted glass concealed the face but not the identity of its well-known passenger.

Many of Churcher's wealthy friends and associates had long ceased using personalized license plates for security reasons. His still read CHURCHCO. It was, he proudly boasted, a conscious measure of his arrogance.

The antenna-studded limousine rocketed down the drive and through the electrically operated gates. The wrought iron tour de force had once greeted the major film stars of the thirties and forties at the studio now owned by Churchco Communications.

The stretched Lincoln accelerated east onto the 290 Freeway, and in less than thirty minutes was hard into the curving interchange where Texas 610—the heavily trafficked ribbon that rings the Houston suburbs—meets the Katy Freeway to downtown.

Characteristically, Churcher was evaluating the problem at hand and the men with whom he would soon meet: Gorodin, a pleasant, accommodating fellow, but cunning; Beyalev, cold, ambitious, and inexperienced, therefore dangerous and not to be trusted; Deschin, an old friend who had the power to make things right—if he wanted to. Churcher hadn't seen Deschin in almost six years. Not since the last problem with their arrangement. Not since the Nugent report.

He slouched in the backseat of the limousine, and shuddered at the memory. *Overdone, heavy-handed*, he thought. Typically Russian. He felt sickened whenever that rainy night in Deschin's Moscow apartment came to mind, sickened by the fear and confusion that he imagined on Dick Nugent's face the night of his death.

The limousine was on the Katy Freeway where it swings across Texas 45, and fast approaching the North Main off-ramp, the major street-level artery that cuts through the heart of downtown.

The Rolex started chirping and brought Churcher back. The repetitious beeping reminded him, over and over again, how he'd been manipulated and used. He let it continue a long time before he clicked it off.

Andrew Churcher flipped a stirrup over the saddle horn and reached beneath the horse's heaving belly. He pulled hard on the cinch loosening it, and slid the hand-tooled saddle from the white Arabian's back. The momentum carried the saddle in a wide arc onto the rail of a weathered fence. A whistle sent the animal romping off into the pasture.

His father's horse had been watered, saddled, and ready to go at 7:15 A.M. sharp, as always. A half hour later when Churcher still hadn't shown up at the stables, Andrew took the Arabian for a run himself.

He was squaring the saddle on the fence when he spotted a rooster tail kicking into the air behind a car in the distance. Andrew ducked between the whitewashed rails and ambled through the mesquite to the road that split thousands of acres of fenced pasture.

Ed McKendrick's car approached at high speed, and nosed to a stop in a dust cloud.

"Good news, Drew!" he boomed, unfolding from behind the wheel of the red Corvette. "Contracts for European distribution just came through."

Andrew jammed his gloves in the back pocket of his jeans, and latched onto the hand McKendrick offered. "That's great," he replied.

"Sure is, kid," McKendrick rumbled. "The old man did a hell of a job convincing the commies that he could sell their Arabians to Wops, Squareheads, and Micks, not to mention the Limeys and Frogs. Didn't leave anybody out, did I?"

McKendrick was Churchco's ramrod. A good-looking iron pumper, and all-American linebacker with a PhD in economics from Notre Dame. Five years ago, Churcher pirated him from the Rand Corporation, the Los Angeles based think tank, as a replacement for Dick Nugent.

Andrew disliked McKendrick's style but knew that beneath the locker-room bluster hummed the most disciplined mind he'd ever encountered next to his father's.

"Geezus, Ed, you're the worst," he said in response to McKendrick's ethnic shorthand.

"Shit," snorted McKendrick, gesturing to the expanse of uninhabited land. "Who the hell's going to hear me out here? Besides, I love 'em all. You know that. Got some great numbers for you, too."

"Numbers?" queried Andrew.

"Yeah. Before you go to Russia, you're going to have to

swing through Rome," McKendrick explained. "And yours truly can recommend some flesh-crazed madonnas you can slip right into."

Andrew shook his head from side to side in mock despair.

"When you're not screwing your brains out, you can sell Arabians," McKendrick went on. "There'll be buyers up the ying-yang at the International Horse Show. And we have a direct line to the guy who organizes it every year. His name's Borsa, Giancarlo Borsa. He's a government honcho, runs the Defense Ministry when he isn't breeding Arabians. He'll be expecting your call. He and your old man go way back."

"I know. Dad introduced me when we were there last year," Andrew replied. "I'll look him up as soon as I get in."

McKendrick pulled a bulging file folder from the Corvette and dropped it on the hood with a thud. "Everything you need's in there," he said.

Andrew hefted the file as though he were weighing it. "That's a lot of numbers," he shot back, teasing.

"Bet your ass," McKendrick said deadly earnest. "Get familiar with 'em." He had completely missed the entendre. His computerlike mind had reset, and he was all business. "This is your shot, kid. Don't blow it."

Andrew felt frivolous in the face of serious matters. *I'll get it one of these days,* he thought. He had made similar efforts of camaraderie with McKendrick in the past, but the timing was never right.

"You're leaving in two weeks," McKendrick went on. "Use the time to bone up on each account. Know the individuals you'll be dealing with. Memorize their backgrounds, business interests, the profile of their breeding stock. What they have. What they need. Am I coming through?"

Andrew nodded earnestly. "Does Dad know?"

"No. I haven't been able to reach him yet today."

"Me neither," Andrew said curiously. "He didn't ride this morning. Didn't call to let me know he wasn't, either. Not like him. Something's going on, Ed. I thought, maybe, these contracts were it."

McKendrick shrugged, then his mind reset again. "Probably

did too much galloping on some little filly last night and took the morning off!'' he cackled.

He turned from Andrew, crossed to the Corvette, and slid his large body behind the wheel.

"Remind me to give you those numbers!" he shouted as he slammed the car in gear. Then he popped the clutch, kicking up a shower of dirt and gravel, and roared off down the dry road.

Andrew tucked the thick file under his arm.

Twice he had flown with his father to Moscow, and then on to Tersk in the foothills of the northern Caucasus, where some of the finest Arabian horses in the world are raised. Both times Churcher had slipped away to "meetings" and had returned ebullient and satisfied, the way he always did after closing one of his deals.

That his father had gone to see a woman didn't occur to Andrew at the time. But, now, he recalled that day at the breeding farm in Tersk—the rapid guttural sound of the Russian auctioneers exhorting the bidding higher and higher; the babble of interpreters keeping clients in the competition for sales that averaged over $150,000; the barrel-chested horses prancing obediently to clipped Russian commands; the stink of hay and animal waste filling his head; the evaporating ammonia, so powerful it burned his eyes, making them water; then, the delicate aroma of perfume cutting through the stench like the scent of Texas lavender that blew through his rooms above the stables when the wind shifted direction—and the woman, willowy, white-skinned, jet black hair, red lips, soulful eyes, and the look—the fleeting current that passed between her and his father when she nodded to the auctioneer and outbid Theodor Churcher for an animal he wanted badly.

That his father had allowed it should have been proof enough, Andrew thought, but the sexually charged glance left no doubt. It had the hallmarks of smoldering intimacy, of nights spent passionately.

Andrew swept his eyes across the pastures that rolled to every horizon, trying to recall her face; but he couldn't.

Chapter Five

Each week the airports that serve the Washington, D.C., area handle a revolving door blur of traffic as over three hundred thousand people arrive and depart the nation's capital.

On this morning, the continuing arrival of representatives from fifteen NATO countries and their retinues packed the terminals, along with welcoming committees, security personnel, and ubiquitous media correspondents.

In the Lufthansa section of Dulles International, West Germany's Deputy Minister for Strategic Deployment Gisela Pomerantz, fashionably attired in a long raccoon coat, and carrying an alligator attaché, strode through the arrival gate.

Her aquiline face, the impact heightened by the blond hair pulled back severely, remained composed and assured despite the microphones, tape recorders, and camera lenses that thrust toward her.

The questions came rapid-fire, in an overlap of English and German: "Do you think the Russians really mean business this time?" "What *are* the chances for disarmament?" "As an avowed hard-liner, can you support a nuclear pullback of the magnitude suggested?" "Do you have specific concerns with regard to negotiating points?"

Pomerantz held up her hands defensively.

"Please," she pleaded, "we hawks can't handle more than four questions at once. It ruffles our feathers," she added with a disarming smile.

Laughter rippled through the crowd of reporters, who appreciated the self-deprecating inference.

"I hope so. —Better than even.—That's what I'm here to de-

37

cide.—Definite concerns," she said, placing crisp pauses between answers and pointing to the reporter who had asked the question to which she was replying.

Her entourage closed around her and began walking through the terminal. The reporters surged after them. One of the more tenacious correspondents thrust her microphone between the jostling bodies.

"Can you be specific about your concerns?" the young woman prodded.

Pomerantz eyed her coolly, and continued walking.

"No," she replied with finality. "I can't discuss them at this time, I'm sorry."

The group pushed through the automatic doors. A protocol officer came forward and directed Pomerantz to a limousine. She took one step into the rear of the vehicle, and paused suddenly.

"Hello, Gisela," Phil Keating said with a warm smile. The chief U.S. disarmament negotiator was tucked into the far corner of the backseat, smoking a cigarette.

"Philip?" Pomerantz mouthed with momentary uncertainty. Keating still had the craggy good looks; but his hair had grayed, and gold-rimmed bifocals bridged his nose. She settled next to him and kissed his cheek. "Good to see you, Philip," she said brightly. "Thanks for coming."

"Good to see you, too," Keating replied, studying her face. He was thinking it was as beautiful as he'd remembered when she flared the fur onto the seat, revealing a black knit dress that hugged her long, shapely torso. His eyes swept over it appreciatively.

Pomerantz noticed and broke into a comely smile. "The last time you looked at me like that Keating, I recall you disappointed me—terribly."

"It was the gelati," he said with the boyish charm that first attracted her to him. "I mean, there's just something about chocolate gelati—no woman has ever been able to compete with it."

"Oh, I know," she said, pausing for effect before adding, "that's why I voted against holding this conference in Italy."

They were both laughing as the big car left the Dulles access road and swung onto the Beltway heading for Camp David in the bare-treed forests of the Appalachian foothills.

Snow started to fall.

"You know," Pomerantz said with a mischievous twinkle, "a spicy sex scandal might give the media something to pick on besides my 'political baggage filled with hawk droppings,' as they refer to my policies."

"Don't count on it," Keating replied. "Indiscretions outnumber lobbyists in Washington these days." He grinned, took a drag of his cigarette, then pressed it into an ashtray, and snapped the lid closed. "To tell you the truth," he resumed more seriously, "I was hoping you'd brought other bags on this trip."

"I brought the only ones I have, Philip. Whether or not I unpack them is up to you," she replied softly, taking his hand much more gently than on that day nine years ago.

"I'll do everything in my power to stop you," he countered, leaving his hand in hers.

They studied each other's face for a moment before their eyes met in silent confirmation of their intense attraction.

On the rear window of their limousine, large flakes of snow were sticking, then slowly fading away, melted by the radiating heat of the electric defroster.

Chapter Six

The drive to the Churchco Tower on Fannin Street took less than the usual twenty-five minutes.

Theodor Churcher rode one of the glass elevators high into the open core of the building to the tower-level executive suites.

Elspeth, his longtime administrative assistant, saw his preoccupation and sensed what was coming.

"Clear the deck, Els," Churcher said without breaking stride. And that was all he had to say. They had their own special shorthand, and this meant he'd be unavailable and incommunicado for the rest of the day.

"Jake called," Elspeth said, knowing that despite Churcher's order he'd want to be told.

Churcher paused thoughtfully, lips tightening as he decided, then nodded. "But nobody else," he said. He crossed to his office, inserted his card key into the electronic reader, and entered. The Van Gogh was waiting on the glass desk.

The intercom buzzed.

Churcher flicked a look to the painting, then pressed the blinking light on the phone and scooped up the receiver. "Jake!" Churcher said, forcing it. "What's going on in Foggy Bottom?"

"Geneva. Current scenario has genuine potential," Boulton replied rapid-fire. At five-six, and a hundred-thirty-two pounds, the director of Central Intelligence had the metabolism of a hummingbird. "Nature of my call is related. Specific interest—your ETA Rome."

"I'm not going," Churcher replied. "Andrew's handling the auctions alone this year. Churchco Equestrian's his division now."

Boulton's eyes widened pleasantly in surprise. "Celebration definitely in order."

"You know it. I never thought I'd see the day. What did you have in mind anyway? The Italians getting out of hand?"

"Negative. Italian Defense Ministry has displayed exemplary toughness despite severe internal pressures. Advent of arms control negotiations prompts Company to ascertain IDM's needs, and affirm our support. Informal conduit to Minister Borsa deemed appropriate."

"Hell, I'd have been tickled to pull things together with Giancarlo for you. Can I help out with anything else?"

"Affirmative. Evaluate capability of newly appointed chief Churchco Equestrian to assume role."

"Sorry. I can't recommend that, Jake. The boy's got the smarts, but he's going to have his hands full trading horses over there. This is his first crack out of the box. I'd hate to see him screw it up."

"Agreed."

"I've got some offshore problems snapping at my heels," Churcher said, glancing anxiously to the Van Gogh. "I'm going to have to drop off."

"Seven-fifteen tee-off, opening day, Eagle Rock?"

"I'll be there."

Churcher hung up. He slipped the fraudulent painting into the portfolio, and zipped it closed with an angry motion. There was an element of danger in what he was about to do. It gave him pause. Not for his own safety, but that of someone for whom he cared deeply. He scooped up the phone again, called Moscow, and alerted her. Then he crossed to a door in the wall of arched windows and exited to an expanse of roof where a helicopter waited.

The high-speed amphibious craft was painted Churchco's corporate black and silver. It was a customized version of the CC-65 Viper, the two-seat attack helicopter Churchco Aero-Space manufactured for the military. The weapons and munitions bays had been gutted, and fitted with auxiliary fuel tanks that greatly extended its range.

Churcher set the portfolio on the vacant copilot's seat, donned safety harness and headphones, and threw a number of switches on the console.

The turbine whined to life, the slack rotors quickly becoming a whirling blur.

Churcher gently pulled back on the joystick.

The chopper lifted off in the familiar forward tilt, revealing the concentric rings of a huge Churchco logotype painted on the roof as a landing target.

In seconds, Churcher was gliding above the Republic Bank Center, and on over One Shell Plaza, Penzoil Place, and the other curtain-walled shafts that stabbed into the morning sun.

Churcher clicked on the radio.

"This is Churchco N653WD to Hobby Field. Request clearance to heading three five zero."

"Cleared to three five zero. Fifteen hundred."

"Fifteen hundred," Churcher echoed.

"Roger," the controller said, then shifting to familiar tone, "This here's Jordy Banks. That you, Mr. Churcher?"

"Sure is. How're you doing, son?"

"Just fine, sir," he drawled. "Churchco's already up three and a half."

Churcher had been so preoccupied that morning he hadn't checked the stock activity as he always did.

"Three and *five-eighths*," he bluffed. "And don't sound so surprised."

Churcher clicked off, punched the throttle, and headed southeast toward the Gulf of Mexico. In twenty minutes he'd covered the distance to a cluster of oil drilling platforms. Each sported the concentric *C*s of the Churchco logotype.

Below, on Churchco 47, bare-chested men in hard hats wrestled with the drilling pipe.

The whomp of spinning rotors signaled the helicopter's approach. It came at an angle toward a landing pad that cantilevered over the sea.

Churcher hovered momentarily, as if he was going to land, then punched the throttle, lifting off again.

The men below shouted and waved as Churcher headed out toward open sea. One of the youngsters turned to the leather-skinned crew chief next to him. "What's that all about?" he shouted.

"That was the boss," the chief hooted. He whipped chain around pipe and pulled hard. "Just his way of letting us know he's out there. Buzzes us all the time."

The new fellow looked after the helicopter, now a distant gull on the horizon. "Son of a bitch—" he said admiringly, punching the air with a gloved fist.

Churcher knew his employees. And he knew they got a kick out of the chairman of the board piloting his own helicopter. And, so did he.

Aircraft had always captivated him. At age twelve, to the consternation of his parents, he skipped farm chores to catch rides in a rickety crop duster. The old bi-wing's pilot was a former World War I flier who filled the teenager's mind with tales of bravery and derring-do. And each time they soared above the endless acres of blight-ravaged crops, Churcher fantasized that they would land in another world far from the dust-bowl poverty in which he lived. And each time the plane touched down on the drought-hardened field behind his family's tiny farm house, he cursed the bitter reality and vowed that no matter what it took, he would one day have unlimited wealth—and he soon realized that the symbol could become the means. Obsessed with learning to fly, but not having the money for formal instruction, he talked the crop duster into giving him lessons in exchange for gasoline—siphoned from the family's farm vehicles. He soloed at sixteen and, a year later, won a scholarship to Houston's Rice University, where he majored in engineering and designed his first airframes. As an OSS operative during World War II, he flew gliders to night landings behind enemy lines and discovered that he thrived on the risks; and now, he was not only a pilot but also a manufacturer of aircraft, including assemblies of the Space Shuttle, and Apollo moon rocket before that; and a lifetime of risk-taking had paid off.

The helicopter left the last drilling rig behind.

Churcher engaged the computerized navigation system, locking the chopper onto a preprogrammed heading—the precise intersection of latitude and longitude which he had passed on during his call to the Soviet Embassy in Washington the night before.

The data transfer had been accomplished by concealing the numerical coordinates in Churchco contract numbers. Churcher's extensive business dealings in the Soviet Union generated many bona fide calls during which contracts were discussed. And for years, both sides had used this method to arrange meetings and specify locations without raising the suspicion of national security eavesdroppers.

The chopper was below any radar now, skimming the surface of the Gulf. Anyone monitoring it would have assumed Churcher had landed on the drilling platform; and of course, the roughnecks assumed its destination another of the Churchco platforms sprinkled over the thousands of square miles of ocean. Churcher counted on that whenever he made this run.

The previous afternoon in Moscow, a TU-144 supersonic jetliner—a civilian version of the Soviet mach 2.3, 9,600-mile-range Blackjack bomber—left Ogarkhov Air Force Base. Six hours later, at 3:35 A.M. EST, it touched down at Castro International in Havana, and taxied to a secured area away from the terminal.

Soviet Minister of Culture Aleksei Deschin and Vladimir Uzykin, his KGB bodyguard, were the only passengers. They hurried down a mobile boarding ramp to a Russian-made limousine parked on the tarmac.

The chauffeur-driven Chaika took the two men to the Soviet Naval Base at Cienfuegos on Cuba's southern shore. They boarded a Soviet Foxtrot class submarine, and went directly to the officer's mess, where Gorodin and Beyalev were waiting.

At precisely 5 A.M., as scheduled, while the four men breakfasted, the Foxtrot slipped from its berth into the main ship channel.

The captain ordered his executive officer to set a southwest course into the Caribbean.

Almost immediately, two hundred and fifty miles out in space, a United States intelligence gathering satellite detected the sub's movement. The KH-11 *Ferret* was the cutting edge of surveillance technology. Circling the planet in Polar orbit, the Ferret took advantage of the earth's rotation, and scrutinized the surface *twice* every twenty-four hours, performing heretofore unimaginable feats of surveillance; its sensitive electronic interceptors monitored up to a hundred telephone conversations simultaneously; its high-resolution camera read the numbers on the license plates of moving vehicles; and its lightning-fast central processor recorded and/or transmitted the ferreted data to ground stations—the top-secret, mission-control-like rooms where technicians and analysts sat at consoles monitoring space-, land-, and sea-based surveillance devices.

The photographic data on the Soviet submarine was instantly transmitted to Anti-Submarine Warfare Headquarters at the Naval Air Station in Pensacola, Florida. ASW intelligence personnel evaluated the information, identified the ship as an enemy vessel, and initiated an alert.

Chapter Seven

The digital clock in Pensacola's ASW Duty Room read 05:23 hours.

Navy First Lieutenant Jon Lowell was the airborne tactical co-ordination officer on duty. The tall sandy-haired Californian was leaning over the pool table about to put away a game of eight ball when the alert sounded. The other members of the crew scrambled immediately. Lowell coolly stroked the winning shot before hurrying after them.

Last to leave, last to arrive, never pressured, Lowell had a patient, methodical nature that made him well suited to ASW. His resting pulse of forty-eight came from running the equivalent of a 10-K each morning in under thirty minutes. He'd grown up in a rambling Santa Barbara beach house, and inherited his exceptional hand-eye coordination from his mother—a talented graphic artist—and honed it in the video arcade on State Street, where, as a teenager, he spent after-school hours destroying alien starships that flew across his video screen.

Within minutes of the alert, Lowell and his crew had collected mission data, and were sprinting across the tarmac to their Lockheed Viking S-3A. The two-engine plane—pilot and copilot side by side on the flight deck, TACCO and sensor operator in aft cabin—was designed to locate and track submarines, and equipped with armaments to destroy them. Primarily carrier based, the Viking's small crew, and maneuverability enabled it to respond quickly to ASW alerts from land bases as well.

The Viking's pilot, Navy Lt. Commander Keith Arnsbarger, was a tall red-faced Georgian. The first thing he put on each morning was the mirror-lensed sunglasses he claimed to be wearing at birth. He had done two carrier-based tours in Nam piloting reconnaissance aircraft, and assignment to ASW was a natural.

Arnsbarger had gone straight from Annapolis to war, and had been living in the fast lane ever since. The endless chain of one-night stands and hangovers ended the day he started dating Cissy Tate, the widow of a fellow pilot whose F-14 vanished during a training mission over the Gulf. Arnsbarger had been living with Cissy and her eleven-year-old son for three years now. Lately, he'd been thinking of the boy more and more as his own, and though he hadn't told anyone yet, for the first time in his life he was considering marriage.

He was imagining what Cissy's reaction to the idea might be, imagining her gentle face coming to life when he got a priority ASW clearance from Pensacola Tower and started the Viking down the north/south runway. Twenty seconds later, the silver and sky-blue bird rose from the tarmac and, wheels still retracting, headed due south over the Gulf of Mexico.

When the Soviet submarine left Cienfuegos harbor, she remained on the surface and headed for open sea. The sounds of her screws pushing water were picked up by SOSUS.

The Sound Surveillance System was a global network of hydrophones anchored to the ocean floor. These submerged listening posts ringed Soviet Naval bases and shipping channels throughout the world. The Caribbean net that covered Central American and Cuban ports detected the sounds of the Foxtrot's cavitation.

This noise—the whine of a spinning propeller creating a vortex, a whirling mass of water with a vacuum at its center—was transmitted by cable to ASW Headquarters in Pensacola.

Within minutes, these sounds were recorded, computer analyzed, and matched against a library of previously recorded acoustic signatures of the Soviet fleet. The submarine's "ac-sig" identified the target vessel as a Soviet Foxtrot.

This data—along with location coordinates, also determined from the hydrophone contact—was immediately transmitted to the Viking in flight.

In the compartment aft of the cockpit, Lieutenant Lowell sat at the plane's electronics-packed surveillance console. The unit is folded vertically about the TACCO's center of vision, presenting him with three equidistant data planes: flashing banks of SOSUS status indicators above, combination radarscope and graphic tracking monitor with attendant controls in the center, computer and communications apparatus below.

Lowell entered the newly transmitted positional coordinates for the submarine.

The computerized tracking system reconciled the data from the satellite and hydrophone contacts, and recalculated the *Fly To Point*, the estimated position of the Soviet submarine, which had been previously determined from the satellite data only. Lowell had just initiated a process of refinement that would continue automatically.

The blip of the Soviet Foxtrot started pinging across the radarscope.

Lowell's pulse quickened; his eyes narrowed; he straightened in the chair.

"Target up," he announced while encoding again.

Three rows of numbers flashed across the screen.

"Range—three point six five miles. Heading—six zero five five. Speed—twenty-five knots," Lowell reported in crisp cadence.

The first light was just bending over the horizon as Arnsbarger repeated the data and dipped a wing, adjusting the Viking's course to the new FTP. The Soviet submarine was still on the surface when Arnsbarger leaned forward in the cockpit and spotted it. A plume of water arched behind the conning tower as it sliced upright through the sea.

"There she blows, bucko," he called out. He increased airspeed, put the Viking into a shallow dive, and started closing.

Below, atop the Foxtrot's conning tower, her captain pulled the stem of an English briar from his mouth and leaned into his binoculars, observing the Viking's approach. "Clear the bridge! Dive! Dive!" he shouted, his voice blaring from loudspeakers in every compartment in the submarine.

The Klaxons wailed their call to action.

The crew scrambled to battle stations in response.

The captain and executive officer came down the ladder from

the bridge into the control room, joining Gorodin, Beyalev, Deschin, and Uzykin, who had assembled in response to the alarm.

"What is it?" Deschin asked. "Something wrong?"

The captain shook his head. "Right on schedule as a matter of
fact," he replied without taking the pipe from his mouth. He
slipped out of his parka, and dropped it onto a hook welded to
the bulkhead. "We're just playing the game," he went on as he
passed them. "We play it every time we make this run." He
smiled, took up his position at the chart table, and addressed the
diving officer. "Negative trim. Take her to two hundred feet,"
he ordered. "All ahead full."

"The game?" Deschin inquired impatiently, turning to the
men around him.

"The Americans expect us to dive and run," Gorodin replied.
"So"—he paused, inhaling deeply on one of the little wrinkled
cigars he favored.

"So we dive and run," Beyalev interjected, taking advantage
of Gorodin's hesitation. "We don't want to break the pattern
we've established and arouse their curiosity beyond the normal."

"What would make them curious about this, this—" Deschin
paused, gesturing to the interior of the sub as he searched for an
appropriately derogatory word "—this rust bucket of obsolete
technology?" he continued, finding it. Though a reliable work-
horse, the diesel-powered Foxtrot class was designed in the fifties
and was far from the cutting edge of Soviet naval power.

"Nothing," Gorodin answered simply, smiling to indicate that
that was the point.

"Precisely," Beyalev snapped, launching into one of his self-
aggrandizing tirades. "Once identified as such—and not a Viktor
Class *III* whose superior speed, range, and armaments intimidate
them—they will lose interest as they always do. Then"—he
made a sharp turn in the air with his hand accompanied by a
whistling noise—"back to base for the Viking."

Deschin let an amused smile indicate no more explanation was
required.

Beyalev nodded and reddened slightly, sensing he may have
overdone it.

Uzykin, the KGB man, had said nothing throughout. He stole

a glance at Beyalev, clearly pleased with his enthusiasm if not his penchant for verbosity.

On the surface, the sea rolled over the decks and conning tower of the Foxtrot as it submerged.

The Viking, jet engines whining, made a low strafing run. Doors in the underside of the fuselage yawned open, dropping sonobuoys into the Caribbean a thousand feet below. Hydrophones within the canister-shaped units began transmitting data that pinpointed the submarine's course beneath the sea up to the Viking.

The tracking-monitor in Lowell's console came alive with a series of green lines: each represented data from one of the sonobuoys; each moved in a staccato rhythm across the screen; all intersected to reveal the position and course of the Foxtrot below.

Lowell tracked the sub for approximately half an hour. He ascertained its course was away from the United States mainland, verified its acoustic signature as that of a Soviet Foxtrot, and transmitted this data to ASW Forces Command.

As the Russians anticipated, once satisfied the vessel was an over-the-hill Foxtrot, and not a missile-carrying Viktor Class III, ASW Command called off the alert, ordering the Viking back to base.

Arnsbarger put the two-engine jet into a looping right turn.

Lowell sat staring pensively at his console. After a few moments, he leaned into the cockpit.

"Where do you think they go?" he asked.

Arnsbarger shrugged. "Search me," he replied. "Probably Castro's weekly nose candy junket to Bogota."

Lowell laughed. "No kidding. This is what? The fourth, fifth time that *we've* tracked 'em. Same sub. Same course. Like every three, four months, right?"

Arnsbarger nodded, swung onto a heading for Pensacola, and pushed the throttles home.

The plane vibrated, then just hummed.

Lowell was deep in thought.

"I think I know," he said.

"Know what?" Arnsbarger asked.

"I think I know how to find out where they go."

Below, the captain of the Soviet Foxtrot waited until he was certain the Viking had broken contact, then changed to a north-westerly course. For the next six hours the Foxtrot headed at top speed into the waters of the Mexican Gulf.

Churcher's helicopter had been cruising at wide open throttle for exactly two hours and thirty-eight minutes. He was thinking about how he would approach Deschin when the ever-changing graphic on the computerized navigation monitor indicated the Viper was directly over the rendezvous spot. Churcher put the chopper into a sweeping turn, and spiraled to a landing on the gently rolling sea.

A thousand yards due east, the Foxtrot's periscope broke the surface and cut through the waters toward the helicopter.

Churcher shut down the turbine and released his harness, preparing to transfer to the submarine.

The black steel hull punched through the surface into a blazing midday sun. The Red Star on the conning tower glowed like an illuminated beacon.

Chapter Eight

A maroon-and-black hearse came through the big curve in Pembroke Street, skid chains drumming on the plowed road in a rhythmic dirge. It slowed at the bottom of a rise and turned into a drive lined with pines. The antenna flicked a low hanging bough, and snow crystals sparkled in the cold light. The hearse pulled next to a car at the far end of the drive, and crosshatched the snow until the rear door was aligned with the entrance to Sarah Winslow's cottage.

Two men, bundled against the cold, got out and went inside. The walls of the tiny house shook as they clambered up the stairs and entered the bedroom.

The driver removed his visored hat. "How goes it, Doc?" he inquired a little too avidly.

The doctor, a boyish fellow with glasses, had made the call that brought them. "It'll be a minute," he replied in a curt tone that dulled the man's fervor.

Sarah lay under the quilt in a fetal curl. The doctor was with her when she died early that morning, her hands clutching the envelope, her head filled with the smell of it—a mixture of ink and onionskin, and time. They triggered a flood of memories, enriching her last moments. Her life ended with a brilliant flash of light and rolling thunderclap—the same bolt of lightning she thought had ended it early in the spring of 1945, in Italy, during the war. The same one that gave rise to the events culminating in the letter.

The doctor gently pulled the envelope from between Sarah's hands, slipped it into a pocket, and went downstairs to use the phone.

The men from the funeral home unfolded the large polypropylene bag with the broad zipper and sturdy handgrips they'd brought, and crossed to Sarah's bed to take her.

Melanie Winslow's loft was a bright, cheerful place in the mornings. Light streamed through the skylights, bathing a jungle of plants and illuminating the numerous dance posters on the walls.

She sat cross-legged on the bed, holding a cup of coffee, the sheet over her shoulders like a collapsed tent. "One-nighters," she said coolly, "are how I make sure I don't become dependent on someone."

Tim propped himself against the headboard, and nodded. "There are—devices, you know," he said facetiously.

Melanie chuckled. "After a couple of bad marriages, a ton of guilt, and too much therapy, they start looking pretty good," she said, adjusting her position on the bed. "Seriously, I got my act together and decided, never again. I don't date. I don't get involved. I don't see anyone more than once. It's that simple."

"Must've been a couple of real losers—"

"Not really. I was as responsible as they were. Selfish. Focused on my career, *and* my body. They wanted kids, which I thought would destroy both. Don't get me wrong, they had their faults, but"—she paused and took a sip of the coffee—"yours truly was no angel. First time, I was nineteen and didn't know anything. The second, I was twenty-eight and thought I knew it all. Funny," she said poignantly, "they both hurt as much."

Tim didn't reply, nor did his expression change to indicate he empathized. He was too intent on studying her face—obliquely, the way men do the next morning.

Melanie had seen the distant uncertainty many times and knew what he was thinking. "I'll save you the heavy math," she said. "I'm forty-two."

She slipped from beneath the sheet, stepped to the floor unclothed, and did a lovely *jeté en tourant* across the sleeping balcony. She held the last position, articulating it, a current flowing through her in the diffused light.

Tim swept his eyes over her elegantly arched figure, easily that of a woman ten years younger.

"You're very beautiful," he said desirously.

"An illusion," she replied, moving back to first position. "The lighting. It's all in the—"

The single clipped ring of the telephone interrupted her.

The answering machine clicked on.

Melanie tilted her head thoughtfully, deciding, and did a little *brise ferme* to the phone. She turned up the volume on the answering machine, heard the end of her recorded message and the electronic beep, then monitored a man's voice.

"Miss Winslow? This is Doctor Sloan. I'm calling about your mother. Give me a call as—"

Melanie snatched up the receiver. "Doc? Hi, it's Melanie," she said rapid-fire. "How's she doing?"

Melanie's highly tuned posture slackened at the reply. "Yes, thank you," she said softly. "I'll come this afternoon." She hung up slowly, and glanced to the skylight in reflection. Her eyes filled.

"You okay?" Tim asked, seeing the change in her.

Melanie nodded unconvincingly and slipped back under the covers next to him. She buried her face in the curve of his neck and cried softly. Her feelings were complex and difficult to sort out. She had never been this aware of her own mortality before. She burrowed in closer to him, and lay there thinking about it for a while. Then, in a small, vulnerable voice, she said, "Make love to me."

Chapter Nine

President Hilliard stood with his back to the huge stone fireplace in the sitting room of the presidential cottage at Camp David, and raised his glass to Phil Keating and Gisela Pomerantz.

"To the birth of a new era—and to those who will inherit the torch of peace."

"And to you, Mr. President," Pomerantz added, holding her glass up to him.

The trio clinked glasses, and sipped the bittersweet vermouth-cassis-and-soda that was the President's favorite aperitif. They had gathered, at his request, prior to a luncheon for diplomats who would represent NATO countries at the upcoming disarmament talks.

"Gisela," Hilliard said, getting to business. "I had a lengthy and frank transatlantic powwow with Chancellor Liebler this afternoon. And I assured him that we were fully aware of your country's *special* interest in the success of the talks."

"I'm certain he was most appreciative," Pomerantz replied. "As the only country on the border between East and West, Germany has been, as you've often said, the linchpin of deployment. Naturally, she should command the same position with regard to disarmament."

Hilliard nodded emphatically.

"The Chancellor and I covered that ground quite thoroughly," he said, going on to enumerate. "We specifically discussed the suspicion long held by some NATO members that the United States had secretly developed defense initiatives designed to confine a nuclear conflict to Europe; Germany's strategic position as *the* point of attack by Warsaw Pact forces in a conventional war;

55

her need to continue selling industrial products to the Soviets and
Eastern block; and, as a divided nation, Germany's desire to
maintain cordial relations with the East, thereby keeping borders
open and separated families in contact."

"You've articulated our concerns very well, Mr. President,"
Pomerantz replied.

"Phil's a good tutor," Hilliard said with a smile. "Now," he
resumed, "Chancellor Liebler agreed that what we're proposing
in Geneva is very responsive to those concerns, and in light of
recent displays of good faith by our side and the Soviets, I asked
him—" He paused to clear his throat, and sipped some of the
aperitif.

"The President's referring to our indefinitely postponing deployment of Pershing IIs in Norway and Belgium," Keating
said, taking over. "And the Soviet's subsequent dismantling of
their SS-20s along the Polish Border in response."

"Yes," Pomerantz replied, brightening. "We were quite
pleased that the disarmed system was one targeted on Europe
rather than one targeted on the United States."

"Which brings me to my point, Gisela," Hilliard said. "In
light of all this, I asked the Chancellor, 'Why is the German
government so—for lack of a better word—uptight?' And he—"

"If I may, Mr. President," Pomerantz interrupted. "Why did
he send *me* to represent Germany, and not someone who is more
aligned with your position? Wasn't that your question?"

"Gisela," Keating counseled, "I think it's a mistake to take
the President's comments personally."

"No, no, she's right, Phil," Hilliard corrected. "And the
Chancellor gave me a damn good answer. He said, he wanted to
be certain our negotiating strength is what we claim. And if we
can convince his resident hard-liner here—" He let the sentence
trail off, and gestured to Pomerantz. Then he turned back to Keating with a veiled look that said—I know what you're thinking
and God help you if you say it. "And I agree with him, Phil,"
the President resumed, with a bold lie. "Nothing wrong with
taking a good hard look at what we're doing before we commit."

Keating, who was thinking—*Bullshit! I don't need anybody to
assess the strength of my position*—caught the look and pre-

tended to concur. "That's a very prudent attitude, sir," he said, forcing a smile.

Hilliard nodded. He had wanted Pomerantz to feel comfortable and wholly accommodated, and was thinking he'd succeeded, when the protocol officer informed them luncheon had commenced.

"Precisely, I am all in favor of prudence," Pomerantz replied as they followed the protocol officer to the door. "You see, after studying the NATO Report, all nine-hundred-fifty-four pages of it, I asked Chancellor Liebler and Defense Minister Schumann a question neither could answer. And that question was—'What ever happened to the *Heron*?'"

"Heron?" the President echoed, looking back at Keating. "Phil, I recall we monitored the testing of that system in the mid-seventies. Right?"

"That's correct, sir," Keating replied smartly. "Soviets never deployed it."

"As best we can determine," Pomerantz corrected sharply, enunciating each word, and neatly tacking the phrase onto Keating's reply. Then she turned to the President and, softening her tone, said, "That's a quote from the NATO Report, Mr. President. I'm sure you'll agree, it's not the kind of wording that inspires confidence."

Hilliard burned Keating with a look. "Is that what it says, Phil?" he asked through clenched teeth.

They were moving into the dining hall now.

The President laid back to enter alone. "We'll talk," he barked before Keating could reply.

Keating nodded. He leveled an apprehensive look at Pomerantz as they separated, and went about mixing with the other representatives in the dining hall.

The President paused and, with effort, transformed his pained expression into an ebullient smile and entered to spontaneous applause.

Chapter Ten

The swell had rolled hundreds of miles across the Gulf before it slapped against the starboard pontoon of Churcher's helicopter. The unoccupied craft rode the crest, settling onto the flat catenary of sea beyond.

Two hundred feet beneath the surface, the prow of the Soviet submarine cut through the black water.

The interior of the Foxtrot always reminded Churcher of Moscow before the snows—cold, gray, and depressing. Portfolio in hand, he was waiting in the wardroom with Gorodin and Beyalev when the door in the bulkhead swung open and Deschin's bodyguard entered.

Uzykin had the head of an eagle. The tip of his broad nose descended almost to the centerline of his lips. He surveyed the compartment and, satisfied all was in order, motioned Deschin inside.

Deschin wore a dark blue suit, square shaped and buttoned over a slight bulge in his waistline, white shirt, and subdued striped tie.

He had put on a few, thought Churcher, but the hollows below his cheeks were still there.

Four medals—Hero of the Soviet Union, the Order of Victory, Marshall of the Soviet Union, and Order of Lenin—hung above Deschin's breast pocket.

He smiled at Churcher and extended a hand. "Ah Theo," he rumbled in his heavily accented English. "You'll forgive an old friend for keeping you waiting?"

Churcher's eyes twinkled, as they always did when he held the cards. He shook Deschin's hand firmly, causing the medals to dance.

"Please, Aleksei, no need to apologize," he replied, pushing the left lapel of his suit jacket forward with his thumb. "See, you outrank me."

Deschin leaned forward, squinting to see the tiny emblem pinned in the notch. He knew that the gold and enameled insignia meant Churcher had been awarded the Distinguished Flying Cross for his heroic piloting of gliders during World War II. "By a margin of four to one!" he roared heartily.

As the soviet minister settled, Churcher unzipped the portfolio, removed the painting, and placed it on the table in front of Deschin.

In the cramped, somber compartment, the impact of the vibrant colors and powerful structure of the canvas was overwhelming—as Churcher knew it would be. For a moment, the four Russians stood blinking and stunned.

Churcher set the portfolio aside, and gestured magnanimously to Deschin. "You have the floor, Aleksei," he said. "I'm quite certain as minister of culture you can explain this."

Deschin took a long moment to think it through, deciding to force Churcher to keep the ball. "We have assembled at your request, Theodor—and at great inconvenience. The first explanation should be yours." He paused locking his anthracite pupils onto Churcher's and added pointedly, "My government doesn't take kindly to being threatened."

"I assume you're referring to my conversation with your people in Washington?" Churcher asked rhetorically. Then nodding compassionately, added, "I can see how it would be upsetting coming so close to the talks."

"I'd say your timing was particularly unnerving," Deschin snapped. "Yes."

"You mean, your people aren't going to put all their missiles on the table?" Churcher asked facetiously.

"Nuclear disarmament isn't my area," Deschin bluffed. "I'm not privy to the strategy, nor will I speculate what they—"

"Then allow me," Churcher interrupted. "Sometime last night, you got a call from—Kaparov? Pykonen? Whoever. And he said, 'What the fuck is going on here, Aleksei? I thought we owned this guy? If Churcher does as he's threatening, we'll lose our edge. The very thing that has prompted us to go to Geneva; that will allow us to trade system for system, missile for missile, warhead for warhead, and still come out ahead will be kaput-nick!'"

Churcher let it sink in for a few seconds.

"How am I doing?" he asked almost mischievously.

"Very well, I'm afraid," Deschin replied.

"Right," Churcher snapped. "The bottom line *is*—the United States representative can't ask to negotiate for something he doesn't know exists."

He spread his arms in a magnanimous gesture.

"So, here we are," he concluded. "My apologies for my tactics, my friend; but had I not used that leverage, Aleksei, would you be here now?" Churcher didn't expect an answer. He matched Deschin's contemptuous glare with one of his own, and continued. "Now *I* don't take kindly to being taken," he said, stabbing the painting with a forefinger. "The currency used to make your last payment and, as best I can determine, to make most of the others over the years"—he paused to emphasize the scope and premeditated nature of the deception—"is counterfeit. All brilliant works, no doubt of that. Works of genius. But, nonetheless, fakes, forgeries."

Deschin stared at Churcher blankly.

"Come on, Aleksei," Churcher prodded. "You don't expect me to believe you didn't know?"

Churcher had him and knew it. Many times in his forty years of dealing at the top, his adversaries tried to put things over on him. A few had succeeded; but sooner or later, he found them out.

Deschin pulled a cigarette from a pack.

Uzykin stepped forward and lit it.

Deschin inhaled deeply, his mind searching for a way to avert this disaster. Finally, he exhaled, and more than credibly, replied. "You couldn't be more wrong, Theodor. I vouch for their authenticity myself."

Churcher shook his head no emphatically. "There's no disputing that this one's a fake," he challenged.

Deschin wondered how Churcher could be so positive. His face darkened at the possibility that crossed his mind. He decided to be direct because he had to know. "You didn't go to someone?" he asked, uneasily. "You didn't have it authenticated by a professional?"

Churcher scowled, insulted by the suggestion. "Of course not," he replied, his drawl thickening as it always did when he lost patience. "We've both known that'd never be possible. And the whole world knows your people have these paintings under lock and key, and won't sell any of 'em. How could I take one to an expert? Where would I say I got it? You took advantage of that, Aleksei. Took advantage of *me*."

Deschin was relieved by the answer, but didn't let it show. "Then what makes you so sure?"

"That," Churcher replied, placing the nail of his forefinger beneath the telltale area of crimson pigment. "Right there," he went on. "The Dutchman would've never done that. He wasn't a fusser. Never would've touched it up like that."

Deschin slipped on his glasses, and leaned close to the painting, examining the spot where Churcher's fingernail was now digging into the paint.

"Very, very astute," he said, his face still close to the textured surface. He straightened, and peered over the tops of his glasses with a professorial air. "You're overreacting, Theo. Really. In spite of what we'd all like to believe, Van Gogh *was* human. He made mistakes, and he fixed them. We all do."

"Fine," Churcher retorted. "How do you propose to fix this one?"

Deschin inhaled deeply on his cigarette, then filled the compartment with smoke. "I'm afraid you're forgetting a most famous American proverb, Theodor. Now how does it go?" he wondered, feigning an effort to recall it. "Ah, yes," he resumed. "'Don't fix something that isn't broken.' You're familiar with it. No?"

Churcher seethed, lifted the painting with both hands, and smashed it over the back of a chair. The canvas shredded. The frame splintered.

The four Russians flinched.

Deschin ducked to avoid a piece of the gilded wood that rocketed past his ear.

Churcher's cold look said, It's broken now!

Deschin settled and brushed flecks of paint and gold leaf from his jacket. "What do you want?" he asked in a tone intended to signify he'd had enough.

"The originals, of course," Churcher replied. "All of them. As we agreed a long time ago."

"Or?" Deschin prodded.

"Or—like I said, I'll be forced to take steps to even out the ante in Geneva," Churcher replied. "Of course, should I meet a sudden and suspicious end, the director of Central Intelligence will receive, under anonymous cover, a complete set of drawings and specifications for the *Kira* conversion. He should be able to figure out the rest from that. I know he will. We play golf. Jake Boulton's a very bright fellow."

"How?" Deschin asked coolly. "How did you get the package of drawings, Theo?"

"I spend a lot of time in your country, Aleksei," he replied, thinking if Deschin was shaken he was hiding it well. "I have friends there."

"The paintings will be a problem for me," Deschin said flatly. "Though many works from the Hermitage and Pushkin have been shown in your country recently, I've managed to withold 'your's' from those exhibitions. But eventually I'll be forced to include them; and they'll be exposed to scrutiny by international experts. So you see, Theo, we can't very well give you the originals and send fakes. There's no other way to resolve this?" he concluded, his tone now more pleading than demanding.

"The paintings were the only reason I got into this. You know that. There's nothing else you people have that I want or can't buy," Churcher replied. "I mean, we have an agreement. And for years, more than *twenty* of them, I've kept up my end." He'd become too hard, too emotional, he thought, and consciously shifted gears. "Look, I'm not here to rub your nose in it, Aleksei," he said, his voice pained, that of a man not wanting to hurt a friend. "You have some problems? Take all the time you want, okay? Weeks, months, whatever. Long as when it's all done, I come away with what I've been promised, just like you. Now, that's fair, wouldn't you say?"

Deschin nodded contritely. "More than fair," he admitted. A section of torn canvas had come to rest on the table in front of him. He stubbed out his cigarette in the pigment, and shook his head in dismay. "I'm sorry, Theodor," he said.

Gorodin knew what was coming now. They had discussed this over breakfast during the voyage from Cienfuegos. He tensed, preparing to move quickly when the signal was given, though what he was about to do was no longer to his taste. To his surprise, Uzykin signaled Beyalev instead. At that very instant, and by that simple gesture, Gorodin knew, to his delight, his days in Cuba would be over soon.

On the flick of Uzykin's eye, Beyalev stepped forward, pulled the 9mm Kalishnikov from his shoulder holster, and brought the steel spine of the grip down hard onto the side of Churcher's head, just above his left ear—all in one smooth, swift motion.

Textbook, Gorodin thought. His mind drifted back to his last kill—a puzzled young fellow in a hotel room six years ago. It was a covert assassination; what those in the trade, on the Soviet side, call a *Mokrie Dela*, literally, a "Wet Affair." It had soured him terribly, and he was more than pleased to keep it his last. Often, in his sleep, Gorodin still heard the muffled crunch of Dick Nugent's body when it landed on the concrete decking around the pool of the Americana Hotel that night in Miami.

Churcher remained conscious just long enough for his eyes to snap open in astonishment. Then, the expression fell from his face, and the chairman of the board of Churchco Industries slumped in Beyalev's arms.

Deschin grimaced. Then nodded.

Gorodin took Churcher's wallet and removed the electronic card key.

Beyalev lowered Churcher to the floor, and pressed the muzzle of the Kalishnikov to his temple.

"No!" Deschin exclaimed.

He and the captain moved with lightning speed. The captain got to Beyalev first and jammed his thumb behind the trigger, preventing him from pulling it.

"We agreed I would seek confirmation from Moscow should a kill appear necessary!" Deschin said to Uzykin sternly. As the bodyguard of a Politburo member, Uzykin clearly outranked his KGB colleague. "Call him off!" Deschin went on. "This decision must be made at the highest level—and with the Premier's concurrence."

Beyalev and the captain were still crouched over Churcher's unconscious body, glaring at each other, hands locked about the Kalishnikov's trigger assembly.

Uzykin nodded to Beyalev, indicating he had deferred to Deschin.

The captain eased somewhat, slowly removed his thumb from behind the trigger, and stood.

Beyalev holstered the weapon.

"Carry him forward," the captain ordered. "We have procedures to efficiently dispose of him if Moscow so decides."

The others moved to take Churcher's body.

Deschin winced, averting his eyes, and headed down a passageway toward the communications bay.

Chapter Eleven

A wind-driven sleet slashed across Red Square into the unflinching faces of the elite Red Army Guard at sentry post no. 1—the entrance to Lenin's Tomb.

Premier Kaparov had been on an emotional high since he and Deschin had revealed the existence of a Soviet missile base in the Western Hemisphere to his chief negotiator. Churcher's threat to forward drawings of the *Kira* to the Americans, thereby alerting them to SLOW BURN, had plunged him to the depths of depression.

"He can't be allowed to do this," the Premier said bitterly.

Pykonen, Anatoly Chagin head of GRU, Sergei Tvardovskiy head of KGB, and two Politburo members representing the military—who were gathered around the table in the Premier's office—nodded dutifully.

"Decades of hard work and excruciating tests of patience will be wasted," Kaparov went on. "When I think of our efforts in Eastern Europe, Southeast Asia, the Middle East, Central America—" He paused, and shook his head despairingly. "For over twenty years those ventures have kept the enemies of the Soviet state chasing the elusive carrot of détente while the threat of cold war alternatives snapped at their heels, kept them busy while we established our position of nuclear superiority—and now, all for naught."

"And needlessly so," Tvardovskiy said. He was a loud, repulsive fellow with capped teeth. He knew the flecks of gold atop the worn incisors reinforced his ruthless image, and left them that way. "These eventualities should have been foreseen, and safeguards developed to deal with them," he went on. He didn't

have to say GRU, and not KGB, had been entrusted with SLOW
BURN's security. "Who knows if the situation is even salvagea-
ble now?"

"*I* do," Chagin said, with the icy stare of a paranoid stoic
whose work fed his neuroses. GRU headquarters was its taberna-
cle. Vicious guard dogs patrolled the grounds. Attaché cases
were prohibited inside. Chagin rarely left the windowless fortress.

While the Churchco dialysis machine cleansed Kaparov's toxic
blood, the group assessed the impact Churcher's threat would
have on the upcoming arms control negotiations if carried out.
They groped desperately for a plan to counter it. But, as Kaparov
feared, they found only one. The Premier left the meeting exhausted, clinging to the hope that Deschin's rendezvous at sea
with Churcher would be successful.

That evening, in the bedroom of an apartment a short walk
down a corridor from his office in the Council of Ministers building, Premier Dmitri Kaparov lay next to his wife of fifty-three
years.

The events of the previous twenty-four hours had severely
drained him, but he couldn't sleep. For hours, he had been staring at the shadows thrown across the ceiling from the lights in
Red Square, thinking about SLOW BURN, and reflecting on its
beginning, on those days when he and Aleksei Deschin were rising stars in the Intelligence and Cultural ministries—agencies
that rarely interacted, save for the KGB's chaperoning of cre-
atively frustrated ballet stars.

However, early in the spring of 1960, the two young lions
were unexpectedly drawn together. An American business entre-
preneur with a passion for collecting art was the catalyst.

Theodor Churcher was in the Soviet Union on a business trip
when he noticed the name Aleksei Deschin on a list of government appointments. They had worked together in the OSS during
the war, and Churcher sought out the new deputy cultural minister. During a vodka-embellished reunion, replete with the telling
of wartime stories, Churcher queried Deschin about the mother
lode of Western art long exiled to the basements of Soviet museums. He expressed interest in quietly acquiring the masterpieces, and he would pay dearly for them—in hard American

dollars. A currency which, both men knew, was highly prized by the Soviet government.

For Deschin, it was an exciting prospect. Who would have thought that a bureaucrat in a nonstrategic agency would be able to make such a tangible contribution to his government?

For Kaparov, the KGB "handling agent" assigned to oversee covert exchanges of paintings for cash, it was humdrum at best. Humdrum until, in a brilliant stroke, he saw the potential to alter history and, with Deschin's assistance, hatched a bold plan.

Kaparov audaciously proposed that the government forego the much sought-after cash, and request another form of payment. One that he knew only *this* American could pay. An American who, Kaparov rightly suspected, wanted the artworks badly enough to pay it. Along with Deschin and Vladimir Semichastny, KGB Chief at the time, Kaparov sold the unorthodox idea to Premier Nikita Khrushchev, and SLOW BURN was born.

The terminally ill Premier's recollection was marred by bitterness. He had planned that the position of unchallenged nuclear superiority would be his legacy to the Soviet people. And now he felt as if a knife had been suddenly thrust into him, with the cruelest timing imaginable. The long thin blade he visualized was slowly piercing his flesh when he heard the footsteps, the knock, and then the slow chatter of the hinge as the door opened, and his aide Vasily entered.

"Excuse me, Mr. Premier," he whispered.

"It's all right, Vasily. I'm awake."

"Minister Deschin is on satellite hookup, sir," Vasily said. "Shall I bring the phone to the bed?"

"No, no," Kaparov replied softly. He knew what the call was about, and had been hoping it wouldn't come. That would have meant a satisfactory agreement had been struck with Churcher. "I'll take it in my office," he said, thinking some decisions are not for the ears of one's mate. He leaned across the pillow and kissed his wife on the forehead. "I will be back shortly, Pushka," he whispered.

"Your robe, Dmitri," she said, awakening. "Don't forget your robe."

"No, I will go stark naked," he teased.

He pulled his stiffened body from the bed and slipped into his

robe with Vasily's assistance. He knotted the waist tie and
stepped into his slippers.

Then, Dmitri Kaparov, General Secretary of the Communist
party, Premier of the Council of Ministers of the Soviet Socialist
Republics, the most powerful man in all of Russia, shuffled fee-
bly to his office to decide whether Theodor Churcher would live
or die.

Chapter Twelve

The Satellite Surveillance Group at the Naval Air Station in Pensacola is housed in K Building, at the far end of the ASW Forces Command complex.

On returning from the Foxtrot alert, Lieutenant Jon Lowell completed his watch and went directly to the heavily guarded and fenced structure. He took the steps two at a time, entered the nondescript lobby, and returned the salute of the Marine guard.

"Corporal," he said, in the laconic tone military officers seem to use with subordinates.

"Morning, sir. How're you today?" the poised youth replied.

"Fine thanks," Lowell said. "Heading for the TSZ."

This meant that Lowell sought access to the Top Secret Zone, where Anti Submarine Warfare, Satellite Surveillance, and Sound Surveillance System headquarters were housed.

The guard examined the ID badge clipped to the right breast pocket of Lowell's uniform. The plastic-laminated card displayed the tactical coordinator's name, rank, serial number, squadron, and photograph. He made a notation on a clipboard, then stepped aside—giving Lowell access to a pedestal-mounted keypad and monitor linked to the base's personnel access computer.

Lowell entered his security clearance code.

The screen came alive with confirming data.

Seconds later, the steel door behind them slid open automatically.

"Go get 'em, sir," the guard exhorted. He was referring to the fact that all K building personnel were involved in a continuing hunt for the enemy.

"Do my best," Lowell replied, stepping through the doorway into the TSZ.

Minutes later, Lowell was in the photographic library, assembling the materials he needed to pursue his hunch about the Soviet submarine's destination.

The walls of the room where Lowell was working were papered with photomurals of incredibly detailed, high resolution KH-11 satellite photographs. A linear network, designating latitude and longitude, was superimposed over each sat-pix, as was a pattern of tiny camera registration marks that resembled plus signs. In the lower right-hand corner, a data block spelled out date, time, navigational coordinates, satellite position, and security classification. All photographs displayed in this decorative manner had long been declassified.

By the time Lt. Commander Arnsbarger, the *Viking*'s pilot, arrived, Lowell was standing at one of the long library tables. The half dozen 18″ x 24″ sat-pix enlargements that he had requisitioned were spread out on the white formica surface. Lowell hunched intently over an illuminated magnifier, moving it slowly over the surface of one of the photographs.

"Well?" Arnsbarger challenged, removing his sunglasses. "Where do these Ruskie bozos go?"

Lowell looked up and shook his head. "Nowhere," he said quizzically.

Arnsbarger questioned him with a look.

Lowell gestured to the magnifier. "Be my guest."

The big pilot leaned to the eyepiece. A silvery oblong shape, heading into the main ship channel from the Soviet naval base, was centered in the cross hairs of the illuminated rectangle. The Soviet captain and his first officer were clearly visible on the bridge.

"That's our sub," Lowell said. "By the way, if you look real close, you can see the captain's got a pipe jammed in his mouth."

Arnsbarger looked up and nodded. "Yeah," he said expectantly.

Lowell pointed to the data block on the sat-pix. "Sailed from port, twenty-eight January at five-thirty. Okay?"

"I'm with you."

Lowell slid a second sat-pix next to the first. He set the magnifier on it and centered the cross hairs on a similar oblong shape that was entering one of the long submarine slips in the Soviet base.

Arnsbarger leaned to the eyepiece again. "Looks like Captain 'Pipesmoker,'" he said, still looking into the magnifier.

"Right. Same sub," Lowell replied. "Returned to port, twenty-eight January at twenty-three forty-five hours," he added, indicating the data block.

"Elapsed time, round-trip, seventeen hours fifteen minutes," Arnsbarger calculated, straightening from the eyepiece.

"Right again," Lowell said. "Figuring an average speed of twenty-five to thirty knots—nine hours out, nine back, and no drift time, the outer mark is—"

"Highly unlikely in that tub," Arnsbarger interjected.

"That's my point," Lowell resumed. "The outer mark is within a two-hundred-fifty-mile radius of port."

"Which is nowhere," Arnsbarger said.

"Damn near," Lowell said thoughtfully.

He moved a few steps down the table to where he had unrolled a chart of Gulf and Caribbean waters. A navigator's drafting compass lay next to it. Arnsbarger watched intently as Lowell placed the pinpoint of the instrument at zero on the scale of nautical miles. He spun the adjustment wheel until the graphite point reached the two-hundred-fifty-mile mark. Then he placed the point of the compass at Cienfuegos and drew a scaled two-hundred-fifty-mile radius circle. The line cut through the Florida peninsula at Palm Beach and barely ticked Mexico's Yucatan.

"Well, we know they didn't torpedo the Boom-Boom Room at the Fountainbleu," Arnsbarger cracked. "What about Cotoche or Cozumel here?" he asked, indicating the Yucatan area.

Lowell shook no emphatically. "I checked every pertinent sat-pix," he replied. "The sub never showed in either port. Besides, considering the elapsed time, that'd really be stretching its range."

Arnsbarger shrugged and studied the map. "Maybe the guys with the white powder meet ol' Pipesmoker halfway," he said facetiously.

"That's what I've been thinking. Some kind of meeting."

"With who?"

"Beats me."

"Could just be a training run."

Lowell grunted with uncertainty. "That's what I've been telling myself till today," he replied. *"Twelve days,"* he said incriminatingly. "It's only been twelve days since we last tracked 'em."

"Good point. Not a whole lot of time between runs; breaks the pattern," Arnsbarger admitted. "Something to think about."

Lowell smiled. "I have another one for you." He tapped a finger on another sat-pix in front of Arnsbarger. "What's that?" he challenged.

Arnsbarger slid the illuminated magnifier to where Lowell indicated and leaned to the eyepiece. "Tanker? Containerized carrier? Hard to tell for sure." He shrugged. "Not exactly our area, bucko."

"Yeah, I know," Lowell said. "Just that digging through this stuff, I noticed that every time our sub makes one of these circuits, that ship's docked in Cienfuegos exactly one week later without fail." He turned his palms up. "Probably nothing."

"Probably," Arnsbarger echoed. "We have an acoustic signature on it?"

"Dunno," Lowell replied.

"Might be worth a look-see," Arnsbarger said. "If we get an ac-sig match off the hydrotapes, maybe we could identify it."

"Yeah," Lowell said.

Chapter Thirteen

Churcher was still unconscious when he hit the water. The cold slap in the face, the chilling of his entire body to 39 degrees Fahrenheit, snapped him awake.

He clawed at the water, fighting to pull himself upward. Fighting the sea, and the darkness. Fighting to stay alive.

He hadn't any idea how far it was to the surface; nor any recollection of the men carrying his limp body and sliding it head-first into the greased tube, the clang of the steel hatch, the mechanical engaging of the breechblock, or the captain's order to "Fire one!"

Those bastards! Those dirty fucking bastards! he thought.

He opened his mouth to scream.

Dark brine rushed in, pulling the tail of his necktie with it.

He couldn't believe they had done this to *him*. True, he'd caught them trying to screw him. Put it to them pretty hard. But he gave them every chance and sufficient time to make things right. Had they just ignored his remark about the *Kira*? About the package of incriminating drawings that would now go to Boulton? Hollow threats weren't his style. Deschin knew that.

The tie and the bitter water choked him.

His voice wailed inside his head. *Christ, thirty fucking years of doing business with them, and it had come to this!*

Churcher had known most of the members of the postwar Soviet hierarchy: Malenkov, Khrushchev, Kosygin, Gromyko, Dobrynin, Chernenko, Brezhnev. Like him, they were self-made men who had an earthy integrity, the sons of farmers and factory workers who doggedly, shrewdly, and, yes, ruthlessly made it to the top. They played by the rules, breaking them only for the good of all the players—as they defined it. None of *them* would have allowed this to happen. None of them would have given the order to terminate Theodor Churcher.

But Kaparov had. Was it not sophisticated equipment manufactured by Churchco's Medical Products Division, and quietly exported at no cost, that kept the jaundiced Premier alive for the last six months? The irony of it! Churcher couldn't help thinking it was his own fault. He should have known better. Kaparov was KGB.

Churcher finally got hold of the necktie and yanked it from his mouth.

Bubbles pulsed from between his lips, trailing behind him in a rapid stream.

He pulled at the water. And kicked at it. And cursed it. And propelled himself up through it. And was beaten by it. Beaten by pain. Excruciating pain. The death rattle of dying cells ripped through him like a bullet fired in a steel box. It tore at his muscles and paralyzed his limbs. But his oxygen-starved body screamed to no avail. The few molecules of the precious gas that remained in his blood were already racing to his brain to keep it alive.

He began to hallucinate, and envisioned a macabre ratchet-toothed monster erupting from within his chest in an explosion of tissue, bone, and blood—and then, blinding strobelike flashes followed by nothingness. An eternity passed before the sight of tiny figures running out of the milky haze heartened him; children giggling as they scampered across the broad lawn of his estate, calling out, "Grandpa! Grandpa!" And as the bright, smiling faces came closer and closer, Churcher filled with pride, and bent to scoop them into his arms—but they ran right through him.

He had one fleeting moment of consciousness. *I'm going to make it!* he thought. *Son of a bitch, I'm going to make it!* He looked desperately for the glow which would signal he was nearing the surface.

But darkness prevailed.

His body continued rocketing upward, gaining momentum like an air-filled drum. Finally, it exploded into the sunlight and splashed into the sea, settling facedown, arms and legs askew in the way dead men float, and was carried off by the current.

The captain had brought the Foxtrot to the surface. An ordnance specialist stood next to him on the bridge shouldering an RPG-7 ground to ground mobile rocket launcher.

"Fire when ready," the captain ordered calmly.

The ordnance specialist pressed his face to the eyepiece and squeezed the trigger.

The RPG-7 rocket came from the launcher with a deadly whoosh, and darted into the fuselage of Churcher's helicopter.

A violent explosion erupted.

For an instant, a brilliant flash, yellow-orange at the center and framed by a purple-green halo that came from the chopper's fuel expanded above the sea in silence. Then came the sound as the thundering fireball completely incinerated what a millisecond earlier had been a twelve-thousand-pound helicopter.

Pieces of the chopper spiked through the air in every direction. Long trajectories arced over the sea. Chunks of flaming debris plunged into the water, emitting puffs of steam.

The captain nodded to the ordnance specialist, then turned to the first officer and said, "Take her down."

Deschin and the others were waiting below in the Foxtrot's control room.

"It's done," the captain reported evenly, as he came off the ladder from the bridge, pushing his pipe between his teeth in a self-satisfied gesture.

Deschin nodded thoughtfully. "Shame," he said. "Churcher should have listened to his board of directors."

The others looked at him quizzically, as Deschin knew they would.

"He once told me they didn't like him flying to the drilling platforms," Deschin explained. "They were concerned one day he would crash."

He said it coldly, without emotion, a simple statement of fact, and of what he had calculated would be perceived should the wreckage of the helicopter or Churcher's body—without a bullet in it—be found.

The men gathered round him nodded smugly.

Deschin swept their faces with disapproving eyes. "He was a son of a bitch," he said. "But he was my friend." He turned and walked slowly from the control room, lighting a cigarette.

The Foxtrot was well below the surface when Churcher's hand bumped into the piece of floating wreckage. He was semi-conscious but could feel the smooth aluminum and instinctively crawled onto the large section of paneling from the chopper's belly. The foamed plastic core had enough buoyancy to keep him afloat. He began coughing violently, and returned a chestful of water to the sea.

Chapter Fourteen

In the cemetery on the hill overlooking Christ Episcopal Church, a few mourners stood, heads bowed above scarf-wrapped necks, while the minister recited final words over Sarah Winslow's coffin.

Melanie lingered as the group dispersed, and watched as her mother was lowered into ground frozen harder and deeper than the diggers could remember. She stood alone between the side-by-side graves of her parents, hoping that the minister was right—that at this very moment their souls were being joyously reunited—though she found it difficult to believe in a Hereafter for herself.

The doctor also remained. He moved forward from behind the flower-covered grave where he had been standing unobtrusively.

"Give you a lift?" he offered in a friendly voice.

"Thanks, no," Melanie replied. "I think I'll walk. It's such a beautiful morning, and I—" she paused, and shrugged halfheartedly.

He nodded that he understood.

"I was with your mother," the doctor said. "It was peaceful. She just fell asleep. Before she did, she asked me to make sure you got this." He removed the envelope from his pocket and handed it to Melanie, adding, "It was her last conscious thought."

Melanie accepted the envelope without looking at it, and smiled appreciatively. "Thanks again," she said. "Thank you for being with her."

She turned, and meandered down the narrow road, between

the headstones, out of the cemetery, and past the white clapboard church that nestled in the snow-blanketed hills.

Moments from her years in this wholesome place came to mind while she walked—fleeting glimpses of eating homemade ice cream on summer nights in the lawn glider, galloping on her chestnut colt through fields of wildflowers, her parents glowing with pride when she danced at a school recital, the rush of passion with her first lover, the train station on the day she left home to audition for a dance company in New York.

She was crossing a field when the chirp of a foraging wren pulled her out of it, and she looked with some surprise at the envelope in her hand. Intrigued, she opened it, and began reading the letter her mother had written so long ago.

> January, 15, 1946
> Dearest,
>   I have something wonderful to share with you! Just before Christmas, I gave birth to a beautiful little girl. She's pink and blue-eyed, and has wispy silken hair. We named her Melanie. Of course, Zachary believes her to be his, and I have said nothing to the contrary. But I'm certain she is really yours, and wanted you to know.
>   I have no doubt of this because I discovered that I was pregnant on the hospital ship taking us home. Funny, we hit some rough weather just after we left, and everyone was seasick. Lord knows, at first, I thought I was, too. But only in the morning? Every morning? For weeks? Even after the seas had calmed?
>   Your daughter is healthy, with straight, strong bones, and has her father's face when she grins. We're all happy, and living in a perfectly wonderful cottage that Zachary built for us.
>   I hope you're happy, too. I think about you, and wonder what you're doing. Are you still in Italy? Will you return to Rome and resume your studies at the university? I hope so. I want so much for this to reach you. I'm sending it under your code name, as I know the military personnel in the sector know you by it, rather than your own. How could they ever forget you? I know, I won't.
>   As ever,
>   Sarah
>   P.S. How could we have known they'd ever find us?
>   Oh, I'm so happy to be alive!

Melanie was stunned by the revelation. The words rang like a bell clapper that wouldn't stop. She sat on the trunk of a fallen tree and read it again, and then again. And then, again, after she resumed walking. She didn't feel the cold. She didn't feel anything except an overwhelming loneliness.

A vague recollection of her mother's face came to her, and as it sharpened Melanie saw Sarah's cheerful countenance replaced by a rather queer, unsettled look. Her father's brother had been the cause of it, she recalled. Uncle Wallace often joined them for Sunday dinner, and on one such occasion he kept remarking how much his ten-year-old niece resembled her father. And each time he said it, Sarah's face took on the strange expression. It made Melanie uncomfortable at the time, and she purposely didn't dwell on it. But it had stayed with her all these years, and now, she understood why.

She had turned into the drive, and was walking through the glade of pines toward the cottage when a gust of wind caught the envelope and scooped it from her grasp. It inflated, and sailed through the air—then, swooping down, danced, pinwheeling across the frozen snow. Melanie chased after it, the pages of the letter fluttering in her hand, her boots crunching through the hard skin of white between the trees. Almost within reach, the envelope suddenly sailed upward and snagged amidst the twigs of a bare hawthorn. Melanie slipped her hand between the branches and carefully picked the envelope from the thorns. Then, she sensed a presence and looked up.

What she saw only intensified her feelings of abandonment— that she had lost both her parents on the same day, one for the second time, and one forever.

There, framed between two mature maples, stood the stone cottage—the cottage she had always been so proud to say had been built by her father.

She approached it slowly and, after walking around it, sat crestfallen on the top step of the porch and read the letter again.

But what she was searching for with each reading wasn't there to be found. It was cruel, she thought. Cruel and tormenting that this staggering revelation was incomplete—that neither the envelope nor the letter itself revealed the identity of the man who had never received it.

*   *   *

It had been an unusually mild winter in the Southwest. March was still a week away and buds were already sprouting on the tips of oak and aspen.

A few wind-stretched clouds hung in the sky as the Piper two-seater came out of the southwest, and made a slow banking turn low over the Churcher estate.

The man next to the pilot pulled a motor-driven, 35 mm camera to his eye and began taking photographs. He trained the tele-photo lens on the grounds, on the surrounding approach and service roads, on the high walls, and on the museum entrance kiosk.

Below, in the study of the Chappell Hill mansion, Andrew Churcher and Ed McKendrick sat in opposite chairs, dwarfed by towering walls of books.

Neither reacted to the drone of the plane.

Andrew stared glumly at the phone on the desk. His father had been missing for three days, and Andrew had slept little. An overall numbness and sense of detachment had gradually set in.

McKendrick fidgeted, his mind wrestling with a decision he'd been hoping he wouldn't have to make. But the mystery of The-odor Churcher's disappearance grew as each day passed. And for reasons known only to McKendrick, he was feeling pressured by it. The time had come. He arched his back against the chair, got up, and went to the oak wall behind the desk. A Cezanne still life hung in the center panel. He swung aside the hinged frame, re-vealing a wall safe. His thick fingers grasped the combination dial and began twirling it.

"What're you doing?" Andrew asked halfheartedly.

"Getting something," McKendrick mumbled.

He realized he had been so preoccupied, he had forgotten about Andrew. McKendrick decided to proceed despite his pres-ence. He finished the combination and brought the dial to a pre-cise stop.

The tumblers clicked into position.

McKendrick turned the lever and pulled open the safe. A flat, square metal box was on a shelf by itself. He removed something from it, and returned the box to the safe, which he immediately closed and locked. Then slapping at the frame with an elbow, he sent the Cezanne swinging back into place with a thud.

McKendrick's brow furrowed in concentration. He turned and crossed the room, flicking a plastic card that he had taken from the safe against his thumbnail.

"What's that?" Andrew asked.

"Card key."

"Yeah?"

"Match to your father's."

"Office, museum—"

McKendrick nodded, and said, "Something I'm supposed to do—" He paused thoughtfully and added, "But I'm not sure."

Uncertainty, particularly admitting to it, Andrew thought, wasn't at all like McKendrick. Even in his numbed state he sensed the weight of his dilemma.

"Do what?" he asked, getting out of the chair and crossing toward McKendrick with more vitality.

"Something—has to be—forwarded," McKendrick replied, picking his words. "But only under certain circumstances."

"Did I miss something?" Andrew asked suspiciously, "Or didn't you just answer my question without telling me anything?"

"Your father didn't want you involved," McKendrick replied flatly. He turned away from Andrew, and slowly crossed the room in thought.

Andrew pursued him. "Christ, he's been missing for three days. He's probably dead. And you've got something to do that I can't know about!" he said emotionally, wondering why his father's confiding in McKendrick had never bothered him until now.

McKendrick stopped walking and turned to face him. "Take it easy, kid," he said calmly, having heard the resentment in Andrew's voice. "*I* don't know about it either. I've got orders, that's what I know. And before I carry them out, I've got to be positive your father's dead and know the circumstances."

"Why?" Andrew asked. "You're still not telling me what I want to know, Ed."

"He didn't say why," McKendrick replied. "Hell, I don't know what to tell you."

Suddenly, Andrew could hear his father's voice—"Articulate. Articulate. Never expect someone to read your mind." He took a moment to compose himself, then stepped around McKendrick to face him. "I have two questions, Ed, and I expect you to answer them," he said in a controlled, businesslike tone.

McKendrick studied Andrew for a moment, gauging the change in him. "Okay," he said, "shoot."

"First, what has to be forwarded?" Andrew asked. "Second, to whom does it go?"

McKendrick considered it for a moment. "There's a package in the museum," he replied. "I have no idea what's in it."

"Yeah?" Andrew prodded impatiently.

"It goes to Boulton," McKendrick replied, half wishing he hadn't.

"Boulton? My father's golf crony?" Andrew blurted, feeling foolish the instant he said it. He could already hear the bite in McKendrick's tone.

"No, Boulton the CIA honch," McKendrick snapped facetiously, not disappointing him. "It goes to the company, Drew, not the country club." He paused and added sharply, "'To be sent under anonymous cover in the event I croak under suspicious circumstances.' That's a quote, and it's all I know."

"Geezus," Andrew exclaimed. He hadn't anticipated the second half of McKendrick's reply.

"My sentiments, exactly," McKendrick said. He winced, thinking Churcher would ream his ass if he wasn't dead and ever found out McKendrick told Andrew about the package.

The two men held a look. Andrew broke it off.

McKendrick fell into a chair, flicking the card key against his thumbnail.

The exchange had shaken Andrew from his lethargy. He paced anxiously and circled to the desk where he straightened the phone—as if adjusting its position might cause it to ring.

Prior to closing the book on his years in Cuba, GRU agent Valery Gorodin had one last task to carry out. The assignment came directly from the office of the Soviet premier. And Gorodin knew it was undoubtedly the most important of his career—the one that could put him back on the road to membership in *nomenklatura*.

For years, direct travel between Cuba and the United States had been indefinitely suspended. Gorodin had been routed through Mexico City, arriving there just after midnight. He spent the evening at the Soviet Embassy on Calzada Tacubaya, securing his cover.

This meant he had to become familiar with an elaborate new identity—personal history, career background, and reasons for travel—and he had barely eight hours to do it. Memorizing "the legend" was much like cramming for a final exam, and Gorodin was a quick study; but using the cover biography, in the off-handed manner of a person who has lived it, was infinitely more difficult.

To sharpen Gorodin's responses, GRU personnel who had been acting as his tutors became his interrogators. They grilled him for hours, asking the same questions repeatedly. They forced him into traps, discrepancies, and incriminating silences until the answers came automatically and seemed natural. It was the most intensive eight hours Gorodin had ever spent.

The following morning, a colleague led him into the bowels of the Embassy and introduced him to the "dry cleaner"—a network of tunnels that branches out from a basement storeroom, providing concealed access to surrounding streets and vice-versa.

"The Company keeps us under constant movements analysis," the colleague warned. "They know about these tunnels, too; but the station chief doesn't have the personnel to monitor each terminus round-the-clock. Let's hope we picked one he's not watching today."

Gorodin hurried anxiously down the damp narrow passageway. It led to a rickety staircase that came up in an alley behind a bordello on Calle San Jacinta. Gorodin opened the door a crack and peered into the alley. An Embassy driver was waiting in a cab to take him to the airport. A bleary-eyed prostitute was leaning against the door, propositioning the driver. *Hooker or CIA case officer?* Gorodin wondered. He waited until the driver got rid of her, then pushed aside the sheet metal door and hurried to the taxi.

The second leg of his journey took Gorodin over the Mexican Gulf. The route reminded him that seven miles below, search and rescue teams were scouring the waters for Theodor Churcher and his helicopter.

The tires of Mexicana Airlines Flight 730 added their black stripes to runway 37N at Dallas-Fort Worth International Airport twenty minutes ahead of schedule, and taxied to the terminal directly.

The time was 11:40 A.M. when the mechanized boarding ramp swung into position and bit into the side of the jet's fuselage.

The passengers spilled into the customs area, gathering around baggage conveyors. A few with carryons proceeded directly to counters where uniformed United States customs agents waited.

Gorodin was in this group. Time was his adversary now, and he was pleased to have arrived early.

In sunglasses, white shirt, tie, and rumpled beige suit, he looked every bit the travel-weary businessman. But it had been years since he had operated in the field, alone and undercover.

A wave of apprehension broke over him as he approached the customs agent. His mouth turned to cotton. A wetness broke out behind his knees.

Gorodin fought to overcome his anxiety, and nonchalantly tossed his two-suiter onto the counter. He presented a bona fide French passport—one that had been surreptitiously procured, and then washed by GRU counterfeiters.

The customs agent, a skittish young woman with close-cropped hair, saw "Republique Francais" embossed in gold on the deep maroon cover. *"Parlez vous, Anglaise, monsieur?"* she asked haltingly.

"Mais oui, madame," replied Gorodin. "When in Rome—" he added jovially in English. He was fully prepared to converse in fluent French but gladly accommodated her.

"Great," she drawled, "because my French is—" she paused and waggled a hand, then opened his passport and matched face to photo.

"Where you coming from Mister—Coudray?" she asked, quickly adding, "I say that right?"

Gorodin nodded amiably, and leaned on the counter.

"Mexico City," he replied.

"City of embarkation was Paris?"

Gorodin nodded again.

"And you're going to?"

"Dallas, New York, Paris."

"Business?"

"Oui, madame," he replied, purposely slipping into French.

"Okay," she drawled, tapping his bag. "Would you open that for me, please?"

Gorodin popped the latches of the two-suiter. His hands were sweaty, and his fingers left smudges on the chrome. He split the halves of the bag and dried his palms in his pockets.

The agent poked through the clothing, seemingly disinterested. But her eyes alertly recorded the labels of French manufacturers on most of the garments. She paused and fingered one curiously.

Gorodin's heart quickened. His mind leapt to all the disastrous possibilities: Had the label been improperly sewn? Had he been given a shirt much too small for him? Had she spotted some silly oversight that had cast suspicion on him?

"Cardin. Great stuff," she said. "Bought the same shirt for my husband. He loves it." She smiled and flipped the bag closed.

Gorodin nodded, and felt somewhat relieved. He was thinking that the hours at the Embassy in Mexico City had been well spent when she made an offhanded observation that threatened to unnerve him. "Your accent, if you don't mind me saying it," she remarked, "sure doesn't sound French."

She's right! Gorodin thought. Despite his language skills, the years in Cuba had imparted a decidedly Latin flavor to his English. Even his Russian had been slightly tainted.

"I am a Basque," he replied proudly, as if he'd been saying it all his life. He snapped the latches on the suitcase closed, punctuating his reply.

The agent stamped his passport and returned it.

"Have a nice day, Mr. Coudray," she said in a singsong cadence.

Gorodin slipped the passport into a pocket, and forced a smile in response to her rhyme. Then, he slid his bag from the counter, and walked quickly into the long tunnel that led to the terminal.

There was a new confidence in Gorodin's stride. Yes, yes, it was good to be back, he thought—back closer to the edge, thinking on his feet, winging it resourcefully. He was hurrying past a newsstand when he noticed headlines proclaiming—"CHURCHER STILL MISSING IN GULF."

Outside, he threw his bag into a dusty Chevy wagon on the arrivals ramp and jumped in next to the GRU driver, a powerfully built young agent named Vanik.

The car pulled away immediately, heading south for U.S. 45, the arrow-straight freeway that connects Dallas, Houston, and Galveston.

The drive to Houston would take approximately four and one half hours. Gorodin would have preferred to fly. But no connecting flight meant no record of M. Coudray ever having gone to Houston. And Gorodin wanted this last task to be as clean as possible.

"Everything's being arranged," Vanik said.

"Good," Gorodin replied. "We have to move fast."

They spoke in Russian.

The long drive ended at an abandoned ranch in desolate country outside Houston. They immediately entered a ramshackle barn where a third man was painting a mobile cherry picker to resemble a Houston County Gas & Electric service truck. That evening Gorodin pored over the photographs of Churcher's estate Vanik had taken from the Piper, and began solidifying the plan to break into the underground museum.

Chapter Fifteen

Dinh Tran Xuyen and his family lived in a steel Quonset hut, one of thousands of makeshift structures dotting the countless islands and estuaries along the Gulf coast of southeastern Louisiana where colonies of homesteaders had sprung up. Most were immigrant fishermen from Southeast Asia who found that the climate and ecological makeup of the area closely resembled the land they had left behind.

Dinh had come to the United States in the mid-seventies with the members of his family who'd survived the war. They started a fishing business and made a living netting menhaden—the yellow-finned members of the herring family which run in large schools in Gulf waters, and are more commonly known as bony fish.

But Dinh wasn't fishing this night. The deck of his forty-two-foot trawler was piled high with discarded refrigerators, bathtubs, and assorted car parts as he headed out into the Gulf. Dinh, his brother-in-law, and their teenage sons ferried the junk into the Gulf and heaved it over the side, marking the spot with an inexpensive navigation device. The submerged Lorans unit emitted a radio signal that would guide them to precisely the same spot with their next load. Indeed, they weren't scuttling junk, but rather building a reef on which vegetation and inert sea life that would attract fish would grow.

Dinh and his family were hoisting the dismantled carcass of a Volkswagen over the side when the fog bank suddenly shifted. The searchlight of a cruising Coast Guard patrol boat pierced the darkness and found them.

"Shut down your engines and prepare to be boarded," the captain barked over the loudspeaker.

Dinh flicked a look to the others and shook no sharply.

This had always been his fear, and he made a habit of working under the cover of darkness and fog to avoid it. Dumping wasn't illegal—dumping without a permit was. And like most Gulf fisherman, Dinh didn't file for one because the precise location of his reef would be marked on charts of local waters, an open invitation to poachers who'd rather fish someone else's reef than build their own.

Dinh and the others quickly muscled the old VW over the side. The instant it hit the water, he punched the boat's throttles home and headed for another fog bank about a mile away.

The cutter accelerated and pursued.

But Dinh's boat disappeared in the dense haze before the cutter could catch it. The captain watched the blip on his radar screen, and decided the fog was too thick to continue pursuit safely.

Dinh kept his throttles to the wall to put as much water between the two vessels as possible. The boat had raced a few miles through the fog when Dinh spotted something dead ahead in the water. He turned the wheel hard, putting the boat into a sharp high-speed turn.

Thirty-six hours had passed since Churcher had climbed onto the piece of floating debris from his helicopter. He'd been carried northward by the South Equatorial current, finally catching the curling flow of the Mississippi River that spun him inland toward the Louisiana coast.

The sharply turning vessel sideswiped the piece of debris, knocking Churcher into the water. Then the stern whipped around right over him, and the propeller bit into his left arm, severing it just below the elbow. He was suffering from exposure and dehydration, and hovered on the edge of consciousness, but he let out a long, piercing scream nonetheless.

Dinh heard it and throttled back the engines, circling the boat while his brother-in-law panned a searchlight across the choppy surface. They quickly found Churcher and plucked him from the water.

Dinh reacted instinctively the instant he saw Churcher's

wound. After the bombings, booby traps, and napalm of the Vietnam War, this wasn't the first severed limb he'd seen.

"Get the first-aid kit," he shouted to one of his sons; then, turning to his brother-in-law, ordered, "Head for home, wide open!"

Dinh ripped open the plastic case his son brought from the cabin, removed a length of rubber tubing, tied it tightly around Churcher's bicep, stemming the flow of blood; then went about bandaging the stump. All the while his brother-in-law had the boat at full throttle heading for the village where they lived.

It was close to midnight when the boat pulled up to a swaybacked dock built on angled stilts that marched into the placid Delta waters.

Dinh's wife ran from the Quonset hut to greet them. She was stunned to see the two men lifting Churcher's lifeless form out of the boat.

"What happened? Is he alive?" she asked as she helped them.

"Barely," Dinh replied. "Propeller."

"I'll get the pickup," she said, assuming they would take him to the hospital.

Apprehensive looks flicked between the two men. But there was no need for discussion. Neither wanted to deal with the authorities who would want to know where they were and what they were doing when the accident occurred.

"No!" Dinh shouted, grasping his wife's arm to stop her. "Get Doctor Phan."

Giang Phan had been a fully accredited physician in Vietnam, and served as a battlefield surgeon. The immigrant families trusted him. He knew their customs, spoke their language, and cared for them. But he had not yet been licensed to practice in Louisiana.

Churcher lay pale and unconscious on a mattress on the floor of the Quonset hut as Doctor Phan examined him.

"He's lost a lot of blood," the doctor said. "He needs a transfusion. He'll die without it. And I don't even have the equipment to type his blood, let alone access to supplies to replenish it."

"We can't take him to the hospital," Dinh said forcefully.

"We can't. Besides, he might die there anyway. Just do your best."

The doctor let out a weary breath. "I'll need a dish or a plate," he said to Dinh's wife. "Line up over here," he ordered the assembled group when she returned with it. Then, pricking the forefinger of each, he "field typed" Churcher's blood—mixing samples from the potential donors with a drop of Churcher's blood on the plate until he found one that blended smoothly and didn't clump, which meant they were the same type.

A direct, donor-to-patient transfusion was made.

Then Dr. Phan turned his attention to Churcher's crudely severed forearm. "I don't know," he said dismayed at the state of it. "I just don't know."

Chapter Sixteen

Four days had passed since Gisela Pomerantz rattled President Hilliard and Keating with her query about the Soviet *Heron* missile system.

Following the NATO luncheon, Keating and Hilliard discussed the subject in the limousine on the way to Capitol Hill. The President was scheduled to meet with auto industry leaders who had been pressing for import quotas, and he was in a testy mood. The three CEOs were averaging just under six million dollars a year, each, in compensation. For that kind of money, Hilliard thought, they should solve their own problems.

"Talk to me, Phil," he ordered curtly.

"I don't know what to say. According to the NIE, the *Heron* was tested, failed, and never deployed," Keating replied, citing the National Intelligence Estimate, a top secret evaluation of the military and economic status of all foreign nations.

"When was all that?" the President shot back.

"Last test monitored—July of seventy-five. We've seen nothing of it since."

"Not like the Russians to scrap an entire missile system, Phil," Hilliard pressed. "I mean, I've waded through more NIEs than I can count. The bottom line is, they just can't afford it."

"Maybe they had no choice."

"Come on, Phil," Hilliard admonished.

"I know, I know. No maybes," Keating responded defensively. "Where do we go from here?"

"Goose Jake," Hilliard instructed. "It's Langley's responsibility. Set something up. Saturday. Oval office. Afternoon. Clear it with Cathleen."

Now, President Hilliard and Chief Negotiator Keating sat in the Oval Office in the White House awaiting the arrival of Jake Boulton, director of Central Intelligence.

The President kicked back in his chair, put a foot against the desk, and propelled himself toward the window that overlooks the Rose Garden. When the chair stopped rolling, Hilliard swiveled, stood, and studied the bulletproof panes for a moment. The temperature outside was so cold that the inside surfaces of the five-and-one-half-inch-thick glass were lightly dusted with frost. Hilliard drew a face on one of the green-tinged panes with a fingertip—a circle for the head, three dots for the eyes and nose. He was about to draw the mouth when he took his finger from the glass and turned to Keating. "Before Jake gets here, run down the last couple of days for me, will you?"

"Well, it's gone pretty much as we anticipated," Keating replied. "All the NATO folks are eager as hell to get out of the deployment game, that's for sure. But they want assurances. Thatcher still has daily antinuke marches in front of Ten Downing. Same for the Italian's over the cruise installation in Sicily."

"I know," Hilliard said. "It's been giving Minister Borsa grief since the day he approved it."

"He's been up against more than protestors lately."

The President nodded knowingly. "I saw the antiterrorist memorandum. Far as I'm concerned, NATO can't tighten the security screws enough. Anything else?"

"Well, the Belgians have been breathing easy since we've postponed. But they're still terrified the talks'll fail, and they'll be forced to deploy. Ditto for the Norwegians, and Dutch who are both—"

"Pisses me off!" Hilliard exploded. "All these years, these damn heads of state have failed to sell the need for deployment to their people; the very people who put 'em in office to protect 'em! If we hadn't been deploying all this time, where the hell would they be now?! I'll tell you where—looking at a stockpile of Russian SS-20s planted throughout Eastern Europe with nothing in the West to force the Soviets to the table. No deterrent— no disarmament. Why is that so hard to understand?"

Keating shrugged.

The President shook his head from side to side despairingly and took a moment to settle himself. "Any problems?"

"A little wrinkle with the Swedes."

"Oh?" Hilliard wondered, smoothing his beard.

"Seems they broke some KGB people who infiltrated their peace movement," Keating responded. "Organizing rallies, pumping in money, the usual agit-prop stuff. The Swedish government wanted to declare 'em persona non grata, and boot 'em. But we convinced them this is not the time to embarrass Moscow."

"Good going. Can't say I blame them. They've had it with Russian subs plying their waters. What else?"

"Nicholson's been kicking up a little dust. Nothing major."

"Nicholson?" Hilliard responded, surprised. "Christ, sixty, sixty-five percent of his suggestions ended up in our disarmament package. Find me another former chief negotiator who's had that kind of input in a succeeding administration. What's his beef?" the President asked, feeling slighted.

"His book," Keating replied, smiling.

"His book?"

Keating nodded. "I told him I'd mention it to you. Seems it was about to go to press and Boulton's censors deleted half of it." Keating let the sentence hang, heightening the President's curiosity, then added, "For reasons of national security."

Hilliard broke up with laughter. "Half of it?" he asked thoroughly amused.

Keating nodded again, and smiled.

"Those two have been banana peeling each other's paths since Nixon was a choirboy," Hilliard chortled. "Their battles on the golf course alone are—"

The intercom buzzed, interrupting him. He chuckled to himself and scooped up the phone.

"Yes?—Send him right in, Cathleen. Thanks." Hilliard hung up, and said, "Jake."

The door to the Oval Office swung open, and Jake Boulton, DCI, popped through it.

"Mr. President. Phil," he said rapid-fire.

"Thanks for coming by, Jake," Hilliard said. "What can you tell me about this damned *Heron*?"

"The SS-16A," Boulton said crisply.

"Whatever the hell the numbers are," the President said impatiently. "The one they supposedly tested and scrapped."

"Right," Boulton said, "the SS-16A. NATO code name *Heron* after the ornithological species of waterfowl. Initially developed for submarine launch. Design goal—solve chronic, unacceptable guidance system performance." The data came from Boulton in clipped, high-pitched bursts.

"What was its problem?" Hilliard asked.

"Best we can determine—" Boulton began.

Hilliard and Keating exchanged glances.

"—the Heron took its namesake too seriously," Boulton went on. "The bird is a patient, tenacious hunter. It waits unmoving for hours, locks onto prey the instant it appears, and—whammo—the target never gets away."

"And the missile?" the President prodded.

"No powers of discretion," Boulton replied. "It locked onto everything and anything. Tendency acutely manifested over water where distracting targets are isolated and clearly defined. Ships, rowboats, buoys, metallic debris, a floating beer can, in one instance, even a fellow missile, and whammo!" He made a diving motion with his hand. "Problem magnified as range increased."

"So it was *never* deployed, right?" Hilliard asked.

"Right. NIE confirms," Boulton replied smartly.

"Is that an—absolutely right? Or an—as best we can determine right?" the President jibed.

This stopped Boulton. He hesitated briefly, feeling suddenly unprepared. "The second, sir," he replied with diminished fervor, anticipating the President's reaction.

"Well, what the hell does that mean, Jake?" Hilliard pressed. "That we have doubts? I mean, how the hell can we start horse-trading with the Russians in Geneva next week if we aren't positive we know about every system they've deployed?"

The President got up out of his chair, almost charged out of it.

"The concept of negotiating is based on total, *total* knowledge of the other side's arsenal, dammit!" he continued heatedly.

"*You* know that, Jake! Geezus, I've got Phil here massaging the hell out of the NATO people, convincing them we're on solid ground; and before he even gets into it, the Germans drop the *Heron* right in our laps!"

"Fortunately," Keating interjected, "it was handled privately, and Pomerantz has agreed to keep it that way until we can get a fix on the facts."

"But if we can't, Jake," the President said, still charged up, "and she drops that tidbit on the other NATO representatives—" he let the sentence trail off, emphasizing the gravity of the situation. "And who would blame her?" he added. Then lowering his voice but maintaining his intensity, he said, "There's no way we can back out of the talks now. None. Not after pushing so hard for them. Even a stall would be unacceptable. It's tightrope time—no matter which way we fall we get screwed."

He moved around the desk, and approached Boulton.

"I want this, Jake. I want it badly," the President said with obsessive fervor.

"Yes, sir. I know," Boulton replied contritely.

"Good," Hilliard said. "Now, these talks are going to go on for months. Use the time. Juice your people. Fine tune your antenna. Wind up a couple of dozen more spooks and turn 'em loose. The *Heron* may be a dead duck, but—as best we can determine, just doesn't cut it. I want to close the loop on this, Jake. Top of the shopping list!"

"Our prime KIQ, Mr. President," Boulton said, smarting, but knowing Hilliard was right. This was a key intelligence requirement if ever there was one.

He did a crisp about-face and headed for the door.

"Jake?" Hilliard called out.

Boulton stopped on a dime and turned. "Sir?"

"Do me a favor, Jake," the President said. "Ask your boys to back off Nicholson, will you?"

"Nicholson?" Boulton broke into a boyishly innocent smile. "I'm not aware of a problem there."

"Glad to hear it," the President said. He knew Boulton's answer was his way of indicating he'd take care of it, without admitting it was necessary.

Boulton exited the Oval Office thinking about the round of

golf he and Theodor Churcher had played at Eagle Rock a few
months earlier. The solid thwack of driver against ball blasted
thoughts of *The Heron,* and Nicholson, from his mind as he pictured his old friend's perfect swing that the DCI had long envied.

Churcher had always been a hell of an athlete, Boulton recalled—a physical fitness maniac forty years before it had become fashionable. They had run cross-country together at Rice in
the late thirties. And it was Churcher who, though totally exhausted and near collapse, would dig down inside himself and
prevail through sheer will and determination. They had been
close all their adult lives, and Churcher's disappearance at sea
had unsettled the DCI. He blew past the President's secretary
without even a nod.

The President waited until the door had closed behind the DCI.
"I'd say he got the message."

Keating nodded.

"Brief Pomerantz," the President said. He turned to the window. The face he had drawn earlier on the frosted pane was still
visible. He put his fingertip to the glass, and drew a hard,
straight line for a mouth. "And make sure she stays zipped."

"You realize that directly contradicts your last order," Keating said with a lascivious smile.

The President burned him with a look. "Dammit, Phil!" he
replied. "This is no time for jokes. The whole thing could blow
up in our faces. And there's too much at stake to let that happen!"

Keating nodded contritely, and left.

The President angrily spun his chair and strode from the office.
He had a half hour before a National Security meeting, and he
knew just how he'd spend it.

"Arlington, sir?" Cathleen asked, sensing his mood.

Hilliard nodded tensely.

Cathleen called the White House garage.

The President had lost his temper, and it bothered him—not
because he'd blasted Keating unjustly, but because whenever the
frustrations became that overwhelming, Jim Hilliard knew he'd
lost his perspective. A walk through the National Cemetery always helped him regain it.

A light rain was falling as the stretched Lincoln proceeded up Memorial Drive.

President Hilliard got out and, declining raincoat and umbrella, walked alone amidst the identical limestone slabs that marched over the undulating terrain to every horizon.

Secret Service personnel followed on foot, maintaining a respectful distance.

The President paused solemnly at one of the water-stained headstones, and bent to straighten the small bouquet of violets that lay beneath the inscription which read:

JANET DAVIDSON HILLIARD

Janet Hilliard had never served in the military, but she had died in the service of her country.

And these were the times the President missed her most—when he needed to confide his fears and cope with his frustrations. And at these times, he would relive that tragic day in Chicago.

The Hilliards had just arrived in his hometown to kick off the campaign for his second term. Jim Hilliard was an extremely popular president. But the latest national polls had shown an unexpected surge for his opponent. And the President and his wife found the tumultuous crowds at O'Hare heartening.

They were acknowledging the cheers when the Secret Service agent saw the swift movement in the crowd, the sudden thrust of hands forward, and the deadly glint of blued metal. He dove at the President, knocking him to the ground an instant before the first sharp crack.

Janet Hilliard was standing directly behind her husband. The action that saved his life exposed her to the assassin's fire. Not for long. Perhaps an eyeblink or two passed before another Secret Service agent had bear hugged her to the ground. But the pistol had kept firing throughout that immeasurable interlude. And Janet Hilliard had been mortally wounded.

The President won the close election that followed.

And voices on the Hill soon began whispering that the tragedy, not his record, was his edge.

The President didn't like it; but he was enough of a realist to acknowledge that maybe, just maybe, they were right. And he privately dedicated his second term to his wife's memory, and made arms control his number one priority so that nations wouldn't one day do to each other what a crazed American did to Janet Hilliard. Nuclear disarmament was to be her legacy, not his, and it was being endangered.

Chapter Seventeen

On an autopsy table in Forensic Center, the Harris County coroner's offices on Old Spanish Trail near the Astrodome, a man's hand, the skin bleached to an opalescent gray, stuck out from beneath a shroud. The highly reflective surfaces intensified the light, which placed an eerie, surrealistic emphasis on details.

The time was 11:22 A.M., Sunday.

Doctor Tom Almquist, M.E., observed as a Houston Police Department fingerprint specialist took the hand and rolled each of the swollen fingers first across an inked pad, then across a pre-printed record card.

When finished, he studied the prints, and nodded to Almquist, pleased. "Better than I expected. A couple of them are real clean. Floaters can be a bitch."

The officer packed his equipment and left, taking the prints with him.

Almquist, a rotund black man with a bushy moustache and patient eyes, thought for a moment, then pulled the green shroud from the table and set it aside. A lower left arm, severed just below the elbow, was all that lay on the cold stainless top. Almquist hovered above the limb, studying the ragged stump.

Shredded tissue, ligaments, tendons, muscle, and blood vessels mushroomed around the crudely snapped radius and ulna bones of the forearm.

Almquist tore the wrapper from a disposable scalpel and leaned to the table. He placed the laser-honed blade on the inside of the forearm and pulled it the entire length, continuing down the wrist, palm, and center of the middle finger to the tip, splaying the tissue. Then, carefully excising the flexor carpi and the

99

extending sheath of muscles beneath, he revealed the radial artery, and went about removing it and the branching digital vessels of the hand and finger—a lengthy, tedious process.

Almquist spent the afternoon completing the procedure and running laboratory tests on the tissue sections and blood samples he'd prepared for analysis.

One result had surprised and baffled him. He ran the test again with the same result, which prompted him to call Houston Chief of Police Hedley Coughlan.

Now, Coughlan, a well-groomed man in a knife-creased suit, was rapping a knuckle on the glass partition to get Almquist's attention.

Almquist pulled the green shroud over his work and, peeling off his surgical gloves, entered an anteroom joining Coughlan, Andrew Churcher, and Ed McKendrick.

While Coughlan made the introductions, Andrew fought a fast-rising nausea brought on by the odor of cold flesh, chemical disinfectant, and death that had followed Almquist into the room—an odor that Andrew Churcher would never forget.

Coughlan noticed, and wrapped an arm around the young man's shoulders. "You all right, son?" he asked compassionately.

Andrew nodded and swallowed hard.

"I'm real sorry about this," Coughlan continued in a paternal tone. "Your father and I—well, you know how close we were, Drew. Whatever I can do."

"Thanks," Andrew said, regaining his composure. "Do we know what happened, Hed?" he asked.

Coughlan lifted a shoulder in a half shrug.

"We do and we don't," he replied. "At first, we figured his chopper went into the drink, but now—"

"Wait a minute," McKendrick interrupted. He was glad Andrew had asked the question; he didn't want to appear overly concerned with *how* Churcher had died, but it was important he know. "You have Mr. Churcher's corpse out there, but don't know what happened to him?"

Almquist and Coughlan exchanged uneasy looks.

Coughlan sucked it up. "We have a—*piece* of him," he said. "A small piece. Part of an arm."

When he called Andrew earlier, Coughlan said there had been
a development, but avoided the details. These weren't the kind
he covered on the phone.

McKendrick winced at Coughlan's answer.

Andrew felt bile rising in the back of his throat.

Coughlan pressed on, to get past the moment. "Way it lays
out," he began in as professional a tone as he could muster,
"yesterday afternoon, on a beach in Louisiana, some kids spotted an arm floating in the surf and notified authorities. The Louisiana State Police fished out that severed limb. There was a
watch still in place on the wrist. Turned out to be a Rolex."

Coughlan produced a plastic evidence bag, opened it, and removed the watch.

"As you may know," he resumed, "Rolex watches are collec-
tor's items. Each has a registration number with the name of the
owner on file. The LSP contacted the Rolex corporation, and
were informed"—Coughlan paused, and grasped an evidence tag
affixed to the watch—"that number 28900371 was registered to
one Theodor Scoville Churcher of Houston, Texas. That's when
they called us."

Andrew stared at the precisely machined luxury timepiece
Coughlan held. It was his father distilled to his essence, he
thought.

"We had the limb and watch airfreighted in this morning,"
Coughlan resumed. "Checked fingerprints first thing, just to be
certain. A match beyond any doubt," he added emphatically.
"Then, Tom began his work-up. That's when the flags started
popping."

"We're looking at a number of confusing discoveries here,"
Almquist said, taking over. "The dismemberment for one. It
could've happened in a crash. That's what we thought after talking to the LSP. But this isn't the pathology we usually see. Impact dismemberment most often occurs at joints, not between
them as in this case. Shark attack's a possibility. Boat propeller's
a third. We think he might have been alive when it happened
because very little blood remained in the limb. In a corpse, it
would've been congealed, and not spilled from veins and arteries
so readily. Nevertheless, the pressure of the watchband around

the wrist trapped enough blood in the vessels of the hand for me to run some tests.''

Almquist paused, and turned to a table behind him to get something.

Andrew was feeling detached, almost as if he was standing outside himself watching through the glass of the anteroom. He had heard Almquist's and Coughlan's words, and had formed appropriately bizarre images in his mind. But the full force of their meaning had yet to register.

Almquist turned back to the three men with a printout he'd slipped from a file on the table.

"This is a computer-generated profile of blood gases," he resumed. "This line here represents nitrogen—an unusually high percentage of nitrogen. And that's what really puzzles me. The only way this happens is via—"

"Rapid underwater ascent from great depth," McKendrick interjected. "I dive," he added in explanation.

Almquist nodded. "Right. Commonly called 'the bends.' This percentage isn't necessarily fatal, but there's no other explanation for its presence. I treated a number of cases in the Navy during the war—mostly frogmen in trouble who came up too fast."

"Doesn't make sense," McKendrick said.

"I agree," Almquist replied. "I'm just telling you what I found."

"We were hoping one of you might shed some light on it," Chief Coughlan said. "Any idea what your father was doing out there that might have put him a couple of hundred feet beneath the surface?"

Andrew thought, shrugged, and shook his head in bafflement.

"Ed?" Coughlan prodded, turning to McKendrick.

"Beats me, Chief," McKendrick replied.

"Not too many ways of getting down there," Coughlan said, thinking out loud.

"What about the chopper?" Andrew inquired. "Maybe it crashed and sank, trapping my father inside. By the time he got out, he was a couple of hundred feet down."

"We thought about that," Coughlan replied, nodding. "It's a possibility, but the chopper would've busted up pretty good on impact, and if not, flotation gear would've kept her afloat." He paused thoughtfully, then resumed, "Which leaves deep-sea gear—scuba, submarine, and cement booties, so to speak."

"What're you getting at, Hed?" Andrew asked. "You're confusing me."

"Sorry, son, not my intention," Coughlan replied. "Just exploring ideas. I mean, anything out of the ordinary happen lately? Anything of an unusual nature come to your attention. Anything? Anything at all?"

"I come up with a big zero on that one, Chief," McKendrick shrugged. "Nothing."

Coughlan swung a look to Andrew, "Drew?"

Andrew shrugged.

"He didn't go riding that morning," he replied. "Usually does."

Coughlan nodded, turned, and paced thoughtfully.

Almquist returned the printout to the file.

Andrew took advantage of their preoccupation to catch McKendrick's eye, and mouthed—Boulton?

McKendrick's eyes widened as if he'd been goosed with a cattle prod, and the vein in his neck was popping. He checked his outrage and shook no sharply.

Andrew shrugged, chastised.

Coughlan turned back to Andrew, took his hand, and placed the Rolex in his palm.

"Hang onto it, son," he said.

Andrew stared at the watch forlornly. Then he raised his eyes apprehensively to the glass partition and the shroud-covered limb beyond. It all hit him at once: the odor, the place, the circumstances, the knowledge his father was dead, that under the shroud lay a piece of him—a piece of him! His father's arm torn from his body!

He felt as if he'd been kicked in the groin. The indescribable hollowness spread excruciatingly through his bowels up into his abdomen. He swallowed hard, turned to a sink nearby, and vomited.

At approximately the same time in Chappell Hill, a maintenance truck with Harris County Gas and Electric markings was bouncing over ruts in the service road that ran outside the northeast

wall of the Churcher estate. The truck came through a turn and
slowed to a stop next to one of the power poles that marched in
an unbroken line to the horizon.

The beam of a flashlight came from within the cab and found a
marker on the pole that read, "NE263."

Valery Gorodin clicked off the flashlight and got out of the
truck.

Two fellow GRU operatives followed. Vanik, who had picked
up Gorodin in Dallas, carried a metal toolbox.

Gorodin climbed up behind the cab and into the bucket of the
cherry picker. He activated the hydraulic controls and swung the
bucket off the spine of the truck, lowering it to the ground.

Vanik handed Gorodin the toolbox and climbed into the bucket
with him. Both wore black jumpsuits and watch caps. The
third—dressed in traditional lineman's attire, hard hat, and
equipment belt—went to another control panel on the truck. He
would take over the operation of the bucket should it become
necessary.

The stone wall was twelve feet high. Eight inches above the
top of it, an electronic surveillance beam projected horizontally
between abutments.

Gorodin maneuvered the bucket upward until it was hovering
above the wall. Then he skillfully bent the arm of the cherry
picker in an inverted V, maneuvering the bucket toward the
ground on the opposite side. The trick was to keep the apex of
the triangle—formed by the arms of the articulated boom—centered over the top of the wall. One jerky move, one over-correc-
tion and the ungainly apparatus would break the surveillance
beam, sending an alarm to security central dispatch and trigger-
ing an armed response.

Finally, the bucket settled silently onto hard-packed soil on the
estate side of the wall.

Gorodin and Vanik climbed out with their equipment. The museum entrance kiosk was far across the grounds. They moved
cautiously in the darkness through a grove of aspen, and hurried
toward it.

Gorodin's stomach butterflied pleasantly as they reached the
kiosk. He had the electronic card key that he'd taken from

Churcher's wallet on the Foxtrot. He inserted it into the reader
next to the elevator.

The doors rolled open.

The alarm system in the museum deactivated.

Gorodin leaned into the elevator cautiously, looking for signs
of surveillance devices. Satisfied the elevator was clean, as he
had expected, he entered.

Vanik followed.

The elevator closed and descended, taking the two Soviet
agents into the museum below.

McKendrick's Corvette screeched up the ramp in the parking
garage beneath Forensic Center.

McKendrick spun the wheel right and glanced sideways to Andrew next to him. "Feel better now?" he asked, in a sharp tone
devoid of compassion.

Andrew slumped in the low seat of the Corvette and nodded
automatically.

"Good," McKendrick replied, "because I'm really pissed
off." The vein in his neck was popping again.

"What?" Andrew asked, baffled.

"You almost blew it in there!"

The car came up onto the street.

McKendrick flicked on the headlights, slammed the transmission into second, and turned west into Old Spanish Trail, heading
for the South Loop.

"What're you talking about?" Andrew snapped, pushing into
a more upright position.

"Boulton? The package in the museum!" McKendrick taunted
angrily. "I knew I should've never told you about them!"

"Back off me," Andrew said. "I didn't say anything. But I
probably should have." He felt like a child unjustly accused of
snitching, and squirmed in the seat.

"No fucking way!" McKendrick exploded. "If your old man
wanted *anyone* to know he was connected to that package, he
would've said so! You think he told me, 'under anonymous
cover,' just for the hell of it? He didn't even want Boulton to
know!"

"Okay, okay, you have a point," Andrew said defensively. "But something's not right here, dammit! I felt it the minute he didn't show up at the stables that morning."

"Shouldn't have said that to Coughlan, either," McKendrick shot back.

"Why not?" Andrew asked, without sounding argumentative.

"Cause I figure you're right," McKendrick replied less vociferously. "Something weird's going on. If you're smart, you'll forget it. Your old man's dead. Nothing's going to change that."

"Forget it?" Andrew exclaimed. "You heard Coughlan. You know my father didn't do any diving. That leaves subs and cement booties, and I don't like the sound of either!"

"Tough!" McKendrick snapped. "It was his life, he lived it his way. Whatever he was into, he knew it was hardball, that's for sure."

"Come on, Ed," Andrew pleaded. "We've gotta do *something*. We just can't—"

"No! *I've* gotta do something!" McKendrick interrupted angrily.

"The package—" Andrew said flatly.

McKendrick ignored him and downshifted.

"Ed," Andrew pressed.

McKendrick tightened his lips, and stomped the gas pedal to the floor.

The Corvette laid down a patch of rubber and took off. Its taillights left a red smear in the darkness.

Andrew lurched backwards, pinned to the seat by the sudden acceleration.

The car rocketed into the on-ramp of the 610 Freeway. By the time it hit the traffic lanes it was doing well over a hundred.

In the underground museum on the Churcher estate, Vanik was crouching in front of a storage room door, positioning a device made of precisely machined stainless steel parts over the lock.

This door and five others—four of which Vanik had already opened—led to climate-controlled rooms where paintings not hung in the galleries were stored. The doors were arranged in a semicircle, and opened onto an atrium from which the galleries fanned out.

Gorodin exited the adjacent storage room.

Vanik questioned him with a look.

Gorodin shook no, disgusted. "Not in there, either," he replied in Russian.

"Two more to go," Vanik said, discouraged. "Maybe Comrade Deschin was wrong. Maybe the package is in the mansion or offices downtown?"

"No," Gorodin said flatly. "Minister Deschin knew Churcher for over thirty years. They were very close. He was positive something this sensitive and important to Churcher would be kept here. Get on with it. We're wasting time," he added impatiently.

Vanik shrugged and returned his attention to the device that he had positioned on the door. He grasped the handle—a long, one-inch-diameter stainless dowel—and spun it. Three mechanical jaws tighted on the edges of the lock's hardened steel faceplate. Additional turns of the handle drove a super-hardened steel drillbit into the keyhole, then gradually retracted it, tearing the lock assembly from the door.

Vanik removed the device and set it aside. Next, he inserted a machined crank-handle into the jagged opening. He engaged the now exposed inner locking mechanism, and rolled back the four dead bolts that penetrated two inches into the metal frame on both sides of the door.

Gorodin pulled it open, reached inside, flipped on the lights, and entered the storage room.

Like the other storage rooms, this one was lined with parallel racks filled with canvases. A long work table with large, flat steel file drawers beneath, took up the center of the space.

Gorodin went to the drawers, opening them bottom to top, searching as he went, and not taking the time to close them. Once certain the package of documents wasn't in the drawers, he crossed to the racks of paintings, and began flipping through the canvases.

In one rack, The New York School—a Rothko, a Klein, a large Pollock, two Rauschenbergs, a Warhol, and three de Koonings. In the next, Impressionists—three prize Tahitian Gauguins, two Monets, Matisse's "Chambre Rouge," four Lautrec lithographs, Van Gogh's "Prison Courtyard," and a Degas. In the third rack, Renaissance masters—a da Vinci, a Raphael, a

Titian, a Giorgione, two Botticellis, four Michelangelo drawings, and a Veronese. In the fourth, a massive Courbet by itself. The fifth was filled with over a dozen Picassos. The sixth contained Russians—three Kandinskys, a Pevsner, three Malevich sketches, and a Chagall, and then, two more Chagalls. These last two canvases were exactly the same size, and stored back-to-back in a tight-fitting clear plastic sleeve—the only works stored in this manner.

Thus intrigued, Gorodin pulled them from the rack and carried them to the worktable.

The flamboyant oils were two of many Chagall had painted in Russia for the Jewish Theater in 1920. At the time, he had already spent four years in Paris, returning to his homeland just prior to the Bolshevik uprisings to court his long-time fiancée. He was made commisar of art for his home city of Vitebsk, where he founded an art school. Its students, like the master who taught them, produced works diametrically opposed to the state-approved Social Realism. And in 1923, Chagall's style was challenged by the new regime.

"Don't ask me why . . . a calf is visible in the cow's belly. Let Marx, if he's so wise, come to life and explain it to you," Chagall replied. He and his bride left Russia soon after, never to return.

Now, sixty-three years after Chagall painted them, GRU agent Valery Gorodin held the two masterpieces that had never been exhibited in Russia or the West. He slipped the back-to-back canvases from the plastic sleeve, and in the space between them found what he was after.

The package was a sealed, nine-by-twelve-inch waterproof mailer. It contained six engineering drawings of the *VLCC Kira*. The thirty-by-forty-inch blueprints had been folded four times in each dimension and fit neatly into the mailer which was devoid of markings and return address. The typing on the plain white stick-on label read:

> J. Boulton
> 2364 Fallbrook Road
> Chevy Chase, MD 20015

Gorodin wasn't an aficionado, but he knew Chagall was an expatriat Russian Jew. He smiled appreciatively at Churcher's selection of a hiding place, took the package, and quickly left the storage room.

The red Corvette swung into the short approach road that led to the Churcher estate.

McKendrick depressed the button of the remote control unit clipped to the car's visor.

The ornate entrance gates rolled back.

The Corvette rocketed between them without slowing, and accelerated up the cobbled drive. In thirty seconds the car had circled the mansion, crossed to the far side of the grounds, and nosed to a fast stop in front of the stables.

Andrew opened the door and got out.

McKendrick leaned across the transmission hump. "Package can't be shipped from Texas," he said. "I'll be gone at least a day. Don't talk to anybody."

Andrew grunted and slammed the door.

The Corvette rocketed off into the night.

Andrew watched for a moment. He felt isolated. The way he did as a teenager after he'd tangled with his father who would bring down a steel door in his mind, shutting him out. Andrew stuffed his hands into the pockets of his jacket, crossed to the stables, and climbed the outside staircase to his quarters above.

Across the grounds, the Corvette came over a rise and pulled to a stop adjacent to the museum kiosk.

McKendrick got out of the car, and walked briskly beneath the kiosk's intricate steel-and-glass roof toward the elevator.

He took the duplicate electronic card key from his wallet, and was about to insert it into the reader. His eyes darted to the status light. It was red, not green, indicating the elevator was in the down position—someone was in the museum. Had to be. McKendrick was turning toward the security phone on the opposite side of the kiosk when he heard the elevator door rolling open.

Gorodin and Vanik appeared in front of him. They froze for an instant, startled by McKendrick's presence, then bolted past him and ran into the darkness.

McKendrick took off after them. He had no idea who they

were, but he'd seen the package under Gorodin's arm, and knew he had to get it back.

The chase led toward the grove of aspen.

Gorodin was in the lead, already short of breath, and hanging onto the package. He was really back now, he thought. It was typical that the task had gone so well, only to be compromised at the last moment. He envisioned Beyalev smiling snidely on learning he'd been caught, and ran even faster.

Vanik was a few steps behind struggling with the toolbox, glancing back at their pursuer who was gaining.

McKendrick's massive arms and legs were churning, his chest heaving. In a burst of speed, he launched his 240 pounds through the air, diving past Vanik for Gorodin who had the package. The ground came up fast and hard as McKendrick landed just short of his target. His hands clawed at Gorodin's ankles as they slipped from his grasp. He had stopped many touchdowns in South Bend with that kind of tackle, but that was twenty years ago and he could see what he was doing.

Vanik got tangled in McKendrick's legs and went down, the toolbox crashing to the ground with him.

Both men scrambled to their feet.

McKendrick marshalled all the power in his weight lifter's body and fired a punch toward Vanik's head, intending to take him out with a single devastating blow and go after Gorodin.

Vanik put the toolbox in front of his face.

McKendrick's fist smashed into the steel surface. The bones in his hand shattered in a muffled crunch. He recoiled, howling in pain.

Vanik raised the toolbox overhead, and heaved it at McKendrick. It bashed him square in the chest, knocking him to the ground.

McKendrick shoved it aside to get up.

Vanik dove at him, slamming a forearm into his throat and a knee into his groin as he landed.

McKendrick gasped, his body arched against the pain. Vanik's fingers clawed at his neck, and vise-locked around it, thumbs crushing his windpipe from both sides, brutally. McKendrick fought to tear them from his throat, but Vanik's strong, expertly trained hands continued strangling him, and he knew he had only a few seconds of consciousness left. He expanded the powerful muscles in his neck and caught a breath, then brought his fists up explosively between Vanik's arms, and slammed them into the underside of his jaw.

Vanik bellowed as the tandem blows landed. The force sent him reeling backwards off McKendrick onto the ground.

The impact on McKendrick's broken hand sent shock waves rocketing up his arm. He got to his feet, despite the pain, and was searching the darkness for Gorodin when Vanik lunged into his legs from behind, knocking him to the ground again.

The two men rolled, and came up grappling at each other's clothing, fighting, clawing to get a handhold, any advantage.

McKendrick's right hand was useless. He exploded from down low, and blasted a left into Vanik's stomach. The punch landed with such force, McKendrick's fist penetrated the triangle beneath his adversary's rib cage to the wrist.

Vanik made a disgusting, wretching sound and doubled over in agony.

McKendrick lunged forward, grabbed a handful of his hair, and brutally smashed a knee up into his face.

Vanik's head snapped backward. Blood was spurting from his nostrils and mouth. He tumbled end over end, arms and legs flailing, and landed in a lifeless heap a distance away.

McKendrick turned to where he last saw Gorodin.

The sharp crack of a gunshot rang out.

McKendrick straightened suddenly, and spun to his left holding his shoulder. A burning sensation exploded across his chest. The searing pain shot up the side of his neck and out the top of his head. He staggered forward, realizing in his zeal to retrieve the package he had made a fatal error; he had never considered the men were armed, though to *assume* it had been drilled into him in the military and had paid off in Asian jungles. Wasn't *he* the platoon leader who warned his men, "Unchecked emotion is an enemy sniper!" Hadn't *he* once sternly lectured a friend who had chased a burglar instead of calling police? Didn't *he* always caution others to—

Another sharp crack rocked the night.

McKendrick saw the blue-orange flash in the blackness at the very instant the bullet ripped into his flesh. He lurched with a yelp. His left leg buckled under him. He dropped where he stood. Blood gushed in spurts from a hole in his thigh.

Valery Gorodin holstered his weapon, a Smith and Wesson magnum supplied by the GRU in Houston, knowing he had waited much too long before using it. The movement of the combatants, the darkness, the difficulty of getting a clean shot would suffice to explain. But Gorodin knew the truth to be different as he hurried to his downed colleague. "Is it bad?" he asked in Russian, the extreme circumstances causing him to slip into his native tongue.

"Nyet, nyet." Vanik lied, through a broken jaw. He pushed up into a sitting position with Gorodin's help, and shook his head trying to clear it.

McKendrick was lying in the grass nearby, the blood draining out of him while his nostrils filled with the smell of cordite. The brief exchange in Russian between the two GRU operatives was the last thing he heard before losing consciousness.

Gorodin dragged Vanik to his feet and, hefting the toolbox and the valuable package, led his battered colleague across the grounds.

Andrew couldn't hear the sounds of the fight in his quarters above the stables. But the sharp gunshots penetrated the stone walls. He was sitting on the bed pulling off a boot when the first crack made him flinch. The second confirmed what he thought he had just heard. He slammed his foot back into the scuffed leather and ran for the door, pausing to take a rifle from a rack next to it.

Andrew came onto the landing at the top of the outside staircase. It took a few moments for his eyes to adjust to the darkness and pick up the two figures running through the grove of aspen a distance across the grounds. He came down the steps, two, three at a time, ran past the stables, along the pasture fences in pursuit, and was cutting across the path that led from the mansion to the museum when his boot hit something slippery. His legs went out from under him. He fell to the ground, and slid through a patch of wet grass. The rifle flew out of his hand, vanishing in the darkness. He came to a stop, smeared head to toe with a viscous substance that tasted sweet on his lips. McKendrick was moaning nearby. Andrew scrambled to his feet, cleaning his face on his sleeve, and hurried toward the sound. McKendrick was lying facedown in the grass when he found him.

"Ed? Ed?" Andrew called out, shaking him a few times before accepting that he was unconscious.

McKendrick's face was pale and battered. His right pants leg was soaked with blood. The crimson syrup poured out the cuff onto the ground in a steady stream, adding to a rapidly expanding pool.

To his horror, Andrew realized it was McKendrick's blood seeping into the grass that had caused him to slip, and that now covered him. Shaken by the sheer volume of the spill, he grasped the bottom of McKendrick's pants leg and ripped the seam to the hip.

Gorodin's second shot had ricocheted off the thigh bone, nicked the femoral artery, and lodged in the mass of muscle and tissue directly behind it.

Andrew pressed his palm over the pulsing fountain that splattered him, temporarily stemming the flow. It was obvious McKendrick needed immediate paramedic attention. But, equally obvious, he would bleed to death while Andrew was summoning them. He quickly removed his belt, wrapped it around McKendrick's thigh above the wound, and pulled it tight. The blood kept coming. He pulled tighter, and tighter still, and pushed the prong of the buckle through one of the holes in the leather to hold the pressure.

The flow subsided slightly. But the highly developed muscles of McKendrick's thigh, which was the size of Andrew's waist, were preventing the artery from compressing. It wasn't nearly enough. At this rate, McKendrick would bleed to death in three minutes instead of two.

The thought of McKendrick dying with him right there, helpless to do anything, plunged Andrew into momentary panic. He fought off the sensation and forced himself to think. McKendrick's left hand was underneath his torso. Andrew pulled it free, bent up the thumb, and jammed it into the bullet hole in his flesh like a cork.

The bleeding stopped.

But within seconds, Andrew could feel pressure building behind it. Lubricated with blood, McKendrick's thumb would pop out soon after he left to seek help. Andrew forced it as far into the wound as it would go, held it there with his knee, and removed his belt from McKendrick's thigh. He rebuckled it around both thigh and wrist, securing the makeshift plug.

Then, Andrew ran like hell to the stables where there was a phone.

Chapter Eighteen

After the funeral, Melanie had taken long walks through the New Hampshire countryside trying to sort things out, trying to cope with the knowledge that someone other than her father was her father—a man without a name, a name she sought desperately.

She spent hours in the cottage looking for it; she searched the attic, every room and closet, and she rummaged through boxes, trunks, suitcases, and drawers.

There had to be something, she thought—another letter, or a note, or a document—something that would provide a clue to the man's identity and help her find him. Indeed, her mother's death had made Melanie all the more aware of her own age. She was barely, but undeniably, on the wrong side of forty—bored with her work, afraid of emotional involvement, confused by her lack of direction, and she hoped that a relationship with her real father, getting to know what he was like, might give her a better understanding of herself and, perhaps, might also help explain her unstable relationships with men.

But Melanie's obsessive search, and the various memorabilia it had unearthed, only drained and frustrated her. The name wasn't there to be found.

The only other link to the past was in plain sight in her mother's bedroom. Melanie was standing in the doorway looking at the desk by the window, imagining Sarah—young, vivacious, "glad to be alive"—sitting there writing the letter, when she saw the WWII photograph. She correctly assumed that the attractive man, possessively hugging her mother's waist, was her real father, and she sat at the dresser studying his face. Her initial excitement gave way to a strange hesitancy. A few uneasy

moments passed before she overcame it and stole a sideways
glance at the mirror. Then, looking straight into it, she began
comparing her face to his. Slowly, tentatively, she brought her
hands to her forehead and ran the tips of her fingers over her
expressively arched brows, across the bridge of her nose, down
along the sides of it, then, tracing the upward cant of her eyes to
the delicately emerging lines at the corners, moved out onto her
pronounced cheekbones and into the hollows beyond, almost as
if examining each feature to prove that what she saw in the picture, and in the mirror, was actually there. Indeed, the resemblance was strong and undeniable. The planes of her face
were unquestionably his.

Though satisfying, the discovery only fueled her desire to
know more, which made her angry. Angry at her mother. Angry
that she hadn't confided in her. Angry that she *couldn't*! Angry at
being denied the conversation that would have answered her
questions. And finally, angry at herself on remembering the
times her mother called wanting to chat, and she was too busy or
uninterested and put her off; the times her mother urged her to
come home for the weekend, and she had chosen to remain in the
city. Maybe one of those times, she thought, maybe all of them,
her mother had been searching for a way to utter that first sentence, after which the dam would have burst, and the rest would
have come in a flood of unshared memories.

Melanie stared at her face in the stained mirror, watching her
anger turn to regret. She removed the photograph from the frame
and put it in her purse, along with the letter and envelope.

She spent the rest of the weekend in Dunbarton and, on Monday, took the afternoon train to Penn Station. It was 10:47 P.M.
when she got out of a cab in front of her building on Gramercy
Park in New York City. The glow of streetlights crept around the
edges of the trees, and sent shadows from the cast-iron fence
stretching across the pavement. A cold, blustery wind was blowing, as it was the morning she left, and she found the continuity
reassuring. She put a hip into the taxi's door to close it, and
hurried toward her apartment, still coping with the emotional up-
heaval caused by her mother's death and incredible letter.

She was physically and emotionally exhausted when she entered her loft. The air had a chill, and the windows were rattling

in their frames. She flipped on the lights, dropped her suitcase to the floor, and locked the two deadbolts, affixing the safety chain automatically. The circular stair to the sleeping balcony seemed endless. She tossed her down-filled coat on the bed, kicked off her boots, and crossed toward the bathroom to shower.

The blinking red light on the answering machine, which indicated there were messages, caught her eye.

She stepped to the phone in her dancer's duckwalk, rewound the tape, depressed the play button, and turned back toward the bathroom.

Her mother's voice stopped her in her tracks like a gunshot. "Hello, hon, it's me," Sarah said from the answering machine in her feeble rasp. "I'm not feeling real well tonight. Actually, I'm feeling awful."

Melanie was stunned. A chill ran through her, and for the briefest instant she reacted as if her mother were still alive, making a mental note to return the call. Then she realized that the morning the doctor called, she left for New Hampshire without checking messages from the previous night; the night she had spent with Tim? Tom? Whomever.

"I'm leaving you a letter honey," Sarah's voice went on. "You'll be shocked when you read it. I apologize, and I hope you'll forgive me." The words came in hurried phrases separated by Sarah's labored breathing. "Something else you should know," she resumed. "Something that's not in the letter. It won't mean much to you now, but it will after you read it. There's a lot more I want to say, but I'm very tired, Mel. So, just remember the name Deschin—Aleksei Deschin." She repeated it, then spelled it out, adding, "And always remember I love you. Bye."

Melanie's heart pounded in her chest—pounded so hard she could hear it. She buzzed with elation. Then she thought to herself, *I love you, too, Mother.*

Chapter Nineteen

More than a week had passed.

In Geneva, Switzerland, U.S. Disarmament Negotiator Philip Keating and his staff had taken up residence at Maison de Saussure, just off Route de Lausanne on Lake Geneva. The eighteenth-century mansion was designed by French architect Francoise Blondel who, in the early seventeen hundreds, designed the ancillary buildings of Versailles. The magnificent estate was a short drive from the United Nations Palace in Ariana Park in the north end of the city where the talks would be held.

Keating checked in twice daily with President Hilliard—the question of the Soviet *Heron* missile still unresolved.

Most of the fifteen NATO representatives, Gisela Pomerantz among them, and their retinues had arrived.

An international pool of media correspondents had followed. They were headquartered just off Avenue De Ferney in the International Conference Center, from where official briefings would be issued.

Soviet Negotiator Mikhail Pykonen had arrived from Moscow fresh from a meeting with Premier Kaparov and Minister of Culture Aleksei Deschin. Pykonen was secure in the knowledge that Theodor Churcher's threat to inform the Americans about SLOW BURN, the secret missile base, had been thwarted. And he was fully confident of leaving Geneva with a world-dominating, first strike nuclear advantage for his country.

The week had been filled with formal dinners, inaugural ceremonies, and an official meeting of the two superpower negotiators.

The trading off of nuclear hardware, the bargaining of warhead

for warhead, the retreat from Armageddon, or so Phil Keating
thought, was about to begin.

Six days ago, after the meeting in the Oval Office during which
the President had caught him unprepared on the status of the
Soviet *Heron* missile, Jake Boulton had gone directly to Langley.
His hide was still smarting from the President's lashing when he
met with his DDO and DDI and other top members of his staff in
the French Room, his private conference area, and did some
lashing of his own. Soon after he had finished, the agency issued
a KIQ directive which when decoded read:

> Z152726ZFEB
> TOP SECRET KUBARK
> FR: DCI
> TO: CONCERNED AGENCIES
> INFO: KIQ FLASH PRIORITY
> STATUS SOVIET SS16-A MISSILE SYSTEM CODE-NAMED
>   HERON
> UNRESOLVED. IMPERATIVE GENERATE HARD EVI-
>   DENCE SYSTEM DEPLOYED OR SCRAPED. DEPLOY-
>   MENT ASSUMES
> SEAGOING BASE. REPORT ANY SUSPECT SOVIET NAVAL
>   ACTIVITY, RELATED SHIP MOVEMENT, OR UNEX-
>   PLAINED
> OCEANOGRAPHIC PHENOMENA LANGLEY IMMED. PER-
>   TINENCE
> AT DISCRETION OF DCI NOT INVESTIGATOR.

In Pensacola, Florida, Navy Lieutenant Jon Lowell, along with
all other ASW personnel with top secret security clearances, had
signed off on the KIQ directive within twelve hours of it being
issued. But none had any reason to think it significant.

Lowell spent his off-duty hours in K building's TSZ organizing a data search for the tanker he had spotted on the sat-pix. The
one that always appeared in Cienfuegos harbor a week after he
and Arnsbarger tracked the Soviet Foxtrot in their Viking.

From the photos, Lowell established at what hour the ship had
arrived in port, then worked backwards to determine approximately when it had sailed through the network of hydrophones

ringing the Soviet Naval Base. This narrowed the search to eleven hydrophone tapes that covered the one-hour-forty-eight-minute window he had established.

Now he faced the task of determining which of the many acoustic signatures on the tapes was the target ship. He had no idea that the one he was after belonged to a tanker of Liberian registry named—the *Kira*.

In New York City, there was not a single Deschin, Aleksei or otherwise, listed in the massive telephone directory which was the first place Melanie Winslow had gone after hearing her mother's voice on the answering machine.

She took the rest of the week off, and spent the time on the telephone and in the library.

In the Genealogy Department at the Main Branch of the New York Public Library on Fifth Avenue and Forty-second Street she learned that the name *Deschin* probably had Eastern European roots. And that it was most likely an amalgamation of two other names which might have been "Desznev" and "Chinova."

Her numerous calls to the Pentagon in search of information about a World War II special operative in Italy, code-named *Gillette Blue*, were met with paranoid evasiveness, bureaucratic buck-passing, and wisecracks. Even the name Aleksei Deschin elicited uncomprehending silences. Indeed, there are ninety members on the Soviet Council of Ministers and four hundred on the Central Committee. Their names are not the sort of information Pentagon clerks assigned to WWII archives commit to memory. Nor from the information Melanie supplied did the clerks have any reason to connect the name to the Soviet Union, or the upper echelons of its government. Indeed, as one said, "I'd love to help you lady, but for all I know Aleksei Deschin's jockeying a cab in Newark."

Driven by an inborn human force, an unquenchable need to know herself, to know those people who had given her life, the need that has seen fortunes and lifetimes spent searching, Melanie became determined to find her real father if at all possible.

Her only solid lead—that Aleksei Deschin had attended the

University of Rome prior to the war—came from her mother's letter.

It had been years since she had taken a vacation, and almost five since she had lived in Paris with the French journalist who had been her second husband. Obtaining a month's leave from the dance company, she fetched her passport from a safety deposit box, turned a chunk of her savings into traveler's checks, and started packing.

In Glen Cove, New York, a seaside community on Long Island's North Shore about twenty-five miles east of Manhattan, Valery Gorodin had spent the week at the Soviet estate on Dosoris Lane.

The forty-nine-room Georgian-style mansion sits on thirty-six heavily treed and fenced acres. Built in 1912 by George Pratt—son of the founder of Pratt Institute, the world-famous art school—"Killenworth" was purchased in 1948 by the Soviets as a weekend retreat for their United Nations personnel.

But located dead center between the commercial and financial centers of Manhattan and the aerospace defense industries on Long Island, Killenworth quickly became a prime Soviet COMINT installation. The acronym stands for communications intelligence, and the space beneath the mansion's slate roof that once quartered servants now concealed electronic surveillance gear and personnel dedicated to intercepting the high volume of sensitive, and often top secret, transmissions that traverse the corridor.

Upon arrival, Gorodin gave the package of *Kira* drawings to a waiting courier for immediate transfer via diplomatic pouch to Deschin in Moscow. Debriefing sessions followed, after which Gorodin swam and played *gorodky,* a popular Soviet club sport which colleagues teased bore his name. Many offered congratulations on his success in Houston. Nevertheless, between sets of gorodky, one GRU colleague who had been involved in the debriefing probed at a nerve he had sensed was exposed.

"Dangerous to leave a live witness, Valery," he remarked.

"It was dark. They were struggling," Gorodin replied nonchalantly, repeating the litany he had recited earlier. "I couldn't get a clear shot."

"Never known you to do that before," the fellow said. He

turned from Gorodin before he could reply, and began positioning the gorodkys—wooden cylinders the size of bowling pins—within a white outlined square. The object of the game is to clear the square of cylinders with a single throw of the *bita*, a striped stick the length of a cane. The colleague finished, handed the bita to Gorodin, and nodded challengingly.

Gorodin saw that the cylinders stood in a nearly impossible pattern. He sensed he had to clear them with one throw to end discussion of leaving a live witness. The throw-line was thirty feet from the "city," as the square is called. He positioned his toe against it, reared back, and hurled the bita toward the cylinders.

It whistled through the air like a boomerang, the stripes blurring in concentric rings, and slammed into the three cylinders on the left. Then it kicked across clearing the center and headed for the wall beyond, leaving one standing. But, as Gorodin had intended, his throw had such force, the striped bita ricocheted off the wall and came back through the city, taking out the last cylinder with a loud thwack.

He swung a victorious steely-eyed look to his colleague. Despite the run-in with McKendrick which blemished the purity of it, Gorodin immensely enjoyed operating in the field again. He was eager for more, and wanted to remove any suspicion that he was unfit.

His evenings had been spent with young Russian women who staff Soviet installations around the world for such purposes. The Kremlin's spymasters encouraged these liaisons to eliminate incidental social contacts. This lessened the chance that an agent might fall into a honey trap—a sexual relationship set by a rival intelligence group which then blackmails the target to do its bidding.

Gorodin found the State-supplied trysts to be sexually extreme, and satisfying. But they left him emotionally empty.

While at Killenworth, he speculated he would be posted to Moscow or perhaps his home city of Kazan, approximately eight hundred kilometers east of the capital on the Volga. He was pleasantly surprised by the nature of his next assignment. He'd never been to Rome, and looked forward to using his Italian.

122   GREG DINALLO

*   *   *

In a Quonset hut in southeastern Louisiana, Theodor Churcher
lay on his back in the dark. He had no idea where he was. For a
moment, he thought he was dead. But the pain that wracked his
body insisted otherwise. The fingers of his left hand tingled and
itched incessantly, but he had no left hand. He stared panic-
stricken at the bandaged stump, trying to reconcile the discrepancy, and prayed what he saw was part of an enduring night-
mare.

Doctor Phan and Dinh's family observed Churcher's survival
with trepidation, concerned he might make trouble for them upon
recovering.

But even in his weakened state, once Churcher's mind started
working again, it started calculating, and he quickly dispelled
their fears. He was pleased the authorities hadn't been notified.
The world, and more importantly the Russians, thought he was
dead, and he'd keep it that way for now.

"You keep my secret," Churcher said to Dinh, "and I'll keep
yours—under one condition. Soon as I'm well enough to leave
here, I want you to go to Houston and fetch somebody for me."

In Houston, Ed McKendrick had been barely alive when the
paramedics arrived at the Churcher estate that night. But they had
started pumping plasma into him immediately, and six hours of
surgery later, his heart was still beating powerfully and his brain
waves were peaking evenly; he had survived.

He had spent most of the time in intensive care at the city's
renowned Medical Center.

Andrew had been to see him a number of times, but today was
the first day McKendrick felt strong enough to carry on a conversation of any duration. He was staring blankly at the television
over his bed when Andrew entered.

"Hey, Drew," he said, brightening. His face was bruised, fist
encased in plaster, shoulder and thigh heavily bandaged; an IV
stabbed into his forearm.

"Come to stick your thumb up my ass again?"

"That was *your* thumb," Andrew replied. "You're too big an
asshole for mine."

McKendrick laughed heartily.

Andrew was pleased that McKendrick was his raunchy self again.

"They're torturing me, son," he rumbled, gesturing to the TV. "That thing's on twenty-four-hours-a-day. Christ, I've been sentenced to death by Phil Donahue." McKendrick took the remote control and clicked off the television. "Thanks, kid," he said, suddenly stone-faced serious. "Thanks a lot for what you did."

Andrew nodded, and smiled self-consciously. Compliments and expressions of gratitude always embarrassed him. He never knew how to respond.

"I've been watching the boob tube all week," McKendrick said. "Nothing new on your old man."

Andrew nodded. "Coughlan called the other night," Andrew said. "He told me some debris from the chopper had washed up east of Galveston. The FAA's running tests. It sounds like it busted up pretty good. He had nothing new on my father either."

Andrew's eyes saddened and fell, momentarily.

"Bastards got away with the package," McKendrick said, purposely breaking the silence.

Andrew nodded grimly, and said, "I looked for it."

"But you didn't—" McKendrick prompted, letting it die out when he saw Andrew understood.

"Not a word to anyone," Andrew replied crisply. "If I'd found it, I would've sent it to Boulton."

"Way to go," McKendrick said.

"I told Coughlan the truth—we came back to the estate, spotted intruders on the grounds, and idiots that we were, we chased them," Andrew explained. "I didn't mention the museum. Couldn't. I didn't know about the break-in until I went looking for the package. Nobody's been down there since that night but me."

McKendrick pursed his lips, impressed. "Got it figured out yet?" he asked, teasing.

"Partly," Andrew replied.

His tone left no doubt he was serious. McKendrick's brows raised in curiosity. He inclined his head toward the door. Andrew reached back and closed it quietly.

"Talk to me," McKendrick said.

"Well, I spent some time poking around the museum," Andrew began. "Sure are a hell of a lot of paintings down there. The rest of the world thinks about half of them are in Russian museums," he added suspiciously.

"No shit?" McKendrick snorted, intrigued.

"Yeah. Gauguin's 'Are You Jealous?' was the tip-off," he said. "It's a beaut. Strong patterns, bright colors, two Tahitian girls, naked of course. Your kind of stuff. I saw it at the Pushkin when I was in Moscow with my father. A few hours of research in our library is all it took to confirm the rest were from there or the Hermitage. Any idea how he got hold of them?"

McKendrick lifted his good shoulder in a shrug. "Hell, he's been doing business over there for years," he replied. "Who knows?"

"After everything that's happened," Andrew said, "it's the *kind* of business I'm wondering about."

"Where're you headed?"

"Well—Churchco's into all kinds of high tech stuff. Stuff that's illegal to export. And—"

"Stuff the Russians are working twenty-four-hours-a-day to get their hands on," McKendrick interjected, warming to the idea. "Interesting theory."

Andrew shrugged, feeling disloyal to his father for suggesting it. "It just occurred to me that the paintings could induce that kind of cooperation," he replied defensively. "I mean, art's always been my father's passion. Money would be the *last* thing that would tempt him," he explained, adding, "Just an idea."

"You've got a wicked mind, son. I like it."

"Hey, you're the one who said something weird was going on," Andrew retorted. "My father said, 'send that package to Boulton, to the *CIA* if I croak mysteriously.' The coroner said, 'rapid ascent from a great depth, possibly a submarine.'" He shrugged and shifted gears, feeling the need to supply a more positive explanation. "Maybe he was working on something with Boulton. They were in the OSS together during the war. I don't know. What's it matter, anyway?" he asked, suddenly aware of the futility.

"What're you going to do next?" McKendrick asked.

"Go to Rome—sell Arabians, I guess," Andrew replied, unenthused and somewhat evasively.

"You guess?" McKendrick prodded.

"Nothing I can do here. You said it yourself, he's gone. Besides, nothing would frost my father more than knowing I was moping around doing nothing."

McKendrick nodded in agreement. "Going to Moscow and Tersk, too," he asked slyly.

Andrew nodded resolutely.

"Horse-trading, huh?"

Andrew's lips tightened in a thin smile. "Mostly."

McKendrick grinned. "You're okay, kid. But watch your ass," he said sharply. "Those two pansies I beat the shit out of last week—?" His inflection rose, and he paused.

Andrew chuckled and nodded, deciding he actually liked the crude fellow.

McKendrick smiled cryptically. "They were Russians—professionals."

Andrew looked at him squarely and said, "Figured that."

BOOK TWO

ROME

"As memory alone acquaints us with the continuance and extent of . . . perceptions, 'tis to be consider'd, upon that account chiefly, as the source of personal identity. Had we no memory, we should never have any notion of . . . that chain of causes and effects which constitute our self or person."

—DAVID HUME, *A Treatise Of Human Nature*

Chapter Twenty

The sun shone with golden brilliance on Comiso, Sicily, an agrarian community sprinkled across a lush southern plateau. A nightingale flew low over the grassy fields, and landed on a vine laden with wild berries. All morning, the bird had been siphoning the sweet nectar and ferrying it to her young, nearby. Now, she heard a distant clanking and stiffened.

About a half mile away, a convoy of earth movers, led by a huge bulldozer, lumbered over the crest of a hill, like an invading army. Indeed, the olive drab equipment displayed military markings, and soldiers from the Italian Corps of Engineers sat in the cabs.

The racket grew louder.

The frightened bird flew off.

A short time earlier, more than a hundred protestors had assembled in the flower-dotted fields. Now they placed themselves between the advancing convoy and the grove where the bird was foraging.

The bulldozer charged down the hill toward them.

For centuries, Comiso's richly vegetated plateaus have been a haven for wildlife and a nesting ground for birds migrating south for the winter from across the continent—an ideal sanctuary due to the area's extreme isolation, predictably mild climate, and strategic location in the center of the Mediterranean.

For these same reasons, experts at NATO, in consultation with the Pentagon, had selected Comiso for deployment of one hundred and twelve American cruise missiles. This site "maximized the potential" for the intermediate-range low-flying weapons to be launched without interference from man or nature, and to strike preselected targets with their nuclear warheads.

A year before, when the Italian government sanctioned deployment, hordes of placard-waving peace demonstrators from across Western Europe descended on Comiso. The diverse group had been assembled by a resourceful young woman named Dominica Maresca.

The daughter of a wealthy Venetian industrialist, Dominica grew up in an opulent palazzo on the city's Grand Canal, and was schooled in local convents. A willowy beauty with the almond-shaped face and long, sharply cut nose of her forebears, she could have been the model for Modigliani's "La Belle Romaine." But behind the serene mask throbbed a recalcitrant vein, and at eighteen, she broke with her family and strict religious upbringing to attend the University of Bologna, where she joined the Italian Communist party, and worked as an organizer in elections. The latter brought her to Rome, where her antinuclear stance came to the attention of Ilya Zeitzev, the KGB *rezident*.

Zeitzev was a ruddy, obese man in his fifties with a lumbering gait, and tiny, tightly gathered features that gave his large face a rather pinched expression. He worked out of the Soviet Embassy—a stone building hidden behind sheets of steel which are welded to the wrought iron fence that rings the grounds—where he was listed as deputy cultural attaché, a cover that gave him diplomatic immunity. This meant he couldn't be prosecuted should his espionage activities be exposed. Indeed, he could commit murder in front of witnesses, and at worst be expelled. More practically, Zeitzev could park anywhere without his car being cited or towed away. And in a city of almost two million vehicles, the DPL license plates were the real payoff.

Diplomatic status also gave Zeitzev an entree to events where government, business, and cultural leaders mingled. At such an event, a fund-raiser for World Peace sponsored by the Italian Communist party, Zeitzev first approached Dominica Maresca.

The benefit was part of the International Horse Show at Piazza dei Siena in the Borghese Gardens. The amphitheater encircled the forecourt of a fourteenth-century castle which housed the exclusive, elegantly furnished indoor boxes—each connected to a private stable beneath—of the leading Italian breeders. Each box opened onto a sweeping balcony that overlooked the arena and flanked the castle's entrance, a massive stone door displaying the crest of the original owner. At the trumpeted call to colors, an ingenious mechanism swung the slab upward into a horizontal position behind the castle's facade, creating a dramatic entrance for the horses. Brightly colored banners ringed the arena, adding to the air of pageantry. That of *famiglia* Borsa, long prominent in international equestrian circles and philanthropies, fluttered from the center pole.

The current scion, Italy's Defense Minister Giancarlo Borsa, hosted the benefit. Tall, with thoughtful eyes and flowing white mane, Borsa exemplified the ideal of noblesse oblige in which he was raised as he strode from his private box, joining the guests assembled on the balcony. As if on cue, the sun moved above a prism built into the tower across the arena and, as Renaissance architects intended, projected a beam of light onto the stone door illuminating the crest. The ambient glow created an aura around Borsa as he held court amidst the guests, Dominica Maresca among them.

"You really think Hilliard's proposal is the answer," the statuesque Venetian said, provoking him.

"Yes. It will force the Soviets to the table," Borsa replied. "I think Italy should deploy. *Will* deploy, as far as I'm concerned."

"I think it's a ruse. Sleight of hand to achieve the very thing Hilliard claims to oppose."

"Young lady," Borsa said somewhat condescendingly, "Perhaps you're forgetting, there are those committed to keeping him honest—myself among them."

"Then it's time you stopped him from using the promise of nuclear cutbacks as an excuse to build up his own arsenal."

"It's obvious you have no understanding of the man's policy," Borsa replied, setting off a chorus of support among the group.

"It's an *indefensible* policy," she retorted.

"An apocryphal one, as well," said Zeitzev, timing his entrance to provide Dominica with an ally just when it seemed there were none to be had. He took her arm and directed her away from the group. "I'm sorry, but I couldn't hold back any longer," he went on as they strolled along the balcony. "You seemed surrounded by the enemy."

"By choice," she said spiritedly. "Best way to turn them around is from the inside."

"I agree. But as they say in my country, 'You can't turn stampeding caribou from the middle of the herd'—not without being trampled."

"Someone has to take the risks."

"I might be in a position to minimize them."

Dominica tilted her head, considering the remark. "Why offer to help me?"

"Because we share the same goals," he replied, going on to say he was impressed by her work, and introducing himself as the Soviet cultural attaché.

The latter was a test. Most responded by asking why he was involved in matters outside his official jurisdiction. Most failed.

"Good. I just wanted to be certain," she said, assuming he was KGB.

A trumpeted fanfare echoed through the arena. The castle's massive stone door rumbled loudly, and began rising. The prized Arabian horses that would be auctioned to raise money pranced onto the red clay.

That was a year ago, and since, with Zeitzev's support, Dominica infiltrated the European peace movement and incited many antinuclear demonstrations. Despite her efforts, the cruise missiles had been standing quietly in their silos in Comiso for months.

Recently, pressure applied by President Hilliard on NATO countries reluctant to deploy nuclear weapons had given rise to increasingly rabid opposition. NATO personnel, as well as business and political leaders outspoken in their support, had become terrorist targets.

Such incidents prompted NATO to issue a directive that antiterrorist measures at all bases be tightened. This meant that the wildlife sanctuaries next to the silos in Comiso had to be cleared of vegetation.

About a week later, when Ilya Zeitzev arrived in his office on the second floor of the Soviet Embassy, deputy *rezident* Antonin Kovlek was waiting for him. Kovlek was a taut man with thick glasses that belied his limited intellect. Prioritizing the influx of intelligence data was one of his responsibilities.

While Kovlek briefed him on NATO's decision to remove the vegetation in Comiso, Zeitzev took a wedge of *taleggio,* one of the Italian cheeses that had become his passion, from a small refrigerator. He lowered his massive body into his desk chair, and began peeling the wrapper from the cheese. He knew the vegetation in Comiso provided cover for his agents who routinely monitored the NATO installation, and—should the Politburo so decide—would also provide a staging area from which to launch a terrorist attack on it.

"When, Comrade? Do we know when?" he asked impatiently the instant he grasped the implications.

Kovlek nodded crisply, and handed Zeitzev a photocopy of a document that displayed the official seal of the Italian Defense Ministry. "The twenty-third according to this directive we obtained," the deputy replied. "That's a Monday."

"A little more than three weeks," Zeitzev calculated in a tone that suggested he was unhappy with the little time he had to counter the plan.

"Yes, but the vegetation is on Italian land. So, the Italian Army will remove it. Therefore, three weeks could easily turn into three months," Kovlek replied jauntily, hoping to mollify him.

"Or three *days,*" Zeitzev snapped, holding up the photocopy. "Did you see the signature on this?"

"Borsa," Kovlek said flatly.

"Borsa, *head* of the Defense Ministry. Borsa, champion of deployment," Zeitzev lectured.

He shook his head and slipped a piece of the cheese between his lips, savoring the nutty flavor that made the roof of his mouth tingle—a timely reminder of how much he enjoyed the advantages of being posted in a Western capital, and of how unhappy his mentors at No. 2 Dzerzhinsky Square would be if NATO curtailed surveillance of the missile base.

"This plan, Comrade—it must, *must* be subverted," he said. "Give it to Dominica."

Now, as the equipment that would remove the vegetation charged across the field, Dominica Maresca, once again, led a group of protestors in Comiso. This time their placards displayed, not antinuclear slogans and peace signs, but catchphrases that lamented the plight of the area's wildlife. Dominica had rallied environmental groups from across Europe to force the government to declare the area a national sanctuary. However, their petitions had been ignored, and the KGB's highly valued camouflage had run out of time.

A representative of the Italian Government rode in a jeep next to the convoy of earth movers. He waited until the bulldozer that bore down on the protestors was a few meters from Dominica before he held up a hand.

She stood her ground unflinchingly as the massive piece of equipment stopped closer than she anticipated. The battered plow arched high above her, clumps of grass and shrubs were jammed between the menacing teeth.

The government man got out of his jeep. "I must ask you to instruct your people to move aside," he said politely.

"And I must instruct them to remain," she replied, a defiant timbre in her voice.

The soldiers who operated the equipment revved the diesels in response. They built the sound to an intimidating cadence, filling the air with acrid fumes.

Dominica raised a bullhorn to her mouth. "Wildlife! Wildlife! Wildlife!" she shouted.

The protestors quickly took up the chant, turned their backs to the convoy, and sat down—heads bent forward, backs curved, arms wrapped around pulled-up knees—like boulders scattered in the field.

"Fucking assholes," muttered the government representative in disgust. He was a mid-level bureaucrat in the Defense Ministry. Procedure called for him to report the stalemate to superiors, and await instructions. Experience taught him it would be days before he had them—days during which Italy's soccer championships would be decided. The tickets had cost him plenty, and no group of bleeding heart ecologists was going to keep him from the match. He made a snap decision to expedite the situation, and signaled the bulldozer with an abrupt wave of his arm.

The soldier started the twenty-five tons of steel rolling, and centered it on a cluster of protestors. He depressed pedals and pulled levers until he had maneuvered the leading edge of the plow beneath a half dozen of the hunched men and women. He scooped them into the deeply curved trough, and yanked hard on another lever. The hydraulic pistons that manipulated the bulldozer's welded steel arms drove the plow upward, swiftly elevating its human cargo five meters above the ground. With a vengeful smirk, he pulled a third lever releasing the compressed air that held the plow in position. It pivoted downward, dumping the protestors like clods of earth atop others below.

Those who weren't injured scrambled to their feet, shouting expletives at the soldier. He laughed and made an obscene gesture. The angry protestors surged forward, surrounding the bulldozer.

Dominica climbed up onto one of the treads.

"Bastard! You bastard!" she screamed in Italian through her bullhorn. "Why did you do that? Why?"

"Bitch!" the soldier shouted.

He reared back and slammed a foot into Dominica's stomach, knocking her to the ground. Some of the men in the group leaped onto the dozer, threatening the soldier. One lunged into the cab and began punching him. The soldier panicked, slammed the transmission in gear, and pressed the accelerator to the floorboard. The bulldozer lurched and charged into the crowd.

The protestors began screaming, and started to scatter. Some stumbled as they attempted to get out of the way. A shriek that segued to an agonized wail silenced the shouting mob. The unmistakably terminal plea announced that the fifty-thousand-pound bulldozer had crushed one of the demonstrators.

Dominica pushed her way through the crowd that formed around the victim. She recoiled at the sight of a twelve-year-old boy beneath one of the Caterpillar treads—his torso pressed into the soft earth, his mouth frozen open in a silent scream, his eyes wide with the puzzled look of someone who had no reason to expect to die. She bent over him and took his hand, which immediately tightened around her's. He tried to speak, but could manage only a muffled gurgle. Blood rose from the back of his throat, and filled his mouth. The crimson lake spilled over his lip and ran down the side of his face onto their locked hands. His last breath was pungent and warm against her face.

Chapter Twenty-one

That same morning, nine hundred and fifty miles to the north, a heavy rain pelted Rome's Leonardo da Vinci Airport as TWA flight 802 from New York dropped out of the clouds and touched down on the slick runway.

The time was 11:26 A.M.

Andrew Churcher was one of the first passengers to come through the boarding ramp into the terminal. A shoulder bag containing the client files McKendrick had given him slapped at his side. He ambled along, making small talk with an older couple who had also traveled first class. They were horse people from the auction circuit who, like Andrew, had come to Rome for the International Show at Piazza dei Siena.

Valery Gorodin had traveled coach, and took steps to avoid being detained by those passengers clogging the aisles while removing carry-on items from overhead compartments. Just prior to landing, he had casually moved from the rear of the plane to an empty seat directly behind the first class bulkhead. A position which would enable him to deplane quickly, and resume close surveillance of Andrew Churcher.

Italian military personnel in gray jumpsuits, black berets, and mirror polished boots provided security inside the terminal. Each carried an Uzi slung across the front of his body.

Andrew cleared passport control, and entered the baggage claim area where those meeting passengers were grouped behind a waist-high security barrier. Some held signs with handwritten names. Almost immediately, Andrew saw the one that read "Churcher." But the sixteen-hour journey from Houston had a disorienting effect, and he continued walking a few steps before he realized that the uniformed chauffeur standing *inside* the barrier next to the automated baggage carousel was there to meet *him.*

The chauffeur's presence reminded Andrew that this was a Churchco operation, everything prearranged by Elsbeth, Theodor Churcher's assistant, to exacting specifications. In the past, Andrew would have bristled at the long-distance control exerted by his father. But now that he was gone, Andrew found it surprisingly reassuring.

Andrew raised a hand to the chauffeur who had been standing impassively. The man's eyes lost their blank expression, and the blue in them twinkled as the casually attired young man approached.

"Welcome to Rome," the chauffeur said in heavily accented English. "I'm sorry about your father," he went on uneasily. He wanted to pay his respects, but was hesitant to bring up an unpleasant topic.

"Thanks," Andrew replied, feeling saddened, and distanced from the stronger emotions that surfaced at the thought of his father having been murdered.

The stocky Italian extended a hand, and, brightening, said, "Fausto."

"Of course," Andrew said, shaking it. "You drove for us last year, didn't you?"

"*Si, si.* And many times for your father before that. He was a very fine man."

Andrew nodded, wondering—as he did last time—why, unlike the others, Fausto was allowed to wait inside the security barrier for his passenger. A loud buzzer that announced the baggage carousel was being activated pulled Fausto away before Andrew could ask.

Gorodin had been watching from the other side of the carousel. He paced a few steps closer to the security barrier, and lit a cigarette. Then he blew out the match, threw it to the floor, and ground it into the gray terrazzo with his heel. A stream of smoke came from his nostrils as he surveyed the anxious faces that looked past him in search of friends and loved-ones. The crack of match against striker, and the whoosh of sulfur bursting into flame, called his attention to a plainly dressed man, with thick glasses.

After lighting his cigarette, Antonin Kovlek disposed of his match in exactly the same manner as had Gorodin, identifying himself as his contact.

Gorodin's eyes directed Kovlek's attention to Andrew. Neither agent openly acknowledged the other. Zeitzev had sent his deputy as a safety precaution, not a welcoming committee. Should Gorodin be delayed by Italian authorities, Kovlek would take up surveillance of Andrew Churcher. If not, he'd keep an eye on Gorodin—Gorodin was GRU.

Fausto carried Andrew's travel bag and led the way toward a row of customs stations, angling toward the one on the extreme left. The uniformed agent broke into a broad smile the instant he saw them approaching. Fausto winked, and said something in Italian that turned the agent's smile into a lewd chuckle. Then, further heightening Andrew's curiosity about Fausto, the customs agent waved them through without even a cursory check of Andrew's passport or baggage.

They had walked a short distance when one of the Uzi-carrying guards noticed, and stepped forward to challenge them. Before Andrew knew what was happening, Fausto had produced his wallet and opened it with a snap of his wrist that emphasized the inconvenience.

To the guard's chagrin, he was staring at a brass shield pinned next to official police identification.

Fausto snapped the wallet closed, ticking the tip of the guard's nose. "Careful!" he barked in Italian. "You lose that, you lose the only thing you have that will get you a promotion." Then he turned and headed for the glass doors that led outside the terminal.

"So, Fausto, you're with the police?" Andrew said. He wanted it to sound like a casual observation, but was unable to suppress the wonder in his voice.

"Retired. Twenty-five years on the Questura," he replied, referring to the detective squad, adding "Twenty-five years of collecting IOUs."

"The customs agent—that wasn't a professional courtesy?" Andrew asked, surprised.

Fausto smiled cagily, and shook no. "He cheats on his wife. He got—how you say?—*busted* in a raid on a sex club. I decided he might be useful and kept his name out of the reports." Fausto chuckled, savoring the memory of it. "He's been eternally grateful," he went on, adding philosophically, "Of course, human nature being what it is, gratitude has always been the seed of resentment." He pulled back his jacket, letting Andrew glimpse the 9mm Baretta that rode on his hip.

The exit door opened automatically.

Fausto led Andrew toward a Maserati *quatroporto*. The black sedan was parked directly in front of the terminal, in a restricted area, beneath an overhang that protected them from the rain.

The Maserati pulled away from the terminal, water spitting from its grooved radials.

Andrew settled back into the soft Italian leather, and stretched out his lanky frame—his body telling him it was night; the brightness, despite the rain, insisting it was day.

Fausto wheeled the big car onto a road that led to the autostrada, and pushed a button on the walnut-paneled console. The electric door locks engaged.

The precise click triggered the memory of a thriller Andrew had once seen. The opening sequence raced through his mind: An airport, a chauffeur with a sign, a businessman, a limousine speeding into the night, fingers pushing buttons. And then, in a frenetic visual barrage—electric door locks activating, the window between passenger and chauffeur ascending, deadly gas filling the rear compartment, the man's eyes widening with terror, fingers clawing at the glass, body falling back onto the seat unconscious!

At the time, Andrew thought it was a damn clever abduction. Now, he thought about McKendrick's warning, "Watch your ass son. Russians, professionals."

Andrew realized he had no proof of anything Fausto had said. He resembled his father's chauffeur; but that was a year ago, and the memory was vague. Anyone could get a police shield and phony ID, especially a pro. Why hadn't he been more alert, more vigilant?! Why hadn't he walked right past Fausto, and taken a taxi? Why *hadn't* he watched his ass? He hadn't been in Italy a half hour and already he had screwed up in a way that, at least in

the movies, had proved costly. Andrew studied his reflection in
the glass that separated him from Fausto, and listened for the hiss
of deadly gas.

The Maserati cut through the sheets of rain, turned onto the
autostrada, and accelerated smoothly on the glistening concrete
ribbon.

Approximately two hundred meters back, Gorodin and Kovlek
sat behind the chattering wipers of an aging Fiat, its engine
straining to keep up with the high performance vehicle it was
tailing.

Chapter Twenty-two

At approximately the same time that Gorodin and Kovlek were following their target, First Lieutenant Jon Lowell was searching for his.

The time in Tampa, Florida, was 8:17 A.M.

The moment he completed his midnight to eight ASW tour, Lowell had gone directly to K building.

Now, he was hunched over a computer console in a SOSUS research lab set up for use by ASW personnel. The electronics-packed facility was adjacent to the main control room where military technicians, on a rotating twenty-four-hour watch, sat at consoles monitoring satellite and underwater cable transmissions. All pertinent data was sent over a land-based communications net to analysts at the National Security Agency at Fort Meade, Maryland, then forwarded to the Central Intelligence Agency in Langley, Virginia.

After shifting his focus to the mystery vessel he had spotted on the satellite photographs, Lowell pulled copies of the twelve hydrotapes that covered the one-hour-forty-eight-minute SOSUS window he'd established. With assistance of Navy Electronics Technician Lew Scofield, Lowell had been searching the tapes for the recording of the ship's acoustic signature. Once located, it would be computer-compared with all others on file in the sonar library. With any luck, it would match one that had already been identified. Lowell and Scofield had searched ten tapes without finding it.

When Lowell arrived that morning, Scofield was threading the next to last hydrotape across the sound heads of the big Ampex reel-to-reel machine. He balanced a slowly growing ash on the

141

tip of a cigarette that never left his mouth. Lowell had been working on and off with the lanky midwesterner for over a week, and had never once seen the ever-present ash fall before the technician could tap it into an ashtray.

"Data up, sir," Scofield announced when he had finished. "We're looking at fifty-fifty today."

"Yeah, odds are getting better. Has to be a set of twin screws on one of these."

"Unless you're off on the tonnage, sir, and the sig we're after's a one banger."

"No way," Lowell replied as he settled in at the console. "Ship scales out somewhere between a hundred forty and a hundred fifty thousand tons. That means we're looking at a tanker or containerized carrier. And either way, something that big has to be pushing twins," he went on, referring to the propulsion arrangement which gave the big vessels otherwise unattainable maneuverability.

Lowell donned a set of experimental headphones he had been testing. They received their signal by infrared light beam rather than by wire, giving him freedom of movement in the lab. And he had been pleased to discover they were more than able to reproduce a broad range of pure frequencies. He flipped on the tape console that was linked to the big Cray X-MP supercomputers used to process and analyze intelligence data, and began scrutinizing the hydrotape.

His ears filled with the overlapping frequencies of moving ships, sealife, and the surging Caribbean.

A little over a half hour had passed. Lowell had gotten up from his chair, and was pacing thoughtfully as he listened. Suddenly, he paused in mid-stride, and pressed the earphone to his head.

Scofield was bringing his Zippo to a fresh Marlboro when he saw Lowell's reaction.

"Low frequency rumble," Lowell said. He listened for a few more seconds, then nodded emphatically, and sat down at the console. "Yeah, yeah we're talking power here. Real big plant. Ship's gotta be in the tonnage range we're looking for."

The target was in his sights now. He could feel the competitive intensity building; just as it did in the Viking whenever the hours of tedious searching paid off in the blip of an enemy submarine pinging across his monitor.

"Patch it through the frequency digitizer," he said to Scofield sharply.

"The what, sir?" Scofield asked uneasily. He was fully conscious of Lowell's intensity and embarrassed he couldn't respond.

Lowell flicked him a sideways glance, and smiled. He knew Scofield was relatively new to the job and welcomed the chance to broaden his knowledge. The digitizer was a piece of equipment Lowell had adapted from submarine surveillance technology. He was an outstanding sonar technician until he decided he'd rather hunt than be hunted, and applied to ASW.

"It's a bunch of chips about that big," Lowell said, indicating Scofield's Zippo. "It reduces the sound waves to digitized pulses, cuts negative feedback to zero, and separates them into a dozen frequency ranges. We can listen to each range by itself."

"Kind of like the graphic equalizer on a stereo."

Lowell nodded, and stabbed a finger at a row of buttons on the console in front of Scofield. "Give me the high end first," he said decisively. If he was right, it would be the only frequency range he'd need.

"Yes, sir. And thanks, I'll remember that," Scofield said, pushing the button labeled 16/40 kHz, rerouting the hydrotape data through the digitizer that filtered out all but the highest frequencies.

The sound in Lowell's headphones changed dramatically. The low rumble of the ship's power plant dropped out, as did the swishing throb of a passing school of barracuda, leaving the high frequency whine of propeller cavitation, the noise made by the ship's blades carving a hole in the water. The singsong rhythm of the whine he'd isolated was all the proof Lowell needed that the vessel was pushing twin screws.

"That's the one," he said triumphantly.

Lowell removed his headphones, scooped up the phone that hung from one side of the console, and punched out Arnsbarger's number.

The phone rang several times before Arnsbarger lifted his head from the pillow. "Cissy? Cissy, get that will you?" he growled, before realizing that she was in the shower and her son had already left for school. Finally, he crawled out from beneath the bedding and picked it up. "Yeah—" he mumbled in a sleepy voice.

"Rise and shine, big fella!" Lowell hooted.

"Christ," Arnsbarger replied, wincing. "Won't be noon for a couple of hours. What the hell's going on?"

"I nailed her!" Lowell blurted excitedly.

"Great. Glad to hear you're not a virgin anymore, son. Now if you don't mind—"

"I'm talking about our mystery ship," Lowell interrupted, laughing. "We just tracked down her acoustic signature."

"Oh," said Arnsbarger, suddenly coming to life. "Way to go. I sure to hell wished it'd taken you a couple of hours longer. On my way."

In the forty-five minutes it took Arnsbarger to shower, dress, and drive to the base, Lowell and Scofield refined the distinction between frequencies, and digitally isolated the acoustic signature of each of the ship's propellers.

When Arnsbarger entered, they had already made separate tracks of each cavitation whine, and Lowell was running them through the graphic analyzer.

Two linear patterns moved horizontally across the console's video screen. Each of the parallel waves peaked and valleyed about a centerline, like an electrocardiogram.

"What do you have up there?" Arnsbarger rasped, looking better than he sounded. "A couple of whales getting it on?"

"Yeah," Lowell chuckled. "You're looking at the hottest pair of twin screws this side of Cienfuegos."

"Separated them out, huh?"

"It was easy. Look at that."

Lowell tapped the screen, indicating the top signature pattern. It was decidedly more frenetic than the lower.

"Hard to port," he went on. "Starboard screw is turning almost half again as many revs. Frequency's more than ten killies lower."

"Well, let's find out if that John Hancock has a match," Arnsbarger replied. "What're we waiting for, anyway?"

"For your head to clear," Lowell cracked.

"Ship'll be a pile of scrap in a Yokohama yard before that happens."

"So will you if you don't give it a night off once in a while."

"You're starting to sound just like Cissy," Arnsbarger teased. "But she's a lot easier to look at. I mean, I could've stayed home and heard that."

"Yeah, but not this," Lowell replied.

He removed his headphones and tossed them to Arnsbarger, who slipped them on. Then Lowell swiveled to the console's keyboard and encoded:

LOG:CX-MP/AC:SIG:LIB-COMP:ANA/2-TRK:SRCH

This linked the computer in Lowell's console to the Cray X-MP in the control room, instructed it to access the acoustic signature library, and run a comparative analysis program on the two-track specimen signature Lowell had prepared.

"Okay. Here we go," he announced, pushing a button that transmitted the data and started the search and match process.

Operating at speeds in excess of one billion instructions per second, the supercomputer compared the specimen acoustic signature with the hundreds of thousands on file. In the time it took Scofield to stub out a cigarette, pull another from his pack, and light it, the Cray had found a match. The laser printer tied in to Lowell's computer came to life:

P103612PMAR
ASW PENSACOLA
ACSIG COMPARATIVE ANALYSIS REPORT 71938647
VESSEL IDENTIFIED AS: VLCC KIRA
CLASSIFICATION: SUPERTANKER TWIN SCREWS
DISPLACEMENT: 145,000 TONS
CARGO: 125,000 TONS
MANUFACTURER: MITSUI YARDS YOKOHAMA JAPAN MAY59
MOTHBALLED: PIROS FINLAND DEC68 FEB72
REOUTFITTED: VASIL'YEVSKIY YARDS LENINGRAD USSR
REGISTRY: REPUBLIC OF LIBERIA 26JUL73
OWNER: LEASEHOLD SHIPPING LTD HAVANA CUBA

Lowell tore the page from the printer, and the three men huddled scanning the data.

Arnsbarger whistled.

Scofield nodded in agreement.

Lowell just smiled.

All eyes were on the third line from the bottom. The connection to Boulton's KIQ directive was strong. They went to the ranking ASW intelligence officer in K building immediately. Within an hour, copies of the acoustic signature report on the *Kira*, the KH-11 recon photographs, and a log listing the sightings of the Soviet submarine that provoked their investigation had been transmitted, via a secure communications link, to Boulton at Langley. In minutes, the best of the CIA's analytical minds were focused on the *Kira*.

Chapter Twenty-three

The weather in Rome had cleared when Melanie Winslow's flight from New York landed later that same morning. She cleared customs and hurried to a bank of public telephones. Her pulse rate soared as she pulled the Rome directory from its hanger, opened it to the *D*s, and frantically turned the pages to the heading *DES*. She ran her finger down the column of names—Descano, Descenta, Descilare. The names jumped from *Desc-e* to *Desc-i*. Not a single *Desc-h*. No Deschin, not a one. Melanie let out a long breath, and admonished herself for believing, even for a moment, that it might be this easy.

She took a taxi into the city and checked into the Gregoriana, a tiny hotel that lies hidden just east of the Spanish Steps on a narrow residential street after which it is named. Its fourteen cozy rooms were coveted by those in the arts who were fond of their intimacy and the bright palette used in their decor. Melanie had stayed here once, years ago, while performing with a dance company at Teatro dell' Opera. She was pleased to find the hotel's ambience intact on her return.

She showered quickly, slipped into jeans, turtleneck, and leather bomber jacket, and took a taxi to the Piazza Cavour, where she rented a motor scooter.

An attendant in coveralls with SCOOT-A-LONG embroidered on the breast pocket gassed the bright green Motobecane, and gave Melanie a map of the city.

"My last one. I saved it just for you," he said flirtatiously.

"Thanks," Melanie replied with a smile. She settled on the scooter and, handling the controls with familiarity, started the engine, prompting the attendant to skip his orientation speech. "Maybe you can tell me how to get to the State Archives?" she asked.

"Ah, *si*, the Sapienza. You want the most direct route? Or the one where the streets have cobblestones?" he asked with a lascivious smile.

"I can see it's time for me to be scooting along," she said sharply. She pushed the scooter off its stand, popped the clutch, and accelerated onto Via Triboniano, which borders the west side of the piazza.

The attendant's remark got her thinking about the first time she had rented a scooter in Italy. She was in Florence and observed to an English painter she had met that "The young women seem so spirited, so—"

"Fulfilled," he offered somewhat smugly.

"Exactly," she said. "They've been liberated. They have jobs, incomes, careers."

"And motor scooters," he added with an enigmatic smile. "They have motor scooters."

Melanie didn't understand.

He teased her mercilessly, and refused to explain, prompting her to rent one. And then she understood: the cobblestone streets, the steady vibration, the stimulating sensation building. As a teenager, she'd made a similar discovery galloping bareback across the New Hampshire countryside on her chestnut colt.

The airy dome of Capella di Sant'Ivo—the fourteenth-century church in Palazzo di Sapienza where Pope Boniface VIII, a Machiavellian churchman who wielded the power of his office with unscrupulous abandon, founded the University of Rome—shimmered in the afternoon light as Melanie approached on her scooter.

The state-funded institution, directly across the Tiber from the Vatican, bestows degrees in the full range of arts and sciences. In 1935, the University was awarded modern accreditation and moved to more spacious quarters. Nevertheless, records are still kept at the Sapienza, which now houses the State Archives.

The courtyard between the two massive wings was clogged with traffic as Melanie cruised the grounds on the motor scooter in search of the records office. The ride and the cold air had reddened her complexion and lifted her spirits.

A sign that read *UNIVERSITA L'UFFICIO REGISTRAZIONE* got her attention. She backed off the throttle and steered the Motobecane into a parking area that looked like a motor scooter convention. She hurried up the steps of the administration building and, after a few wrong turns in the maze of corridors, found the Records Office.

The room had Renaissance proportions and had once been a refectory. Beneath the vaulted ceiling, its plaster darkened from centuries of burning tallow, stood several cluttered desks, rows of file cabinets, and a modern glass enclosure that created a private space for the supervisor.

Melanie paused to evaluate the student clerks behind the service counter, and approached the one she judged had the most easygoing nature of the three.

The young fellow looked up from the file cards he was methodically alphabetizing.

"*Prego signora?*" he said.

"*Si,*" she replied. "*Parla inglese, per favore?* You speak English?"

He held his thumb and forefinger about a half inch apart. "*Capisco un po'*—I think," he replied, breaking into the friendly smile she had anticipated.

Melanie smiled back, relieved. "I'm trying to find someone," she said slowly in a louder than normal voice, making the assumption—for whatever reason most people do—that comprehension increases with volume. "He was a student here in the late thirties."

"Thirties?" the clerk exclaimed.

He wasn't a day over nineteen, and as far as he was concerned, she could just as well have said 1300s.

"Yes, the years just prior to the war. His name's Deschin. Aleksei Deschin."

Melanie took a piece of paper and pencil from the counter, and began neatly printing the name.

In the rows of gray steel cabinets behind them, another clerk was filing document folders that were in a wheeled cart. Marco

Profetta had no reason to pay attention to their conversation—not until he heard Melanie say, "Deschin." His eyes flickered at the first mention. He mused when she repeated it, then coolly resumed his filing chores, covering his reaction.

Melanie finished writing Deschin's name on the slip of paper, and handed it to the clerk.

He stared at it blankly for a moment.

"You do have records that go back that far, don't you?" she prompted optimistically.

The young clerk shrugged, and splayed his hands.

"Can you find out? Is there someone who might—"

"*Aspetti un momento*," he said, interrupting her. He turned from Melanie, crossed the room, and entered the glass enclosure. A slim, fashionably attired woman was working at a computer terminal.

Melanie couldn't hear what was being said. But she could see the clerk explaining, and the woman responding with a pained expression, and making quick little negative movements with her head. Melanie decided it was time to be more assertive, and walked around the counter to the glass enclosure.

"Tell her I'm trying to find my father," she said, addressing the clerk. "Tell her it's very important."

The supervisor looked up with a slightly piqued expression. "I'm sorry, but we can't accommodate you," she replied coolly, in excellent English. "Current records are on the computer. Those from recent years, though inactive, are filed here as you can see. But anything from before the war—" she let the sentence trail off, shaking no with the same quick movement of her head she had used with the clerk, then resumed, "—*they* would be almost impossible to retrieve."

"But you do have them," Melanie said, undaunted.

"Some," the supervisor reluctantly admitted. "But it could take days, even weeks, in the archives just to find the proper volume. *If* it wasn't destroyed in the war. I'd like to help you, but—"

"Then please hear me out," Melanie interrupted in a desperate voice. "The only thing I know about my father is that he was a student here. That and his name. Maybe the records *were* de-

stroyed in the war. Maybe *he* was destroyed in it," she added
glumly. "Or maybe he fell out of bed twenty years ago and
broke his neck. I don't know. Look, I realize the chances of
finding him are pretty slim. But I have to try. I have to find out
as much about him as I can. And I have nowhere else to start.
Nowhere. You're all I've got. I'd appreciate whatever help you
can give me."

The supervisor was visibly touched, her expression more sym-
pathetic now. "Perhaps Gianni can find the records for you,"
she said, shifting her look to the clerk.

"I have class," he said, glad to have an excuse to avoid the
dank, musty caverns beneath the Sapienza. He turned to
Melanie, and lifted a shoulder in an apologetic shrug. *"Ciao,
Signora,"* he said as he left.

Melanie thought for a moment, then brightened with an idea.
"Suppose *I* look for them?" she said, turning back to the supervisor. "If the records are in the archives, I'll find them, believe
me. I don't care how long it takes. Would that be okay?"

The supervisor considered the suggestion for a moment, and
smiled. "I don't see why not."

"Thank you. Really, I can't tell you what this means to me,"
Melanie said.

"There is a form you must fill out first," the supervisor said,
reverting to a more businesslike manner. "We are very cautious
about releasing data on our alumni, and to whom."

She got up from her chair, and stepped to the opening in the
glass enclosure.

"Marco?" she called out to the clerk who was still filing documents in the rows of steel cabinets. *"Marco, venga qui?"*

Marco didn't look up from the folders in the cart immediately.
When he did, he pointed to himself, indicating he was uncertain
she was addressing him.

"Si, Marco," she replied. *"E mi porta un forma requi-
sizioni?"*

He closed the file drawer and came toward them in a floating
saunter, using an effeminate flick of his wrist to take an information request card from the counter on the way. He had heard her
call him the first time, but feigned he hadn't. It was preferable

that they didn't know he'd been observing them from the moment he overheard Melanie say, "Deschin, Aleksei Deschin."

The name didn't mean anything to the clerk or the supervisor. They had no reason to know the name of the Soviet minister of culture.

But Marco Profetta did. To him it meant money.

Chapter Twenty-four

The Maserati was traveling fast on the S201 Autostrada toward the city when the rain let up and the skies started to brighten.

To Andrew's relief, no deadly gas had filled the rear compartment, and no attempt had been made to abduct him. The turn in the weather prompted him to go to Piazza dei Siena—the outdoor amphitheater in the Borghese Gardens where the horse show would be held—prior to checking in at his hotel.

Fausto adjusted his course, left the S201, cutting through the Trastavere District to Ponte Garibaldi. He crossed to the east bank of the Tiber, and headed north on the Lungotevere, the broad boulevard that snakes past the townhouses fronting the river. At Ponte Cavour, he angled into Via Ripetta, and continued to Piazza Del Popouli, just west of their new destination. There, the Maserati's progress came to an abrupt halt. The piazza was congested with traffic. Hundreds of vehicles were gridlocked about the Hellenic obelisk at its center.

Andrew lowered the window for a better view of the limestone needle that split a backdrop of evergreens.

The sharp crack of a gunshot rang out behind him.

He spun to the rear window of the Maserati.

The tinted glass framed Santa Maria Dei Montesanto and Santa Maria Dei Miracoli, the churches that divide the streets which fan out from the south side of the piazza. Befittingly, the baroque twins were clothed in a matching latticework of construction scaffolding.

Another gunshot echoed through the stone piazza.

As the sharp pop rang in his ears, Andrew wondered why neither pedestrians, nor workers crawling about the scaffolding, had reacted or taken cover.

Silvio Festa knew why. Silvio was the smoothly muscled construction worker using the Ram-set, a gunlike tool that anchors things to concrete. He fired it dozens of times each day, and the sharp report had become just another sound in the noisy piazza.

Silvio was ruggedly handsome; and in sweat-stained tank top, faded jeans, and tool belt slung low on his waist, he exuded a raw sexuality. Indeed, women found him irresistible. He slept with them all and bragged they were *fazzolettini di carta*— Kleenex. But one had a sassy elusiveness that captivated him, and unlike the others, *she* controlled the pace of their relationship. Silvio patiently planned to consummate it. She had been in Sicily for a few days on business. This evening, he would pick her up at the airport, take her to dinner, and fill her veins with Frascati, a smoky local wine. This evening, Dominica Maresca would be his.

Silvio pushed a spike into the barrel of the Ram-set, then opened a small steel box. It contained rows of color-coded cartridges that resembled .22 blanks. He selected a powder load, thumbed it into the chamber, inserted the breech plug, and snapped the tool closed. The muzzle had a square safety guard. He positioned it on a two-by-six he was anchoring, pressed down to release the safety, and pulled the trigger.

The Ram-set fired with a loud bang. The spike pierced the hardened lumber, pinning it to the concrete.

Silvio stepped back from his work, thinking about his elusive woman, thinking about Dominica's long limbs wrapped around him, her generous mouth devouring his, and went about reloading.

Fausto had finally maneuvered the black Maserati through the traffic jam in the piazza. He made a right into the Viale del Mauro Torto, the main road that runs just inside the wall of the Gardens, and accelerated beneath a tunnel of evergreens.

The Fiat in which Gorodin and Kovlek were following was still locked in traffic. They watched the Maserati zigzagging between the angled vehicles up ahead, losing visual contact when it exited the piazza through the arched gateway at the north end.

Kovlek leaned on the horn in frustration.

The driver of the car in front of him stabbed an arm out the window and gave him the finger.

Gorodin was too tired to be angry, and broke into an amused smile.

"Where's Churcher staying?" he asked.

"I don't know," Kovlek replied, feeling chagrined and trying to hide it. "A hotel, I imagine. I don't know which one."

"Okay, head for the Embassy," Gorodin said wearily, his tone born of severe jet lag.

"My orders are to maintain surveillance," Kovlek protested, angered by Gorodin's lethargy.

"So are mine, comrade," Gorodin replied. "But the fact remains—we haven't."

"Which means we do whatever is necessary to reestablish contact," Kovlek snapped. "And I don't see how returning to the Embassy will accomplish that."

Gorodin had anticipated the rivalry. It was always this way between the two agencies. GRU and KGB were no different than other organizations when it came to territorial imperatives. He was tired, and had hoped to stave it off. But he knew exactly how to reestablish contact with Andrew Churcher, and decided to dispense with Kovlek quickly.

"Pull over there," he said in a commanding tone, pointing to a line of taxis at a stand.

"What?" Kovlek blurted indignantly.

"Drive aimlessly in search of Churcher if you wish, comrade, but you'll do it alone. I'll be at the Embassy. And I guarantee you, within minutes of arriving I'll know where to pick up his trail."

Kovlek looked surprised.

"Don't be alarmed," Gorodin continued. "Before leaving to resume surveillance, I'll be sure to inform your *rezident* of Churcher's whereabouts"—he paused, letting Kovlek chew on the barb before he gaffed him—"in case, for some absurd reason, he'd want you to continue backing me up."

Gorodin smiled as Kovlek angrily downshifted the Fiat and turned the wheel hard, pulling out of the piazza into a street that led to the Embassy.

*   *   *

Fausto sat patiently behind the wheel of the Maserati that was
parked in the entrance tunnel of Piazza Dei Siena. Within a few
days, the amphitheater in the southeast quadrant of the Borghese
Gardens would be overrun with international horse traders. The
clatter of hooves, prancing before the breeders private boxes,
would fill the air.

But now it was empty and silent.

The red clay was still moist from the rain. The musky scent
mixed with the fragrance wafting from the pine forest that surrounded the fourteenth-century castle.

Andrew was standing alone in the show ring in front of the
massive stone door, thinking McKendrick would be proud of
him. As exclusive agent for the prized, and therefore higher
priced, Soviet Arabians, this was where he would be competing
for millions of dollars in orders. And like a battlefield commander on a reconnaissance mission, he was getting a feel for the
terrain on which he would soon be fighting. But at the moment,
Andrew's capacity for strategic planning was limited. He was
tired, and wanted nothing more than to curl up in a sleeping bag
on the bed of pine needles that lay beneath the towering trees.

He settled for Suite 610 in The Hassler-Villa Medici, the su-
perdeluxe hotel perched imperiously above Piazza de Spagna on
Via Sistina. The luxurious cluster of rooms in the northwest corner had been his father's private enclave whenever he was in
Rome. The broad expanse of windows overlooked the dome-
studded southern half of the city.

It was just after 3 P.M. when Andrew checked in and found a
stack of phone messages; one was from Giancarlo Borsa. Andrew went to the suite and locked the door behind the departing
bellman. The phone was on a credenza next to the bed. He took a
banana from a bowl of fruit, and deftly slipped it into the telephone cradle as he removed the receiver to make certain the pins
remained depressed, and a connection was not made.

He unscrewed the plastic mouthpiece exposing the diaphragm.
No bugging device or additional wiring indicating a tap was visible. He turned the receiver over, and shook it gently. The diaphragm dropped into his palm with the same result. He
reassembled the receiver and hung it back on the cradle.

Then Andrew went about the room examining picture frames, lamps, headboard, television, chandelier, a vase of flowers; but found no listening devices. It struck him that the flowers had no scent. He leaned closer to an Astramarium, one of dozens of the hybrid lilies in the arrangement. The speckled blossoms looked authentic. They felt authentic, too. But they were made of silk, as were all the others in the vase. Each a brilliant example of the flower-maker's art.

From the moment he entered the suite, Andrew had assumed that the flowers were neutralizing the aroma of furniture polish, cleansers, and starch that make hotel rooms the world over smell the same. But they weren't. The competing fragrance, he realized, was the vestige of a familiar perfume.

The exotic blend of essences took Andrew back to that day at the auction in Tersk. And he knew that his father's woman, the aristocratic Russian swathed in sable, the one whom Theodor Churcher had allowed to outbid him, the one whose face Andrew couldn't recall, had been here—in his hotel room, that afternoon.

The phone rang.

Andrew was deep in concentration, and jumped at the sound. He let it ring again, then scooped up the receiver.

"Hello?"

"Mr. Churcher?" The voice was dusky—a woman's accented English.

"Speaking," he replied.

The woman said, "This is the housekeeper. The writing equipment you requested is in the desk," and hung up.

Andrew listened to the dial tone for a few seconds, then lowered the receiver to its cradle. He was puzzled. He hadn't made any special equipment requests. The gilded antique desk stood against the north wall. He lowered the hinged front that served as a writing surface, revealing a portable typewriter inside. A sheet of paper had been rolled halfway into the platen. Andrew studied it for a moment, then grasped the knob on the side of the typewriter and turned it slowly, rolling the sheet upwards. Four clicks brought the tops of letters into view. A snap of his wrist revealed the single line that had been typed across the page—and then rolled back behind the platen to conceal the message. It read:

HE WAS MURDERED. I KNOW WHY. PIAZZA DI TREVI. 6PM.

The phone rang again. A single, startling ring.

Andrew backed his way across the room, unable to take his eyes off the typewriter.

His hand found the phone and lifted it.

No one was on the line.

Chapter Twenty-five

While Andrew was checking in at the Hassler, Kovlek's Fiat pulled up to the gates of the Soviet Embassy. A sergeant in the Red Army Guard stepped smartly to the car and bent to the window.

"*Nomyer sveedam namorye?*" he challenged.

"*Nyet, skandeetsianyeram,*" Kovlek replied, matter-of-factly, supplying his half of the day's password.

The guard nodded and rolled back the gates, allowing the Fiat onto the grounds.

Kovlek led the way to the Embassy's *rezidentura*.

Gorodin obtained a copy of the Rome yellow pages; then commandeered Kovlek's secretary, Ludmilla, a robust woman who spoke fluent Italian, and conducted a telephone survey of Rome's luxury hotels. She placed the calls alphabetically, asking each hotel if Mr. Andrew Churcher had checked in yet. The Ambasciatori, Cavalieri, Eden, Excelsior, and Grand proved negative.

Andrew was in Suite 610, staring in chilled silence at the one-line message in the typewriter, when Ludmilla called the Hassler.

"Yes, yes, I believe he has," the operator said.

The phone rang once.

Ludmilla tapped the line button with the receiver in a lively gesture that disconnected the call.

"The Hassler," she said triumphantly.

"The Hassler," Gorodin echoed, glancing to Kovlek. "Shall we resume surveillance, comrade?"

The intercom buzzed before Kovlek could respond.

"*Da? Deptezche rezident,*" Ludmilla answered. She nodded

several times, and hung up. "Comrade *rezident* wishes to see you both," she said. "Right away."

A surveillance specialist was leaving Zeitzev's office as Gorodin and Kovlek approached. She climbed a staircase to the electronics-packed room beneath the Embassy's roof. Here, as in Glen Cove, GRU conducted extensive COMINT operations: Listening devices planted throughout the city were monitored; communications of the Italian government, other embassies, and domestic and multinational corporations were intercepted.

All data was recorded.

When the recorder that the specialist had been monitoring clicked off, she transferred the data to cassette, and brought it to the *rezident*'s office. She and Zeitzev listened to it several times on a sound system built into a modular storage wall that also housed a television and videotape recorder, shelves of albums and cassettes, reading matter, and the refrigerator filled with cheeses. Zeitzev spent long days in the heavily furnished room. The wall was his escape.

The office smelled somewhat rank as Gorodin and Kovlek entered. The big florid-faced *rezident* turned to them and broke into a broad smile. His suit looked like he'd slept in it, which he hadn't.

"Welcome to Rome, comrade," he said, extending a hand to Gorodin. "We're looking forward to assisting you in whatever way we can."

You lying slob, Gorodin thought as he locked onto Zeitzev's beefy fist and shook it. "This is a fairly straightforward task. I can manage alone if you're shorthanded," he replied, reaching for his cigarettes.

"I wouldn't hear of it," Zeitzev said.

Gorodin nodded, and forced a smile. GRU ran the COMINT operation; but field personnel were in short supply in Rome, and he'd be forced to work with KGB backup. He would have been delighted if Zeitzev had taken the out, but he didn't really expect he would.

Zeitzev's ebullient mood caused Kovlek to assume events had gone well in Sicily that morning. And nothing would please him more than to be praised in front of Gorodin. "Comiso?" he asked solicitously.

Zeitzev's eyes tightened in a cold stare. "It was a mess down there. Horrible," he said, explaining about the bulldozer incident. "Dominica was devastated when she called, and quite obsessed with avenging the boy's death." He paused in reflection, and smiled. "I was quite intrigued by how she proposed to achieve it." Then, in order to prevent Kovlek from pursing the matter in front of their GRU rival, the *resident* turned immediately to Gorodin. "Now, to other business. *Your* business," he said, crossing toward the storage wall. "Recorded less than fifteen minutes ago," he added, intending to impress him. "Listen."

Zeitzev depressed the start button on the cassette player, and the ring of a telephone came from the big speakers. Once, twice, then—

"Hello?"

"Mr. Churcher?"

"Speaking."

"This is the housekeeper. The writing equipment you requested is in the desk."

Zeitzev clicked off the tape deck. "The man, of course, is Andrew Churcher," he said. "But who's the woman? We know she isn't who she says she is because the housekeeper at the Hassler is named Vincente."

The color drained from Kovlek's face. He couldn't believe what the existence of the tape implied. He felt like a fool.

Gorodin burned the stunned deputy with a look. He couldn't believe it either; but, on second thought, he could. It was a classic example of KGB paranoia run rampant—Zeitzev had found out where Andrew Churcher was staying; had technicians bug the hotel room; but hadn't informed Kovlek.

"Well?" Zeitzev said, like a prodding schoolmaster.

"The accent," Gorodin said. "It's slight but—"

"Everyone in Italy has an accent when they speak English," Kovlek interrupted scornfully.

"Not an Estonian inflection," Gorodin said, weary of his denseness. He was referring to the Scandinavian lilt of the Russian spoken in the Baltic Republics.

Zeitzev heard the certainty in Gorodin's voice, and nodded, "My assessment, too," he said in an outright lie. He'd detected the accent, but couldn't place it. "The Baltic Republics definitely." He lifted the phone and buzzed his secretary. "Bring me The List," he said.

Since the Revolution, secrecy and control had been the mechanisms of the Soviet state. Ideas, art, music, and literature were censored; computers, copiers, printing presses, and typewriters were controlled; the movement of citizens strictly regulated.

Guaranteed the right to rest in Article 41 of their Constitution, Soviets vacation at government-operated resorts. Few travel outside the Iron Curtain. Those who do are on The List. The names in the green leather binder, found in Soviet embassies the world over, are updated daily. Travel itineraries and extensive biographical data are noted next to each.

Zeitzev's gangly secretary entered with the binder, and leaned across the desk to whisper to him.

"He'll have to come back," Zeitzev replied, a mild irritation in his voice.

"I *told* him you were busy, comrade," she said defensively. "He said he has something important, and insisted on waiting."

Zeitzev's expression softened. "All right," he said, reconsidering.

The secretary nodded and left.

Zeitzev opened the binder, and began running a finger down the columns of names. "Eight from Baltic Republics," he announced. "Three cleared to Italy. One woman. Birthplace: Tallinn, Estonia. Residence: Moscow."

"Estonians," Kovlek said with disgust. "They do nothing but complain of religious persecution, and watch Western television programs from Helsinki. Unpatriotic swine each and every one."

"Well, this swine has *blat*," Zeitzev said, using Russian slang for clout. "Winner of three Olympic medals in equestrian events. Father, chairman of the Arabian Breeders League. Reason for travel, International Horse Show, Rome. All things considered, I'd say the chances that Comrade Raina Maiskaya was Churcher's caller are rather high, Gorodin, wouldn't you?"

Gorodin nodded cautiously, pushed another cigarette between his lips, and lit it.

"But if she's here to horse-trade with Churcher," Kovlek said, "why impersonate the housekeeper?"

"Precisely," Zeitzev said, mulling it.

Kovlek moved around the desk to look at The List. "She's staying at the Eden," he announced. "I'll pick her up, and question her."

"No, comrade. I'd prefer you *observe* her for a while," Zeitzev said, and shifting his eyes to Gorodin, ordered, "*Maintain* surveillance of Churcher." He used the emphasis to remind him that he hadn't, adding, "I'll be happy to define the concept if you wish."

Gorodin took the reprimand stoically. He had no need to retaliate. The Churcher "account" was his. He recognized the name Raina Maiskaya. It had been mentioned on and off during the years that he'd forwarded artwork from Deschin in Moscow to Churcher's helicopter at sea. Gorodin knew she was Churcher's Soviet lover. But he decided neither of his KGB rivals had a need to know. They worked for him, not vice versa. *His* sanction came from Moscow. He was GRU.

Zeitzev nodded, indicating the two operatives were dismissed, and buzzed his secretary on the intercom.

"Send him in," he said, referring to the man who had been waiting in the outer office.

Gorodin and Kovlek were approaching the door when it opened, and Marco Profetta floated into the office.

"This will cost you," he announced in prissy Italian that went with his walk. "Lady's looking for your minister of culture. You know, your boss?" He slipped a file card from a shirt pocket, and held it up to Zeitzev. It was the Official Information Request Card Melanie Winslow had filled out, and had a Polaroid snapshot of her affixed.

Gorodin's Italian was fluent. He stopped on a dime, stepped back into the office, and closed the door, shutting out Kovlek who had already exited.

"I'd better hear this," he said to Zeitzev.

Zeitzev considered confronting Gorodin over the presumption, but decided against it. He held out a hand to Marco for the file card.

"Five hundred thousand lire" the wirey student said, fixing his price.

Zeitzev scowled, snatched the card from his hand, and studied it as Marco told the story of Melanie's appearance in the Records Office, and how she strode boldly into the glass enclosure to confront the supervisor.

"But what does she want?" Zeitzev interrupted.

"I couldn't hear what they were saying," Marco replied in a perplexed whine. "But I can find out."

Gorodin swung a skeptical look to Zeitzev.

"It's the truth," Marco said, seeing it. "What reason would I have to make it up?"

"I can think of at least five hundred thousand," Gorodin said. He grasped one of Marco's arms, and pushed up the sleeve. The veins ran in pale gray streaks. He shrugged at the absence of needle marks.

"Maybe, this Miss Winslow is the prevaricator," the *rezident* ventured.

"Are you suggesting she's a professional?"

"It's possible."

Gorodin shook his head. "It doesn't sound like the Company's way of doing business. Besides, what could Boulton find out about Comrade Deschin that he doesn't already know?"

Zeitzev's eyes speculated.

Gorodin nodded grudgingly at the implication.

"The usual hundred thousand lire," Zeitzev said, dismissing Marco. "My secretary will take care of it."

Marco sighed and left the office, closing the door after him.

Zeitzev crossed to the half-fridge and opened it. The rank odor in the office intensified. He removed a wedge of cheese, and unwrapped it. "We'll have to find out what this Miss Winslow's up to," he said, then clarifying, added, "But she's my problem. You deal with Churcher."

"My orders are to refrain from interfering with Churcher as long as he sticks to business," Gorodin replied, deciding he'd better establish his authority. "Moscow doesn't want to raise suspicion that the services were involved in his father's death."

"Yes, my briefing included that task, but not why it was necessary," Zetizev replied solicitously.

"With good reason," Gorodin said sharply. "Its classification prohibits it. I *can* tell you, comrade, that the Politburo wants the flow of hard currency from the Arabians to continue. They're counting on Andrew Churcher to peddle them. And we have no proof he's doing otherwise."

The *rezident* nodded, accepting the sudden turn in their positions reluctantly.

"Who will you use on the woman," Gorodin asked, purposely maintaining the reversal.

"Marco."

"The *schpick*?"

"He's the best student on my roster," Zeitzev said. "And he's already in position."

Gorodin let out a weary breath, and shrugged.

Chapter Twenty-six

After filling out the official requisition forms, Melanie Winslow followed the supervisor through a thick wooden door that led to the rooms directly below the university's Records Building. They went down an old staircase that twisted back on itself. Bare light bulbs threw angled shadows across the walls. Cobwebs hung like drapery from darkened corners. The eerie descent brought them into a damp stone room, where they walked between rows of wooden tables that held cloth-bound ledgers.

Melanie was thinking of the reclusive men who had spent lifetimes in such places, painstakingly inscribing each entry by candlelight, when the supervisor stopped walking and gestured to a table beneath a bare bulb.

"You can work there," she said.

Melanie's head was filled with musty air, her skin was crawling with the dampness, and she was having second thoughts about her suggestion.

"Have any idea where I should start?" she asked. The anxiety had dried her throat, and her voice cracked when she spoke.

"Well, it doesn't look like whoever brought all of this material down here was big on alphabetizing," the supervisor replied. "But *those* might be what you're after."

She pointed to an alcove where boxes and file folders and ledgers were piled on wooden tables. The stacks tottered and leaned threatening to fall, the floor littered with those that already had.

"Good luck," she said.

"Thanks, I'll need it."

"You'll be fine," the supervisor said with a smile. "By the way, I'm Lena, Lena Catania."

Melanie grasped the hand she offered, and shook it lightly, feeling a little more relaxed. "Where'd you learn your English?"

"California. I think I was four when we moved there. My father was working for a wine exporter at the time. Well, see you later." Lena turned to the staircase, paused, and turned back. "We leave at five, and the door is locked. Make sure you're out by then."

"Thanks," Melanie replied as she sat at the wooden table, like the monks she had imagined. She didn't know exactly when Aleksei Deschin had attended the university, so she began with the first class of the modern era, a thick folder dated 1935. It gave off the dank odor of mildew, and the turn of each page filled the air with particles of dust that made her throat scratchy. The folder contained not only academic qualifications and evaluations but also personal histories and family backgrounds, the kind of information she sought, which heartened her.

She had been at it for several hours when she heard a creaking sound above, and cocked her head curiously. "Lena?" she called out. "That you?"

There was no response.

Melanie shifted in her chair uneasily, and looked at her watch. It was almost four thirty. A few pages remained in the folder she was examining. She decided to leave now, and take it with her. That's when she heard footsteps on the stairs. First one, then another, like someone carefully placing each foot, to make as little noise as possible. She got up from the table and crossed to the staircase.

"Lena?" she called out again.

Again no response.

She started up the stairs. Cautiously, at first, craning to see around each turn as she approached it. Then, anxiety building, she started climbing faster.

Suddenly, there was a loud click and the lights went out, plunging the space into absolute blackness.

Melanie froze on the staircase.

"Excuse me?" she called out. "There's someone down here! Please wait!"

Now the footsteps ascended—quickly, noisily.

She grasped the railing, and started running up the stairs in the darkness. Her shins smacked into the treads. She groped and stumbled and fell. The door hinge creaked above. She got to her feet and resumed climbing. Faster and faster, through one turn in the twisting staircase, then another. It couldn't be much further now. It couldn't. Oh God, it could! She shuddered at the memory of demons chasing her up a staircase that had no end; night after night as a child, she had climbed it in sweat-soaked terror until her father would hear the thrashing and hold her in his arms until she was sleeping peacefully again. She came through still another turn. The door lay dead ahead. A shaft of light came from between the frame and the thick wooden edge. It was still open! She dashed up the last few steps, and lunged for it.

On the opposite side, Marco Profetta listened as the onrushing footsteps came closer and closer. He waited until the very last moment, and then he slammed the massive door shut, and threw the deadbolt home.

Melanie's palms slapped against the wood just as it closed with a heavy thud, and clang of the bolt.

"There's someone in here!" she shouted. "Open the door, please! Lena! Marco! Anybody?"

Marco stepped back from the door, and snickered. A short time ago when Zeitzev called, Marco assured him he'd find a way to deal with the pushy American woman. And he derived a perverse pleasure from the method he'd chosen. He turned, and sauntered back to the rows of gray steel cabinets, and resumed filing.

Though the time was barely 4:40 P.M., no one else was there to hear Melanie's pleas for help. A short time earlier, Lena and the others had been quite pleased that Marco had volunteered to stay until five and cover for them. In Rome, the chance to get a headstart on rush hour traffic, especially on Friday, is not taken lightly.

Melanie stopped shouting and leaned against the door. The thought of being locked in the dank obsidian basement for the entire weekend made her shiver.

* * *

The scent of perfume no longer permeated Suite 610 in the Hassler. After removing the page with the astonishing message from the typewriter, Andrew put a match to one corner, tossed it into the wastebasket, then flushed the ashes down the toilet. Traces of the acrid fumes still hung in the air.

Andrew had fallen onto the huge bed to nap; but he was restless and anxious, and every five minutes, or so it seemed, he checked his watch to see if it was time to leave—time to meet the Russian woman whom he assumed had typed it; then called, alerting him to it.

He returned phone calls to pass the time. Most clients just wanted to be assured that he'd still be attending the auctions in the Soviet Union despite his father's death. He'd returned Borsa's call first. But Italy's Defense Minister was working the weekend, and left the number of his office in the Quiranale, the Seat of Federal Government. The line had been busy for hours, and Andrew tried it a half dozen times before he finally got through.

"Minister Borsa?—Andrew Churcher."

"Andrew," Borsa said in a solemn voice, "I am stunned about your father. My sincere condolences."

"Thank you, sir. I know how close you both were, and how much he respected your leadership in the equestrian community. Your help will be invaluable."

"I'd been planning to assist you, Andrew. And, under the circumstances, I feel doubly bound to do so; but I'm afraid my time at the show will be greatly diminished this year. That's why I called."

"I'm very sorry to hear that, sir. What's the problem?"

"Always the same—Americans and Russians."

An ironic smile broke across Andrew's face.

"I'm returning to Geneva tonight," Borsa went on. "But I plan to be in Rome next week to host the benefit auction for World Peace, as I do every year. And I *am* in need of some breeding stock from Tersk. Would it be possible for us to meet, then?"

"Absolutely. At your convenience."

"Good. Tuesday, around noon. Come to my private box in the

amphitheater," he said. "Perhaps I will sell *you* a horse. It is a most worthy cause."

Andrew made a few more calls, then he started feeling light-headed and realized that he was somewhere over the Atlantic when he'd last eaten. He was reaching for the phone to call room service when he decided he couldn't spend another minute in the suite. Earlier, he had promised Fausto that he would let him know if he was going out, but Andrew wanted to be alone; he wanted to walk, and get some fresh air, and think about the woman he'd be meeting; the woman who had made the bold claim—"He was murdered. I know why."

Andrew grabbed his jacket, and an apple from the bowl on the credenza, and left.

Valery Gorodin was in the bar off to one side of the Hassler's ornate lobby. A copy of *Le Monde*, the French evening newspaper, was spread out on the table in front of him. Indeed, it was as M. Coudray that he lifted a glass containing the dregs of a Campari and soda, and rattled the ice cubes at a passing waiter.

"*Garcon?*" Gorodin called out. "*Garcon, en outre, s'il vous—*" he paused, feigning he was correcting himself, and said, "*Encora. Encora per favore.*"

Hours ago, too many hours ago Gorodin thought, he had settled at this table along the glass wall from where he could monitor the bank of elevators. In his enthusiastic return to field work, he had conveniently forgotten about the waiting, the boredom, the effort to remain alert while trying to appear disinterested and casual, that are often part of it. His right calf had fallen asleep. He had reached under the table and was massaging it when he spotted Andrew coming across the lobby from the elevator.

Andrew plucked a street map from the concierge's desk, and headed toward the doors that led to the street.

Gorodin almost cheered at the sight of him. He casually folded his paper, tossed some lire on the table, and limped out of the bar into the lobby.

Andrew came out of the hotel onto Via Sistina, studying the map; then crossed the street and started down the Spanish Steps, heading for the area of knotted streets around Fontana di Trevi. The city was alive with vehicles and pedestrians, and the crisp twilight of the cold night raised his spirits. He jammed his hands in his pockets and quickened his step.

Gorodin gauged Andrew's direction from within the lobby. Then he exited, crossed to the top of the broad staircase, and watched him descend. His calf was still all pins and needles. He shook his leg in an effort to restore the circulation, and waited until Andrew had reached the piazza below before starting down himself.

About a half mile away, a battered Fiat was parked adjacent to the high stucco wall that parallels Via Ludovisi, opposite the Hotel Eden. Kovlek sat in the darkness, next to a KGB driver, patiently watching the windows of a second floor room. Occasionally, a shadow could be seen moving across the sheer curtains. In less than an hour, Raina Maiskaya would leave the hotel for her meeting with Andrew Churcher.

Chapter Twenty-seven

That afternoon in Geneva, Switzerland, Philip Keating and Gisela Pomerantz sat opposite each other at a long table beneath a canopy of chandeliers in the United Nations Palace. The disarmament negotiators were meeting for their first bargaining session.

Mikhail Pykonen, the wiley Soviet, held up a copy of the book by former U.S. Negotiator Arthur Nicholson—published after Boulton eased CIA censorship—entitled *THE KEY QUESTION*. On the cover was a photo of a hand inserting a launch key in the arming mechanism of a Minuteman Missile.

Keating sighed, anticipating a windy tirade on how past negotiators distorted Soviet positions.

"A most powerful work by Mr. Nicholson," Pykonen began. "And to open these proceedings, I would like to read a scenario he has hypothesized, one which may well be prophetic should these talks fail."

Pykonen paused dramatically, opening the book.

"Mr. Nicholson writes—'The precept of mutual deterrence should be held inviolable. The unchecked deployment of advanced first-strike weapons will undermine this cardinal rule, and breed preemptive strategies. Within this "do it to them before they do it to us" mentality lurks the ultimate nuclear threat. And one day, a Russian or an American military strategist will be forced to make such a recommendation—*because* of the technologies thrust upon him.' Then Mr. Nicholson goes on to ask the key question—'Are leaders in Moscow and Washington willing to recognize this threat and defuse it?'"

Pykonen swept his eyes over the group. "Yes!" he said fervently. "Those in Moscow are. Those in Moscow will."

The delegates around the table broke into applause.

"And they now propose," Pykonen went on, "an immediate bilateral freeze, during which deployed systems will be verified on-site, those in development divulged, followed by elimination of first-strike weaponry and deployment of bilateral strategic defense systems."

This elicited another round of applause—which Phil Keating hoped would be lengthy. He needed time to think. Despite the dying Soviet Premier's obsession, Keating hadn't expected his negotiator to discard the standard hard-line attitude so early on. And Keating had prepared remarks to counter it. Now, he had to abandon them, and make an extemporaneous reply. He had recently seen a PBS production of Chekhov's *The Three Sisters,* and as the faces around the table turned to him, Keating's mind leapt to the Soviet dramatist.

"Minister Pykonen has most generously quoted an American author," Keating began. "I would like to quote one from his country, in turn. Though not a disarmament expert, Anton Chekhov unknowingly outlined the crux of our task in a letter to his friend A. S. Souvorin when he said—'Remember, a gun on the wall in the first act is sure to fire in the third.'"

Keating paused, catching a look from Pomerantz, who was thinking, *Chekhov?* Bleak, pessimistic, futile Chekhov?

"We are well into the first act," Keating resumed. "And there is not one, but thirty thousand guns on the wall—thirty thousand nuclear warheads between the two superpowers alone."

Pomerantz brightened, thinking, *not bad.*

"And each carries almost ten times the yield of the bomb that destroyed Hiroshima," Keating went on, building to his finish. "Unlike Chekhov, our job is to structure an imperfect drama; to make certain that neither his precept nor Mr. Nicholson's scenario become part of it. Our job is to make certain that not one of those thirty thousand guns ever fires."

When the ensuing applause subsided, Keating added, "And in light of Minister Pykonen's remarks, I have no doubt we can do just that."

                         *   *   *

The sun had gone down, and a thin wash of purple light reflected from the winter sky when the DCI's armored limousine pulled up to the south portico of the White House. The results of an intensive DDI analysis of the data transmitted earlier that day from ASW were contained in Boulton's briefcase, and in a slide projector carried by an aide. The two men stepped from the limousine to an entrance that gave them direct access to the Oval Office.

The President was on the phone with Keating in Geneva. When he hung up, he tilted back in his chair and leveled an apprehensive look at his DCI.

"That was Phil," he said. "The Russians are—*different* this time. They're not rigid anymore, not frightened. They put it all on the table first crack out of the box. Phil thinks they're up to something."

"That's a given, sir."

"What do you have for me?"

"An intriguing anomaly, sir," Boulton replied, handing him copies of the ASW data. "Vessel in question—tanker. Cargo, one hundred twenty-five thousand tons of crude. Documents analysis reveals a one-thousand-ton discrepancy between rated and delivered tonnage," Boulton replied in his cryptographic syntax.

"Which means—" Hilliard pressed, sorting through the pages of data.

"Various scenarios that invite scrutiny arise," Boulton replied, finishing the President's sentence. "Conclusion due to *unwavering* consistency of discrepancy. Precisely one thousand tons each time." He unbuttoned his suit jacket, and sat on the edge of the President's desk. "Consider, Mr. President," the DCI went on more conversationally, "That when the *Kira* was reoutfitted, a one thousand-ton-sized compartment was carved out of her hold—a compartment for 'cargo' other than oil, so to speak."

"Jake," the President said a little impatiently, "are you telling me that *Herons* are deployed in that tub? That a hundred-fifty miles off our shores, there's a tanker loaded with nukes on a Caribbean cruise?"

"No, sir. Theory considered and dismissed," replied Boulton, reverting to his staccato delivery. He stood and, with a flick of a thumb and forefinger, rebuttoned his suit jacket. "DDI calculates said compartment could provide only marginal deployment capability, that is, one *Heron* and attendant support."

"Hell," the President said. "The Russians didn't go to the trouble of reoutfitting a tanker just to deploy one missile."

"Agreed."

Hilliard's face clouded over at the thought that occurred to him. "Christ, Jake—what are the chances we're looking at a fleet of 'em?"

"Negative. Scenario dictates a missile-to-launch-crew ratio of one-to-one. Submarine deployment is twenty-five-to-one. Limited supply of qualified technical personnel eliminates the option."

"Yes, the Kremlin's worse off than we are. And they're not competing with a private sector that triples the pay in the military. They can't afford to take crews from subs carrying twenty-five birds and assign 'em to tankers with one. I agree."

Hilliard flicked a glance to the slide projector Boulton's aide had set up. "What's the feature presentation?"

Boulton nodded to the aide who dimmed the overhead lights, and flipped on the projector.

A glowing chart of Gulf and Caribbean waters appeared on the wall opposite the President. The landmasses of Cuba, Central America, and the Gulf coast of the United States were delineated.

Boulton took a pointer from his pocket, telescoped it open, and traced a big triangle on the projection as he spoke. "*VLCC Kira* runs a triangular circuit, sir. Havana, Gulf, Puerto Sandino, and back. Pick up crew, take on crude, pump off crude, *ad infinitum.*"

"Sounds like maybe we're looking at a missile delivery truck," the President ventured.

"Indeed, a prime scenario, sir. Moscow ships hardware to Cuba. *Kira* picks up and, under legitimate cover, delivers to Soviet missile base in Nicaragua, *but*—" Boulton advanced the slide, and a satellite surveillance photograph of Nicaragua replaced the map —"analysis of KH-11 reconnaissance indi-

cates''— Boulton zoomed in to the distinctive geometry of a
baseball field; long shadows of personnel in strategic positions
indicated a game was in progress —"that said scenario is nega-
ted.''

"Because of a baseball diamond?'' asked the President somewhat incredulously.

"Yes, sir,'' Boulton replied smartly. "The import here is—
Russians play soccer. Baseball is a Cuban game.''

"Pardon me?'' Hilliard said, offended by the DCI's Cubaniza-
tion of the national pastime. The President grew up in Chicago,
and spent as much time at Wrigley Field as he had at the U. of
C. Law School. Ernie Banks was his hero, and it still irked him
that the guy who hit five grand slams in one season, led the
league in home runs and RBIs four times, and was voted MVP
two seasons running had never played in a World Series. "Let
me tell you, Jake,'' he went on, "if this means that Abner Dou-
bleday really grew up in Havana, I'm going to be real upset.''

"I'll put someone right on it, sir,'' Boulton said deadpan.

The President laughed.

Boulton nodded to his aide, who flicked off the projector and
brought up the room lights.

"So what you're telling me,'' the President concluded, "is
that baseball means we have a Cuban, rather than a Soviet, presence in Nicaragua.''

"Correct, sir.''

"And the soccer team would never turn its nuclear hardware
over to the baseball team.''

"Correct again.''

"Okay—back to the *Kira*. False alarm, pack of trouble,
what?''

"Trouble—situation demands that conclusion.''

"Until we verify one way or the other.''

"Exactly.''

"How?''

"Visual inspection.''

"Board her?''

"Affirmative. It would require a finding, sir.''

The President nodded thoughtfully. "Very well, I'll sign it.
But we can't get caught, Jake,'' he warned. "No gaffs. I don't

want people telling the truth when they should be lying. Not now.''

"Not ever, sir," Boulton replied grimly.

The President drifted off for a moment, then tightened his lips and caught Boulton's eye. "If we're right, Jake. If the Soviets have *Herons* deployed out there somewhere, that means they wouldn't break-even in Geneva—they'd *win*. What would result?"

"World domination; unreasonable demands—without option," Boulton replied, angered by the idea. "Consider bilateral disarmament in place—a year, two, three—*then* imbalance is insidiously revealed," he paused unexpectedly, and broke into a curious smile.

The President stared at him, baffled as to why.

"Consider, sir," Boulton went on, delighted by his vision, "consider the import if positions were *reversed*."

"Yes, yes, of course," Hilliard said, sharing it. "We would have them out of eastern Europe so fast it'd make their heads spin." He paused, then added, "For openers."

"Affirmative," Boulton said, the smile gone now.

The President nodded, decision made. "Go to it."

Boulton and his aide packed up and left.

The President pressed a button on his console. "Cathleen? Get me Phil, will you?"

The *U.S.S. Marathon*, a Navy patrol gunboat, sliced through the icy waters of Lake Geneva, pulling streaks of red and green light through the darkness behind it. The swift vessel, armed with ordnance and electronic surveillance gear, was assigned to provide offshore security for the U.S. disarmament contingent housed at Maison de Saussure.

After making his report to the President, Keating had joined Gisela Pomerantz in one of the mansion's private dining rooms. Lights on the opposite shore twinkled through the mist. The silver and crystal between them shimmered in candlelight, adding to the romantic aura.

Pomerantz raised her glass in a toast. "To two-act plays," she said, gazing alluringly over the goblet at Keating.

He smiled knowingly at the reference, and touched his glass to

hers. "To two-act plays," he said, thinking the years had given
her a radiance that made her all the more attractive to him. Then,
in an effort to lighten the mood, he added, "You know, I think
that might come in handy during tomorrow's session."

She continued staring at him, not as if puzzled, but as if she
hadn't heard what he'd said. Then she smiled, and asked, "What
might come in handy?"

"The way you're looking at me," he replied with a grin,
"Take my word for it—it's very disarming."

"I was hoping it would have that effect on you, Philip," she
replied seductively.

"Gisela—" he said, feigning he was taken aback by her
boldness. "Surely, after all these years you know better than to
expect the promise of carnal pleasures to cloud my judgment.
I'm a highly trained professional, sworn to uphold and defend the
Constitution of the United States—a married one."

"I didn't know the Seventh Commandment was part of it,"
she replied, breaking into a wry smile.

"Well," he said, matching it, "I have to admit the framers
were rather passionate when it came to separation of church and
state, but I—"

"Very passionate, as I understand it," she said, interrupting.

"And you're suggesting we take full advantage of their
wisdom—"

"—And exercise our freedoms to the fullest," she said, finishing Keating's sentence in a sensual tone. "Yes."

"Well, I've always been in favor of exercise—" he replied
thoughtfully, as if considering what she'd proposed. Then, the
desire in his eyes matching hers, he dipped a fingertip into the
champagne, brought it to her mouth, and began moistening her
lips with the vintage Cristal, while softly adding "—And passion
can have its moments."

"I've been waiting years for this one," she replied in a
breathy whisper. "The sight of you has always made me—" she
paused, licked a droplet of champagne from the corner of her
mouth, then, leaning forward until her lips were inches from his,
purred "—has always made me wet."

A tingling sensation rippled across Keating's midsection and
spread down into his thighs. He wanted her now, wanted her

more than ever as he took her face in his hands, fighting the temptation to touch his lips to hers. He was thinking that they would be soft and eager and, moistened with the champagne, would fuel the passionate rush, as he'd always imagined, when someone knocked on the door.

Keating and Pomerantz froze momentarily, then settled back into their chairs with wistful sighs.

"Yes?" Keating called out.

The door to the small dining room opened, and one of his aide's entered. He smiled at Pomerantz, then bent to Keating, and whispered something.

"Tell him I'm on my way," Keating said.

The aide nodded and hurried off.

"The President's calling," Keating said.

"I'll be here."

"Could be awhile."

"I'll be here," she replied seductively.

No more than fifteen minutes had passed when Keating returned, accompanied by his aide, and, with cautious optimism, briefed Germany's minister for strategic deployment on the *Kira*. Despite the short interval, the President's call had turned Keating's mind firmly to business, and the intimacy had been forever lost.

Chapter Twenty-eight

Raina Maiskaya stepped out of the elevator into the Hotel Eden's handsome lobby, pulling on short leather gloves. In fur hat and tailored wool coat that went below the calves of her boots, she looked like the wealthy Roman women who came to the hotel's chic rooftop restaurant with their lovers—as she had many times with Theodor Churcher.

She didn't know she was being watched; she assumed it, and planned to use the long walk to Piazza di Trevi to lose any surveillance. The Eden's revolving door spun her into the cool night. She walked east on Ludovisi. East was the wrong direction. But Ludovisi is a one-way street, and walking against traffic would prevent a vehicle from tailing her.

Kovlek and the KGB man were across the street in the Fiat. They drove to the intersection, made a left into Pinciana, and went around the block. The Fiat was on Aurora approaching Ludovisi when Raina came around the corner into the glare of its headlights. When the oncoming traffic passed, they made a broken U-turn and followed at a distance.

At the next intersection, Raina turned west into Liguria. A third of the way down the steep slope, she angled into a cobbled alley behind the shops.

The Fiat drove a short distance past the alley, stopped, and started to back up.

"No, she'll hear the car," Kovlek said. "And it's a rat's maze in there—staircases, narrow passageways."

The driver pulled the Fiat to the curb.

Kovlek removed two palm-sized walkie-talkies from the glove box, and handed one to the driver.

"I'll let you know where we come out," he said.

Kovlek walked up the incline into the darkened alley. Light spilled from a few windows onto the piles of trash and cars that hugged the buildings.

Raina followed the twisting alley to a court from which other passageways branched. She was going down a staircase when she heard footsteps and looked back. A shadow stretched high across a wall above her. Then a figure shrouded in darkness appeared atop the steps. The man paused, unsure of the route she had taken from the court. Raina held her breath in the shadows until he stepped back to examine the other passageways; then she hurried down the steps to an adjoining lane.

Up ahead, two men were unloading a bakery truck. One dragged sacks of flour onto the tailgate. The other stood in the street, stacking them on a dolly. Raina hurried between the truck and the building, startling him as she passed. The sack slipped from his grasp, hit the ground, and burst, broadcasting the flour across the cobblestones. The two men began arguing heatedly in Italian.

Footsteps were coming down the staircase behind her now— but Raina couldn't hear them.

Andrew was at a stand-up counter in a coffee bar, a few blocks from Piazza di Trevi when the city's bell towers began pealing their solemn call to vespers. He glanced to his watch, washed down the last bite of a brioche with his second cup of espresso— to keep him alert—folded the map, and hurried into the dark streets that swirl around Piazza di Trevi. He heard the fountain before he saw it, and moved in the direction of the roaring waters.

Valery Gorodin passed the time window-shopping, and had become virtually captivated by a display of lingerie. Italian men loved it and their women loved to wear it, and their shops knew how to sell it. The window was filled, not with stiff plastic torsos, but with photo blowups of luscious Italian models in seductive poses, wearing the risqué fare. Gorodin had given his imagination full rein when he noticed a reflection rippling across the glass, and realized Andrew was leaving the coffee bar.

Gorodin had lost his concentration, and almost missed him. He
waited until his anxiety subsided, then followed.

Indeed, Piazza di Trevi is one of Rome's major shopping dis-
tricts. And the semicircle of boutiques opposite the fountain are
among the busiest, especially on reopening after the midday shut-
down. By six o'clock, the well-lit piazza was crowded with
shoppers and strolling Romans taking their *passeggiata*.

For this reason, and for the many escape routes in the knot of
surrounding streets, Raina Maiskaya had picked this time and
place for the meeting. She was feigning interest in some shoes on
a sidewalk display when she saw Andrew come loping into the
piazza.

Getting out of the hotel had settled him, but now his apprehension returned, and his stomach was churning. The impact of the
immense monument in the tiny piazza—the powerfully muscled
Tritons charging through the swirling waters on their steeds—
gave him a tourist's demeanor that concealed his nervousness.

Raina watched him, wondering how anyone who looked so
much like Theodor Churcher could be so different in tempera-
ment. She recalled the time Churcher complained, "The kid's an
eccentric, a cowboy who won't join the club," and how she
gently suggested he involve Andrew with the Arabians, and how
it delighted Churcher when the horses brought them together, as
she'd predicted.

Andrew saw the striking woman coming across the piazza.
Yes, yes, he could see *her* on his father's arm. He had no doubt
she was the woman that day in Tersk. And when her long strides
brought her beneath the light, he saw she had a cool, mysterious
beauty—sharp features set against luminous porcelain, like
Steichen's portraits of Garbo. He stared, unable to imagine how
the image had ever escaped him.

Raina quickened her stride, broke into a little run, and threw
her arms around him in an expression of sympathy and affection.
And he returned it. Moments earlier, he was anxious and alone in
a strange city. Now, he was holding this woman who had held
his father, who he sensed shared his feelings and concerns, and
whose presence bolstered him. He had no idea that her gesture,
though genuine, also established a cover.

"Were you followed?" she asked, still hugging him. Her voice had the dusky lilt he heard over the phone.

"I don't know. I didn't see anyone."

"*I* was, but I lost him."

"If you don't mind me asking," Andrew said in a whisper as they pulled back from each other, "how'd you get into the suite?"

"Don't whisper. It attracts attention," she warned. "With a key—your father had given me."

Andrew smiled, feeling a little naive. "How do you know he was murdered?" he asked.

She blinked at his directness, took his arm, and started walking around the curve of the piazza. "He called me that morning. He was furious, and said he was going to 'kick Aleksei's butt.'"

"Sounds just like him," Andrew said with a little smile. "Who's Aleksei?"

"Aleksei Deschin, cultural minister, Politburo, and very close to the Premier. Your father 'did business' with them for years."

"He was paid in paintings, wasn't he," Andrew said. It was a statement.

"Yes. That's where the problem arose. He discovered the 'payments' were fakes."

Andrew nodded with some understanding now. "Payments for what?"

"Cooperation—in matters of national security. That's all he ever told me. For my own protection."

Andrew was stunned by her reply. "That's, that's just unbelievable," he finally muttered, the words sticking in his throat. "I don't know what to say."

To his extreme dismay, she had confirmed his darkest suspicions about his father. His hopes of disproving them, if only to himself, had just been undeniably shattered. The realization was anguishing, and, despite the evidence, fueled his unwillingness to accept the idea that his father had hurt his country.

Theodor Churcher was a patriot, and war hero, not a traitor; and try as Andrew might, he couldn't reconcile his view with Raina's; the data refused to compute. If she was right, the world might soon learn that his father had sold out to the Russians. The thought was more than painful—it was mortifying.

He walked in silence until the impact wore off, then his face softened with a question.

"What's your name?"

"Raina, Raina Maiskaya," she said lyrically.

"Who killed my father, Raina?" he asked with quiet intensity.

"Glavnoe Razvedyvatelnoe Upravlenie," she said, bitterly enunciating each syllable.

Andrew stared at her baffled.

"GRU," she said. "They're like KGB—just as ruthless but more cunning." She shook her head, dismayed. "It should never have happened. There was a package. Your father was totally confident it would protect him." She saw a flicker of recognition in his eyes. "You're aware of it—"

"Yes," he said cautiously, hearing McKendrick's voice warning him.

"Then I assume that it has been—"

"No," he said, anticipating her question.

"They got it," she said flatly.

Andrew nodded grimly. "You're familiar with the contents?" he asked.

"Drawings. Engineering drawings of a tanker."

"A tanker? I don't get it."

"Nor do I. Your father wanted the drawings. I got them for him. That's all."

"*You* got them—"

"Yes, from a man I know. A Jew. He's a marine engineer in Leningrad. A refusenik. His job sensitivity is used as an excuse to detain him. He wanted his son to get out of Russia before he could be conscripted."

They had crossed the piazza and were a few steps into the darkness of a narrow street. Raina swung him around, and started walking in the direction from which they had just come.

"What is it?" he asked at the sudden reversal.

"Nothing. Just a precaution. I don't like to be predictable. To make a long story short, I heard about my friend's problem, and used my connections to get his son out—in exchange for the drawings."

"They killed my father before they had them."

"He must have endangered something of very high priority for them to take that chance."

Andrew nodded, thinking his father had trusted her completely—and he would now. "The highest," he said. "My father wanted that package to go to the CIA."

Raina flicked him a look.

"McKendrick took two bullets trying," Andrew went on. "Now it's my turn."

"How?"

"You got the drawings for my father. Get them for me."

"Impossible."

"I'll be in Moscow in a week," he said, ignoring her reply, and, in a commanding tone, added, "Find a way."

Raina's face hardened at his brashness, then eased into a smile. *Pure Theodor Churcher,* she thought.

Kovlek had been watching from the steps of a church across the piazza, and casually tailed them when they walked off together. Now, all of a sudden, they were coming right at him. He was positive she hadn't seen him earlier; positive she had no reason to suspect him. He would handle this boldly, as if he had as much reason to be there as they. And so, he came at them, at a brisk cadence.

As expected, Raina took no notice of him as they passed within a meter of each other. As a matter of fact, she averted her eyes. For no special reason. Just a quick glance to the ground that fell atop the granite pavers where he stepped, that fell atop his shoes, atop the flour that filled the crease between the upper and sole and dotted the polished black toes. She knew a man had followed her into the alley; and she put the pieces together, and knew Kovlek was that man.

"I was wrong," she said, pulling Andrew closer, and wrapping her arms around him, as if they were lovers. "The man with the glasses—"

Andrew's eyes flicked in Kovlek's direction.

"Don't stare," she warned.

She pulled him to her and kissed him. Hard. On the lips. "I'll contact you again," she said as she broke it off. Then gently brushing the hair from his puzzled face, added, "I'm sorry for what I had to tell you, Andrew. And very sorry for this.'' He didn't understand until she reared back and slapped him across the face. "Animal! Filthy animal!'' she shouted, implying he had suggested something tawdry. She turned on a heel and stalked off in the direction of a dark narrow street.

The blow caught Andrew by surprise. He recoiled, backing into a row of sidewalk display racks.

Most observers laughed, assuming, as Raina intended, that she had just dispatched an overzealous gigolo.

Kovlek stiffened, and took the walkie-talkie from his pocket.

Gorodin was watching from a shadowed doorway. He winced, realizing Kovlek was about to apprehend her. Left alone, she would think her charade had worked and maintain contact with Andrew, which Gorodin much preferred. He whistled to get Kovlek's attention, and shook no vehemently to dissuade him.

Kovlek had had his fill of his GRU rival. And having blown the surveillance, he shuddered at the thought of facing Zeitzev empty-handed. He ignored the warning and clicked on the walkie-talkie.

"Vladas? Vladas, are you there?'' he barked to the driver in the Fiat.

The walkie-talkie crackled with a reply.

"She spotted me!'' Kovlek went on. "She's heading west on Sabini! Move in! We have to pick her up now! Hurry!'' He clicked off and charged after Raina.

Andrew had spotted them running across the piazza. He had just started to pursue when Gorodin stumbled purposely into his path.

"*Merde!*'' Gorodin shouted as they went down in a tangle of limbs. He made certain he landed atop Andrew to further delay him and, as they got to their feet, acted as if the collision was Andrew's fault.

"*Idiot!*'' he exclaimed, throwing up his hands. "*Ce n'est pas ma faute! C'est vous qui l'avez fait. Idiot!*''

"Okay, okay!'' Andrew said, trying to placate the incensed Frenchman.

Suddenly, the screech of tires and blast of headlights came from behind them. The Fiat roared past, following Raina and Kovlek into the narrow street.

Andrew whirled from Gorodin, and ran after it. The piazza was cluttered with displays and shoppers, which slowed his progress. He threaded his way through them, rounded the corner, and ran into the narrow street. His footsteps echoed in the tunnel of hard surfaces. Hell-bent, he ran a long distance in the darkness before realizing the street was empty. The man and the car and Raina Maiskaya had vanished into the night. Andrew pulled up abruptly, then reversed direction and hurried back to the piazza.

Gorodin was gone.

The fountain's waters roared.

Andrew was alone.

Chapter Twenty-nine

A pastel moon hovered in hazy twilight as Alitalia Flight 776 from Comiso descended toward Leonardo da Vinci, and taxied to the domestic terminal.

Silvio Festa, the single-minded construction worker whose "gunshots" had gotten Andrew's attention earlier, was waiting for Dominica Maresca when she deplaned. But alas, upset by the day's events in Sicily, Dominica wasn't in the mood for the evening Silvio had planned, and insisted he take her home.

When he parked in front of her building on Via Campagni in the Tributino district, she leaned over and put a light kiss on his mouth, flicking her tongue beneath his upper lip as she broke it off. "Thanks. I knew you'd understand," she said in a soft, seductive voice. And then, making certain he glimpsed her bare breast through the scooped neck of her blouse, she turned, got out of the car, and walked toward the building.

Silvio hungrily eyed her swaying hips as she climbed the steps and went inside. Then his desire shattered the fragile dam that contained it. He charged out of the car, into the building, and up the stairs after her. He had never raped before. He had never been denied before. Not like this.

Dominica was opening the door to her apartment when she heard the rush of footsteps. Silvio lunged for her, his momentum carrying them into the vestibule. He landed on top of her, tearing at her clothing in a passionate frenzy. She pummeled him, and squirmed and struggled, trying to fight him off, and, finally working a leg out from beneath him, kicked the door closed.

For in truth, Dominica was emotionally charged by her ordeal in Comiso, and wanted nothing more than to scream in ecstacy and drive the painful memory of it from her mind. But she was consumed by it. Consumed by what had happened to that boy, by the image of his body pressed into the earth, the life squeezed out of it by steel treads—and *she* had put him beneath them. His death was on her soul, as his blood had been on her hands; and she still had the smell of it, and the smell of his last breath in her nostrils. From the moment they pried his body from the soil and took him away, she had been planning her absolution.

Silvio finally pinned her to the floor and plunged into her like a lust-crazed stallion. It didn't occur to him that she was still controlling the pace; she who knew that women's rights had become fashionable in Italian courts, that men who treated their women like *fazzolettini di carta*, like Kleenex, were vulnerable; she who planned to use him, and had.

Soon she had him in her bed, and held him in her arms; and now, while her long fingers made him ready to love her again, she made her next move.

"He will never know this," she said softly, with a haunting sadness.

"Who?" Silvio wondered, tilting his head up from her breast so he could see her face.

"That poor boy in Comiso," she replied. "He will never have a lover, or a family, or anything."

"Ah, Dominica," he said with a philosophical tone, "there is nothing you can do."

"Don't say that," she pleaded, stealing a glance at him to assess the effect.

"Dominica," he said comfortingly, gently touching her face, "it will be all right. It will pass."

"Exactly," she replied. "Soon, it will be as if he never existed, a forgotten child, a wasted life. I don't want to live with that, Silvio. I can't."

"Well, what are you going to do?" he asked, giving her the opening she sought.

Dominica considered her answer for a long moment.

"Give his death meaning," she replied, choosing her words carefully. "Force Giancarlo Borsa to pay for that poor child's sacrifice, so that those who plan nuclear war in the name of peace will think of him every day and never forget he died for their sins.''

"How?" he asked facetiously. "Plaster his picture on milk cartons and buses, like they do with missing children in America?"

Dominica shook her head from side to side, and smiled tolerantly.

"With a symbol. We will use a symbol, Silvio," she replied, enthusiasm building. "One that already exists. Millions of them, all over the country."

Silvio pushed up on an elbow.

"Well then, it should be easy to point out one of these 'symbols,'" he said, challenging her.

Dominica smiled knowingly, almost mischievously. She had him now, she thought. She leaned over him, and ran her tongue over his hardening penis.

Silvio moaned and forgot all about his question.

Dominica answered it anyway, continuing to lick a path from his loins to a sweat-filled hollow on his chest where a tiny crucifix lay. She took it between her teeth and jerked her head, snapping the thin chain.

Silvio blinked, startled.

Dominica bounced up from the bed, and put a leg over him, straddling his hips. The cross was still in her teeth, the chain dangling above Silvio's face like golden tinsel in the moonlight. Her eyes narrowed in a wicked glint as she put her hands on her bare hips and thrust her breasts forward, declaring victory.

Silvio smiled acknowledging it. He reached up to her mouth and, gently forcing his thumb between her soft lips, took the crucifix from them.

"See?" she said. "Now, all we have to do is—connect the symbol to the event."

"I can think of at least a thousand ways," he said facetiously.

"I'm not surprised. I have a feeling you have a real flair for what I have in mind. Matter-of-fact, I know you do."

"Really? So, tell me, what is it that—"

Silvio sighed, then shuddered as she reached down between their bodies and slipped him inside her.

"I will, Silvio," she purred. "I'll tell you exactly. But not now. Ohhh, Silvio, not now."

She arched her back as he came up to meet her, and stayed with him like this until the sounds he made told her he was close. Then, she purposely slid off him before he finished, and moved forward onto his chest until her wet thighs were on either side of his head. And as she had hoped, he did what she wanted without protest or prompting. Dominica was sure of him now; sure there would be no need for coercion—for the threat of criminal proceedings as she had planned—to obtain his assistance. Silvio Festa would do whatever she asked, because he wanted to please her.

Chapter Thirty

Andrew had been stunned by the abduction, stunned by the swiftness of it. Raina had been on his arm one minute and gone the next. Actually, in *less* than a minute, he had calculated. From the time she saw the man with the glasses to when she vanished in the narrow street couldn't have been more than forty-five seconds. Andrew had been wandering Rome's dark streets for much longer than that, now. He turned a corner and found himself in front of Police Headquarters on San Vitale. He stood blinking at the whirling roof flashers on the Fiats that pulled up with the evening's collection of drunks, prostitutes, and petty thieves—wondering what he would tell the police if he went inside.

"Excuse me, but I was having a clandestine meeting with a Russian woman when she was abducted."

"You actually witnessed this abduction?"

"Well, sort of, I mean, I chased the car, but—"

"You *didn't* witness it."

"No."

"What was this meeting about?"

"My father's espionage activities."

"Your father's espionage activities—"

"Well, you see, she was his lover; but he was recently murdered, and now, I'm trying to—"

Andrew zipped his jacket against the cold, shoved his hands deep into the pockets, and walked on, deciding en route to return to the hotel and call Fausto.

The two had been in Suite 610 for over a half hour now. Fausto had bawled Andrew out for not calling him before leaving the hotel. Andrew had briefed him on events that led to his meet-

192

ing with Raina, and running on adrenalin, he was still pacing, and still talking.

"Where? Where would they take her?" he wondered.

"Soviet Embassy, most likely," Fausto replied in his heavy accent. He was slouched in a club chair, and gesturing to another, gently added, "Andrew, maybe you should sit down."

"Let's go there and ask to see her," Andrew pressed on, ignoring Fausto's suggestion.

Fausto shook his head. "They'd deny she was there," he replied. "We wouldn't even get through the gate."

"Damn. I finally had a way to go with this. I mean, Raina had connections. We were going to meet in Moscow and—" He threw up his hands. "I might've stopped them if that Frenchman hadn't clobbered me."

"You might have stopped a bullet," Fausto suggested sagely.

Andrew's fervor cooled in acknowledgment. He dropped into a chair opposite Fausto, thinking about what had happened to McKendrick.

"You're sure he wasn't one of them?" Fausto asked.

"The Frenchman?"

Fausto grunted.

"I don't know. I don't think so," Andrew replied. "What's it matter anyway?"

"I was thinking, they might be watching you, too," Fausto replied. "If they are—" He paused, and swung a glance to the phone. "Did the woman call you?"

Andrew nodded.

Fausto's brows went up.

"But we didn't talk about a meeting," Andrew said, seeing his reaction. "And she didn't identify herself. Besides, I checked the phone."

Fausto nodded sagely, pulled himself from the cushions of the club chair, and went toward the phone.

Andrew swiveled on the chair, watching him. He smiled when Fausto lifted the receiver, replacing it with one of the bananas from the bowl on the credenza.

"You're wasting your time," he said genially.

Fausto unscrewed the mouthpiece, and let the diaphragm drop into his palm. No bugging device. No wires. He peered into the hollow plastic shell. Same result. He shrugged, then glanced around the room.

"I checked the rest of the place, too," Andrew said, knowing what he was thinking.

Fausto sat puzzled for a moment, then considered the diaphragm in his palm. He turned to the lamp on the nightstand, and began tilting the diaphragm at various angles, so its surfaces caught the light.

Andrew's curiosity got the better of him. He stood, and crossed to Fausto. "What're you doing?"

"*Aspetti.*"

Fausto was holding the diaphragm steady now, adjusting the angle just so. "Ah, look."

Andrew leaned closer and saw the legend KIZ/1MCR inscribed in the metal casing. "Yeah—" he said, not understanding.

"Koehler Industries, Zurich—one-thousand-meter range cellular relay," Fausto said slowly, relating each word to the legend. "*That's* your bug."

"You replace the diaphragm in any phone with this diaphragm, and it's bugged."

"*Diaphragms,*" Fausto said, emphasizing the plural as he unscrewed the earpiece revealing another. "One in each end of the handset—to hear both sides of the conversation. They're the best on the market. And, perhaps you've noticed, not easily detected by the untrained eye."

Andrew broke into an embarrassed grin.

"They work in tandem with a recorder or relay unit," Fausto went on, reassembling the phone and leaving the bugs in place. "Better if they don't know we found them," he explained. "*Capisco?*"

"Capisco," Andrew echoed.

Fausto's face suddenly clouded with concern. "You called me from here—"

Andrew nodded grimly. "I didn't do anything right, tonight. I probably *should have* gone to the police."

Fausto shook no. "What makes you think *their* inquiries wouldn't be met with denials? Remember, an Embassy is sovereign territory. It can't be searched."

"*Legally*," Andrew said, his eyes brightening with an idea.

"*Che pazza!*" Fausto snapped, knowing what Andrew was thinking. You'll get shot on sight—*legally*."

"Maybe I could get in on the pretext of business," Andrew went on undaunted. "Make up a story about the Arabians. You know some problem that—"

"Forget it," Fausto interrupted. "Nobody does business at this hour. Besides, they know you were with her. They'd see right through your pretext."

Andrew took a deep breath and let it out. "I guess you're right," he said, suddenly hit by exhaustion. "What do you think'll happen to her?"

"I don't know. I'll need some time to—how you say—*scavasto*." He made a churning gesture with his hands while he searched for the word. Then, literally translating the Italian, said, "Excavate."

"You mean, do some digging."

Fausto nodded. "Get some rest. Sell some horses. I'll call you," he said, adding, "so to speak."

"Thanks."

Fausto patted him on the cheek and left.

Andrew fell facedown across the bed. Thirty-two hours had passed since he left Houston, and aside from a catnap on the plane, he hadn't slept. He lay on his stomach, staring at the intricately woven patterns in the oriental rug until he fell asleep.

When he woke, it was with a start. He was on his back looking straight into the blazing chandelier above the bed. He lay there disoriented for a few moments. Then it all came back, in a rush, with an overwhelming sense of urgency. He sat up suddenly, and glanced to his watch. It was almost eleven thirty. He had slept for over two hours. It felt like two minutes. He took the map from his pocket, and began searching for the Soviet Embassy.

Chapter Thirty-one

Melanie stood on the top step of the staircase in the Archives beneath the Sapienza, pounding on the door with her fists, and screaming for help at the top of her lungs. It was more out of frustration now. She'd been doing this on and off for hours to no avail. Finally, she overcame her anxiety, sat down again on the steps in the darkness, and started thinking.

She had survived New York's Streets and subways for twenty years, not to mention the blackout in sixty-seven. She was in her early twenties and new to the city at the time, and spent that night backstage at the Odeon, a dumpy theater on Houston Street in the East Village where she'd gone to audition for *Oh, Calcutta!* on a dare. But that evening, others had groped through the blackness with candles and bottles of wine and pizzas, and it turned into quite a party.

This was different. She was alone, hungry, and softened by middle-aged comforts. She'd expected her eyes to acclimate and bring vague suggestions of steps, and walls, and light fixtures into view. But after the first hour, she still couldn't see her hand in front of her face. The absence of light was total, as if she was suddenly struck blind.

She was digging through her purse for a package of gum to alleviate the dryness in her mouth when she began thinking about the footsteps she had heard earlier and recalled the sequence of events: whoever locked the door had come down the staircase a short distance, *then* the lights went out, and *then* footsteps ascended. That meant the switch was on *her* side of the door! She ran it through her mind over and over, trying to hear the footsteps, trying to count them.

With one hand on the rail, the other on the wall, Melanie started down the steps in the pitch blackness. It took several tries, first one wall, then the other, sliding her palms over the dusty surfaces before her fingers found a run of electrical conduit which led her to the rotary switch—Click! The bare bulbs exploded with light, sending the angled shadows up the walls and illuminating the cobweb tapestries.

She was startled by the sudden brilliance. It took a few moments for her eyes to adjust and focus on the eeriness, which she found comforting now.

Bolstered by the triumph, and resigned to her incarceration, Melanie decided to make use of the time. She descended the twisting staircase to the stone room and resumed her search for Aleksei Deschin's records.

Marco Profetta spent the evening at Allegro, a gay bar on Paccione, not far from the Sapienza. For hours, Marco had resisted the advances of a barrel-chested businessman who fancied the wiry sleekness of his body. Marco would have liked nothing better than to let the big German take him back to his room in the DeVille, and pound him mercilessly into the sheets. But Zeitzev had agreed to pay Marco the 500,000 lire that he wanted for the Information Card to deal with Melanie Winslow. And his work wasn't finished.

It was 11:23 P.M. when he left Allegro to return to the Sapienza. He cruised the courtyard in his red Alpha. The headlights revealed dozens of motor scooters still parked in the area. Some were clustered near the entrance to the Records Office. Marco got out of the car, and examined them. His eyes darted to the words *SCOOT-A-LONG* stenciled across a green Motobecane. A tag displaying the distinctive logo had dangled from the key ring clutched in Melanie's fist that afternoon. He smiled at his cleverness, lifted the scooter's molded plastic engine housing, and began the next phase of his plan.

Hours of searching still hadn't turned up the elusive name Melanie sought. She was opening another folder when her head snapped up in reaction to the creak of the door hinge above.

"Pronto? C'e qualcuno qui?" came the prissy voice from the top of the staircase, "Hello? Hello, anyone down there?"

"Yes! Yes, there is," Melanie shouted back.

She grabbed her purse and ran like hell, her dancer's legs taking the stairs three at a time.

"Yes, wait! I'm coming," she shouted as she climbed.

Marco stood to one side of the opened door, hands on hips, smiling slyly at the relief he heard in her voice. She would be so grateful.

The dashing footsteps got louder, and suddenly, Melanie charged through the open doorway, past Marco, into the records office.

"Signora!" he exclaimed. "We thought you had left," he said, feigning confusion.

"Somebody locked me in," she replied breathlessly. "I shouted and shouted. I can't imagine no one heard me."

"Ah," Marco said, knowingly. "Janitor, *sordo,*" he went on, cupping a hand behind his ear, indicating the fellow was hard of hearing. *"Sordo."*

"Oh," Melanie said, understanding.

"I came back for my book," he said, holding up a text. "I saw light under the door."

"Thank God," she said in a more subdued tone.

"You need a ride?"

"No, I rented a scooter," she replied. "Thanks."

She took a moment to collect herself, and they went outside together.

"Ciao, signora."

"Ciao, Marco. *Molto grazie."*

Marco waved and sauntered toward the parking area.

Melanie stood in the courtyard for a few moments, drawing the cool, fresh air into her lungs. Then she walked quickly toward her motor scooter.

Marco got into his car, and watched expectantly.

Melanie dropped onto the Motobecane's seat, fishing through her purse for the key. In ten minutes, she thought, twenty if she detoured to one of those cobblestoned streets, she would be standing under the hot shower in her room; after which, she'd go down to the cozy hotel bar. God, how she wanted a tall, frosty gin and tonic that would wash the musty taste of the archives from her mouth. She found the keys and, in her haste, stabbed the key at the ignition upside down. She fidgeted with it for a moment until she realized her mistake, then, all in one motion, reversed the key, pushed in, and turned it. The engine kicked over, but refused to start. She waited a few seconds and tried again. Nothing. She sighed, slumped on the seat, and noticed headlights approaching.

Marco leaned out the window of the Alfa coupe which pulled up next to her.

"Walk-A-Long strikes again," he said, chuckling.

"I'm afraid my sense of humor's been dealt a fatal blow," she replied with a thin smile.

"Where are you staying?"

"At the Gregoriana."

"Come on, I'll take you."

"What about the scooter?"

"Call them, and they'll pick it up. Come on."

Melanie gathered her things, and got into the Alfa next to him. Marco smiled and drove out of the parking area, heading north on Della Scroffa.

"What are you looking for down there, anyway?" he asked offhandedly.

"Information about my father."

"Oh," he said, filing it away. "My father went to the university, too; graduated in fifty-eight, I think."

Marco took Copelle to del Tritione and started up the hill. Many people had already left the city for the weekend. And traffic was light at this hour. It took less than ten minutes to drive to the Gregoriana.

"Thanks again, Marco," Melanie said as she popped the Alpha's door.

"*Prego, signora,*" he said magnanimously. "What time shall I pick you up tomorrow?"

"Tomorrow?" Melanie replied, puzzled.

"Yes, I'll be your driver."

"Oh, that's not necessary. You've already done enough. I'll get another scooter."

"Please, *signora,*" he insisted. "In Rome, a man who rescues a woman becomes responsible for her. It's an old custom. You have no choice. So, your wish is my command—almost,'' he joked charmingly.

Melanie smiled and looked at him thoughtfully.

"Well, there *is* something you can help me with," she said. "The Records Office is closed for the weekend, isn't it?"

"Si."

"I'd like to get back in there tomorrow, and Sunday instead of waiting. Can you arrange it?"

"Of course, I have the key. What time shall I pick you up?"

"Ten?"

"Si. Le dieci."

Marco had her perfectly positioned, now. Why follow her, and chance being spotted or losing her in traffic on that scooter when he could chauffeur her instead. He watched her go into the hotel, then drove back to the Sapienza, and descended into the Archives. He had until 10 A.M. the next morning to find Aleksei Deschin's records.

Chapter Thirty-two

The back of Kovlek's hand landed on Raina Maiskaya's cheek with a loud smack.

She lurched backwards, almost toppling the chair, in Zeitzev's office to which she was bound. Kovlek was standing over her. Zeitzev, and Vladas, the KGB driver, were slouched in stuffed side chairs. They had removed Raina's outercoat, and the rope that held her to the chair crisscrossed the center of her chest, pulling her silk blouse tight against her breasts.

"Well?" Kovlek shouted.

Raina lifted her head to the defiant angle it held prior to the blow. Four red welts were already rising on the side of her face.

"I told you," she replied evenly, "Mr. Churcher and I were talking business. Arabian horses."

"Liar!" Kovlek shrieked, slapping her again.

Raina recovered and eyed him with an odious smirk.

"Then why did you strike him? Why did you run?"

"Because he offended me," she replied. "He made a filthy sexual suggestion."

"Another lie! What were you trying to cover up?"

"Nothing."

"Why did you say you were the housekeeper when you called him?"

"I never called him."

Zeitzev pulled his huge frame from the chair and lumbered toward her. "Madame Maiskaya," he scolded gently, "we have a recording of the conversation."

"Impossible."

"It is your voice," he insisted.

"Impossible."

"Listen." He popped a piece of cheese into his mouth, and nodded to Kovlek.

The deputy placed a set of headphones over Raina's ears. He turned to the stereo unit behind her, and depressed the play button on the cassette deck.

Raina heard the two rings of the phone, followed by the exchange between she and Andrew.

"Well?" Zeitzev prompted.

"That's not me," she lied.

"Listen again," Zeitzev said insidiously.

Kovlek had already rewound the tape. He pressed play, and cranked the volume to the maximum setting.

The first ring exploded in Raina's ears at a full 150 watts per channel. Her eyes snapped open like she'd been stabbed. At the second, she lurched against her bonds as if an electric current was surging through her body. Her head snapped from side to side in a futile effort to shed the headphones as the voices screamed inside her skull unable to get out.

When the tape ended, Zeitzev approached her, dropped to a knee, and removed the headphones.

Raina began shaking her head trying to clear it.

"Now, madame," Zeitzev said more sternly, "your actions with Churcher have been highly suspect. It's very important we know what he's up to. You will tell us." He stood, walked a few steps, and paused. "Oh, yes," he went on as if he'd forgotten, "we have other tapes, *special* ones designed to induce cooperation. Entire symphonies, if you will, that last for hours. You see, Madame Maiskaya," he went on, embellishing the scenario, "sound is a truly unique sensory stimulant. Dentists use it to increase pain thresholds. We use it to exceed them. Indeed, the human nervous system is extremely sensitive to auditory invasion, which makes sound a most potent form of torture. I'm sure you'll be pleased to know it leaves no visible marks or scars, but be advised, its power is unlimited, and its effect can be lasting and traumatic."

Raina eyed him coldly, with hatred. "I can't hear a word you're saying," she said facetiously.

"That may well be your fate," was his icy reply.

A short time earlier, Andrew came out of the Hassler, carrying a manila envelope. He got into the first taxicab in the line at the curb, stuffed some lire into the driver's hand, and gave him the envelope.

"Deliver it to the American Embassy, okay?"

The cabdriver smiled at the lire, and nodded.

Andrew slipped out the opposite door of the taxi and hurried into the darkness.

The cabdriver didn't know the envelope was empty, and the addressee fictitious, nor would it have mattered if he had. He pocketed the money, and drove off.

Seconds later, Gorodin hurried from the hotel and jumped into the next cab, exhorting the driver to follow the first.

Andrew watched the two vehicles heading north on Tinita di Monti, then walked to the Soviet Embassy.

He was standing beneath a tree, in the silent blackness of the small park opposite the Embassy gates, now. Lights burned in many windows of the staid building. Andrew wondered behind which Raina might be. He crossed the street, angling away from the gate where a member of the Red Army Guard cradling an AK-47 was posted. The high fence was topped with razor-wire; and the sheets of steel welded over the decorative ironwork, not only blocked sightlines, and bullets, but also hand and footholds, as well.

Andrew had walked a short distance in search of a way over it when a vehicle turned the corner and caught him in its headlights. He ducked back against the fence as a taxi passed and pulled up to the gates. Gorodin got out and slammed the door. Andrew didn't know that the U.S. Embassy was a short drive from the Hassler. He picked it because he knew any cabdriver would understand. Gorodin realized immediately upon arriving there that Andrew had shaken him, and headed here. He approached the guard and displayed his identification, which drew a cursory glance.

"*Nomyer sveedam namorye?*" the guard challenged.

"*Nyet, sbalkonam,*" Gorodin replied flatly.

The guard nodded and opened a personnel door to the right of the gate, allowing Gorodin onto the grounds.

Andrew observed the lax check of identification, and overheard their conversation. The tone suggested it was an exchange of passwords, which it was.

"A room with a view of the sea?"

"No, with a balcony."

"Nyet, sbalkonam," Andrew repeated to himself. Perhaps the password would get him onto the grounds, he thought. And the fact that he was doing business with the Soviet Union might cover him if challenged once inside. At worst, he'd be denied entry. He was an American. They couldn't abduct *him* off the street.

The needles in the VU meters of Zeitzev's stereo were slammed so hard to the right they appeared to be stuck.

Raina's long body arched in the chair against the pain that stabbed into her from the headphones. The precise frequency of fingernails on a blackboard had been screeching in her ears for over a minute now. Her entire body was vibrating. But it hadn't moved since her pelvis thrust forward at the first chilling tone. The movement had hiked her dress up around her thighs, exposing her vulnerably opened legs.

"Best orgasm she's ever had," Zeitzev chortled.

"Yes, yes," Kovlek slobbered. "But wait till she gets a taste of the microphone!" he roared, thrusting his groin forward, prompting vulgar laughter.

Raina couldn't hear it. She had no thoughts, made no sounds, and saw only violent electronic patterns, as if her mind had become a television screen that had gone suddenly haywire. Her posture gradually became even more explicit, allowing the three Russians to glimpse tufts of pubic hair curling from beneath the lace edges of her lingerie. They were so consumed by their perversity that they jumped when the door opened, and Gorodin entered.

Zeitzev saw the disgust in his eyes and decided to take the offensive. "Why aren't you on Churcher?"

"He's tucked in for the night," Gorodin lied.

His head snapped to Raina. The frequency in the headphones

had just changed to an oscillating bass resonance, and her stiffened body had suddenly started to buck and gyrate convulsively.

Gorodin grasped the cord from the headphones and snapped it with his wrist, like a bullwhip, unplugging the jack from the amplifier.

Raina slumped into the chair as if it was her body that had been unplugged.

"She refuses to tell us what she and Churcher were discussing," Zeitzev said defensively.

"She would have if this idiot had left her alone," Gorodin snapped, gesturing to Kovlek.

"She's my account," Kovlek countered loudly.

"She was Theodor Churcher's lover, and that makes her mine," Gorodin retorted. "What happens between her and Churcher's son is GRU business, not yours." He swung a searing look to Zeitzev. "I told you it was classified!" he went on. "Contact Moscow Center! Ask Tvardovskiy for verification, if you wish. But I'd think twice before rousing him at this hour."

The three men exchanged frustrated glances, itching to challenge Gorodin, but knowing better.

"Well, you're not as stupid as I thought," he said, sensing their capitulation. "Now, get out. I want to talk to her alone."

Zeitzev thought for a moment, nodded to Kovlek and Vladas, and the three of them left the office.

Gorodin crouched, and untied Raina from the chair. She was barely conscious. Her complexion was waxen; her clothing soaked with sweat. He filled a glass with water from a pitcher on the desk, cradled her head, and poured some onto her lips, then gently onto her face.

"Can you hear me?" he asked.

Her eyes were open in a blank stare.

"Can you hear me?" he asked again a little louder.

She made a pained expression, and nodded slightly.

"I know who you are, Raina Maiskaya," Gorodin said. "Your silence could inflict untold damage on your country. Do you understand?"

Raina nodded.

"Good. You are going home," he went on. "You think about what I said on the way. It will be the most important decision of your life, and should you decide wrongly—the last."

Nomyer sveedam namorye? the guard would challenge.

Nyet, sbalkonam, Andrew would reply.

Nyet, sbalkonam.

Nyet, sblakonam.

Nyet, sbalkonam.

Andrew had remained in the darkness, repeating the words. He was concerned that he might skew one of the sounds and change the meaning by mistake. He recalled the time he had said "conscientious," and his listener heard "contentious." Ironically, he was applying to Rice, his father's alma mater, and the interviewer was impressed that Andrew had inherited the tycoon's gall.

The Russian guard noticed Andrew approaching, turned his head slightly, and swept his eyes over him.

Andrew studied the stern marble-hard face in search of a crack, and decided the fair-skinned, blue-eyed, bow-lipped guard would look like a cherub if he smiled—but he didn't. The rigid fellow personified the monolithic hold the Soviet Union has on its people, Andrew thought. And his admiration for Raina grew, strengthening his resolve to help her.

He was reaching for his wallet and poised for the guard's challenge when the headlights of a car came from inside the grounds. The guard turned from Andrew, and rolled back the gates allowing it to pull forward, then stepped to the driver's window and shone a flashlight across the faces inside.

Andrew was stunned as the light moved onto the ashen, catatonic mask between Gorodin and Zeitzev.

Raina's head turned. She looked right at Andrew, right through him with her blank eyes.

Andrew froze, unable to move or utter a sound. He watched as the car roared off into the darkness.

The guard closed the gate, and turned to him.

"Yes, what do you want?" he asked in Russian.

Andrew eyed him for a long moment.

"Go to hell," he said bitterly.

Andrew turned and walked away—walked along the welded sheets of steel. He was barely four years old when America's thirty-fifth President went to Berlin, but he'd seen documentaries and news clips, and now, the distinctive cadence rang in his ears—"*We* don't have to build walls to keep our people *in*."

Chapter Thirty-three

It was a warm, humid Saturday morning in Pensacola. Lt. Commander Keith Arnsbarger was in his backyard, hitting grounders to his girlfriend's eleven-year-old, when the Naval intelligence officer arrived and Cissy brought him out back. Arnsbarger hit the Little Leaguer one last big hopper, mussed his hair, and tossed him clothes and all into the pool.

Cissy was howling, and the kid was laughing like hell as Arnsbarger and the officer moved off toward an orchard of fruit trees. The brush-cut courier informed Arnsbarger he'd been dispatched to take him to a meeting with the director of Central Intelligence, who was arriving in Pensacola within the hour.

"Can't make it," Arnsbarger cracked. "The President's on his way over to shag some flies. Baseball's his sport," he went on, assuming Lowell or another of his buddies was playing a joke.

Lowell was jogging on Coastline Drive, and well into the ten miles he ran every day when the officer dispatched with *his* orders caught up with him. The lanky Californian thought maybe he had overdosed on beta endorphins, and was as incredulous as Arnsbarger.

"Will you repeat that, please?" he asked. "You caught me in the middle of a runner's high."

He hadn't expected any feedback to his response to the KIQ directive, let alone one as direct as a meeting with the DCI himself. It had been barely eight hours since the data had been transmitted to the NRO in the Pentagon. Lowell couldn't imagine what, but he had no doubt something extraordinary was in the works.

The previous afternoon, during the short ride from the White

House to his office, DCI Jake Boulton came up with a scenario to accomplish on-board inspection of the *Kira*. He met with agency strategists at Langley and ascertained from the ASW data on hand that if the *Kira* adhered to schedule, she would be leaving Havana in six days for Gulf oil fields to take on cargo. Details of his plan were solidified during the night. And the next morning, Boulton—who still held the rank of Rear Admiral, and never missed a chance to get back into a flight harness—departed for Pensacola in the pilot's seat of a Navy F-14 Tomcat.

Now Lowell and Arnsbarger paced anxiously in "The Tank," a secure conference room in K building's TSZ, waiting for Boulton. They snapped to when he, and the aide who had been at the meeting with the President, were shown in by the ranking naval intelligence officer. The same one who had transmitted the KIQ response.

The DCI was a commanding presence in a flight suit. "As you were, gentlemen," he said smartly. "Sacrifice of free time appreciated."

He glanced sideways to the intelligence officer.

"Carry on, colonel," Boulton said, dismissing him. "I'll reestablish contact before departure."

The colonel had expected to be included in the meeting. The thought of having appeared presumptuous in front of the DCI unsettled him. He banged his knee on a chair, making a less than graceful exit.

Boulton didn't react.

Arnsbarger and Lowell surpressed smiles.

"Take seats," the DCI said. He went on to brief them on his meeting with the President; specifically, the need for immediate visual inspection of the *Kira* to ascertain the existence of a compartment carved out of her hold, and its contents—or lack thereof.

"Mission objective—satisfy Commander in Chief's primary KIQ," he concluded. "Supersecret classification dictates four criteria. One—highly unorthodox scenario. Two—minimum personnel exposure, which means inclusion on need-to-know basis only. Colonel will be briefed eventually to handle ASW liaison during execution. Three—zero equipment profile."

"In other words, we're talking hardware that's compatible

with operational climate," Arnsbarger said, sensing where the DCI was headed.

"Affirmative," Boulton said. "Enemy vessels expect Viking S-3A overflights. No stigma attached. Four—the import of one through three. ASW data initiators become optimum mission candidates."

"We're honored, sir," Lowell said smartly.

"Seconded, sir," Arnsbarger said. "We can have our bird on the flight line by—"

"Negative, Captain," Boulton interrupted. "Mission hardware will be supplied."

"Perhaps, I misunderstood, sir," Arnsbarger said. "I thought the Viking was the key to creating the appearance of routine, details not withstanding."

"Affirmative, Captain," the DCI replied. "Bird supplied will be a Viking S-3A envelope—minus TACCO and classified airborne navigational equipment."

"Gutted," Lowell said.

"Gutted," Boulton echoed. "Operational climate is high risk. Lead time, minimum. Support negligible. Acknowledgment upon completion unlikely. Logic will become manifest upon briefing. Briefing contingent upon—confirmation of enlistment by personnel."

Boulton had just given them a chance to change their minds. He leveled a look at Lowell, then flicked his eyes to Arnsbarger.

"Enlistment confirmed, sir," Lowell said evenly.

Arnsbarger nodded crisply. "Count me in."

Boulton smiled and nodded to his aide, who stepped forward with briefing materials.

"For openers, gentlemen," the aide began, "you'll be taking several refresher courses designed to polish and tune skills essential to the success of this mission—you'll start with jump school."

Chapter Thirty-four

Andrew was exhausted when he returned to the Hassler from the Soviet Embassy, and slept soundly. The next morning he was lying in bed half awake, wondering if he'd imagined it all, when Fausto arrived and reported that one of his airport contacts had seen a Soviet citizen, "A woman who had taken ill on a business trip," put aboard a flight for Moscow. Andrew was angry, but not surprised. It was time to get back to business. The drawings of the tanker were in the Soviet Union, and a thick file of orders for Arabians was his visa.

At Piazza dei Siena, Andrew went about working the balcony, the stables, the private boxes, wherever breeders gathered. And though Borsa wasn't there to provide an entreé, as sole representative for Soviet Arabians, Andrew had no trouble writing orders. The horse-trading took place over bidding authorizations to fill those orders at Soviet auctions—a "not to exceed" limit negotiated with each client. Andrew knew the elitism, the perfectionism that drives breeders, and he played the quality and scarcity of Soviet stock against it. However, one American, new to horse breeding, presented a unique challenge.

"Russian Arabians?" the man said with patriotic fervor. "I don't buy Russian horses. I don't buy Russian vodka. I don't buy Russian anything!"

Andrew knew from studying the files that the wealthy fellow owned a number of professional sports franchises, a baseball team among them, which gave him an idea. "Well, it was a little before my time—" Andrew began, "—but I heard people used to have a similar attitude about baseball. Then somebody changed their minds. I think the guy's name was Jackie—Jackie Robinson."

The fellow studied Andrew for a moment, impressed by his shrewdness. "You're telling me the Russian Arabians are the best available," he challenged.

"I know they are," Andrew replied, undaunted. "You think Dr. Hammer's franchise would have paid a million dollars for Pesniar if they weren't? Muscat, a recent U.S. National Champion, was Russian bred, too."

The fellow thought it over for a moment. "I need a franchise maker," he confided intensely. "You find me a Fernando, a Gooden, a Reggie Jackson, and I won't care what *that* stallion costs me."

"You'll have him," Andrew said earnestly, adding, "especially if that wasn't just a figure of speech."

The client confirmed the unlimited authorization. Throughout the weekend, Andrew convinced many others to do the same. This meant he would have little trouble turning the orders into purchases, and handsome profits for Churchco's Equestrian Division.

Rome's streets were once again gridlocked, the air filled with honking horns, expletives, and exhaust fumes. It was morning on Monday.

Fausto was sitting in the black Maserati, parked in Piazza dei Cinquecento in front of Stazione Termini, Rome's classic, postwar train station.

Andrew was in one of the public SIP transatlantic booths, talking to McKendrick on a phone that he correctly assumed wasn't tapped.

"Twenty million in four days," Andrew reported.

"Orders are only as good as the authorization-to-bid that backs 'em," McKendrick challenged.

"Unlimited good enough?" Andrew replied coolly.

"Damn well is, Drew."

"Thanks. How're *you* doing?"

"Real good," McKendrick enthused. "Been walking for over a week; jogging starts tomorrow."

Almost three weeks had passed since the shooting, and

McKendrick had been moved to a room in the Medical Center's rehabilitation wing. He sat next to a window, squeezing a rubber ball in his left hand as he talked.

"Hear anything more about my father?" Andrew asked.

"Chief Coughlan wrangled a look at the preliminary FAA report. Those pieces of debris were jagged and charred, which means something made that chopper go boom."

"Try the Russians."

"Are you sure?"

"Positive. Did you know my father had a mistress?"

"Raina—"

"Yes. She contacted me as soon as I got here. She was giving me important information when they grabbed her. For all I know, she's in the Gulag by now."

"Drew, you're doing fine. I'm impressed."

"I'm scared."

McKendrick laughed heartily, and leaned forward to the window, eyeing the tight bottom of a shapely nurse hurrying past on the sidewalk outside.

"Sounds like you need to unwind, son. You check out those numbers I gave you?"

"No time for numbers, Ed. I'm meeting with Borsa tomorrow, then leaving for Moscow. I'm thinking about stopping in Leningrad after the auctions."

"Why? What's in Leningrad?"

"The guy who supplied that package."

"You *are* doing okay," McKendrick said, his tone suddenly devoid of levity.

"I'll call you as soon as—" There was a click, and then an open line. "Ed? Ed?" Andrew said.

"Drew? Drew you there?" McKendrick said as he turned from the window and saw two wiry Asian men standing behind him. Dinh had a finger on the phone, disconnecting the call. His brother-in-law was standing against the door. Dinh put a finger to his lips, and said, "Mr. Churcher needs your help."

McKendrick's jaw slackened at the import, then his look hardened. "Mr. Churcher's dead," he said challengingly.

Dinh shook his head no. "He said to tell you not to send the

museum package if you haven't already done so. Either way, he
wants you to come with us.''

McKendrick studied him for a moment; then his doubt removed by their knowledge of the package, he broke into a smile
and started dressing.

In the Soviet Embassy in Rome, Valery Gorodin sat alone in a
cubicle in the *rezidentura*'s communications room placing a call
to Aleksei Deschin through the *Vertushka*, the secure switch-
board in the Kremlin.

The weather in Moscow had been gloomy. Premier Kaparov
had nearly collapsed at a Politburo meeting and spent the weekend in the hospital, and Deschin was feeling unusually morose.
He was in Lubyanka—the prison block at the rear of KGB headquarters—observing an interrogation of Raina Maiskaya, which
was doing little to change his mood, when Uzykin, his eagle-
beaked bodyguard, informed him Gorodin was on the line.

"Andrew Churcher is back to business," Gorodin reported.

"Good. Let's keep it that way," Deschin replied. "So far
Madame Maiskaya hasn't revealed a thing. As Theodor
Churcher's lover, I suspect she had a hand in getting him the
package of drawings. I'm concerned she might do the same for
his son."

"I agree. How shall we proceed?" Gorodin asked, shrewdly
deferring his own proposal.

"The drawings are the only thing that can hurt us," Deschin
said. "Hard currency or no, I think we should revoke his visa
and deny him access."

"A sound approach, Comrade Minister," Gorodin replied.
"But if I may, I would counsel the opposite. I suggest we make
certain Andrew Churcher has no trouble entering the Soviet
Union."

"That is highly unorthodox, comrade," Deschin warned. "I
assume you have good reason?"

"Yes, I think you'll agree, I do," Gorodin replied. "If, as
you suspect, he plans to obtain a similar package, he can lead us
to the original source."

"Yes, yes," Deschin replied enthusiastically. "He will undoubtedly have to contact the same traitor who gave the drawings

to his father. And once we identify that person, we can forever eliminate the threat to SLOW BURN.''

Gorodin went directly to Zeitzev's office after he hung up. He briefed the *rezident* on the plan, warning him to make certain Kovlek didn't interfere again. He was about to leave when Marco Profetta arrived.

Marco reported what Melanie Winslow had said during the short drive from the Sapienza to her hotel Friday evening.

"Looking for her father?" Zeitzev exclaimed.

"That's right," Marco insisted. "And as far as I can tell, that's *all* she's doing."

"Could still be a cover," Gorodin said.

"A good one," Zeitzev said. "I mean, who could be so cold-hearted as to deny information to a woman who's looking for her father," he went on melodramatically.

"I can't imagine," Marco simpered as he opened his shoulder bag and removed a dusty, water-stained folder that he placed on Zeitzev's desk. "I spent most of Friday night in that slime pit. But it paid off."

Zeitzev quickly undid the frayed tie, removed the documents, and thumbed through them.

"Minister Deschin's records," he said, playing down the fact that he was surprised.

"Don't you love it?" Marco exclaimed gleefully. "She spent the weekend looking for those. And they've been in my car all along! Under her seat while I was driving her!" He broke up, unable to contain himself. Zeitzev laughed with him. Even Gorodin had to smile.

"Excellent, Marco," Zeitzev said. "I'd say, we can forget about Miss Winslow becoming a problem." Then, turning to Gorodin, he asked, "You really think she's Minister Deschin's daughter, comrade?"

Gorodin was thinking he had just been handed the most promising piece of biographic leverage of his career. It had *nomenklatura* written all over it. "Perhaps," he replied, concealing his reaction. "But I can't imagine a Soviet citizen so foolish as to confront a Politburo member with the matter of illegitimate offspring—let alone *American* illegitimate offspring," he went on, planting the fear in Zeitzev's mind. "Can you?" he asked pointedly, reinforcing it.

"Comrade," Zeitzev admonished, "as one of Moscow's most eligible bachelors, I imagine Minister Deschin has affected the populations of cities to which he's traveled, but the affair is none of my concern."

"I applaud your pun and your wisdom," Gorodin said. "It's undoubtedly the wellspring of your lengthy tenure." He smiled cagily, and left the office.

Zeitzev paid Marco and dismissed him, then his mind turned to other matters. That morning he had briefed Kovlek on what Dominica had proposed when she called from Comiso—the proposal he had avoided discussing in front of Gorodin. Now, brow furrowed with concern, the *resident* reached for the intercom and buzzed his deputy. "This thing with Borsa," he said gravely, referring to Dominica's vengeful plan. "I don't want us linked to it if it goes wrong."

Indeed, thanks to Marco, Melanie had wasted the weekend and most of Monday in the archives. She emerged exhausted into the Records Office above, and Lena wrapped a compassionate arm around her.

"You need a drink," she said.

"Two," Melanie replied.

"On me," Lena said, and led the way to Columbia, a trendy little cafe across from the Sapienza. They sat at a table in the corner close to the window.

"I've been through every folder," Melanie said dejectedly. "I'll probably never find it. Besides, I don't think I can spend another minute down there."

"What are you going to do?" Lena asked.

Melanie took a long swallow of a gin and tonic, shrugged, and opened her purse, removing the WWII photograph that had been on her mother's dresser.

"Well, I have this. That's my mother, and that's him—that's my father," she said, getting goose bumps. It was the first time she ever just said it unthinkingly.

Lena studied the photograph, comparing Deschin's face to Melanie's. "He sure is," she said, indicating the cheekbones and upward cant of the eyes that had once caused a dance reviewer to observe that Melanie reminded him of Leslie Caron.

Melanie smiled poignantly, and shrugged. "Maybe I should make copies of that, and distribute them around the city," she said, referring to the photograph.

Lena nodded, then suddenly focused on another face in the photograph.

"What is it?" Melanie asked.

"I mean, I could be wrong," Lena said, indicating someone in the photograph, "but he looks familiar."

Melanie slid her chair around next to Lena, who was pointing to a tall man standing behind Sarah and Deschin. The young fellow's wavy black hair flowed from a widow's peak, giving him a visionary air.

"Who is he?"

"A very important man in Italy, if I'm right," Lena said, taking a copy of the *International Herald Tribune* from her shoulder bag. She thumbed through the newspaper, and found what she was after. "Look." Lena held the WWII photograph next to one in the paper. The hair was white and receding now, which made the widow's peak stronger; but the thin face had the same sharp-edged nose, wry smile, and haughty tilt.

"Giancarlo Borsa, defense minister, departing for Geneva—" Melanie said, reading the caption.

"If it isn't him, it's his twin," Lena said. "He gives political science lectures sometimes."

"Uh-huh," Melanie said inattentively, still scanning the article. "Where's Piazza dei Siena?"

"In the Borghese Gardens, just up the hill from your hotel," Lena replied. "Why?"

"It says he's expected back on Tuesday to host some benefit there."

"Yes, he's involved in—" Lena paused suddenly. "You're not going to just show up?" she asked, having heard the intention in Melanie's voice.

"Why not?"

"Could you get to see your secretary of defense at a benefit in—say—Madison Square Garden?"

"I don't know; I've never tried," Melanie said with character-

istic spunk. "What else can I do? Call him and say, 'Hi, Mr.
Defense Minister, you don't know me, but I'm a nice, honest
American woman looking for my father, and I have this picture,
and I thought maybe you might be able to tell me about—"

"It's a nice walk," Lena said, capitulating.

The next morning, Melanie walked Gregoriana to Trinita dei
Monti and climbed the splendid staircase to the Pincio and
Borghese Gardens beyond. The sun shone brightly, and a stiff
breeze whistled through the pine forest around the amphitheater,
causing the banners to snap loudly. She made her way to the rear
of the castle and approached the entrance to the stable area. A
uniformed armed guard was posted in a gatehouse, where a sign
proclaimed, *PRIVATO VIETATO INGRESSO*.

"*Prego?*" he asked.

"I'm looking for Minister Borsa," Melanie said.

"This area is private. Is he expecting you?" he barked in Italian, sticking a pipe in his mouth, as if that was all he'd need to
say. It had a short curved stem that let the bowl rest against his
chin.

Melanie couldn't understand a word he said, but she nodded
just to be polite.

"Yes, well, you see, he doesn't know me, but—"

"*Prego,*" he said, taking the nod as an affirmative reply,
adding, "*Ministro Borsa stabili in mezzo.*"

Melanie hurried past the gatehouse and down a dirt road lined
with horse vans to the stable. She entered beneath the Borsa
crest, walked between the stalls, and up a staircase. The private
box was a shuttered wood-paneled room, lushly furnished with
priceless antiques, Persian rugs, paintings of horses, and countless show ribbons. She stepped through it lively and out the
arched door to the balcony. In the show ring below, Borsa, in
natty equestrian attire, and a stableboy were adjusting the saddle
on an Arabian.

"He's beautiful," Melanie called out to get Borsa's attention,
after watching for a few moments.

"Thank you," Borsa replied, climbing a staircase to join her.
"You're rather early," he went on, assuming she was there for
the benefit, which wouldn't start for hours. He towered over her
as he stepped onto the balcony, and Melanie introduced herself.

She was clearly taken by his presence, and offered an awkward apology for the intrusion. Then, quickly capturing his attention with the WWII photograph, Melanie told the story of her search for her father.

"My God," Borsa said in an amazed whisper. "Look at us—Sarah—Aleksei—Your parents you say?"

"Yes," Melanie replied, heartened by his reaction.

"I knew them both," he said poignantly. "Aleksei was an art student from Russia who came to study in the heart of the Renaissance. We were classmates at the university. He was trapped here when the war came."

Melanie was stunned. She didn't hear a word after "from Russia." She wasn't sure she even heard that.

"And as you can see, we fought together," Borsa continued, reflecting on the photo. "Against the Nazis, *and* the Fascists," he added proudly and, seguing into an afterthought, asked, "Do you ride?"

"Pardon me?" Melanie asked, still in shock.

"Do you ride, are you a horsewoman?"

"Oh," she replied coming out of it. "As a matter of fact, yes. Yes, I am."

"Good, I was about to take him for a run in the Gardens," Borsa said, referring to the Arabian. "And we have a mare who could use some exercise. We'll ride, and I'll tell you what I can remember." He called down to the stableboy, who hurried off to fetch the animal.

At that moment, a horse van arrived at the entrance to the stable area. The guard came from the gatehouse.

"I have a horse for the auction," Dominica said from behind the wheel. "Give me a hand will you?"

She wore a black balaclava—a fitted orlon hood with an oblong opening for the eyes, worn by climbers and race drivers—and large dark sunglasses. The effect was more that of a trendy fashion excess than a device to conceal her identity, which it did.

The guard grunted and waved the van into the courtyard beyond the gatehouse, following after it. When the van stopped, he opened the rear door and poked his head into the darkness in search of an animal that wasn't there. That's when Dominica shoved him into Silvio's arms from behind. The powerful construction worker pulled an oat sack down hard over the startled guard's head, and dragged him into the van. By the time Dominica closed the door, the guard had succumbed to the chloroform that had been liberally splashed into the sack. While Silvio— wearing headgear similar to Dominica's—bound the guard, she returned to the cab and drove the van toward Borsa's stable.

Kovlek had been watching from his Fiat on the approach road. He smiled at their progress, left the car, and walked toward the gatehouse.

In the show ring, Melanie took the reins of a magnificent dappled Arabian from the stableboy, and swung into the saddle. She followed Borsa across the red clay and through a tunnel to the bridle paths that interlaced the surrounding pine forest.

"It was spring, 1945, when that picture was taken," Borsa said, "but it was that February when it all began. And what I remember most vividly, is rain—torrents of endless, bone-chilling rain."

Chapter Thirty-five

The winter of 1944 unleashed violent rainstorms across all of Western Europe.

In Italy's Elsa Valley, Aleksei Deschin blinked at the flash of lightning and clap of thunder that rolled through San Gimignano, an ancient mountain town. Rain came off his pancho in sheets as he leaned into the torrent and continued up Via San Matteo, a narrow street in the north end. Three men trudged uphill behind him—a Russian, an Italian, and two Americans—searching for a German supply depot in the downpour.

The storm front ran from Rome through Florence to the north—the same line taken by the allied offensive to liberate central and northern Italy. The chilling deluge had eroded the morale of troops on both sides. But it was the Germans—running out of ammunition, food, and fuel—who were in retreat on every front.

Contrary to this trend, divisions under Field Marshall Albert Kesselring were holding their own in the Elsa Valley against the U.S. Fifth Army. These units, commanded by General Mark Clark, were to push east through Volterra and San Gimignano to Florence. They would join Eighth Army forces advancing west, and attack the Gothic Line, the Wermacht's final defensive position, fifteen miles north. But the well-fueled and fortified German divisions, with an endless supply of ammunition, had stopped Clark's Fifth Army cold.

Adolph Hitler's spirits soared at the news. "This is the turning point!" the Führer exulted. "As *I* told you it would be!"

And he had. Just a year ago, the Führer overruled his general staff, who thought San Gimignano too far west, and insisted the supply depot be located there. The ninth-century city, with its thick walls and lookout towers was not only impenetrable but also strategically located above the roads from the coast to Florence.

Allied Command wanted the depot destroyed. But they had to find it first, and had been working closely with Italian partisans who had infiltrated the valley.

Deschin, the sharp-minded Russian the Americans had code-named Gillette Blue, was in charge of partisan liaison and intelligence. Numerous reconnaissance missions into heavily fortified enemy areas had failed to locate the depot, and he had shifted his focus to San Gimignano. Few German troops were billeted there. Perhaps, Deschin reasoned, it was a ploy to divert attention from the depot. Now, he led the group up San Matteo in search of it.

A stone wall sealed off the top of the street. Much of the soil behind it had been excavated, creating a bunker that concealed two German soldiers and a machine gun. A few flat stones had been removed from the wall to provide a slit for the muzzle. Rain pinged on the corrugated steel roof as the Germans watched Deschin's group enter a bombed-out granary. The German private trained his weapon on the entrance, waiting for the four men to come out.

"Nein," the sergeant warned, seeing his eagerness.

"But, they will be like bottles on a wall," the private protested.

"Nein," the sergeant said more sternly. "You know our orders. Only if they cross toward the church."

Unlike other buildings in the city, neither the church, the magnificently steepled Cappella Di Santa Fina, nor the German storage depot in the catacombs beneath had been touched by allied bombs. Crates of weapons and ammunition, and drums of fuel, were safely concealed in the network of rock tunnels. But months of rain had saturated the porous stone to the limit, and water began seeping through cracks and fissures. The gradual trickles had become unending cascades; and German troops were working frantically in ankle-deep water, covering the precious supplies with tarpaulins.

Deschin's group had finished searching the granary and, having come up empty, was back out in the rain, advancing up San Matteo.

"What do you think?" he asked, eyeing the church.

Giancarlo Borsa looked up at the thousand-year-old structure, rain pelting his sharply cut features. He had organized the resistance in the area and brought Deschin into the group.

"I doubt it, Aleksei," he replied. "Kesselring has respected our artistic treasures. And we can't afford another Monte Cassino," he went on, referring to the sixth-century Benedictine monastery near Naples that the Allies had reduced to rubble only to discover the Germans had never used it for military purposes.

"Maybe that's why Kesselring thinks he could get away with it here," Deschin replied incisively.

"Good point," Borsa said. "But I hate to think of what will happen if you're right."

Theodor Churcher threw back the hood of his pancho angrily. "Horseshit!" he bellowed in a thick drawl. "Not a building on earth worth saving if it's endangering men's lives, let alone American lives!"

The lanky Texan had just turned twenty, a brash, ambitious, unpolished hayseed who thought the sun rose and set on Texas and the United States—in that order. He challenged the others with a look, and set out purposefully toward the church.

"On my signal," the German sergeant ordered in a tense whisper. The private nodded, hugged the stock of his weapon, and wrapped his finger around the trigger.

That morning, during a break in the weather, an Air Force C-47, *Dakota*, headed down a makeshift runway north of Rome with a Waco glider in tow, and began climbing. Three hundred feet back in the Waco, pilot Ted Churcher and spotter Mike Rosenthal were fighting to keep the glider from catching the tug's turbulence, and pinwheeling at the end of the nylon towline.

About eight months ago, Churcher had completed his junior year at Rice and had come home to Lubbock for the summer. He was flying crop dusters, as he did every vacation, when he heard the Army Air Force opened its combat glider school on the outskirts of town. Churcher graduated number one in his class, and flew over a hundred reconnaissance missions behind enemy lines in North Africa and Sicily.

When Captain Jake Boulton, OSS liaison with Fifth Army Intelligence, called for glider-recon to locate the German storage depot, Churcher volunteered.

Now, 4,500 feet above the Tuscan countryside, he checked his landmarks and nodded to Rosenthal.

"Time to part company," he drawled. He clicked on an intercom that ran on a wire wrapped around the towline. "Thanks for the ride, Jake."

"Anytime," Boulton—who was at the controls of the *Dakota*—replied. "Matter of fact, you find that Kraut depot, and we'll tow you all the way back home to Lummox if you like."

"That's *Lubbock,* Jake," Churcher retorted. "And you can bet the farm we'll find it. We'll just keep riding the elevator till we do," he added, referring to the air currents that take a glider back up to altitude.

He pulled the towline release. The metal fitting unlatched with a loud clank. The Waco cut free from the C-47 and soared, gaining altitude, the *whoosh* of air rushing over its surfaces the only sound now. Churcher put it on a glide path to the target ten miles away.

Made of canvas over a tubular steel frame, the gray-green Waco had an 85-foot wingspan that gave it a rate of descent of less than 2 feet per second—slower than a soap bubble in still air. Riding thermals, the bird could stay up for hours, needing barely 150 feet to land when it came down.

Churcher came in over San Gimignano against the camouflage of clouds, and made a silent pass over the multi-towered city. Rosenthal panned his binoculars in search of vehicle tracks or troop activity that would reveal the location of the enemy storage depot. During the next few hours, Churcher made a half dozen passes, lowering the altitude each time. Finally, Rosenthal turned from his binoculars in disgust.

"We're wasting our time, Ted."

"Yeah, the Krauts must move the stuff out at night. The rain washed away the tracks before we got here. Maybe, if I came in lower, you could—"

"Lower? Any lower we'll leave the family jewels hanging on one of those pines."

"Impossible. We're coming in below them. Matter of fact,

Rosenthal, I'm treating you to a bona fide South Texas ass scraper.''

Churcher put the Waco into a steep dive and swooped down over the north end of San Gimignano.

Flocks of ravens roosted in many of the city's towers. The German lookout in the northernmost one saw what at first appeared to be a hovering bird. When he saw it had a shiny Plexiglas nose, he opened fire.

Rounds splintered the plywood floor behind the Waco's cockpit, pinging off the steel tubing and ricocheting out the top of the canvas fuselage.

"Son of a bitch!" Churcher exclaimed as he put the glider into a diving turn, keeping a wing tip to the tower to present as small a target as possible.

The German fired another sustained burst.

The rounds perforated the Waco's right wing. The air began tearing the canvas off the tubular structure, unbalancing the lift and threatening to flip the Waco over on its back. The shredded fabric was chattering like a jackhammer as Churcher fought to maintain control.

"Get behind me!" he shouted.

Rosenthal scrambled from the copilot's seat. The weight shift helped settle the Waco down. Churcher put it into a wobbly dive toward a field a few miles away, just beyond a walnut grove. Gnarled branches began racing past the bottom of the Plexiglas bubble. The landing gear snagged the tops of the last row of trees and tore out of the bottom of the fuselage.

The instant the glider cleared the grove, Churcher got the braking flaps full up, and dropped it onto the tall grass. The Waco tilted forward onto the nose skid, and began sliding over the wet chaff. It had skidded about a hundred meters, and was losing momentum when what was left of the landing gear snagged a wire fence. The glider came to a sudden stop, and pitched over into the mud, burying the nose—which was the way out.

Churcher was stunned by the impact. Rosenthal, who had been out of his harness, was trapped in the tangle of tubing that had been the cockpit. But neither was seriously injured. Churcher was trying to get out of his harness and go to Rosenthal's assistance, when he heard rustling in the grass outside. He pulled his .45 side arm and whirled, just as a bayonet stabbed through the canvas and slashed the fuselage. Churcher held his weapon with both hands and leveled it at the spot where the bayonet continued slashing the canvas to ribbons, making a large opening. Aleksei Deschin's distinctive face peered into the glider.

"Anybody in here need a shave?" he asked in his heavy Russian accent.

"Yes, but we're all out of blades," Churcher replied tensely, training the .45 on him. "You have some we can borrow?"

"The best. Gillette Blue," Deschin replied, completing the exchange of passwords.

Then Churcher relaxed, and lowered the gun.

"Geezus!" he howled as Deschin and Borsa entered the glider. "You guys should've said something before you started slashing. I thought you were Krauts."

"After that landing," Borsa teased, "we didn't think you were in any shape to hear us."

Deschin and Borsa had been waiting in the walnut grove in a mud-splattered truck. Boulton had alerted Gillette Blue to the glider recon-mission, and arranged for partisans to rendezvous with the Waco and get the crew back to Allied lines. And Churcher had skillfully piloted the crippled glider to the landing zone.

The group quickly freed Rosenthal and took cover in the walnut grove, where Ettore, an old partisan who drove the truck, supplied the Americans with civilian clothes. Introductions were made as they pulled the coarse garments over their uniforms, then the talk turned to the German storage depot.

"You know," said Churcher thoughtfully, "we were up there for a long time, and nothing. But soon as we made a pass over the north end, whammo!"

This confirmed Deschin's theory. He and Borsa decided they would drive the Americans back to their lines, then check out that area of the city. But Churcher and Rosenthal insisted on coming along.

"Not until I clear it with command," Deschin replied.

"No need," Churcher said. "Jake Boulton and I are buddies. He'll think it's a great idea."

Deschin eyed him skeptically, and began cranking the handle of his walkie-talkie.

"This is Gillette Blue to Safety Razor. Gillette Blue to Safety Razor. Come in Safety Razor."

"We read you, go ahead," Boulton replied.

"Nest has fallen," Deschin reported. "Both birds are safe and want to help locate the elusive worm."

"Negative, Gillette Blue," Boulton said. "Repeat, negative. Return birds to friendly nest, immediately."

Churcher took the walkie from Deschin. He cranked the handle creating static, then replied, "Negative. Transmission garbled. Repeat, transmission garbled. Say again." He cranked the handle, obscuring Boulton's reply with static, then clicked off the walkie. "I told you Jake'd think it was a good idea," he drawled, grinning. "Let's find us that Kraut depot, Gillette."

The group drove off in the old truck. They were approaching the outskirts of San Gimignano when the cold rain began again. They left Ettore with the truck, continuing on foot to avoid enemy patrols.

Now, Churcher strode boldly toward Cappella di Santa Fina in the downpour. The others strung out behind him. Deschin was in the rear. His eyes caught a flicker of movement in the stone wall at the top of the street. But there was nothing growing between the stones that might have caused it. Then he saw the gun site tracking them slowly across the slit where the stones had been removed.

"Down! Get down!" Deschin shouted.

The German private squeezed the trigger, spraying the street with machine-gun fire.

Churcher dove to the ground, bullets whizzing past him. He landed in the gutter, muddy water gushing into his face. A round had gone cleanly through his left arm. The flesh burned as if pierced by a hot poker. The pattern of fire moved toward the middle of the street. Countless rounds ripped into Rosenthal in the space of seconds, each snapping him in a different direction. He grabbed at his stomach as it exploded into his arms, and fell face down onto the cobblestones. The deadly burst caught Borsa next, popping into his legs, knocking him to the ground, and

continued across toward Deschin, who dove into the bombed out
granary. The rounds pockmarked the broken facade, missing
him; but flying chips of stone cut his face. He hid behind the
rubble until the firing stopped, then craned up, surveying the
street.

Churcher was lying motionless in the gutter when he caught
Deschin's look, and waggled his hand to indicate his condition.
The Russian pointed up the street, and Churcher turned his head
slightly to see the two Germans coming out of the bunker. He
looked back to Deschin, who signaled how they should proceed.

The two Germans came down the hill, each with a weapon in
firing position, cautiously scanning the street for signs of life.
The sergeant looked to the granary. Deschin's apparently lifeless
body hung facedown over the rubble. The private pointed to
Churcher on his belly. The Germans concluded both were either
dead or badly wounded, and continued toward Rosenthal and
Borsa in the center of the street.

The private pushed the toe of a muddy jackboot beneath Rosenthal's chest, and rolled him over on his back. The young flier's
head flopped back and splashed in a puddle. His eyes stared un-
blinking into the rain that pelted his face. The Germans stepped
over him to Borsa who was on his back, conscious, but in shock.
He managed to raise his hands in a defensive gesture. The sergeant angrily knocked them aside with the barrel of his Luger
pistol and placed the muzzle against his forehead. The Italian
closed his eyes prepared to die.

But the sharp crack Borsa heard came from behind him. His
eyes popped open to see the German sergeant pitching forward.
The bullet from Deschin's carbine had cut in beneath his helmet,
chipping the paint from the lower edge, and continued on an
upward path through his neck, blowing pieces of bone, teeth, and
tongue out through a large hole that had been his right cheek.

The second crack followed a microsecond after the first.
Churcher had gradually pulled his .45 into firing position, and
placed the bullet just in front of the left ear of the German private. He dropped like a marionette whose strings had been cut all
in one snip.

Deschin ran to the bodies in the street. He grabbed Borsa beneath the arms, and dragged him across the wet cobblestones toward the granary.

Churcher climbed out of the gutter and, ignoring his own wound, did the same with Rosenthal's body. "Bastards!" he said bitterly as they dragged the two down a short flight of steps into the basement of the bombed-out granary. "It's the church, Gillette. You were right."

A few miles away, on a broad plain that stretches beneath San Gimignano, an Allied Field Hospital had been set up. Rain drummed on the canvas tents. Water gushed in runoff trenches cut beneath the sagging overhangs. Tent flaps snapped noisily in the wind.

Sarah Winslow dashed between rows of wounded men on stretchers and entered a supply tent.

A doctor and nurse, in blood-spattered operating whites, were standing in two inches of water, working feverishly on a wounded GI. He lay on a stretcher set across two fifty-gallon fuel drums. A tray containing medical instruments lay atop a third. Light came from a bare bulb hung from the apex of the tent. A gust of wind followed Sarah inside and set the bulb swinging, creating moving shadows in the operational field.

"Dammit," the doctor said. "Steady that light."

Sarah grasped it and stopped the movement. "Sorry, I didn't expect you'd be in here."

"OR's jammed up. He couldn't wait," the doctor replied, and indicating the soldier's bloody abdominal cavity, added, "Pull back on that retractor."

Sarah did it automatically. "I've got a kid out there," she said, looking torn. "He's bleeding to death."

"So's he," the doctor replied curtly.

Sarah felt like she'd been punched. She'd been in the field almost a year, but the idea of young men dying because they couldn't be treated in time still devastated her.

"Thanks, Sarah," the doctor said when he had things under control. "Do what you can for your kid. I'll come find you when I'm finished."

On his first word, Sarah turned to the shelves behind her and

filled her haversack with the medical supplies she'd come for
originally.

She hurried from the tent into the downpour, and ran to a
wounded GI. Her knees plopped into the mud next to the
stretcher. Blood seeped from beneath it, mixing with the rainwater. Sarah gently peeled away the GI's tattered shirt, exposing
a massive chest wound. She took packets of sulfur from her
haversack, tore off the tops, and dumped the yellow powder into
the hole.

"What's your name, soldier?"

The kid grimaced, holding off the pain. "Cochran, ma'am,"
he answered. "Tommy Cochran."

Sarah smiled. Despite lack of sleep and stress, her face still
glowed with a special beauty. "Mine's Sarah." She made some
gauze pads into a thick wad, pushed it into his chest, and held it
there.

The soldier's lower lip was trembling like a child's. "I'm not
going to make it, am I?"

"Sure you are, Tommy," she replied. "I've seen a lot of
these. You're going to be as good as new."

She only half-lied, she thought. She *had* seen similar inju-
ries—but seen few GIs survive them. Her mind drifted to Zachary, who was somewhere in the Pacific. And she hoped with all
her heart that no one was doing for him what she was doing for
Tommy Cochran right now. They had been married about a year
when Zack enlisted in the Marines. And Sarah quickly knew she
couldn't sit home in Dunbarton waiting, wondering. She was
working for a doctor in private practice, and the day he was
drafted, she enlisted as an Army nurse.

She looked down and saw blood had soaked the gauze pads
and was oozing in thick pools between her fingers.

"Got a cigarette?" Cochran asked weakly.

"Sure," she said, hiding her concern. She slipped a cigarette
from her pocket, lit it, and took several deep drags, then put it to
Cochran's lips. But he didn't respond. All along she could feel
his heart pushing beneath her palm—and now she felt it stop.

A muddy truck pulled to a stop nearby. Deschin jumped out
and helped Churcher from the cab. He slung an arm over the
Russian's shoulders, and they started walking between the tents.

Sarah pulled Cochran's pancho up over his face, and hurried after them. Churcher was stumbling in the ruts when she caught up and wrapped an arm around his waist to help support him.

"This way," she said commandingly, leading them toward an aid station. Another nurse met them at the entrance and directed them inside to a cubicle, where she went about tending to Churcher's wound.

Sarah moistened some gauze pads with a disinfectant and brought it to the cuts on Deschin's face.

"No time," he said, pushing her hand aside. "I left a man in San Gimignano. He's badly wounded."

"I'll go with you."

Deschin shook his head no emphatically. "Too dangerous. It's behind enemy lines."

"They don't shoot nurses," Sarah replied.

"No, they rape them."

"Not this one."

Deschin studied her, taken by her spunk. "Hurry then," he said, turning to leave.

"Aleksei!" Churcher's voice rang out from where the nurse was working on his arm. "Don't leave my copilot to the Krauts."

"You have my word," Deschin said.

Sarah grabbed a haversack of medical supplies, went back to the truck with Deschin, and got in next to Ettore. Deschin was about to follow when a motorcycle ground to a stop in the mud next to him. The courier had a dispatch addressed to:

> Gillette Blue
> Sector 43-N
> By Courier

Deschin removed the dispatch which read:

> STATIC MY ASS! SAFETY RAZOR.

Deschin laughed and got into the truck. It was soon sloshing through rivers of mud that had once been cow paths and back roads. Flashes of lightning flickered behind the mountains. The three drove through the rain in silence. Deschin's hand clutched his carbine, eyes searching the terrain for German troops.

Sarah was leaning back studying the intense Russian out of the corner of her eye. He'd brought wounded partisans to the field hospital several times. And she was reflecting on how their eyes had met, and how she'd found his unique looks and fractured English appealing. But she was very much in love with Zachary.

The rain intensified as the truck pulled up behind the bombed-out granary. Sarah slipped an arm through the strap of her haversack. Ettore took a stretcher from the truck, and they followed Deschin through the trees, over rubble that surrounded the granary, and down the staircase into the basement.

Borsa and Rosenthal lay amidst burlap sacks filled with flour and unmilled grain, where Deschin and Churcher had left them. Deschin had put one of the sacks beneath the Italian's legs to keep them raised and minimize blood loss; it was stained crimson now, prompting Deschin to hurry to Borsa's side.

"Giancarlo? Giancarlo, can you hear me?" Deschin asked intensely.

Borsa nodded slightly, and grimaced in pain.

The vacant stare of the dead American caught Sarah's eye as she knelt next to Borsa. She bit a lip, prepared a syringe, pushed up Borsa's sleeve, and shot the morphine into him. Deschin had already taken a bottle of plasma from her haversack, and Sarah pushed the needle into Borsa's vein. The blood on his pants had congealed, and they'd become matted to his legs. She scissored the bullet-torn fabric loose, then cleansed, disinfected, and wrapped the wounds in temporary bandages.

Throughout, Deschin watched admiringly at the efficient manner in which Sarah worked. Her eyes darting, evaluating, deciding; her hands moving with swift precision. When she finished, Deschin and Ettore slid Borsa onto the stretcher, carried it across the basement, and up the staircase into the rain.

Sarah crouched next to Rosenthal's body, and closed his eyes. Then she wrapped a pancho around the flier's horribly gutted torso to enable Deschin and Ettore to more easily carry him when they returned.

They were sliding the stretcher into the truck when a shot rang out. The round whistled between them, punching a hole in the sheet metal. They whirled to see three German soldiers moving along the side of the granary in the downpour. One raised his rifle and fired again. Deschin and Ettore scrambled behind the truck, rounds chipping into the trees behind them.

"I'm going back," Deschin said.

Ettore nodded that he knew what to do and leaned out from behind the truck, firing bursts from his carbine, pinning down the German patrol.

Deschin took off between the trees. Despite Ettore's cover, one of the Germans popped up firing. Deschin dove headlong into the entrance that led to the staircase as rounds powdered the stucco facade.

"Sarah? Sarah come on!" he shouted as he ran down the stairs into the basement of the granary.

"What about him?" she exclaimed, gesturing to Rosenthal's body.

"German patrol!" Deschin interrupted. "Come on!"

Sarah hesitated momentarily. And in that instant, a blinding flash of lightning, followed by a primordial crack of thunder that sounded as if it split the earth, illuminated San Gimignano like a dozen noons. Traveling over one hundred million feet per second, the jagged bolt stabbed from billowing thunderheads ten miles up, and, like the wrath of an angry deity, struck the spired campanile of Cappella di Santa Fina.

The carillon's bells glowed like huge Christmas tree ornaments as fifteen million volts of electrical current coursed through the bronze. Crackling blue fuzz zigzagged along cracks and licked at the edges of stone as the current raced down the church's wet facade and surged into the porous rock beneath.

In the limestone catacombs, the German soldiers, working to cover the crates of ammunition and drums of fuel with tarpaulins, watched horrified as the current darted out of fissures and crevices, and crawled across the moist surfaces buzzing with high energy. For the briefest instant, the caverns glowed with an ultraviolet fluorescence. Then the bristling voltage discharged in angry sheets across the ankle-deep water and through the ammunition and fuel at temperatures close to 50,000°F. The entire cache exploded in a chain reaction that accelerated through the network of tunnels beneath San Gimignano.

The whole town shuddered as if struck by a devastating earth-
quake. Buildings crumbled. Streets buckled and collapsed.
Church bells rang wildly. Flocks of ravens erupted from the towers, filling the air with their angled black shapes. Thousands of
cats darted wildly through the streets. Townsfolk and German
soldiers ran panicked into the heavy rain.

The German patrol, advancing along the side of the granary,
was buried in an avalanche of rubble as the wall above them
collapsed. Ettore jumped into the truck and drove off with his
badly wounded passenger.

Deschin had just grasped Sarah's hand to drag her from the
basement when the granary came crashing down around them.
She screamed as a huge section of the concrete-and-stone slab
overhead fell, knocking them to the ground in a shower of dust
and grain. Tons of rubble cascaded down, mercifully burying
Rosenthal's body. Then the frightening roar and quaking gave
way to an eerie silence, and the sounds of rain.

Sarah and Deschin were lying on the floor, a short distance
apart. But neither could see the other through the dust-filled air
and darkness.

"Sarah?" Deschin called out.

"Here," she replied. "Over here."

Deschin crawled in the direction of her voice. His fingers
found her hand, and he kept going until they were face-to-face.

"Are you hurt?"

"No. I'm okay," she replied. "You?"

"Okay," he parroted.

"What happened?"

"The German supply depot must have blown," Deschin replied, smiling and sniffing at the air that was thick with the
pungent odor of cordite and fuel.

He worked himself into a sitting position, and helped Sarah do
the same. His smile vanished when he saw they were encircled
by a wall of rubble and grain sacks, capped by the slab above.

The falling concrete floor had slammed into the sacks, which
had been stacked high around them. The uppermost bags burst,
absorbing the impact; while those below supported the weight,
keeping the slab from crushing them to death.

"We're trapped," Sarah exclaimed, a tremor in her voice. "We're buried alive, Aleksei. There's no way out of here."

"I've already found two," he said brightly.

"Two?" she wondered, with a puzzled look.

He took her hands in his, and held them up for her to see. "Now there are four!" he said. "We're going to dig our way out."

She smiled, the tension eased by his charming manner and undaunted optimism.

Deschin paused to get his bearings, then began drawing in the dust on the floor. He calculated the location of the staircase relative to their position, and crawled to that section of the rubble, carefully working free a jagged piece of stone.

"That way," he announced.

He removed another piece of rubble, and then another, sliding each behind him to Sarah, who pushed it aside. In a few hours they had dug a narrow tunnel about five feet deep into the densely packed rubble. But night fell quickly, and soon they were working in total darkness, and numbing cold.

Sarah fell back against the sacks of grain. "I'm cold, Aleksei. I'm cold and tired."

"So am I," he replied wearily. "My hands are numb."

He fell against the sacks next to her, and huddling for warmth, they slept. They awoke hours later to see a few pencil-thin shafts of light that pierced the tons of rubble overhead. Heartened by the new day, they ate some of the grain and sipped water from his canteen, then emptied Sarah's haversack of medical supplies, using it to collect the rainwater that dripped from above.

And Aleksei dug. Hour after hour, he tunneled through wet stone, brick, and mortar, shoring up the walls of the narrow shaft with pieces of wood he unearthed along the way. Patiently, cautiously, he dug, until his hands were raw and bloodied; until Sarah had used up all the soothing medication and bandages; and until having dug far enough to reach the staircase, having every reason to believe their release was imminent, Sarah heard Aleksei's angry, frustrated wail coming from the far end of the tunnel.

"Aleksei? What is it? You all right?"

He emitted another agonzing bellow in reply.

She crawled the length of the tunnel and found him clawing at a wall with his fingers; clawing futilely at the thick, unmoving concrete and stone surface against which the shaft had ended—instead of against the base of the staircase as they had hoped. Aleksei heard her behind him, and turned from the wall. She took his bloodied hands in hers, and they knelt in the cramped tunnel, silently staring at each other for what seemed like an eternity.

Then, their spirits crushed, they crawled back to their space beneath the slab; and as their terror gradually subsided and was replaced by a forlorn acceptance of their fate, they fell into an exhausted embrace, heads buried in each other's shoulder, drawing strength and support. And finally, in what they believed to be their last moments of life, in the absolute blackness of night, without a word being spoken, they lifted their heads slowly, their cheeks delicately brushing until their lips touched; and then, bringing the spark of life to the cold, damp hellhole that entombed them, they became lovers.

It was slow, unhurried lovemaking, not wildly passionate or frenzied, more like a gentle, tender, everlasting embrace; as if, perhaps, seated face-to-face, rocking back and forth in each other's arms, in vibrant silence, they might ignore the rising stench of death, and forget where they were and why, and fall asleep in a warm, blissful haze, and never wake up, and never know they had died.

Chapter Thirty-six

Giancarlo Borsa had developed a slight limp as he walked through the pine forest. He had lived with it for almost forty years, and concealed it expertly; but the topic intensified it. He and Melanie had ridden the Arabians for a while, and the more he talked about Sarah and Deschin, and the more Melanie pulled the details of those desperate moments out of him, the more they felt the need for an intimate exchange. So they dismounted and were strolling side by side on a bridle path that ran along a bluff, the city far below, the Arabians clomping along behind them solemnly, as if sensing the tenor of their conversation.

"Your parents were fiercely brave," Borsa said in conclusion. "They almost lost their lives. But the Germans fell quickly once the storage depot was gone. And Ettore returned for them with *partizani*."

Melanie was touched and fulfilled by the tale, and her eyes had become watery, as had Borsa's.

"That's so incredible," she said softly, almost to herself. "Did they spend time together after that?"

"They were inseparable," Borsa replied. "I recall, Aleksei was devastated when your mother decided to return to the States. It took him a year to get over her; and then, all of a sudden, something happened that plunged him back into the gloominess. He wouldn't talk about it, and went back to Russia shortly thereafter. Your mother seemed much more able to manage it than he, more self-possessed, mature."

"Sounds like mother," Melanie said fondly. "She was always the strong one, always in control."

"Indeed," Borsa went on. "One day, I went to her tent to say

237

good-bye. She was packing, holding the picture, studying it. Her
eyes told me she was deciding something. She tightened her lips,
then folded it in half, almost as if folding Aleksei out of her life,
and put it in her trunk." He sighed wistfully, adding, "We were
all children really, barely in our twenties, and we went our ways;
that's how it was."

Melanie nodded, sensing why her mother had kept it inside all
those years, sensing that Sarah knew talking about it might create
yearnings for something that was forever gone.

"Do you know what happened to my father?"

"Oh, yes. We've maintained occasional contact over the
years. He's a very important official in the Soviet Union, now.
Minister of culture."

"Could you help me get in touch with him," Melanie asked,
feeling overwhelmed.

"I'd be happy to," he replied, bringing a smile to her face. "I
can see you assume he'll be joyfully pleased to know of you, and
indeed, he should. But, keep in mind that your father's position,
and the society in which he lives, could cause quite the opposite
reaction," Borsa added gently, "Regardless, you'll *need* help.
You couldn't reach him the way you reached me. These men
aren't public figures. They don't get involved the way we do here
in the West," he went on, and glancing to his watch, added,
"Which reminds me, I have a benefit I must host. Shall we?"

Melanie nodded, and they mounted the Arabians and headed
for the amphitheater.

Piazza dei Siena was filled with spectators now. Well-heeled
bidders and their guests were milling on the long balcony in front
of the private boxes. In the stables below, grooms were preparing
the horses that would soon be auctioned. A huge banner proclaiming *PACE MONDIALE* hung on the tower opposite the massive stone door through which the horses would make their
dramatic entrance.

Borsa and Melanie came through the tunnel from the bridle
paths on the Arabians and cantered across the show ring toward
his stables.

"Ciao, Olmo! Lucianna! Buongiorno!" he exclaimed, waving
to a couple he recognized on the balcony as he and Melanie dismounted. He automatically held out the reins to the stableboy,

who wasn't there; then looked around puzzled and went beneath the overhang, calling out, *"Paolo? Paolo, venga qui!"* He waited briefly, then shrugged in disgust.

"We'll have to stable them ourselves," he said to Melanie apologetically. "I hope you don't mind."

"I spent my childhood in stables," she said, smiling.

They led the horses inside, removed saddles and bridles, and put them into stalls, then climbed the stairs to the private box above.

Borsa entered first. He walked briskly across the Persian rug to the balcony door, and discovered it had been locked from the inside, ornate key removed. That's when he noticed the shutters had been closed; and when Melanie noticed the hooded figure behind her locking the door to the stables; and when Borsa whirled to see the two faces concealed by the black balaclavas and sunglasses that gave them the look of giant insects. They had been hidden in plain sight amidst the elegant trappings—Dominica in a wing chair, high back to the door concealing her, Silvio on a leather sofa in an alcove to one side.

"What is this!" Borsa demanded angrily. He had walked right past Dominica on his way to the door, and was facing her now.

"Quiet, please," she ordered, her voice muffled by the balaclava. "Just do as you're told," she went on, remaining seated, calmly leveling a handgun at him.

"I'll do what I came here to do," Borsa replied. "I'm going to start this auction, *now*. And—"

"Yes," Dominica interrupted. "Go and *deploy* your horses, Mr. Defense Minister. Then return here, alone. Any trickery—your stableboy, your guard, and your ladyfriend will die."

Silvio pushed a gun against the side of Melanie's head. Her eyes darted to it fearfully. They had been speaking in Italian, and she had no idea what they were saying, which made her even more frightened.

"Go!" Dominica ordered.

Borsa flicked a torn glance at Melanie.

"Be calm," he advised. "Don't confront them."

Dominica unlocked the door, opening it just enough to allow Borsa through. He strode past and down a short flight of steps to the balcony.

The crowd in the amphitheater broke into applause.

A TV crew with a mobile minicam followed Borsa through the crowd to a podium at the edge of the balcony. Paparazzi surged around him, motor-driven cameras whirring and clicking noisily.

"Welcome to the Benefit Auction for World Peace," Borsa began as the applause subsided. "Again, it is my pleasure to host this worthy event. And I ask that you bid generously for the magnificent animals we have for you today. And now"—His voice cracked as he forced it to a climax—"to officially open these proceedings—" he peaked and gestured broadly to the arena.

A trumpeter in medieval silks raised the long instrument to his lips and played a spirited fanfare. The banners of the prominent breeding families snapped in the wind, filling the pauses between the stanzas.

Behind the castle's facade, an attendant listened for the last note to trail off. Then he grasped a thick hawser that hung from the upper reaches of the castle and pulled down, as if ringing church bells.

The heavy rope was affixed to a shaft that ran between two large cogwheels. The teeth engaged the links of a heavy chain that ran from the top corners of the stone door to huge counterweights hanging above it. The attendant's pull lowered the weights just past the balance point. They began a slow, steady plunge, raising the immense slab upward and back—like the door on a residential garage—into a horizontal position behind the facade.

Centuries ago, when so raised, the door served as a bridge over which medieval archers marched to battle stations on parapets along the wall. When lowered, it sealed the portal from enemy hordes, *and*—bridge thus removed—prevented invaders who scaled the walls from crossing into the castle proper.

The first group of horses to be auctioned, each with numbered tag affixed, had been massed behind the door. Now, they galloped dramatically through the suddenly opened door and down a ramp into the arena.

Borsa waved to the applauding crowd and began walking toward the entrance to his private box.

"Giancarlo? Giancarlo, you're leaving us already?" one of the wealthy bidders asked.

"I must phone Geneva," he said, making up an excuse. "I may have to return this afternoon."

Fausto's black Maserati approached the gatehouse at the entrance to the stable area. When the guard didn't appear, Fausto drove through, and Andrew got out to ask a groom for directions to Borsa's stables.

A taxi came to a stop a distance down the street behind the amphitheater. Gorodin paid the driver and strolled casually toward the gate-house. Tapes of Andrew's calls made prior to discovery of the bug revealed he would be meeting Borsa at the amphitheater, and the connection to Geneva caused Gorodin to decide to maintain distant surveillance.

Andrew waved to Fausto to remain parked, and began walking down the dirt road, lined with horse vans.

Kovlek was positioned behind the line of vehicles, from where he could keep an eye on Dominica's van—the guard and stableboy imprisoned inside—as well as the entrance to Borsa's stables. Anyone but Andrew would have been stopped. Kovlek had the dictum of noninterference drummed into him by Zeitzev and Gorodin, and let him enter unchallenged.

Andrew was crossing to the staircase inside the stables when one of the Arabians snorted, getting his attention. He detoured to the stall and was rubbing a palm over the spirited animal's coat when he heard footsteps and turned to see two hooded figures coming down the stairs with Borsa and Melanie. Both carried handguns, and one also had a small gym bag.

Andrew's adrenalin surged, prickling his skin. *Terrorists!* he thought as he ducked behind the Arabian. *Terrorists are kidnapping Italy's Defense Minister!* They stopped on a landing halfway down the stairs. Melanie turned in protest as they prodded her through a door, and for a brief instant, her eyes caught Andrew's in an anguished plea.

Andrew could feel the silent terror in them. He waited until the door closed, then hurried to a phone on the wall of the stable, and dialed the operator.

"Pronto? Che cosa vuole?"

"Yes, please the police! Get me the police!" he said in an urgent whisper.

"*Ah, si, polizia. Vuole Carabinieri? Vigili Urbani? Questura? O Polizia Stradele?*" the operator asked, running down the list of police organizations.

"The police! Emergency, I have an emergency!"

There was a click, and then a man's weary voice growled, "Pronto, Polizia Stradele"—The operator translated emergency to accident, and connected Andrew with the traffic police—"*Voi avete un incidente?*"

"This is an emergency. There's a kidnapping in progress at the amphitheater. Terrorists are—"

"*Scuse, signore,*" the officer interrupted. "*Non capisco l'in-gelese. C'e qualcuno qui la parla Italiano?*"

Andrew groaned in frustration and hung up. He started to the entrance, intending to alert Fausto. But he realized the terrorists might be long gone with their hostages by then. He reversed direction, dashed to the landing, and slipped through the door, finding himself at the base of a staircase. Distant footsteps and voices came from above. He climbed the stairs that led to a maze of maintenance passageways built within the stone caverns to service utility and climate control systems in the private boxes and stables. Then catching up, he watched as they went up a short run of stairs and through a door.

Andrew laid back momentarily, then advanced to find it locked, and came back down the stairs. The system of chains and counterweights that operated the castle's big stone door filled the space around him. Service platforms connected by a network of catwalks were suspended at various levels. He climbed onto one of them and saw the terrorists prodding their hostages along the parapet above the door. Borsa angrily yanked an arm free as they moved behind it. They were out of Andrew's view now, but he could hear them arguing in Italian. Their voices echoed through the vaulted cavern amidst sounds of pushing and shoving and the clatter of hooves as horses thundered into the arena far below.

Andrew dashed to the end of a catwalk, and craned up to see heads, shoulders, arms, the brusque movement of figures scuffling—scuffling directly on the face of the horizontal stone door above. Then he heard a loud groan, and a thud, and a woman screaming, and a gunshot. He grasped one of the cables that suspended the catwalks, and climbed up onto the railing. Another shot rang out as he stretched upward, peering just over the edge of the stone slab.

But he couldn't get onto the slab from the catwalk. Even if he could, the terrorists were armed. Andrew studied the immense mechanism around him, the function of the parts simple and clear. The hawser hung just out of reach. He leaped from the railing, clutching at the coarse hemp with his arms and legs, sliding down a ways before getting a purchase. His weight started the counterweights moving, and the massive stone door began closing.

Melanie took advantage of the distraction and sent one of the terrorists sprawling across the door with a shove, weapon skittering off the edge. The other scrambled to get back onto the parapet before the door dropped too far below it. Melanie ran in the opposite direction, to the high end of the slowly tilting surface, the remaining terrorist crawling after her. Melanie jumped down a long distance to a service platform, landing on her feet, and rolling into a shoulder tumble to break her fall. The hooded figure landed behind her, came up standing, and came at her.

Melanie dashed right beneath Andrew, who was coming down the hawser. He let go, driving both feet into the terrorist who went over the railing, falling into the herd of Arabians thundering into the arena below.

Andrew landed on the platform next to Melanie, grasped her hand, and led the way to a door at the far end of one of the catwalks.

It was exactly noon. The prism in the tower projected a brilliant beam of light across the arena above the prancing Arabians onto the stone door, right on schedule.

The spectators began shrieking in horror.

There on the slowly closing slab—his head centered in the spotlight, leonine mane aglow, arms painfully outstretched, palms pierced by the spikes driven into the thousand-year-old stone by Silvio's Ram-set, there, like Christ crucified, naked against the hard slab—hung Giancarlo Borsa.

He was unconscious. Blood ran down the stone from his palms

in long streaks. A sign proclaiming *PACE MONDIALE* was affixed above his head.

The TV crew had come down the staircase from the balcony, and was running between the horses. The cameraman dropped to one knee in front of the stone door, and began recording the event for the evening news. Paparazzi surged around him, shouting in Italian, pushing, shoving, maneuvering for the best angle.

Andrew and Melanie were coming through a door from the catwalk into the maintenance passageways. The remaining terrorist ran past spotting them, whirled on the move, and opened fire. Andrew and Melanie took cover behind an abutment, the rounds chipped into the stone until the pistol clicked empty and the hooded figure ran. Andrew pursued.

Fausto had left the Maserati and was stretching his legs in the courtyard when the guard's pipe caught his eye. Anyone could have dropped it, but Fausto had thought it curious no guard was on duty. He crossed to the gatehouse and saw little piles of ash on the ground outside where the guard often rapped the pipe to empty it. Something wasn't right. He dialed an emergency number on a sticker affixed to the gatehouse wall.

In Borsa's stables, the door on the staircase exploded open, and the hooded terrorist ran onto the landing, Andrew a few steps behind. He dove through the doorway at the hooded figure. They both tumbled down the stairs into the stable, the Ram-set skittering across the floor.

Melanie came through the door onto the landing, and watched terrified as they grappled below.

The terrorist came out on top, grabbed a handful of Andrew's hair, slammed his head to the floor, and ran. Andrew got up and dove into the fleeing legs from behind. Again, the hooded figure went down, then, all in one motion, made a catlike swipe at the Ram-set, lunged upward, jammed the muzzle into Andrew's chest, and pulled the trigger hastily—before the safety depressed. It clicked, but the charge and spike Silvio had loaded earlier to pin Borsa's feet to the stone door, didn't fire.

Now they stood face-to-face, hands wrapped around the deadly tool, fighting to control it. Andrew had come within a millimeter of having a sixteen-penny spike planted in the center of his chest, and the thought of it made him overpoweringly aggressive. He charged forward, shoving the Ram-set up and away, and drove his adversary backwards against a stall. The abrupt movement caused one of the terrorist's gloved hands to slip. The opposing force suddenly removed, the Ram-set pivoted up and back in a rapid arc that slammed the muzzle flat against the balaclava above the sunglasses; the impact depressed the safety shoe, and jammed a finger against the trigger, causing it to fire.

The sixteen-penny spike ripped through the terrorist's brain, boring a path between the halves of the cortex and shattering the limbic system beneath. Then exiting, it blew a piece of skull out the back of the head, and pinned it and the balaclava to the stall.

Melanie flinched and screamed in fright at the sharp report.

Andrew was frozen by the suddenness with which it all happened. He stood watching the terrorist slide downward against the stall, looking in growing horror at the head that pulled slowly out of the balaclava, at the anguished expression, and the tiny puncture in the forehead that caused it—just above where the brows grew together. The massive exit wound left a long bloody smear on the stall, and there, at the bottom of it, like the period beneath an exclamation mark, was Dominica Maresca's oval face.

A short distance away, the Arabians that had been galloping into the ring when the massive stone door unexpectedly closed trapping them were still spooked, and their hooves were still trampling Silvio Festa's broken body.

In the stables, Andrew was staring in shock at Dominica's face when Melanie screamed again.

"No! No, look out! Look out!" she shrieked at him.

He whirled to see Kovlek, handgun drawn, charging into the stable, a terrifying, fast-moving blur leveling the weapon at him.

The operation had gone wrong, and Andrew was the cause of it. Kovlek had decided *no* witnesses would best insure the KGB came out clean as Zeitzev had ordered.

Andrew's reaction was a mixture of fear and confusion. The KGB agent who had abducted Raina Maiskaya was going to kill him. He didn't know why, and didn't have a chance of stopping him. He was thinking McKendrick would be furious when he found out he had gotten himself killed when a shot rang out.

Kovlek stiffened and rocked back and forth for a moment.

Then the life went out of him, and he collapsed where he stood, revealing Gorodin crouched behind him in the doorway, both hands on his Kalishnikov.

Andrew was too stunned to be relieved, and had no idea what to expect next. Gorodin holstered his weapon, and gestured with his head for them to go. Andrew put an arm around Melanie as she came off the stairs, and they ran from the stables, Gorodin right behind them.

Fausto was hurrying down the road toward Borsa's stables after making the call from the gatehouse. He heard the shots, pulled his pistol, and leveled it at Gorodin, who appeared to be chasing them.

"No, Fausto! No!" Andrew shouted.

"Who is he?" Fausto asked as he turned and ran with Melanie and Andrew toward the Maserati.

"The Frenchman! He saved my hide!"

"What happened?"

"Terrorists! They crucified Minister Borsa in there," he replied. "Literally." He paused as they reached the Maserati, then with a weary nervousness added, "I killed one of 'em. Maybe two."

"We must go," Fausto said decisively.

Andrew nodded, yanked open the rear door, pushing Melanie in ahead of him. The surging scream of sirens began rising as Fausto started the engine. He slammed it in gear, and was starting to pull away when Gorodin yanked open the front passenger door and jumped in next to him. Fausto slammed his foot to the floor, and the big car ripped across the courtyard, past the gatehouse through the entrance, and accelerated down the street behind the amphitheater.

The sirens grew louder. Police vehicles, roof flashers strobing, came through the turn up ahead and screeched to sideways stops, blocking the street. Uniformed officers leaped out drawing guns. Fausto slammed on the brakes as they advanced toward the Maserati. An officer pushed a gun through the open window into his face. Fausto shoved his police identification under his nose in reply.

"Set up a checkpoint at the gatehouse," he barked in Italian to the chagrined officer, adding, "Question everyone who comes out!"

The officer replied with a crisp affirmative, and ordered the police vehicles moved aside, allowing the Maserati to continue through onto the streets.

Melanie sat in the backseat hunched beneath Andrew's arm, shaking, shocked by all she had seen.

Andrew was numb and woozy, heart pumping his blood so rapidly it was blurring his vision.

"You okay?" he asked, blinking to clear it.

"I think so," she whimpered, looking up confused. "Who are you?" she asked. "Who's he?" she indicated Gorodin, who was turned sideways in the front seat.

"Please, allow me," Gorodin said in slightly accented English before Andrew could reply. "Andrew Churcher—he sells horses for my country. Melanie Winslow—she's looking for her father there," he said, introducing them; then gesturing to himself, added, "Valery Gorodin—KGB." He loathed saying it, but knew it would instantly communicate.

Melanie looked at Andrew in stunned silence.

"I can help both of you get into Russia," Gorodin concluded.

"I'm leaving for Moscow tonight," Andrew said sharply. "I don't need help."

"Yes," Gorodin said, matching Andrew's tone. "Only because you've already had it."

Andrew nodded pensively in acknowledgment. "Thank you," he said in a subdued voice. Then he held Gorodin's look, and asked, "Why?"

"Because it's in the best interests of my country. Your business dealings are very high on the Politburo's list of priorities."

Indeed, choosing between Andrew and Kovlek was easy. Gorodin had no doubt whatsoever who was more valuable to the Soviet Union. At worst, Andrew would keep the hard currency coming. At best, he'd divert from business, and lead Gorodin to the source of the *Kira* drawings.

"And me?" Melanie asked, having regained some degree of composure.

"Because you're here, and it's within my power. Unless you'd rather wait six months for a visa, maybe a year. After what happened today—maybe never.''

"He's right," Fausto chimed in. "You should both get out of Italy, immediately—before the Questura finds out you were involved and holds you as witnesses. In Italy, once the wheels of justice start grinding, they grind for all eternity.''

"Then, that's your choice, Miss Winslow," Gorodin said knowingly, "eternity or—tonight.''

Melanie studied him for a moment suspiciously.

"Are you saying you know my father?'' she challenged softly. "That you'll take me to him?''

"Impossible," Gorodin lied, with finality. "He's a very important man. A member of the Politburo. He doesn't even know I exist.'' Gorodin knew she'd have no chance of getting anywhere near Deschin. He also knew timing was the key to exerting biographic leverage for maximum gain. He wanted her in Moscow, stalled and desperate, so that when he was strongest and Deschin most vulnerable, he could play his card. "Besides," he went on, burnishing the deception, "*Rome* is my post, Miss Winslow. Once in Moscow, you're on your own.''

Melanie digested his comments for a moment, then glanced to Andrew.

"Why not?" he said reassuringly. "You have nothing to lose.''

She shifted her look to Gorodin and nodded.

The timing was perfect. Gorodin wouldn't even have to deal with Zeitzev on the matter. The *rezident* would have his hands full trying to cover the shooting of Kovlek in Borsa's stables, and the questions it would raise about Soviet involvement in the terrorist attack on Italy's defense minister—just as disarmament talks were commencing.

In the few hours it took Gorodin to force march Melanie's visa through the Embassy bureaucracy, Fausto drove Andrew and Melanie to their hotels to collect their things, then to the Embassy to pick up the documents, and lastly to the airport.

Inside the packed international terminal at Leonardo da Vinci, travelers clustered around newsstands, snapping up the evening papers that had photos of the ghastly crucifixion splashed across the front pages. Others collected around television sets in the bars—watching the videotape of the stone door closing, revealing Giancarlo Borsa hanging on it. Commentators speculated on the affiliation of the terrorists, their motives, and their objectives, and waited for word on the defense minister, who had been taken to a Rome hospital in critical condition.

And as purple shadows crept across the glittering domes of the eternal city, Aeroflot INT-237 to Moscow came down the runway in a light ground fog, and climbed into the Roman sky.

Andrew sat pensively staring out the window.

"You okay, Andrew?" Melanie asked, after watching him for a few moments. She found his thoughtful gentleness calming, and was attracted to him despite the difference in their ages.

"No," he replied in a whisper. He couldn't get Dominica's face out of his mind. No matter where he looked, her almond-shaped death mask seemed to be looking back with haunting vulnerability.

"Sometimes it helps to talk," Melanie said.

"Sometimes," he said, thinking all the talk in the world wouldn't change the fact that he'd killed two people. Then, realizing he was being insensitive, he turned to Melanie. "I'm sorry," he said, feeling relieved as her face replaced Dominica's. "You've been through a lot today, too. Tell me about this search for your father."

"It's—painfully simple," she said, choosing the words, and forcing a smile out of him. "For forty-two years, I thought I was Melanie Winslow, daughter of a New Hampshire carpenter. Then, my mother died, and I found out my father is a *Russian*, a government official named Aleksei Deschin."

An anxious ripple went through Andrew, though he concealed it, and was certain she didn't notice. Three weeks ago, his jaw would have dropped to his chest, and he would have said something like, "My father knew him. Your father is the *Russian* who probably had him killed." But he had become immune to surprises, and was more calculating now. He knew Gorodin had been assigned to him because he was Theodor Churcher's son, and had no doubt Deschin had ordered the surveillance. So he knew Gorodin had lied to Melanie, and was up to something. He decided to say nothing—for the time being, anyway.

"It's such a strange feeling," Melanie went on. "I mean, this

man, Zachary Winslow, gave me his name, read me bedtime
stories, and held me when I had nightmares. He taught me to ride
horses, paid for my dance lessons, and—I mean, this wonderful
man I called daddy"—she shrugged uncomprehendingly—"isn't
my father. And the man who really is—who's my flesh and
blood, my genes, my roots, my traditions, *my face*—turns out to
be somebody I never knew. And it's—" she paused, sensing Andrew's distance. "I'm sorry," she said. "I didn't mean to run on
like that. It's just sort of overwhelming to find out your father is
someone other than you thought."

Andrew nodded slightly, a sad irony in his eyes, and said, "I
know."

BOOK THREE

MOSCOW

"Life does not give itself to one who tries to keep all its advantages at once. I have often thought morality may perhaps consist solely in the courage of making a choice."

—LEON BLUM, *On Marriage*

Chapter Thirty-seven

Weeks had passed since a cold, harsh rain blasted over the Urals from Siberia, and scrubbed the grime from Moscow streets, heralding an early spring.

Aleksei Deschin was sitting in his study in the once grand building on Proyzed Serova Street in his robe and pajamas, angrily reading KGB reports on the day's events in Rome, when the door buzzer rang.

It was 10:17 P.M.

He peered through the security peephole, then opened the door, letting a young woman into the apartment.

Neither spoke.

He led the way to the bedroom. Then he sat on the carved walnut bed, watching her undress.

She was young, maybe twenty, twenty-two, Deschin calculated, with a taut robustness, white flesh, and pink up-turned nipples that aroused him. She was state-supplied. And like the countless others who had been dispatched into the night whenever he made the call, he'd never seen her before and would never see her again.

When she was naked, she bounded across the room, climbed onto the bed, and, kneeling between his legs, put her face close to his and tried to kiss him.

He leaned away, and, gently pushing her head down into his lap, said, "My needs are simple, and I prefer them quickly satisfied."

She hid her disappointment. She'd expected to spend the night. It was her profession, and proud of her specialties, she was anxious to perform fully for a member of the Politburo who might recommend her.

But this was all Deschin ever wanted from any of them. Sex had long ceased to be more than a mechanical release. He couldn't remember the last time he'd been an active participant, or made love to a woman, or been with one in a way that might resemble a procreative act.

The rhythm of the blond head bobbing between his knees quickened. There was a dressing mirror opposite the bed; but with each of these young women, Deschin couldn't help thinking, *She's somebody's daughter*, and he never watched. The surge was rising now. He began arching his back against the headboard, and as she brought him to the moment, he grabbed two handfuls of her hair, keeping her head just where he wanted it. His body was sagging back against the pillows when he thought he heard the phone ring, and when she looked up at him to ascertain if she had pleased him, it rang again. He closed his robe, and nodded wearily, and she understood and handed him the phone.

It was the Premier's aide, Vasily. The call Deschin long dreaded had come.

Twenty minutes later he was fully dressed and hurrying in the darkness to a waiting sedan. The cultural minister rarely went out at such a late hour. When Uzykin saw Deschin's grave expression he knew his destination was the Kremlin.

The black Chaika crossed Dzerzhinsky Square, accelerating beneath a latticework of cottonwoods into Karl Marx Prospekt, and headed west in the center lane reserved for vehicles of government officials.

The mature one-hundred-foot trees, planted by Stalin at Franklin D. Roosevelt's suggestion, were already budding. Moscow's streets would soon be dusted with snowy pookh, the tufts of silky fiber released by the female cottonwood.

Deschin sat glumly in the Chaika, wishing the problem he'd be facing could be eliminated as easily as the flammable pookh which, as every Moscow schoolchild knows, ignites at the touch of a match, and vanishes instantly in a brilliant flash.

The Chaika came out of Karl Marx Prospekt, crossed Gorkovo, and approached the Kremlin.

The bureaucratic citadel is a sixteenth-century walled fortress. Dark red brick, twenty feet thick in some places, stretches almost eight hundred meters between corners of an inverted trapezoid. Golden onion-shaped domes of four cathedrals swell above the crenellated walls, and countless towers spike skyward, the five tallest thrusting illuminated red stars aloft—into a heavy mist that diffused them.

The Chaika drove the length of the wall to the southwest corner, and entered the Kremlin through a gate at the base of the Borovitsky Tower. It continued up the steep hill, past the Great Kremlin Palace, and beneath the arch of the Council of Ministers Building, stopping inside the triangular courtyard.

Deschin entered via an ornate bronze door, walked beneath the gilded dome, and hurried down a long corridor to Premier Dmitri Kaparov's apartment.

The Premier's wife; aide, Vasily; and personal physician, along with Anatoly Chagin, head of GRU; and KGB Chief Sergei Tvardovskiy were gathered in the bedroom where the Soviet Premier lay near death.

A tangle of tubes and wires snaked from beneath the bedding to vital signs' monitors and life-support systems. The ping of the EKG monitor alternated with the asthmatic hiss of the dialysis machine.

"When?" Deschin asked softly as he entered, his nostrils filling with the suffocating smell of illness.

The doctor turned from the equipment and shrugged.

"Morning, midday at the latest, Comrade Minister," she said.

"Poor Dmitri," his wife whispered sadly, adding almost apologetically, "he thought he had more time."

"We all did," Chagin said, his lips barely moving.

"Yes, you said three months," Tvardovskiy growled, challenging the doctor.

"I know," she replied. "I'm afraid the recent stress accelerated his deterioration."

Deschin stepped to the bed and studied Kaparov's ashen face, knowing his friend would not live to see SLOW BURN realized. He took the Premier's hand and squeezed it gently. He was about to let go when Kaparov squeezed back—hard, as if he knew who it was. Deschin's lips tightened in a thin smile. He turned to the

Premier's wife and hugged her. Then he crossed the room and led Vasily, Chagin, and Tvardovskiy down the corridor to the Premier's office.

Vasily entered the ornate chamber last, closing the door. As the Premier's longtime aide, matters of protocol, such as the arrangements for a state funeral, were his responsibility. "How shall I proceed?" he asked, careful not to direct the question to one man over the others.

"The procedures are clearly outlined in Article Twenty-seven, comrade," Tvardovskiy snapped. "I suggest you follow them."

"No," said Deschin decisively. His title was minister of culture; but when it came to SLOW BURN, his power was second only to the Premier's. "Things are going too well in Geneva. We can't appear to be without leadership, now. We can't lose our momentum."

"I agree," Tvardovskiy said. "But the Americans know of the Premier's condition. They—"

"How? How do they know?" Deschin interrupted rhetorically. "Not by what they see."

"Of course not," Tvardovskiy replied impatiently. "The opposite has always been their only gauge."

"Exactly," Deschin said. "When they don't see the Soviet Premier, they conclude he's ill. But they have no way of determining degree. Tomorrow, he will have recovered sufficiently to leave the Kremlin. Find a military pensioner, preferably a senile one. Dress him in the Premier's greatcoat and hat. Put the old fellow in his limousine and get it out in the streets—where their press people can see it."

"Fine, Aleksei," Tvardovskiy said. "But how long do you think we can—"

"—A day, two, ten," Deschin snapped. "Every *hour* we give Pykonen before making the announcement brings the unchallenged nuclear superiority Comrade Dmitrievitch wanted for his people that much closer."

"I'll do it," Chagin said. He turned and left before either of them could reply.

Tvardovskiy started after him.

"Sergei?" Deschin said sharply, waiting until he had paused

and turned to face him before continuing. "You spoke to Zeitzev?"

Tvardovskiy winced, revealing the gold edges atop his incisors. He'd been hoping the subject wouldn't come up.

"Giancarlo Borsa is an old friend. And heavily involved in Geneva," Deschin went on tautly. He paused, then, with quiet outrage, asked, "How? How the hell did that happen?"

Tvardovskiy stared at him for a long moment while he brought his temper under control.

"It will be taken care of," he said gravely. He was about to warn Deschin not to use that tone when it occurred to him, he might just be addressing the next Soviet Premier.

Aeroflot INT-237 from Rome had flown a northeasterly course across the Adriatic, Yugoslavia, Hungary, the eastern tip of Czechoslovakia into western Russia, and was on final approach to Sheremetyvo International Airport, in the desolate flatlands twenty-six miles northwest of Moscow.

"By the way," Andrew said, taking Melanie's hand, "in case you've heard those stories about Russian air traffic controllers looking at their screens through glasses of vodka—"

"I was just wondering about that," she replied, amused rather than alarmed.

"No problem," he concluded. "The ATC system here was manufactured by Churchco Electronics. It's the best in the world."

"Churchco—" she said, connecting his name to the conglomerate. "You're—"

"Theodor Churcher's my father," he said, nodding. "As they say, I made my money the old-fashioned way—" he cut off the sentence, leaving the joke unfinished. It was the first time he had actually thought about inheriting the billion-dollar empire.

Sheremetyvo was a modern, efficiently run airport, and in minutes they had landed, deplaned, and cued for passport control. A young inspector with a sullen face and brown uniform processed Andrew's travel documents, then began digging through his bag. He unzipped one of the pouches, removed an electric razor, and held it up.

"Is for what?"

"Shaving?" Andrew replied, making the motion over his face with his hand.

The inspector eyed him suspiciously, then shifted his eyes to the shaver, looking for a way to open it; finally he took a penknife from a pocket.

"Hold it," Andrew said, concerned he would damage it. "I'll do it, okay?" He took the shaver and popped off the rotary heads.

The inspector shook his head no, unsatisfied. "Where is cord?" he challenged.

Andrew understood, now. The shaver was a battery-operated model, and had multicolor indicator lights, nine shaving modes with calibrated selector, and sleek packaging. To the inspector it looked suspiciously high tech and electronic, as its designers intended.

Andrew turned it on and ran it across his face, trying not to appear smug about it.

The inspector eyed him coldly, and shoved his bag aside, dismissing him. Melanie was next. He swept his steely eyes over her. "Papers please."

He's probably going to take it out on me, she thought, as she handed them to him.

The inspector examined and stamped her passport, then brusquely unfolded her visa. His eyes widened, his expression softened, and he handed it back, waving her on without checking her bags.

"Mr. Warmth must have a thing for older women," Melanie said as they walked off.

"Does your visa have a small green crest stamped across the signature?" Andrew asked.

"Yes, it does—"

"It's a special clearance. My father's visa had one. It took him years to get it."

"Now we know what Gorodin meant when he said it was within his power."

Andrew nodded, reflecting on his suspicions.

"So much for middle-age charm," Melanie concluded.

The Tupolev 134 had taken three hours and twenty minutes to

cover the fifteen hundred miles between Rome and Moscow. With the two-hour loss of time, it was well after midnight when they arrived at the Hotel Berlin on Zhadanova Street in the theater district.

The Berlin's lobby was deserted and quiet.

They were both too exhausted to appreciate the plush Victorian decor as they trudged to the check-in desk. The clerk was off to one side doing paperwork, and didn't notice them. Andrew lightly tapped the bell.

"Dobriy vyecher," the clerk said as he looked up and approached them. *"Mozhna pamagat?"*

"We'd like to check in, please," Andrew replied. "Mr. Churcher, Miss Winslow."

"Oh, yes, Mr. Churcher," the clerk said.

He took their passports, slipped a card from a file box, and gave it to Andrew to fill out. Then he prepared a *propoosk*—a hotel pass that contains one's name, length of stay, and room number—and pushed it across the mahogany counter to Andrew.

"Give this to the hall attendant on your floor," he said. "She'll give you your key. Reverse the procedure when you leave. The propoosk must be given to the doorman to be allowed to leave the hotel."

"Yes, thanks, I know," Andrew replied.

"I'll have someone bring your bags," the clerk said. He smiled, and returned to his work, assuming Andrew and Melanie were together.

Melanie saw Andrew was about to say something, and touched his arm, stopping him.

"Don't," she said warmly.

Andrew studied her for a moment, then smiled wistfully and turned back to the desk.

"Excuse me, but the lady's checking in as well."

The clerk reddened, apologized profusely, and went through the check-in procedure with Melanie. In a few minutes, she and Andrew, propoosks in hand, were walking a long empty corridor to the elevator.

"I'm sorry, I didn't mean to embarrass you," she said.

"You didn't. I was just being cautious."

"I don't understand."

"They tapped my phone in Rome."

"Why?"

"That's how they do business," Andrew said with a shrug, not mentioning that he suspected his father's collaboration with the Russians was the cause. "The guidebooks say, 'Hotel Berlin, cozy, Victorian elegance, favorite of businessmen,'" he went on. "The truth is, they favor it because they have no choice. The government wanted me here, and that's where Intourist put me. And why does the government want me here?"

"To watch you—"

"That's right."

"But we would just be lovers."

"I know," he said softly, letting his eyes catch hers before adding, "And I'd like that—"

Melanie returned his look and smiled.

"—but they're always looking for an edge. For something they can use against you."

"Well," she said, teasing, "I wouldn't want them to destroy your reputation by revealing you're sleeping with an older woman."

"That's how they work," Andrew said with a grin. "Seriously," he went on, "they're experts at using the most innocent situation to make trouble."

"The KGB?" she whispered.

Andrew nodded, and said, "Don't whisper, it attracts attention." His remark started him thinking about Raina Maiskaya, and he saw her blank eyes staring at him, staring right through him as the car whisked her away on that bleak night in Rome, and wondered if she'd been tortured and imprisoned, or if she was even still alive. The elevator door opened and snapped him out of it. He leaned his head closer to Melanie's as he followed her inside.

"Don't ever forget where you are," he warned.

Melanie nodded.

The door rumbled closed, and he kissed her.

Chapter Thirty-eight

The *USS Finback,* a Sturgeon-class hunter/killer submarine, cut through South Atlantic waters at a depth of seven hundred and fifty feet.

The *Finback*'s captain, Commander Burton C. Armus, was an unpolished bear of a man, ill-suited in size for submarine duty. But he had the devious, calculating mind it takes to hunt in the dark. The *Finback* was as far from the South Bronx as he could get, and he loved it.

Armus was in the process of "tickling" a Soviet Alpha-class submarine off Puerto Rico. The titanium-hulled alpha is the swiftest and deepest diving sub yet built. Armus had spent weeks sparring with his Russian counterpart to learn about its capabilities, and he had learned a lot. He was hunched over a chart in the *Finback*'s control room, plotting the alpha's course and planning a countermove, when the communications officer handed him a teletype from ASW Pensacola which read:

TOP SECRET
FLASH PRIORITY
Z143803ZAPR
FR: ASW PENSACOLA
TO: USS FINBACK
1.DISENGAGE PRESENT TARGET IMMED.
2.PROCEED TO 80W 22N ASAP. INTERCEPT TANKER VLCC KIRA DEPARTING CIENFUEGOS. TRACK TO CONFIRM GULF DESTINATION. REPORT EVENT ASW PENSACOLA IMMED.

Babysit a fucking tanker? Armus wondered.

As a security precaution, the orders were sent without a mission overview. And Armus' reaction, if not eloquent was understandable. He had the alpha going in circles—an "underwater mind-fuck," as he called it—and it killed him to let the Soviet submarine off the hook.

At about the same time, the *Kira* was slipping from her berth at the Soviet naval base in Cienfuegos. *VLCC* means "Very Large Crude Carrier," and measuring longer than four football fields, the *Kira* was properly classified. Her hold was empty of cargo, and she rode high in the water with ungainly majesty as the harbor pilot guided her through the channel. It was 4:07 P.M. when Captain Rublyov took over the helm.

Ostensibly, Fedor Rublyov was the civilian captain of an oil tanker. But he was actually a commander first rank in the Soviet Navy, one of their finest—which was why the *Kira* had been entrusted to his command.

He brought the huge vessel to starboard, and headed west into the orange fireball that sat on the horizon.

The *Finback* was waiting for her just outside Cuban territorial waters. The sub's BQQ-6 bow-mounted sonar picked up the rumble of the *Kira*'s power plant and her twin screw cavitation the moment her engines went all-ahead-full, and she headed out to open sea.

The *Finback* tracked the *Kira* in a looping arc below Cuba's southern shore to its western-most tip. Crawling at a speed of eighteen knots, it took the tanker almost fifteen hours to reach the Yucatan Channel, where she swung north into the Mexican Gulf.

The *Kira* was still 750 miles from its offshore oil field destination when Armus brought the *Finback* to periscope antenna depth. Per the ASW directive, he contacted Pensacola—via SSIX, the geosynchronous satellite dedicated to U.S. submarine communications—and reported the *Kira*'s destination as the Gulf of Mexico, and position as 86W 22N. Almost immediately, the *Finback*'s printer came to life with a reply.

BRAVO FINBACK. CONTINUE TRACKING. GUIDE ASW VIKING TO TARGET AND MAINTAIN PERI-CONTACT TO VERIFY RENDEZVOUS. REPORT EVENT ASW PEN-

SACOLA. TAKE NO OTHER ACTION. REPEAT NO OTHER
ACTION

"Something weird's cooking," Armus said, handing the directive to the deck officer.

"We're guiding an S-3A to a rendezvous?"

Armus shrugged. Both were reacting to the flip-flop in procedure—a Viking S-3A can detect submerged submarines, locat-
ing a surface vessel the size of the *Kira* would be child's play.
Neither knew the Viking had been gutted of all electronic tracking gear.

In Pensacola, Lowell and Arnsbarger were on twenty-four-
hour alert when the *Finback* confirmed the *Kira*'s destination.
Within minutes, they had their Viking S-3A in the air on a southeast heading over the Mexican Gulf. Lowell was in the copilot's
seat instead of the TACCO bay behind. It was 7:05 A.M. EST.

They had been training for two days when Cissy remarked that
Arnsbarger's schedule had changed.

"We're running tests on some new sub-tracking gear," he had
replied offhandedly.

"Oh," she had said, letting it go. She was a military brat, and
knew how to read between the lines.

The night before, Lowell had called his folks in Santa Barbara.
He'd been planning on checking in; the high-risk nature of the
mission prompted him to do it now. He had a long chat with his
parents and younger sister, but nothing was said about the upcoming flight.

The Viking had been in the air a little over two hours when
Arnsbarger locked the radio onto the SSIX band and flicked on
his pipestem.

"This is ASW Viking, Alpha Charlie nine-four-zero, to *USS
Finback*, over."

"This is *Finback*. We read you, Viking."

"Request data update on target, over."

"Location 86.25W 22.37N. Heading three-one-zero.

"Roger."

"What's your ETA, Viking?"

"Estimate visual contact, eight minutes."

The *Finback*'s radar man had been tracking the Viking on the BPS-15 surface search scope.

"Thirty-five miles and closing," he reported.

Armus had his big face pressed to the eyepiece of the periscope. "Viking sighted," he announced about five minutes later. "Let's talk to Pensacola."

While Armus was reporting that the Viking/*Kira* rendezvous was imminent, Lowell and Arnsbarger had gotten a visual fix on the *Kira*.

Arnsbarger reset the radio to the international emergency band. "Let her rip," he said.

Lowell pulled a remote control unit onto his lap. It resembled a minicomputer with a special keyboard, and had a procedure control list affixed inside the cover. The PCL enumerated three sequential event codes.

Arnsbarger looked back at the wing expectantly as Lowell keyed in the first code, and hit the SEND key.

There was a loud bang as an explosion blew a section of the cowling off the port side jet engine.

"Holy shit!" Arnsbarger exclaimed, in case anyone was listening. "We got us a fire in number one!"

"Must've blown a fuel line!" Lowell said.

Flames were licking at the exposed turbine, and smoke was streaming from the exhaust end of the nacelle, leaving a long trail in the sky.

In the *Finback*, Armus was staring wide-eyed through the periscope, and reining in his impulse to surface and take rescue action. The communications officer came running into the control room with an ASW directive, the meat of which read:

> MAYDAY IS PLANNED EVENT. TAKE NO RESCUE AC-
> TION. VERIFY TWO MAN VIKING CREW TAKEN ABOARD
> KIRA.

Armus' brows went up. "Son of a bitch," he said softly, and turned back to the periscope.

In the Viking, Arnsbarger and Lowell were watching the *Kira* coming closer and closer far below.

"About time we got rescued," Lowell said, grinning.

Arnsbarger nodded, and flicked on his pipestem again. "Mayday!" he said. "This is USN Viking *Alpha Charlie* nine-four-zero. We're on fire! Mayday! Mayday!"

On the *Kira*'s bridge, the first officer had spotted the crippled Viking's smoke trail and notified Captain Rublyov. He was leaning into his binoculars when the *Kira*'s radio officer joined them.

"We have received a Mayday, Comrade Captain," he said in Russian. "The pilot has identified as a U.S. Navy Viking."

"A Viking—first we've seen this voyage," the captain said, adding facetiously, "The Americans always make certain we aren't torpedoed by Soviet submarines."

"Do we respond, Comrade Captain?" the officer asked.

"Of course," Rublyov replied. "We are the vessel nearest the Mayday, and will act accordingly. To do otherwise would create suspicion, and invite an inquiry. Put the bridge on the Viking's frequency."

The communications officer hurried off.

A smile broke across Rublyov's pocked Slavik face. "Prepare to rescue crew *and* salvage craft," he ordered the first officer. He knew the Viking S-3A carried top secret surveillance gear—and the *Kira* had a crane capable of hoisting the plane aboard, and acres of deck space to store her. "And have the CMO report to the bridge," he added, scooping up the phone.

"Viking? Viking, this is *VLCC Kira*," he said in heavily accented English. "We read your Mayday, and have you sighted. Do you read? Over."

"Affirmative! Affirmative, *Kira*," Arnsbarger replied. "We're on fire. We're going in. Over."

"Suggest you ditch off our port bow, and remain with your craft if possible."

"Affirmative. Port bow. We have visual fix. We'll pancake her in."

Lowell questioned Arnsbarger with a look. What the Russian captain had suggested was standard rescue procedure—but it wasn't part of the scenario.

Arnsbarger winked. He suspected what the Russian captain was planning, and was playing a game with him.

Rublyov was still smiling when the chief missile officer reported to the bridge. The diminutive fellow wore blue clean-

room coveralls and looked more like he'd come from surgery
than the bowels of an oil tanker.

"Yes, Comrade Captain?"

"Secure your area, comrade," Rublyov ordered. "The crew
of that Viking will soon be aboard, and with any luck, so will
their craft."

"A Viking—" the CMO said, eyes brightening. He headed a
team of missile electronics technicians who Rublyov knew were
more than qualified to evaluate the Viking's surveillance gear.

"You'll have to tarp her, and work at night, but you'll have
sufficient time to pick her clean," Rublyov went on. "*If* we can
get her aboard, and *if* we can—"

A loud boom from the Viking interrupted Rublyov. He and the
CMO looked up to see a hole blown through the fuselage, black
smoke rushing out of it.

Seconds earlier, Lowell had keyed another sequence into the
remote control unit, setting off an explosive charge in the fuselage just aft of the flaming wing.

"Geezus! We're losing the hydraulics," Arnsbarger exclaimed. The explosion had no such effect. Nor did the damaged
fuselage compromise the Viking's ability to maneuver. The
puncture and blown fuel line had been meticulously engi-
neered—for effect only. The Viking was totally airworthy as
Arnsbarger put it on an erratic flight path, making it appear out
of control.

"*Kira? Kira,* this is Viking. Negative on that ditch,"
Arnsbarger said, resuming the scenario. "We just lost our
hydraulics. I can't control her."

Rublyov and the CMO exchanged pained looks.

"Read you Viking. You're positive you can't set down on the
sea?" Rublyov prodded.

"Negative," Arnsbarger said sharply. "I have no controls.
We're bailing out."

"Shit—" Rublyov said under his breath.

Arnsbarger clicked off and started to chuckle, picturing the
look on the Russian captain's face.

"You ready?" he asked.

"Yeah, but I wouldn't mind skipping this part."

"Ditto. Let's set it up and get out of here."

Lowell nodded crisply. There would be no more talk. They had practiced this dozens of times. Now both moved with precision and speed. While Arnsbarger put the Viking on autopilot, Lowell keyed another sequence into the remote unit, and hit the TIME DELAY key. Then, he placed the unit on the floor and nodded to Arnsbarger. The pilot's gut tightened as he reached for the bright yellow ejection seat lever and pulled it.

The tinted canopy blew off before Arnsbarger's hand had released the lever. An instant later, the side by side ejection seats exploded upward from the Viking's flight deck at slightly divergent angles. In a matter of seconds, they both had reached the apex of their trajectories and began plunging toward the sea.

Lowell was falling like a rock, when the chute blew out of his backpack, unfurled behind him, and mushroomed with a loud *whoosh*, bringing his free-fall to a sudden stop. The jolt jerked the harness hard up into his groin, then the pressure eased and he began floating toward the sea. He looked up to see Arnsbarger's chute mushroom, then glanced to the Viking. It was diving toward the sea, like a spent rocket-casing, when the remote unit sent the delayed signal. Two hundred pounds of plastic explosives packed into cavities in the plane's airframe erupted. The Viking disintegrated in midair, and showered the sea with debris.

Rublyov winced, then barked to the first officer, "Get the launch over the side."

Lowell splashed down, and popped his harness. He was floating in his Mae West amidst an ever-widening slick of shark repellent. A liferaft was in the water behind him and had already started inflating. A long tether ran from it to Lowell's wrist. He reeled it in, pulled himself over the side, and broke out a paddle.

Arnsbarger was still high above the sea; he saw the bright yellow shape below, and began working the control lines of his chute angling toward it.

The *Kira*'s engines were at full stop now. Her launch hit the water with the first officer and three crew members aboard. The diesel roared to life, and the launch pulled away from the huge vessel, cutting through the swells toward the bobbing raft about a thousand yards away.

Arnsbarger splashed down closer to the raft than he ever thought he could, shed his chute harness, and started swimming.

Lowell paddled toward him, and in no time, Arnsbarger was crawling into the raft.

"You okay?" Lowell inquired intensely, as he helped him over the side.

"Yeah," Arnsbarger grunted, flopping next to him like a boated tuna.

"Nice jumping."

"Thanks. I spotted a welcoming committee coming this way just before I went in."

"Great," Lowell replied. "This thing's going like clockwork."

"That was the easy part," Arnsbarger said. "Wait and see what kind of welcome we get if they catch us looking for those damned missiles."

Chapter Thirty-nine

The fifth floor hall attendant in the Hotel Berlin was a pudgy middle-aged woman who had learned a bit of English from the hotel's business clientele. It was mid-morning when she glanced down the corridor and saw Melanie approaching in her springy splayfooted walk.

The prior evening Melanie and Andrew whetted their appetites and promised to satisfy them soon. She lay awake thinking about that—about how long it had been since she felt a rush at the thought of being with someone, since she allowed herself such a feeling. She enjoyed it, but she didn't trust it. Events of extreme intensity had brought them together, and she thought perhaps they were the reason. The feeling gave way to an uneasy awareness of where she was and why, and she fell asleep thinking about the need to become acclimated and to plan a course of action.

On waking, she did just that, and as always, the first step was the phone book. But she couldn't find one in her room, so she went to the hall attendant, who not only keeps the keys but also takes messages, calls taxis, and serves as general advisor to her charges.

"Dobraeoota," Melanie said hesitantly, trying out one of the four Russian words she had memorized that morning as part of her plan.

"Good morning," the attendant said. She pointed to Melanie's feet, their turned-out position confirming what her walk suggested, and added, "You're a dancer."

"Yes, yes I am," Melanie said.

"I love ballet. But it's so expensive, and—" The hall attendant heard the elevator opening, and before seeing who exited, she cut off the sentence, and got back to business. "May I help you, now?" she asked.

"Oh sure," Melanie said, seeing her uneasiness but not understanding it. "I'm looking for a phone book."

"I'm sorry, I don't understand," the attendant said blankly, ignoring a nod from a maid who had gotten out of the elevator.

"Tye-lye-fon-niy spra-vach-neek?" Melanie said, resorting to the words she had memorized.

"Tyelyefoniy spravachneek?" the attendant said, still without comprehension.

"It's okay. I'll ask downstairs," Melanie said, trying to exit gracefully. She gave the attendant her room key in exchange for her hotel pass, and exhausting her Russian vocabulary, said, "Spaseeba." Then she smiled and headed down the corridor.

As soon as Melanie stepped into the elevator, the hall attendant took a small journal from the drawer of her key desk, and made a notation.

Earlier that morning, Andrew departed for Tersk from Vnukovo, the domestic terminal south of Moscow. Two hours later, Aeroflot SU-1209 landed in Mineral'nye Vody, a resort area below the foothills of the Caucasus. An Intourist car and driver were waiting for him.

The battered Moskvich station wagon headed south on a narrow concrete ribbon that climbed gradually toward the towering mountain range in the distance.

Yosef, the driver, spoke no English and smiled at everything Andrew said. His pulpy jowls shimmied along with the Moskvich, which rattled despite the smooth road. He was flabby, simpleminded, and wholly unthreatening. Too much so, Andrew thought, deciding Yosef had to be KGB—which he was.

After about fifty miles, the road forked west into the Olkhovka Valley. Here, the flat terrain gave way to Tersk's gently rolling pastures and bubbling springs that provide the nutritious bluegrass and rich mineral water on which Soviet Arabians are raised.

Nikolai Dovzhenko, Tersk stud manager, greeted Andrew with a hug and heartfelt sympathy. Theodor Churcher had been literally his first international client, and the depth of Nikolai's sorrow was testimony to their long friendship. The burly Russian directed Andrew to a pavilion—crowded with buyers—that overlooked a lush paddock and rows of barns beyond. The sounds, the smells, the long wait for the auctioneer to call the first Arabian to the block while attendants primed the buyers with caviar and chilled vodka, were all as Andrew remembered.

More than three hours and countless vodkas later, twenty-five horses had been sold—eight to Churchco Equestrian. A murmur went through the group as the stableman led another Arabian into the paddock.

"Perkha," Dovzhenko said, announcing the name of the magnificently conformed stallion.

The purebred's rippling muscles gave its alabaster coat the look of undulating stone. Its hooves lifted the instant they touched the soil, barely leaving an imprint. The stableman stopped walking. The Arabian did the same—without command and without allowing the tether to slacken—and stood unmoving like a breathing Michelangelo.

The auctioneer opened the bidding at 250,000 dollars, setting 25,000 as the minimum increase.

Andrew knew that Perkha was the franchise maker he sought, and bid 300,000 right off. The price quickly escalated to 600,000. Andrew had just made it 625 when someone called out, "I challenge that!"

Andrew whirled in his seat. He was stunned, not by the remark, but by the voice.

Raina Maiskaya strode forward commandingly. She had arrived after the auction had begun, and remained silent and unseen at the rear of the pavilion.

"Challenge it?" Dovzhenko asked, perturbed.

"Indeed," Raina snapped, fixing Andrew with an angry stare. "Mr. Churcher is acting as a broker here. And I for one would like assurances that those he represents have authorized such extravagant bids, and have deposited currency to cover them in one of our banks as prescribed by law."

"This is most unusual, Madame Maiskaya," Dovzhenko replied. "For years Theodor Churcher was one of our—"

"We're no longer dealing with *Theodor* Churcher," Raina in-

terrupted. "How do we know *he* is worthy of the trust and respect earned by his father?"

"You're unjustly impugning this man's integrity," Dovzhenko
said, referring to Andrew.

Andrew was puzzled by Raina's attack. It tempered his delight
at seeing her alive and whole, and made him wonder if her ab-
ductors had turned her. Had she been brainwashed into working
for them? Or was that what she'd been doing all along? Regardless, he decided he had no choice but to respond to her challenge. "Thank you, Nikolai. I agree," he said, and, glaring at
Raina, added, "But, as *my father* would say, I have the cards,
and I'd like to play them."

"If that means you have the documentation," Raina said
sharply, "I'd very much like to see it."

"You shall," Andrew said.

"Good." Then shifting her look to Dovzhenko, she prompted,
"I'm sure there's an office we can use to settle this matter privately."

"Of course," Dovzhenko replied. "We'll suspend bidding for
a short time." He gestured the attendants pour vodka for the
other buyers, then led Andrew and Raina from the pavilion. They
crossed the grounds—passing the graveled parking area—and
approached a dacha that served as an administration building.
Nikolai opened the door, directed them inside, and started walking back toward the pavilion.

The moment he was out of sight, Yosef got out the Moskvich
and hurried toward the dacha.

"A phone book?" the desk clerk in the Hotel Berlin said somewhat incredulously.

"That's correct," Melanie replied. "I'd like to see a telephone
directory."

The clerk shook his head no. "Nowhere in Moscow is there
such a book."

"You're serious?"

"Yes, this is not kidding."

"All right," Melanie said, perplexed. "Is there a number I
can call for information?"

"The Intourist Service Bureau can give you information about museums, restaurants, ballets, tours."

"No, no, telephone information. I mean, suppose I knew your name and wanted to call you, but I didn't have your number. What number do I call to get it?"

"You mean enquiries," he said. "Not in Moscow. Only in Leningrad is there such a number."

"I don't understand. How do you get a person's phone number or address if you don't have it?"

"From the person you want to call. If I want you to have my number or address, I'll give them to you, won't I?" he said slyly.

Melanie studied him for a moment thinking that in any western city a hotel desk clerk would have been flirting with her by now, suggesting it was really *his* phone number and address that she wanted.

"Look, suppose, just suppose," she pressed on, "you didn't know I wanted to call you, *but* you would really want me to, if you knew I did. Then what?"

"Well, there are the *spravkas*—the kiosks you see in the street. Some will *sell* you phone numbers, but *private* ones are very difficult." He splayed his hands. "You're familiar with baseball?"

"Yes," she replied, a little impatiently.

"I think you just made strike three."

"I get the point," she said, opening her bag and removing her mother's letter and the WWII photograph. "You have a copying machine here I can use?"

He recoiled as if she had said something vulgar. "No copying machine," he said coldly.

"I'm sorry to be such a bother," Melanie said. "I'm asking you because there aren't any phone books. If there were, I'd look under *copying* and there'd be a list of shops, and I'd find one close to the hotel and go there. Maybe you could tell me where the nearest one is?"

"We don't have such places. All duplicating equipment is under State control. It's against the law for private citizens to have it."

"A crime to have a copying machine—" She said it flatly, with disbelief.

"*Shussh,*" he said, and whispering, explained, "Only those involved in *samizdat*—underground literature—have them, but they will be arrested."

"Oh—" Melanie said, almost to herself. "Well, thank you for explaining it to me." She turned from the desk and began walking across the lobby, trying to comprehend the idea that there were no phone books and no copying services in Moscow.

"Excuse me," a man's voice called out.

Melanie turned to see a three-piece suit, wing tips, attaché, and Burberry coming toward her—*an American businessman,* she thought. The rumpled fellow had been standing at the far end of the desk, hurriedly going through papers in his attaché. "I hope you don't mind," he went on, in a soft Southern drawl, "but I couldn't help overhearing some of that. Have you tried our Embassy? They might be able to help you."

"No, I haven't, but I will. Thanks."

"You'll have to excuse me," he said, starting to move off. "I'm running late. I never get used to the time change. Hang in there. Nothing here is easy."

The Embassy—it had never occurred to her. It had been less than a day since she learned who Aleksei Deschin was and where to find him. And her departure for Moscow had been sudden and traumatic. She wasn't prepared. Despite her planning that morning, she hadn't really stopped to think. She decided the lapse was due to what she called "the curse of creative people," who, by nature, invent new ways to do things even when perfectly serviceable ones exist.

She crossed back toward the desk.

"Hi—"

The clerk eyed her apprehensively.

"Got an easy one for you."

"Yes."

"Where's the United States Embassy?" she asked, quickly adding, "And don't tell me there isn't one."

She figured her luck had changed when he smiled.

*   *   *

Yosef, the flabby KGB man, moved down the main corridor of the dacha with surprising quickness and stealth. The first office was open and empty. He heard the *snap-snap-snap* of a typewriter coming from another across the corridor. The upper half of the wall was windowed. The blinds were lowered; the slats open slightly. Yosef peeked through them and glimpsed a woman's hands moving over the keyboard. He assumed it was a secretary at work, and continued down the corridor listening for Raina and Andrew's voices.

But the hands Yosef saw were Raina's. She was typing— "Now is the time for all good men to come to the aid of their country"—in Russian, typing it repeatedly to keep up the noise and the deception. She'd just finished explaining to Andrew that her challenge had been a cover, a way to buy them some time alone; and though still a little uneasy, he had decided to follow her lead.

"My driver," he whispered, indicating the rotund shadow moving across the blinds. "I thought he was KGB. Now, I'm positive."

"I've no doubt of it."

"This whole thing feels like a setup."

"It's possible. You want to forget it?"

Andrew shook his head no. "We'll just have to be careful. I mean, why else would they let you go?"

"Because they had no proof. I stuck to my story, and told them nothing. Besides," she sighed forlornly, "they can arrest me whenever they want, now. They've taken my passport. I can't leave the country."

"I'm sorry," he said, pacing nervously to the other side of the desk. "Raina, I have to find that man in Leningrad," he went on. "How do I—"

"Pardon me?" she interrupted. "I'm sorry, you must stay on this side, my right ear has not come back."

"Bastards," he said, moving around her. "The refusenik you told me about. How do I find him?"

"His name is Mordechai Stvinov," Raina replied. "He lives on Vasil'yevskiy Island. The shipyards are there. Number Thirty-Seven Denyeka Street."

Andrew took a pad and pencil from the desk.

"No, it's all here," she said, indicating she was typing the information amidst the other sentences. "When will you go to Leningrad?"

"As soon as I can. But I have to get there without a watchdog. They'll know if I fly or take the train. And if I hire a car, they'll stick me with another KGB driver."

"Then drive yourself," Raina suggested. "There are checkpoints along the way, but no schedule. In between, you could take hours or days. They have no way of knowing. They lose track of you, then."

Andrew shook no emphatically. "Intourist is the only place I can rent a car. They'll notify the KGB. They probably *are* the KGB."

"Most of them," she replied. "You'll take my car."

"Your car—can I do that? What happens at the checkpoints?"

"You have an international driver's license?"

"Of course. You know Elspeth. She doesn't miss a trick."

"Good," Raina said. "You could get one here if you didn't, but that would alert them." She stopped typing, rolled the page from the typewriter, and handed it to Andrew. "Give that to Mordechai, and he'll know I sent you. Leave the rest to me."

Andrew broke into a smile.

Yosef had searched the dacha and, not finding them, had gone out the back door to look over the grounds. He was coming back down the corridor when an office door opened.

"I hope you're satisfied, now," Andrew said to Raina sharply as he came through it.

"I apologize for any inconvenience that I—"

"Apology not accepted," Andrew interrupted. He stalked off, leaving Raina standing in the doorway, and blew right past Yosef without acknowledging him.

"Americans," Raina said to Yosef in Russian. "Their business acumen is exceeded only by their arrogance."

"No, by ours," Yosef said slyly, holding her eyes with his.

The desk clerk at the Berlin suggested Melanie take the Metro to the U.S. Embassy. But her New York paranoia surfaced, and she balked until he explained it was a clean, efficient, and safe mode of transport.

She left the hotel, giving her pass to the doorman, and headed for the Metro stop on Karl Marx Prospekt.

A man with a peaked cap exited after her and walked in the same direction. He had no pass, yet went unchallenged by the doorman. Pedestrians knew he wasn't a hotel worker because employees must use a monitored security entrance which discourages pilfering of food and supplies. Indeed, Muscovites know those who leave hotels via the main entrance without surrendering a *propoosk* to the doorman are secret police.

Melanie took the Metro to Tchaikovsky Street, one of the boulevards that make up the Sadovaya Bulvar, the outermost ring of Moscow's spiderweb. The United States Embassy at numbers 19/23 was a few blocks north. Her pace quickened the instant she saw the stars and stripes flying above the neoclassic, nine-story building.

The Marine guard checked Melanie's passport, then unlocked the access gate and directed her to the Citizen Services Section of the Embassy, which deals with Americans traveling or living abroad.

Lucinda Bartlett was the officer on duty. She listened intently as Melanie told her story with emotional fervor, and asked for assistance in contacting the Soviet minister of culture.

"It's all so lovely, so romantic," Lucinda said when she finished. The young woman spoke with a slight sibilance that made her esses whistle, and reminded Melanie of the well-groomed girls who attended Bennington College about twenty miles from where she grew up. "But I'm afraid, the Embassy can't get involved in this," Lucinda concluded.

"Why not?" Melanie asked, baffled. She could see Lucinda was moved by her tale, and thought she had finally found someone who would help her.

"Well, first, yours is a personal matter. The Embassy's role is primarily—bureaucratic. Citizen Services deals with the practical needs of American tourists and businessmen. Second, try to put yourself in the Embassy's position for a moment. Someone claims the Soviet minister of culture is her long lost father, pres-

ents an old photograph and letter, which she says was written to
him forty years ago—a letter *and* envelope without an addressee,
which could have been sent to anyone—and asks for help in
contacting a high government official. You see?" she asked, implying it would make perfect sense even to a child. "You have
no proof whatsoever of what you say. The Embassy can't take
action without it."

"Do I strike *the Embassy* as someone who would make this
up?" Melanie replied indignantly. The American presence had
revived her hope, and this was the last thing she'd expected. "I
didn't come all the way to Moscow to play a game. I'm spending
time, money, and energy to find my father. You have no idea
what I've been through to get this far."

"Oh, I can imagine. And I didn't mean to suggest you were
making it up. I'd like to help you, but you must realize what
your story implies. If I may make an analogy, you're asking the
Embassy to approach a member of the President's Cabinet with
something that could very well turn out to be—rather embarrass-
ing. The Embassy can't afford to get involved unless—"

"The Embassy won't help me contact Minister Deschin?"
Melanie interrupted.

"Not without substantial proof of what you say. And even
then, it won't be as simple as you seem to think. Chances are the
Ambassador himself would have to be consulted. As I said, it's a
highly sensitive matter. I'm sure you can appreciate that."

Melanie nodded grudgingly, and let out a long breath while
she regrouped. "Would it be possible to have copies of those
made here?" she asked, indicating the photo and letter.

"Certainly," Lucinda said a little too brightly. She flipped her
hair back over her shoulder and, turning in her chair to stand,
added, "The Embassy can take care of *that* right away."

"Good. I'd appreciate it if you could give me the address of
the Cultural Ministry, too," Melanie added.

Lucinda paused thoughtfully, and swiveled back to Melanie.
"I don't know what you have in mind, Miss Winslow; but I
advise you to avoid rash or aggressive action. Government buildings and personnel are off-limits, and American citizens abroad
are subject to the laws and judicial procedures of their host coun-

try. If you should be arrested here for some reason, the Embassy could do little to help you.''

''I understand,'' Melanie replied. ''I'm going to send Minister Deschin a letter, and ask him to contact me. There's no law against that, is there?''

''Not that we know of,'' Lucinda replied, pointedly.

The man with the peaked cap was feeding pigeons in a park across the street when Melanie left the Embassy. She returned to the hotel, purchased some stationery at the tourist concession, then hurried to the elevator. The man waited until the floor indicator started moving before taking a seat on the far side of the lobby.

Melanie's room was a tiny space crammed with an eclectic mixture of worn European furniture. She sat on the bed and wrote a letter to Aleksei Deschin. She wrote many of them—in a frustrating effort to explain the situation, and who she was, and what she felt. None satisfied her. She just couldn't get it right. It was late afternoon when she wrote:

Moscow, April 6, 1987
Dear Minister Deschin,
    Though I'm often told I inherited my mother's spirit, I'm afraid I wasn't as fortunate when it came to her gift for expression. So, I will let her words speak for both of us. Suffice to say, I am in Moscow at the Hotel Berlin, and want very, very much to meet you.
Your daughter,
Melanie

She attached the note, and a passport photo of herself to the copies of Sarah's letter and WWII photograph, and addressed the envelope to:

Minister Aleksei Deschin
Ministry of Culture
10 Kuybysheva Street, Moscow

A few minutes later, the man in the peaked cap saw her come from the elevator, and watched as she crossed the lobby and

queued for the postal service window. Then he went to the hotel
manager's office to use the phone.

That afternoon, Valery Gorodin had flown from Rome to Moscow, and went directly to the eight-story brick monolith at No. 2
Dzerzhinsky Square, expecting to meet with Tvardovskiy. But
the KGB chief wasn't there.

Here, as in Rome, the scope of Gorodin's task, and the authority of his sanction, gave him highly coveted "hyphenate"
status. This meant he had on-demand access to KGB personnel,
facilities, and pertinent documents. He knew Tvardovskiy hated
having GRU personnel loose in his domain, and purposely
walked the corridors to maximize the number of sightings.
En route, he observed the place was buzzing with rumors
that something big was happening in the Kremlin, but no one
knew what.

Gorodin settled into an unused office with some briefing
memos. One informed him of Andrew Churcher's departure for
Tersk, the other of the *Kira*'s rescue of Arnsbarger and Lowell.
He was reading the latter when the phone rang.

The man with the peaked cap quickly briefed Gorodin on
Melanie's movements, and latest action.

"Good work," Gorodin replied. "On my way."

The postal queue moved slowly, and it took almost a half hour
for Melanie to advance to the window. The ruddy-faced worker
dropped the envelope onto an old scale, flicking the counter-
weight along the balance arm with a forefinger. "Ten kopeks,"
he said.

Melanie paid, and thanked him. A hopeful feeling came over
her as she crossed the lobby. Not only did she have her father's
name and address, and was in the city where he lived, but at long
last she had taken action to bring them together—action that she
expected would provide knowledge of what her father was like
and deepen her understanding of herself. It was within reach
now, and perhaps soon, she thought, the pain from her failed
marriages would be dulled and the fear of meaningful relationships, along with the loneliness and unhappiness it had
brought, would be over. Indeed, at the age when most women

were coping with college age children, a ding in the Mercedes, and a workaholic husband, she was without parents, siblings, husband, or children of her own. The thought of getting to know her father, and the sense of belonging it promised, had comfort and appeal and, most importantly, might get her life back on a happier course.

The postal worker had affixed the stamps to Melanie's envelope, and was methodically rubbing his coarse thumb over them when the door behind him opened.

Two men entered the small room.

"You're not allowed in here," the postal worker said sternly.

The man with the peaked cap closed the door and stood against it, insuring no one else could enter.

Valery Gorodin took the postal worker aside, presented his GRU identification, and confiscated Melanie's letter.

Chapter Forty

It was an almost balmy morning in Washington, D.C. The reflecting pool on the mall was glass smooth, and the District's notorious humidity was coaxing the cherry trees to blossom.

President Hilliard was at a breakfast meeting in the situation room in the White House basement, with his national security advisor and secretary of state, when informed the Viking S-3A was airborne. He joined DCI Boulton in the Oval Office, where a secure line had been tied in to the laser printer the President used with his word processor. The two men anxiously monitored the exchange of communiqués between ASW Pensacola and the *USS Finback*. Finally, the message they'd been waiting for printed out:

TOP SECRET
FLASH PRIORITY
Z114604ZAPR
FR: USS FINBACK
TO: ASW PENSACOLA
VIKING BLEW UP IN MIDAIR. TWO CREWMEN EJECTED.
TAKEN ABOARD KIRA. FINBACK WILL CONTINUE TRACKING.

The moment was jubilant, but signaled the start of another vigil—Lowell and Arnsbarger's search of the *Kira*. Some pressure had been eased by suspension of the disarmament talks through the upcoming weekend due to the attack on Italy's defense minister. This meant Keating wouldn't have to stall the fast-moving Russians while waiting for word.

He had flown in from Geneva late that afternoon. Now, he and the President were watching the evening network news broadcasts. All three reported that Minister Borsa's condition had improved and he was expected to survive; Italian police still did not know who was responsible for the deaths of the two terrorists; the American woman believed taken hostage with Minister Borsa had not been located.

CBS's Rather paused to take a slip of paper from an aide, then said, "This just in—the man found shot to death with terrorist Dominica Maresca in Piazza dei Siena is now believed to have been a Soviet KGB agent."

Hilliard bolted upright. "Geezus," he said. He scooped up his phone and buzzed Cathleen. "I need the DCI—Good—Yes, immediately." He hung up, raised his brows curiously, and said, "Already on his way."

A file photo of a Viking S-3A on the ABC monitor got the President's attention. He used the remote to mute Rather and Brokaw, and listened to Jennings.

The President had an affinity for the ABC anchor. Years ago, Jennings had been given the job prematurely, then axed, but worked hard as a foreign correspondent, and made it back to the top. Hilliard liked that. He liked people with resilience, and he liked Jennings' thoughtful, urbane handling of international events.

"A U.S. Navy Viking S-3A on a routine flight over the Gulf of Mexico burst into flames and exploded early today," Jennings reported. "Two of the four-man crew were able to bail out prior to the blast. Lt. Commander Keith Arnsbarger and First Lieutenant Jon Lowell were rescued from Gulf waters by an oil tanker that picked up their Mayday. The names of the other two crewmen are being withheld pending notification of next of kin."

"Tough to lose two men," Keating said solemnly.

The President smiled. "We didn't," he said, softly. "We considered concocting a story about a special training mission with a reduced crew, but we wanted it to appear totally routine, and decided against it."

"Jake's people are providing cover?"

Hilliard nodded. "They've put together backgrounds, service records, photos of the 'deceased' fliers, and even a distraught relative or two if we need them. You know, Company people who we've—" He paused at the knock that preceded Boulton's entrance.

"Mr. President, Phil—"

"Jake," Hilliard said. "Been watching the news?"

"Yes, sir, en route."

"And—"

"Confirmed. KGB agent killed in Rome."

"What is Moscow saying?"

"Standard denial," the DCI replied, and anticipating, added, "Company source is irrefutable."

"What's the import of that with regard to Geneva?"

"Salient factors suggest purposeful disruption."

"That's hard to believe, Jake. You know as well as I do, Ka-parov wants this before he kicks the bucket."

"Premier was seen this day—in transit," Boulton said pointedly.

The President's head snapped around. "Kaparov's recovered? We know that for a fact?"

"Negative sir. Passenger obscured. Positive identification of vehicle only."

Hilliard mused for a moment, smoothing his auburn beard. "Phil, you think the Kremlin called the shots on this thing in Italy?"

"No, sir. If they did, Pykonen deserves an Oscar for his performance. He was visibly stunned when he was told. I'm sure he knew nothing about it."

"Prosecution rests," Boulton said slyly.

"Jake's got a point. We have an entire Cabinet, the Secretary of the Navy included, who believe one of our Vikings went down in the Gulf with a faulty engine, killing two men. You know, it seems to me all of this is neither here nor there until we get feedback from our men on the *Kira*. What's your ETA, Jake?"

"Carrier-based chopper will rendezvous with *Kira* at o-seven-thirty. DCI will contact Oval Office immediately upon return to carrier—mid-morning."

"You intend to be aboard?"

"Affirmative. Debriefing of rescued personnel will take place en route to carrier. FYI—the *Kira*'s captain suggested immediate rendezvous, since he isn't making mainland port. But—"

Boulton smiled cagily, "—ASW declined night landing on deck of unfamiliar vessel, insuring our personnel ample recon time frame."

"Sounds like the captain wanted to get rid of them," Keating said. "Like maybe he's got something to hide."

"That's what we're going to find out," the President said.

After confiscating Melanie's letter, Gorodin and the man with the peaked cap—whom he called Pasha, a respectful and affectionate form of the surname Pashkov—dined at Lastochka, where twenty-five years before Pasha had recruited him for GRU. It had since become Gorodin's favorite restaurant in Moscow. At the time, Pasha had taken special interest in the young language expert and a father-son type of relationship had developed. Pasha was semiretired now, and worked primarily as a domestic GRU courier.

Yesterday, when Gorodin called from Rome and said he needed a favor, Pasha asked no questions of his former protégé. Indeed, his surveillance of Melanie Winslow was carried out unofficially, and, along with the confiscated letter, would remain between them.

After dinner, Gorodin declined the lift Pasha offered. Instead, he set his fedora at a jaunty angle and walked along the Moskva. He hadn't worn a hat in years, but resumed the habit, unthinkingly, on returning to Moscow. He strolled the length of the Kremlin wall, across the lumpy cobbles of Red Square, down Twenty-fifth Oktabraya that leads directly to Dzerzhinsky Square and the statue of its namesake, and returned to his office. He was talking with Yosef, who called from Tersk to report on Andrew's activities, when a driver arrived with orders to take Gorodin to the Kremlin.

The chimes in the Spassky Tower were ringing, and the rococo hands of the big clock were moving onto 11 P.M. when Gorodin walked the corridor to the Premier's office, knocked, and entered. Deschin, Tvardovskiy, Pykonen, Chagin, and Admiral Pavel Zharkov, Naval Chief of Staff, were seated around the leather-topped table.

"Ah, Valery!" Deschin said, embracing him. "Too much pasta," he joked, holding his arms in a big circle. Then, turning to the others, he added, "We have Comrade Gorodin to thank for keeping the *Kira* drawings out of American hands. And now, it's up to us, all of us, to see that SLOW BURN is brought to fruition."

"Unfortunately, we've already made mistakes which endanger it," Tvardovskiy said. "First off, Andrew Churcher should have never been allowed into the country."

"He's here for good reason," Deschin snapped.

"Yes, yes, I know," Tvardovskiy said impatiently. "But the plan is unsound. It could backfire!"

"I must respectfully disagree, comrade," Gorodin said. "Your man in Tersk reports Churcher is behaving as anticipated. I assure you the source of the *Kira* documents will soon be exposed, and their threat finally eliminated."

"We'll see," Tvardovskiy said. "In the meantime, what about the Americans aboard the *Kira*? They should have been left to drown like rats!"

"They will be gone by first light!" Zharkov said angrily. "Rublyov made the right decision. You would have caused controversy. Furthermore, the Americans are being watched. And, I have ordered that anyone caught searching the *Kira* is not to leave her alive."

"He's right, Sergei," Deschin said. "Though I must admit my initial reaction was similar to yours. But now that the decisions have been made, what purpose can possibly be served by rehashing them?"

"Obfuscation," Chagin said, eyeing Tvardovskiy accusingly.

"Yes," Pykonen chimed in. "You decry the mistakes of others, Sergei, but forget your own. Everything was going smoothly until this mess in Italy."

"Then you should have taken action to prevent the talks from being suspended," Tvardovskiy retorted.

"Dammit Tvardovskiy!" Pykonen erupted. He was a gentleman, not given to outbursts, and startled them. "Your people erred gravely in this matter! They handed the Americans the very thing we had denied them—time to think, and consult, and question and—agghhh!" He threw up his hands in disgust, then shifted his look to Deschin and, lowering his voice, added, "I did what I could, comrade. But the momentum is gone."

Deschin nodded glumly and flicked a solicitous glare at Tvardovskiy.

"My apologies, comrades," Tvardovskiy said, concealing that the slowdown in the talks more than pleased him. "Point well-taken."

He had no trouble prioritizing. Despite the KGB's global agit-prop and intelligence gathering operations, internal activities take clear precedence. The Service knows its power is centered in the need to keep the 270 million Soviet citizens—spread across nine million square miles in fifteen republics and eleven time zones—suppressed. And suppressing dissatisfaction with the quality of life long sacrificed to cold war militarism is the major task. Tvardovskiy knew nuclear superiority might tempt a new Premier to loosen the economic reins, thereby diminishing the KGB's power; and the educated, worldly Deschin would be more prone than others to do so. He also knew that Deschin's swift stewardship of SLOW BURN would enhance his candidacy in the eyes of the Politburo, and that delays would weaken it.

"Just to be the devil's advocate," Tvardovskiy went on, "perhaps we should back off in Geneva until the situations I noted are rectified."

"I've often pictured you as *his* advocate, Sergei," Deschin replied slyly, "But never advocating retreat." Deschin hadn't thought of the premiership often. But faced with Kaparov's death, he had become acutely aware of his strong position, and knew the game Tvardovskiy was playing. "No, we must think aggressively now," he went on. "We must find a way to regain that momentum."

"Easier said than done, comrade," Zhakrov replied.

"Yes, but Comrade Deschin is right," Gorodin said. This was the first he'd heard of the Premier's poor health. He was quite certain the biographic leverage he held—the recently confiscated proof tucked in his pocket—assured his long sought membership in the elite *nomenklatura*. And his ascendency could only be enhanced by Deschin's. "We must push forward," he went on. "This is no time to embrace defensive strategy."

"Well put," Deschin said. "As our beloved Dmitrievitch would say, 'We must turn adversity to advantage.' And he is the key to it."

The group questioned him with looks, as he expected they would.

"The poor man is but a corpse," Pykonen said compassionately.

"Precisely," Deschin replied. "We'd been keeping him alive to preserve our momentum. Now we will let him die to recapture it. Yes, in memory of our deceased Premier, for whom disarmament was all, we will announce to the world that Dmitri Kaparov's dying words were a plea that the talks be resumed immediately, and that they proceed with renewed vigor and dedication until mankind is at long last free of the threat of nuclear annihilation." He paused, assessing the idea, then nodded with conviction. "Comrades—"

He left the office and slowly walked the long corridor to the Premier's apartment.

Mrs. Kaparov was sitting next to the bed, holding her husband's hand, when Deschin entered. She turned slightly as he leaned, putting his head next to hers, whispering something. The tiny woman nodded sadly, her eyes filled with tears. Deschin straightened, glanced thoughtfully to Kaparov's inert form, then tightened his lips and nodded to the doctor decisively.

She stepped to the cluster of medical equipment.

The sounds of artificial life stopped. The peaks and valleys of vital signs were two straight lines now, the synchronized beep a continuous, mournful tone.

Chapter Forty-one

After being plucked from the sea and brought aboard the *Kira*, Lowell and Arnsbarger had taken steaming hot showers, and exchanged drenched flight gear for denims, sweaters, and sneakers from the ship's stores. Then they joined Captain Rublyov in the communications room, and contacted ASW Pensacola. They reported their rescue, the midair explosion of the Viking S-3A, and the "tragic loss" of two crewmen. After which, Rublyov made his suggestion of immediate pickup; and ASW replied it would be dark before a U.S. Navy search-and-rescue chopper could rendezvous, and postponed it until morning for reasons of safety.

"You're both very lucky," Rublyov said as they came from the communications room and climbed the companionway that led to the bridge.

"Yeah, I know," Arnsbarger replied morosely, feigning sadness over the loss of his fellow crewmen. "Somehow, I don't feel much like celebrating."

When the three reached the landing at the top of the companionway Lowell put one foot up on the railing, the other far out behind him, and began stretching out the muscles in his legs.

"How long is this tub anyway, Captain?" he asked, casting a conspiratorial glance toward Arnsbarger.

"Four hundred forty-five meters is this tub."

"Let's see," Lowell said calculating, "that's about two laps to the mile. Any objections to me wearing a groove in your deck?"

"A groove?" asked Rublyov, not understanding.

"He's a runner," Arnsbarger chimed in.

"Ten-ks, marathons," Lowell added, continuing the pre-run stretching ritual.

"Ah," Rublyov said, catching on, "Not a good idea. The deck is a maze of pumping equipment and hoses. I'd be concerned for your safety."

"Piece of cake compared to my usual route," Lowell replied. "No cars, no attack dogs, no kids with garden hoses." He turned and ran down the steps into the passageway, and kept going.

Arnsbarger shook his head in dismay. "Like somebody once said, every time I get an urge to exercise, I lie down till it goes away."

Rublyov broke into an amused smile. He had no reason to suspect that Lowell's request was part of a plan to search the *Kira*. He'd rather Lowell stayed off the deck, but couldn't object strongly without tipping he had something to hide.

In developing the plan, DCI Boulton and analysts at CIA Headquarters in Langley had deduced that if a Soviet Heron missile was concealed aboard the *Kira,* causing the thousand-ton discrepancy they'd detected, it couldn't be housed astern beneath the bridge and living quarters because the tanker's engine room and fuel tanks were located there. Nor for reasons of safety, when taking on and pumping off crude, would it be amidships surrounded by the five cargo compartments that held 25,000 tons of oil each. If one of those *had* been modified, creating the discrepancy, it would be the forward-most compartment in the bow—far from where they knew Lowell and Arnsbarger would be quartered. Hence, the need for subterfuge to get onto the deck with far-ranging mobility.

Now, Captain Rublyov stood on the bridge, his binoculars trained on the tiny figure almost a quarter of a mile away on the *Kira*'s bow.

Lowell was running laps around the perimeter, between the pipe-and-cable railings and the massive hose fittings used to fill and empty the *Kira*'s compartments of crude. He had worked up a sweat and removed the sweater, tying it around his waist. His long, easy stride, and the fact that he was breathing as easily now as when he started running, confirmed he was a long-distance runner as he'd claimed.

Arnsbarger came up the companionway onto the bridge with a

fresh cup of coffee, joining the captain and first officer. "Still at it, huh?"

"Yes, he's most determined," Rublyov replied.

"Compulsive type. Most TACCOS are."

"Taccos?" Rublyov wondered, taking the bait and lowering the binoculars.

Arnsbarger made the remark to disrupt Rublyov's scrutiny of Lowell. While Arnsbarger discoursed on the personality dynamics of those who can sit at a console and maintain their concentration hour after hour, Lowell was concentrating on the *Kira*'s deck.

Both men had been schooled intensively in the design, layout, and construction details of the tanker. And lap after lap, Lowell methodically swept his eyes across the companionways, bulwarks, hatches, and pumping equipment, searching for something that didn't belong, particularly in the bow area.

Dusk was falling as Lowell finished the last lap. He returned to the bridge and signaled Arnsbarger with a look that he had spotted something. But it was after dinner before they could return to their compartment and talk without being overheard.

Arnsbarger turned on a small fan that was affixed to the bulkhead above his bunk. Then, in case their quarters had been bugged, he bent the housing until the tip of the spinning blade chattered noisily against it.

"Find us some nukes?" Arnsbarger whispered as he settled across from Lowell on the opposite bunk, their faces no more than a foot apart.

"Maybe. I found a hatch up on the starboard side, and a companionway that goes below decks next to it," Lowell replied in equally hushed tones.

"We talking a launching hatch?"

"Dunno. But the deck was cut away to put them in."

"A modification."

"Yeah, the rivets are smaller, and the welds are different than on the rest of the ship. And the pipe railing on the companionway isn't the same either."

"Up in the bow, right?"

Lowell nodded grimly.

"That's a long way from home," Arnsbarger went on. "Even in the dark it'll be hard to get back there without being spotted."

"I know. There's only one way to get on deck from our cabin, and it's right below a lookout station."

"And you can bet Rublyov's got one sharp-eyed Ruskie posted just for us." Arnsbarger thought a moment, then broke into a cagey smile. "Be a shame for that lookout to sit out there in the cold all night with nobody to talk to."

They decided to wait until captain and crew were quartered for the night, and make their move after the 2400 watch change. That meant they'd have four hours to search before *two* crewmen would be on deck again.

"This sure is different," Lowell said. "I mean, I'd give anything to be up there hunting subs right now, instead of down here hiding."

"Decided we're a coupl'a wing nuts, huh?"

"Seriously, you thought about what we're doing?"

"Seriously?" Arnsbarger leveled a thoughtful look at Lowell and nodded. "It scares the hell out of me."

"Good."

"That's what Cissy'd say. She's always telling me it's okay to let my feelings show."

"She's right. What's going on with you two, anyway? You going to make an honest woman out of her?"

"Been thinking about it a lot, but—"

"Come on, come on," Lowell said, knowing what was coming and drawing it out of him. "But it—"

"Scares the hell out of me," Arnsbarger said with a boyish smile. Lowell joined in on the last few words, and they were both still laughing as Arnsbarger reached up and turned off the chattering fan.

Hours later, the air temperature had dropped and a stiff breeze had come up. The seaman on lookout didn't hear Arnsbarger purposely slam the hatch on the landing below and noisily bound down the steps of the companionway. By the time the Russian had spotted him, Arnsbarger was already on deck and moving astern.

Lowell was in the passageway behind the hatch, listening for the lookout and wondering why he hadn't gone after Arnsbarger.

Why hadn't he taken the bait? Lowell had just opened the hatch a crack in an effort to ascertain why the diversion wasn't working, when the seaman suddenly came down from the lookout and hurried after Arnsbarger. Lowell waited until the Russian was out of sight; then quickly, stealthily, he slipped through the hatch, and went down the companionway.

Clouds covered a crescent moon, and the *Kira* was cutting through the Gulf in total darkness as Lowell hurried along the immense main deck. He had never felt so alone. It was eerie and desolate, he thought, like being on a floating steel desert. A cold wind stung his face, and blew his slicker flat against his body as he worked his way between the huge hatches and pumping equipment toward the bow.

Arnsbarger was leaning against the rail near the stern, looking out into the blackness, when the Russian seaman caught up with him.

"Can't sleep?" the lookout asked amiably. He'd been instructed not to challenge the Americans unless they threatened the *Kira*'s security. To do so might raise suspicions that the tanker was something other than her appearance suggested.

"Yeah, I guess I'm still a little uptight," Arnsbarger replied.

"Ah," the Russian said. "I have a bottle of *slivovitz*. You know slivovitz?"

"Nope. Can't say I ever met her."

"Is plum brandy. A few shots and *out* like a bulb of light." Why stand outside in the cold watching for them, the fellow thought, when he could be inside drinking with them. "The bottle's in my cabin."

"Okay, you got it," Arnsbarger replied.

A steady spray was coming over the forecastle when Lowell reached the bow. He leaned into the salty drizzle and soon located the hatch and companionway he'd found earlier; then glancing around uneasily, he started down.

The staircase led below decks to a passageway that went off in two directions. Neither had prominence. Lowell made a quick decision and was just moving off when the sound of boots on steel echoed up ahead. There were no doors, no hiding places in the smooth-walled passageway. He reversed direction and hurried back toward the companionway.

A guard carrying an AK-47 turned a corner. He strode down the passageway at a slow cadence, and paused at the base of the companionway.

Lowell had taken cover in the deeply shadowed well behind it. He was watching the guard through the spaces between the treads, and nervously eyeing the deck where his wet sneakers had left prints.

The stairwell was open to the sky. The guard glanced up longingly, then climbed a half dozen steps stopping inches from Lowell who could reach between the treads and touch him. The guard filled his lungs with the sea air, came back down, and continued his rounds.

The instant he was out of sight, Lowell came out from his hiding place and hurried off in the opposite direction. He soon came to a hatch in the dimly lit passageway, opened it cautiously, and heard the hiss of high-volume filtration used in air locks. An intense glow came from the far end of the L-shaped interface. He crept along the wall to the corner, and peered round it. A window overlooked a brilliantly illuminated clean room beyond.

A Soviet SS-16A Heron missile was suspended in the cavernous space like an immense torpedo.

Lowell was staring right at the business end of the sleek weapon; and despite mission objectives, the discovery startled him. The bulbous graphite nose had been removed, revealing the pointed black cones of the missile's seven warheads. It was like looking into a cup filled with gigantic just-sharpened pencils— each capable of unleashing nuclear destruction.

Banks of lights encircled the rocket's finned titanium skin. The blinding halogens were focused on open access hatches, where components of the guidance and propulsion systems were visible.

Most of the technicians had long retired. But a few, in pale blue coveralls, were still monitoring test equipment. Lowell watched as one of them went along a catwalk to a landing and entered an elevator. The late hour and the fact that many vessels used bow space for crew quarters led Lowell to assume the technician was headed for his cabin—but Lowell was wrong. Missile group quarters were adjacent to, not below, the clean room. Lowell had only seen half the picture.

A numerical keypad on the wall next to the hatch—ostensibly requiring an access code—prevented him from entering the clean room. And he decided to leave before the guard returned.

Arnsbarger was with the Russian in his cabin. The seaman pulled the bottle of slivovitz from a hiding place beneath his bunk, held it aloft triumphantly, and headed out the door.

"Hey, where you going?" Arnsbarger asked.

"What about your friend?"

"Sound asleep," Arnsbarger said, hiding the surge of adrenalin that hit him. "All that jogging knocked the shit out of him. Come on, let's drink that here."

"Maybe he woke up," the Russian insisted, heading down the passageway. Arnsbarger was right behind him.

In the bow, Lowell had eluded the guard, scurried up the companionway, and started the long walk back on the main deck.

Arnsbarger and the Russian had come from crew quarters in the stern, crossed the deck, and climbed the companionway to the guest compartments.

The Russian opened the door and entered, then looked back at Arnsbarger.

"He's not here," he said suspiciously. "I thought you said he was asleep?"

"Guess he must've gone to the head," Arnsbarger bluffed. The bedding was appropriately mussed, but he could see the Russian wondering what, if anything, was going on. "You going to crack that open or hug it?" he asked, trying to keep him from going to look for Lowell. He flipped up the foldaway table and set two cups on it. "There we go," he said, taking the bottle. He pulled the cork, filled the cups with the clear, thin brandy, and offered one to the Russian who shook no warily. He was about to leave the compartment to search for Lowell when the lanky Californian entered from the companionway.

"Here he is," Arnsbarger said, concealing his relief and, using his eyes to warn Lowell, added, "My friend, here, brought us a little nightcap."

"Great," Lowell said as he took off his slicker and dropped it on a hook.

"Does he always wear his slicker to the head?" the Russian asked facetiously.

Arnsbarger forced a chuckle.

"I went for a walk on deck," Lowell replied nonchalantly. He fell on a bunk flicking a nervous look to Arnsbarger, who returned it confirming the Russian was suspicious.

"You have to try some of this," Arnsbarger said, fetching a cup for Lowell.

"Yeah, maybe it'll help me crash."

"Crash?" the Russian wondered.

"Sleep, I haven't been able to get to sleep."

The Russian's eyes widened in alarm. He shifted his look to Arnsbarger. Lowell didn't understand the reaction, but Arnsbarger did. Not fifteen minutes earlier he'd said Lowell was sound asleep. Now, he knew the Russian was thinking about that—thinking that Arnsbarger had lied.

"What do you call this stuff, again?" Arnsbarger asked, trying to bluff past it. "Kivowitz?"

The Russian didn't answer. He had stepped to Lowell's slicker and was running a fingertip through the drops of seawater which told him Lowell had been to the bow—which confirmed his suspicion Arnsbarger's lie was a cover—which meant the Americans were up to no good. He looked at them accusingly, and for a brief instant, all three froze in anticipation. Then the Russian bolted from the cabin and ran down the passageway.

"Shit!" Arnsbarger said. A look of terror flicked between him and Lowell—neither would leave the *Kira* alive if the Russian revealed what he knew.

Arnsbarger grabbed the bottle of slivovitz and shoved it at Lowell. "Hang on to this!" he said as he ran past him into the passageway after the Russian, and, calling back, added, "And go barf on the deck!"

He was thinking, he'd catch the Russian and throw him into the sea. They'd empty the slivovitz, plant the bottle in the lookout station, and return to the cabin. At watch change, the Russian would be reported missing and the bottle and the vomit would be found, leading the captain to assume that he'd been drinking on duty, stumbled to the side to vomit, and fell overboard.

The Russian ran down the companionway onto the main deck. Arnsbarger came out the hatch onto the landing and jumped over the railing onto his back. They both went sprawling across the deck. Arnsbarger got to his feet. The Russian charged into his midsection, driving him backwards into the railing—and over it.

Arnsbarger caught one of the pipe rail posts in the crook of an elbow as he went over. He was dangling high above the sea, clawing at the deck with his other hand to get back up. The Russian slammed a foot into his wrist. Arnsbarger lunged, wrapped an arm around his legs, and tried to yank him into the sea.

The Russian went sliding feet first beneath the steel cable that ran between the pipe rail posts. Both hands grasped it as he went under. He came to an abrupt stop hanging over the side, his arms fully extended, his back against the hull.

The abrupt action had torn Arnsbarger's arm loose from the post. His fingers hooked the edge of the deck, stopping his fall. For an instant, the two hung there side by side, their faces inches apart, glaring at each other. The Russian was just starting to pull himself up when Arnsbarger lost his grip and clawed at him frantically, trying to get a handhold as he fell. His fingers shredded the Russian's shirt and hooked behind his belt. The shock of the sudden stop and the added weight caused the cable to begin cutting into the Russian's hands. He started kicking at Arnsbarger to knock him loose.

Lowell was coming down the companionway with the bottle of liquor when the two went over the side. He ran to the railing, flattened himself on the deck, and reached down past the Russian, groping for Arnsbarger.

Arnsbarger tightened his grasp on the Russian's belt and pulled himself upward. Then, holding his position with one hand, he released the other and reached for Lowell's. Their fingertips inched closer and closer together, finally touching, their hands now tantalizingly close to grasping.

Lowell was about to make a lunge for Arnsbarger's wrist when a few crewmen who had heard the noise arrived next to him.

Arnsbarger's eyes widened when he saw them. There was only one way to prevent the Russian from being rescued or shouting out what he had heard.

Lowell saw Arnsbarger's reaction, and was thinking, *No! Dammit, no!* when Arnsbarger withdrew his hand and making a fist smashed it into the Russian's groin. The seaman bellowed, and let go of the cable.

Lowell watched helplessly as the two men dropped out of sight into the darkness, and into the sea.

Chapter Forty-two

The morning after Melanie mailed the letter to Deschin, she took a map from the Intourist desk in the Berlin's lobby and told herself she was going sight-seeing. Most tourists head directly for Red Square. Melanie made a beeline for Number 10 Kuybysheva Street, but the numeral was nowhere to be found. The street was lined with mundane government buildings. Each had a sign, and indeed, one read Ministry of Culture. But which one? Like all signs in Moscow, they were written in Cyrillic, which bears little resemblance to the Roman alphabet. The few characters that do are unrelated in sound: *B* is pronounced as "V," *E* as "Y," *H* as "N," *P* as "R," *X* as "K," which made communicating next to impossible.

Melanie passed the building a half dozen times before a passerby finally identified it for her. She stared at the severe monolith thinking Deschin was in there somewhere and wondering if her letter had been delivered yet. Chauffeured black Chaikas and Volgas arrived and departed through gates patrolled by Red Army guards, giving rise to hopes that she might glimpse him. But to Melanie's dismay the passengers were always tucked in the corner of the backseat, shrunken into turned-up collars, faces obscured by *borsalinos* and newspapers, as if hiding from someone, or something, she thought. Her hopes swiftly faded.

Aeroflot SU-1247 from Tersk arrived at Vnukovo at 12:56 A.M. The flight was nearly empty, and at that hour, the taxi stand in front of the terminal was deserted. Andrew approached with shoulder bag and carryon. A black Volga sedan—engine running, lights on—was parked a short distance down the arrivals

loop. The driver had no trouble recognizing the rangy young
American. He drove forward and pulled to a stop next to him.
Andrew saw the large letter *T* set against a checkered background
on the door that identified it as a taxi, tossed his bag into the
backseat, and got in.

"Hotel Berlin, please," he said.

The driver grunted and pulled away, heading for the M2 highway. The taxicab's radio was set to MAYAK, Moscow's state
radio station. Shostakovich's fiery Symphony No. 7, written in
1941 during the German siege of Leningrad, overwhelmed the
tiny speaker.

Andrew had spent four days in Tersk. They were extremely
successful ones for Churchco Equestrian. He had filled all his
clients' orders—acquiring the franchise-maker for $825,000—
and purchased breeding stock for his own stable as well. The
stud farm threw a post-auction bash to celebrate forty million
dollars in sales; then Yosef drove Andrew back to Mineral'nye
Vody, where he caught the last flight to Moscow.

The cab was turning off the M2 into the Sadovaya outer ring
road when the symphony suddenly faded. A long silence was
followed by a somber Chopin dirge.

The Chopin better suited Andrew's mood. Despite his success
in Tersk, he was unable to relax and savor it. Raina had left for
Moscow immediately after their "altercation" to make arrangements for his trip to Leningrad. And he was preoccupied with the
upcoming drive, and how he would go about making contact
with refusenik Mordechai Stvinov.

Fifteen minutes later, the taxi had ringed the city, and was
driving south on Zhadanova, approaching the Hotel Berlin, when
the Chopin segued to the score from *Boris Godunov,* Mus-
sorgsky's sorrowful opera.

"Ah," the cabdriver said, nodding as if something he had
been wondering about had just been confirmed. *"Y'hero myortviy oonyevo."*

"Pardon me?" Andrew asked.

"Groosvniy, groosvniy," the driver said, drawing out the
vowels mournfully. He pointed to the radio to indicate he was
referring to the sad tone of the music. *"Kermanska Dmitrievitch
Kaparov myortviy."*

"Your Premier has died?" Andrew asked.

"Da, da, died."

"Oh, I'm sorry," Andrew said, realizing there had been no Russian spoken on the radio, no news report. The sudden change in the nature of music *was* clearly the message. *Odd,* he thought, *in this brusque blue-collar nation, that the government announced the death of the Premier to its workers so gently, in such subtle highbrow fashion.* He decided it went hand in hand with a self-proclaimed godless society living in cities packed with cathedrals and churches—over 150 in Moscow alone.

The cab arrived at the Hotel Berlin. Andrew paid the driver and got out. The cab pulled away. Andrew was putting the change into his wallet when he noticed the slip of paper amongst the rubles the driver had given him. He picked up his *propoosk* from the doorman and hurried into the hotel. The hall attendant was in a chatty mood, and was slow to exchange it for his room key. Once inside, he locked the door, sorted through the currency, and found a note—it outlined when and where Raina would meet him with her car, how to get there, and exactly how to proceed on arriving.

The next morning, Melanie stood in her bathtub in the Hotel Berlin—the plastic flowered curtain pulled around her in a little circle—taking a shower. The water was lukewarm, and came in a limp rain from the old shower head. But she hardly noticed. She was just feeling good—a little anxious perhaps, but very optimistic. She closed her eyes, the water running over her lithe body, and thought about Andrew. He was due back, and she was anxious to tell him about the letter she'd sent to her father. The fact that she wanted to share things with Andrew, and hadn't been able to get him out of her mind the last four days, caused her to start trusting her feelings.

The shower suddenly got hotter. Melanie arched her torso, letting the water wash the soap from her long hair. When finished, she stepped from the tub and wrapped herself in one of the huge bath towels. She was thinking Russian girth must have dictated their size, when she heard the knock. The hall attendant with a message from her father? Could it be *him*? Whoever it was knocked again as she hurried, barefoot, across the worn runner to the door.

"Yes?"

"Melanie? It's Andrew."

Her apprehension turned to elation, as she unlocked the door and opened it.

Andrew stood there for a moment and stared at Melanie, almost as if seeing her for the first time. They had spent barely twelve hours together; tense, hectic ones. And he'd never really just stopped and looked at her. The fresh scrubbed rawness he saw made her all the more appealing to him.

"Good morning," he said with a little smile.

"I agree," she said as he entered and closed the door. He reached to embrace her, and she opened the towel and pressed her naked body against him, enfolding them both in the yards of coarse terry cloth.

Andrew buried his hands in her wet hair, his head filling with the clean scent that made him desire her all the more, and kissed her passionately.

They fell back onto the bed, their hunger for each other surging undeniably now; and soon, his lean body was naked and sliding against hers. She shuddered and arched her tiny frame, her breaths quickening as his tongue gently circled her breast, spiraling toward its center while his fingers, tracing down across the smooth planes of her torso, found the slick wetness they sought. Melanie moaned softly at their touch and dissolved into a sultry liquid haze, surrendering to the overwhelming rush. She felt no compulsion to be in control, no need to suppress her emotions; he was consuming her, and she was pleasureably surprised to learn that she could allow it, indeed enjoy it. He kissed her deeply, then slipped between her thighs, setting off a chorus of blissful sighs. Soon, he had found the slow, rolling rhythm that brought her, achingly, closer and closer. And then, as if suspended in time, they were adrift in the romantic ether until, deliriously inflamed, they were overcome by wave after wave of blinding passion, and lay embracing in the afterglow.

"Hello—" Melanie finally purred, her face radiant. "You free for breakfast?"

"I wish," Andrew whispered in a tone that left no doubt he wasn't.

"Why not?"

He shook his head no mysteriously, and put his finger to her lips. "Let's take a walk," he said softly.

She nodded, and, lingering in his arms for a few moments, told him about the mystifying lack of phone books and copying services, and sending the letter to Deschin. "I thought it was my father at the door when you knocked," she concluded.

"Now I know why you were so disappointed when you saw it was me."

Melanie laughed. "All I could think of was, I'm wearing a towel, and look like a drowned rat."

"A *middle-aged* drowned rat," Andrew teased, covering the strangeness he felt talking about Deschin. He wanted to confide in her, but decided it wasn't necessary; and even if it was, this wasn't the time.

The city was awash with colorless northern light as they came from the hotel and crossed Karl Marx Prospekt to the little park that connects the Moskva and Metropole hotels.

"I'm leaving again," he said.

"For where?"

"Leningrad."

"Business?"

"In a manner of speaking. Better if I don't tell you. You understand?"

"No, but it's okay. When will you be back?"

"I don't know." He paused briefly, thinking if things went well in Leningrad and he got the package of drawings, he'd be on the next flight to Helsinki, and added, "I may not be returning to Moscow."

Melanie's eyes fell in disappointment. They continued walking in silence beneath the cottonwoods. "When do you go?" she finally asked.

He stopped and looked at her, and she saw the answer in his eyes. "We'll see each other again," he said. "Here or back home. We will."

She stared at him vulnerably, and nodded. He kissed her; then backed away and hurried across the grass sprinkled with snowy pookh that fell from the trees.

A park attendant had raked some into a little pile. He tossed a match into it as Andrew passed, and with a *whoosh*, the white mound flashed brightly and vanished into wispy smoke.

The beverage vendor at the north end of the park sold fruit juices, various mineral waters, and kvass. A group of men were gathered around the stand, chatting. Pasha was sipping a large glass of pulpy apricot juice. Gorodin was savoring his first mug of the malty kvass since his return. He turned his back and tilted his head to be certain the fedora concealed him as Andrew hurried past on the far side of the beverage stand. Pasha flicked him a look, and went for a walk in the park where Melanie lingered. Gorodin drained the last drops of kvass, and followed Andrew.

Raina Maiskaya's apartment was in a subdivided eighteenth-century mansion overlooking the Moskva River in southwestern Moscow—a charming quarter that had once been the enclave of the nobility. She pulled her black Zhiguli sedan out of the garage and headed east along the river on Kropotinskya Street.

Raina had purchased a Zhiguli because of its reputation for starting reliably in subzero weather. And it did. The "Zhig" had only one problem as far as Raina was concerned—it was black, and had a funereal quality; every speck of dirt showed, and she hated it. But today black would have its uses.

Raina drove with one eye on the road, the other on the rearview mirror. She worked her way across Kalinin Prospect and into central Moscow's streets that were always crowded with vehicles at this hour, mostly black ones. And she knew the congestion of fast-moving Volgas, Moskviches, and Zhigulis would make hers inconspicuous and difficult to follow.

But Raina couldn't see the gray panel truck that had been parked around the corner, nor the KGB driver, expert in such matters, who waited until the Zhiguli was well underway before following.

As Raina had outlined, Andrew left the park, walked through the Alexandrov Gardens that parallel the west Kremlin wall, and past Trinity Gate to the main Metro station next to the Lenin Library on the corner of Frunze. The platforms beneath the barrel-vaulted ceilings and crystal chandeliers were crowded with early morning commuters—one of whom was Gorodin.

Andrew deciphered the color-coded legend, found the Kirov-Frunze line, and took it four stops to Komosomol Square. The immense plaza northeast of the outer ring is bordered by three major railway stations, the Leningrad Hotel, international post office, and acres of parking lots. Andrew rode the escalator from the Metro platform to street level. It was Saturday, and the square was a frenzied bustle of vehicles and pedestrians. Gorodin tailed him to the parking lot east of the Kazan Station, and watched from a distance as Andrew made his way between the tightly spaced cars, counting the aisles as he walked.

Raina's Zhiguli was parked in one of the spots in aisle seven of the crowded lot. She was sitting behind the wheel, and watched Andrew approach and walk past. She waited briefly to see if anyone was following him before pulling out. Andrew heard the car approaching from behind, but kept walking until it came to a fast stop next to him. Raina popped the driver's door, and slid across to the passenger seat. Andrew quickly slipped behind the wheel and pulled the door closed.

"Hi. Where do I—go?" Andrew asked, a little taken aback when he saw her. The European high fashion had given way to plain, almost mannish, clothing, and for an instant he wasn't even sure it was her.

"Circle the lot and make a right into the square," Raina replied, and, seeing his expression, explained, "I thought it best to play down the change of drivers—just in case." She opened the glove box and removed some documents. "I need your driver's license."

"In my wallet," he replied, indicating his shoulder bag on the seat between them.

Raina found Andrew's international license and affixed an official Russian insert. "Now you are a legal driver," she said; then referring to the other documents, added, "Vehicle registration, ownership papers, route map, *and* your Intourist itinerary."

"Where'd you get it?" he asked as he swung the Zhiguli into the busy square.

"Intourist, where else?" She replied smugly.

"What happens if the police check it out?"

"Nothing," she replied suddenly serious.

"You really got it from Intourist, didn't you?" he said, realizing she meant it.

She nodded, her face coming alive with delight. "Bureaucracies," she said. "Somehow the copy to be filed with KGB has been—misplaced."

"I won't ask," he said grinning.

The Zhiguli exited the parking lot, passing within twenty feet of Gorodin who was now watching from inside the gray panel truck that had parked across the street.

Raina pointed to the Yaroslavl Railway Station on the left side of Komosomol Square. "Pull in there," she said. "You're a friend dropping me at the train."

Andrew angled toward the center lane, and pulled into a designated passenger unloading zone.

"Good luck," Raina said. "Say hello to Mordechai for me." She smiled, then got out and walked off in her long, confident stride.

Andrew watched her until she had disappeared into the crowds pouring into the station, then drove off.

The gray panel truck waited until the Zhiguli was moving into traffic, then followed.

Melanie was sitting at a table in a little café in the Moskva Hotel, just off the park. Andrew's departure had left her feeling blue. The cafeteria was crowded and lively, and being around people bolstered her. The Turkish coffee was strong and bracing; the *bleenis* with honey and sugar were vaguely reminiscent of crepes, but much heavier, and she didn't finish them.

Pasha had another glass of juice.

Melanie headed back through the park, thinking about how she would spend the day, and made her way alongside the Historical Museum into Red Square.

The domes atop the patterned turrets of St. Basil's Cathedral sent pointed shadows across the cobblestones toward her. A solemn queue of Muscovites started at Lenin's Tomb and snaked the length of the Square to the east corner of the Kremlin Wall. The two uniformed sentries posted at the entrance had been joined by a contingent of Red Guard soldiers. The flinty-eyed, pale-skinned young men were stationed at intervals along barricades that paralleled the queue.

One of the stocky babushkas sweeping the cobblestones saw Melanie taking it all in. "Tourist?" she asked in a heavy accent.

"Yes, I'm an American," Melanie said, not knowing what to expect.

"Ah, I saw you looking," she said. "It is always a sad day when a Premier dies."

"Oh—I didn't know," Melanie replied. "What's going on over there?" She pointed to a cluster of VIP Chaikas next to the mausoleum that were ringed by a second contingent of Red Army sentries.

"Those are the Politburo's cars," the old woman said proudly. "They are paying their respects today."

"The Politburo is in there right now?" Melanie asked, suddenly coming alive.

The woman found Melanie's enthusiasm amusing, and broke into a gap-toothed smile. "Politburo, yes."

"All the ministers are in there?"

"Yes. It is traditional. They comfort the Premier's family from the noon hour to three."

"So, if I got in line I could see them."

"Yes. That's what they're all doing," she said. "We mourn our beloved Dmitrievitch, but we queue to see the Politburo. On May Day they are but specks high above Lenin's Tomb. Today they'll be as close as he." She inclined her head toward one of the Red Army guards who was standing nearby.

"Thanks," Melanie replied brightly. She hurried off past the line of mourners, turned the corner, and stopped suddenly. The queue extended along the Kremlin Wall as far as she could see.

The Moscow-Leningrad Highway is a two-lane blacktop that stretches 391 miles between Russia's major cities. Andrew drove the Zhiguli onto the flat plains north of Moscow that fell into rolling valleys, then across the stilted causeway that spans the Volga, past endless miles of stunted flax, and through the dozens of drab towns that dotted the route—all beneath the vigilant eyes of the state police, whose intimidating observation posts cropped up at precise thirty-mile intervals.

Andrew had made swift progress through the gamut of checkpoints where his passport and the documents Raina had provided received routine inspection. It was mid-afternoon when the Zhiguli left the low stucco buildings of Novogorod behind. Leningrad was seventy-five easy miles north. Andrew was thinking he'd be there before dark when he saw State Police Headquarters looming atop a rise up ahead. Dozens of garish yellow cars slashed with broad blue stripes were lined up outside the sprawling complex.

Andrew slowed as he approached a line of concrete-block-and-glass kiosks that paraded across the highway.

One of the jackbooted policemen manning the checkpoint waved his billy club, gesturing he pull over.

Andrew parked in the designated inspection lane, where other policemen leaned to the windows of vehicles, questioning the drivers.

The policeman's dark blue greatcoat flowed behind him like a cape as he strutted toward the Zhiguli. He glowered at Andrew through the window, prompting him to lower it faster.

"Gdye vi vadeet mashinoo?"

"I'm going to Leningrad," Andrew replied, realizing this was perhaps the tenth time he'd been stopped, and the tenth time a policeman asked exactly that question in exactly that tone, without a hello, or greeting of any kind. They were robots, he thought, knowing the next question would be in English, and would be—

"Why?"

"I'm a tourist."

"Passport, driver's license, and Intourist travel plan," the policeman said. He noticed Andrew had the documents ready, and snatched them from his hand. He examined each methodically, more than did previous inspectors, Andrew noted. Then retaining them, the policeman circled the Zhiguli, sweeping his eyes over it, pausing briefly to study the license plate.

"This isn't an Intourist car," he said in an incriminating tone as he returned to Andrew.

"Yes, I know," Andrew replied, trying to conceal his nervousness. "A friend loaned it to me. I have the ownership papers here."

The policeman gave them a cursory inspection, and nodded, satisfied. "Do you know how far Leningrad is from Moscow?" he asked.

"Yes, about four hundred miles."

"Six hundred and twenty-four kilometers."

"Okay," Andrew said, mollifying him.

"It is illegal for a tourist to drive more than five hundred kilometers in a single day," the policeman noted pointedly.

"It is?" Andrew replied surprised, his mind quickly calculating. He'd already exceeded the limit—not by very much—but he had exceeded it.

"You're not aware of this law?"

"No, no, I'm not, really."

"Intourist Travel Service didn't inform you of it when you picked up your itinerary?"

"No, they didn't," he said, concerned he would say something that would reveal he'd never been there.

"Here, as in your country, ignorance of the law is no excuse for breaking it. Get out of the car, please."

Andrew was tempted to argue, but did as ordered.

The gray panel truck was approaching in the distance as the policeman led him inside the main building. He ushered Andrew to a windowless room—ten feet square, unpainted concrete block, a single chair, small table, and mirror—and left him there.

A few moments later, a large woman wearing a red arm band entered. She had short-cropped hair, a pig-eyed countenance, and stocky, hard-packed torso that strained the belts that girdled her black uniform.

Andrew took note of her abundant facial hair. *I'm going to the mat with an Olympic shot-putter*, he thought.

"Do you have any drugs?" she asked suddenly, in a Kissinger-like rumble.

"No," Andrew replied, annoyed with himself that she'd caught him off guard, and he sounded defensive.

"A gun?"

"Of course not."

She studied him for a moment, then dumped the contents of his shoulder bag onto the table, and sifted through them. She picked up his wallet and began peeking into the various pockets.

Andrew's heart raced as she removed an assortment of receipts. The typed page that contained Stvinov's name and address was concealed among them—just another piece of paper among many, he had reasoned. Now, it was literally in the hands of the enemy.

The policewoman paused, scrutinizing some of the receipts, but to Andrew's relief she shuffled past the folded page, and returned the receipts to his wallet. "So, no gun," she said with a disarming smile as she scooped everything back into the bag. "Don't you believe your government's stories about the evil Soviet empire? Aren't you afraid?" she asked, sounding as if she didn't believe them either.

"No," he replied, thinking her self-deprecating tone meant he was off the hook, and started to relax. "I find people here are very helpful and friendly."

"Good. Remove your clothes," she ordered.

He almost gulped out loud. "Pardon me?" he asked, his voice cracking. "I mean is that really—"

"Take them off," she interrupted. She folded her arms and watched, like a stolid Buddha, until Andrew was standing in front of her barefoot, in his shorts.

She gestured brusquely that he was to remove them.

Andrew winced, stepped out of the shorts gingerly, and stood with his hands folded in front of him, feeling degraded and vulnerable as she intended.

"Turn, and spread your legs," she said sharply.

Andrew shuffled his feet on the cold floor and separated them apprehensively. He was looking directly into the mirror now, and the humiliated face that stared back confirmed what he was feeling.

"More," she said, slapping the inside of his legs until Andrew responded. Then she bent, and reached up between his thighs and grabbed his scrotum, handling it roughly as if looking for something concealed inside.

"Bend over."

Andrew flinched at the squeek and snap of surgical rubber behind him, and hesitated. His heart pounded in his chest. "Look, I don't know what you think I—"

"Bend!" she shouted. She grabbed the back of his neck and forced him to bend at the waist, then crouched behind him. She grasped his buttocks with her thick fingers, and spread them wide, hard, hurting him.

"You have drugs?"

"No. I told you before that I—" he yelped as she stabbed a gloved forefinger up inside him.

In the adjacent room, Gorodin turned away from the one-way mirror. "You think he's convinced?" he asked the policeman who had flagged Andrew down.

"I can't imagine he'll think he's having too easy a time of it after that," the policeman snickered.

"If he does," Gorodin said slyly, "I'm sure the notion will be dispelled by morning." He glanced back to the one-way mirror.

Andrew was dressing—in record time. When he finished, the pig-eyed policewoman grasped his arm tightly, led him from the room, and down a corridor lined with detention cells.

He wanted to protest that his rights were being violated, and demand to talk to someone at the U.S. Embassy; but he knew that would end his mission.

She opened one of the solid steel doors and shoved him through it. He stumbled forward into the cell, kept his balance, and turned to the door as it clanged shut, shouting, "Hey?! Hey, how long am I going to be in this—" He let the sentence trail off when he saw the other prisoner—a slight young man with matted hair, and pale, gaunt face—huddled in a corner, trying to keep warm.

His forehead and right cheek were badly bruised; he had a cut across the bridge of his prominent nose; and one of his eyeglass lenses had been shattered.

Andrew saw the fear in his eyes—then he felt his own.

Chapter Forty-three

Lieutenant Jon Lowell stood at the *Kira*'s rail with the bottle of slivovitz, staring blankly into the dark sea, envisioning Arnsbarger drowning. The incident had traumatized Lowell, and he was frozen to the spot. The crewmen who had joined him on deck were shouting "Men overboard! Men overboard!" in Russian, and were dashing to life preservers and searchlights.

Rublyov arrived on the run, joining the group at the rail. "What has happened here?" he demanded.

Lowell stared at him blankly for a long moment, then held up the half-empty bottle, and blurted, "One of your men brought this to our cabin—wanted to share it. He and Arnsbarger got into it pretty good—got into politics—into an argument—I tried to stop them—shoved me aside—went outside to settle it. They went over just as I got here. I tried, I—" He groaned, and threw up his hands in frustration.

Though the story was a fabrication, the emotions were real, and Lowell knew they gave it veracity.

Rublyov nodded pensively, examining the bottle. He knew seamen kept their private stock concealed, which meant the only way Lowell could have acquired it was as he said. He glanced to the others solicitously.

"He was trying to help them back up when we got here," one replied in Russian.

"They fell before we could do anything," said another. The rest nodded in silent confirmation.

Lowell had no idea what they were saying. His eyes flicked between them apprehensively. He concealed his relief when Rublyov said, "I'm sorry, Lieutenant. These things happen."

The *Kira* circled the area for more than an hour, her crew sweeping the powerful searchlights over the choppy waters.

Finally, Rublyov ordered, "Abandon search, resume course."

"What do you mean?" Lowell replied. "They've got to be out there somewhere." He protested because he thought it was expected. But all along he knew they wouldn't be found. He knew Arnsbarger would never let that Russian seaman get to the surface to be rescued.

Thirty-six hours had passed since the *Finback* contacted ASW Pensacola, and confirmed the *Kira*'s destination as the Gulf of Mexico. At the time, the *USS Carl Vinson,* a Nimitz-class aircraft carrier, was in the Caribbean off the coast of Nicaragua, 530 miles southwest of the sub's position in the Yucatan Channel. Under ASW direction, the carrier changed course and steamed north toward the Gulf at thirty knots—more than ten knots faster than the *Kira*'s top speed—and was now 175 miles off the supertanker's stern.

The *Kira* had maintained its heading for Gulf oil fields, and was 615 miles southwest of Pensacola, as expected—well out of range for land-based helicopter rendezvous, hence the need for carrier interface.

One of the *Vinson*'s radar operators was tracking the *Kira* on the SPS-10/surface system. The other had the long-range SPS-48/air locked on to a U.S. Navy F-14A Tomcat. The Grumman swing wing fighter had taken off from Pensacola forty-seven minutes earlier, at exactly 5:00 A.M., and now was eighty miles starboard of the carrier, streaking through the darkness at 910 mph.

"Five-thirty to touchdown," the flight officer announced.

DCI Jake Boulton throttled back the Tomcat's twin turbofans. The computerized flight control system automatically adjusted the wing sweep to cruise mode. Boulton radioed the *Vinson*, and got an immediate CTL from Primary Flight Control. He lowered the F-14A's flaps, and minutes later he had the "meatball" in the center lens, and the nose on the line of blue chasers strobing in the darkness far below, and the Tomcat was in the groove. The screaming fighter came over the fantail at a steep angle, lights flaring in the mist, and slammed into the carrier's deck at 140 mph. The tail hook caught the second arrester cable, and the Tomcat jerked to a dead stop, 1.3 seconds after her wheels first ticked the rubber-streaked armor.

The air boss nodded, impressed. "Whoever's on that stick knows his stuff."

Only three people aboard the *Vinson* knew the pilot's identity, and why the carrier had been redeployed: the captain; the communications officer, who received the ASW directive with Langley's cryptonym KUBARK; and, as the directive specified, the "best chopper pilot aboard."

The time was 6:07 A.M. when Boulton popped the Tomcat's canopy.

"Nice flying, sir," the flight officer said.

"Thanks. Like to keep my hand in," Boulton replied, snapping off a salute. He climbed down the ladder that the greensweatered handling crew had just hooked onto the cockpit, and sprinted across the flight deck to a waiting helicopter.

The rotors of the Navy Sikorsky SH-3H *Sea King* were already whirling as Boulton went up the steps. A crewman pulled the door closed after him. The *whomp* accelerated to a crisp *whisk*. The twenty-thousand-pound chopper lifted her tail, then rose at a sideways angle into the first rays of daylight.

An hour and seventeen minutes later, the sun had crept over the horizon, and the *Sea King* was starboard of the *Kira*, and closing fast.

"Target dead ahead, sir," the pilot reported.

"Captain said you were his top gun," Boulton said.

"Captain never lies, sir," the pilot said, smiling.

"Let's find out."

The pilot put the *Sea King* into a sweeping turn and came astern of the tanker, making his approach from behind and above the broad superstructure. This put the expanse of deck, and one-hundred-eighty degrees of unencumbered sky in front of the chopper should an abort be necessary. Then, hovering forward of the bridge, the pilot picked a spot on the cluttered deck and started the precarious descent.

One of the *Kira*'s crewmen ran toward the area. He guided the pilot between the hose booms that cantilevered above the deck, and made certain the landing gear avoided the array of pumps and fittings below.

Rublyov and Lowell stood below the bridge, watching. The latter had returned the borrowed clothing and was wearing his Navy flight suit now. The instant the *Sea King* touched down, Lowell shook Rublyov's hand, shouted a farewell over the *whomp* of the rotors, and dashed in a crouch toward the chopper, carrying a duffel bag that contained Arnsbarger's flight gear.

Rublyov winced as he watched Lowell go. He'd been up half the night searching for a way to keep the American from leaving the *Kira*. The first officer suggested they simply throw him overboard; but the US Navy had already been notified that *two* men had been safely plucked from Gulf waters. Arnsbarger's death would be a delicate enough matter to handle. Rublyov also considered charging Lowell with the murder of the Russian seaman, locking him in the *Kira*'s brig, and refusing to release him to American personnel when they arrived. But such action would firmly focus global attention on the *Kira*, threatening her mission, and if that happened, Rublyov faced the possibility of disgrace and disciplinary action. He decided letting Lowell go was the lesser of all evils, and took it.

Boulton swung a baffled look to Lowell as he climbed aboard. "Scenario indicated two men," he said.

Lowell shook his head from side to side, grimly.

Boulton stared at him for a long moment, nodded to the pilot, and the chopper lifted off.

When airborne, Lowell briefed the DCI in detail on his discovery of the *Heron* missile and clean room in the *Kira*'s bow, the events that led to Arnsbarger's death, and the tense, uncertain moments that followed. "I still can't believe it, sir," Lowell concluded. "We were home free. I should've ditched that damn slicker. Arnsbarger'd be alive if I had. I blew it."

"And he'd confirm that?" Boulton asked flatly already knowing the answer.

Lowell let out a long breath. "Probably not."

Boulton put a compassionate hand on Lowell's shoulder, and the two of them sat listening to the whomp of the chopper's rotors for a long moment.

"Man's a hero," Boulton said finally.

"Yes, sir."

"Candidate for a CMH—" Boulton went on, letting Lowell nod, before adding "—save for covert scenario."

Lowell sensed Boulton's thrust, now. "What *will* go on his record, sir?" he asked.

"What you and Captain Rublyov report."

Lowell nodded thoughtfully. "The Captain's already written his, sir. Did it all by the book. Covered his ass right away." Lowell took a folded, pale green form out of a pocket in his flight suit. "International Maritime Certificate of Death at Sea— Next of Kin Copy," he said. He caught Boulton's eye, and added, "It says Captain Arnsbarger died in a drunken brawl with a Russian seaman."

The DCI nodded crisply.

Lowell's eyes widened in protest.

"Your report must coincide, Lieutenant," Boulton said pointedly. "Must. You understand?"

Lowell tightened his lips and nodded glumly.

President Hilliard stood next to the window in the oval office reading a letter that was typed on Kremlin stationery and bore the chairman's seal. It had been delivered to the U.S. Embassy in Moscow following the official announcement of Kaparov's death, and forwarded immediately by diplomatic courier to the White House.

The President finished reading, and handed it to Keating who was sitting on the edge of the desk. "You're not going to like it," he said.

The intercom buzzed.

Hilliard scooped up the phone. It was Boulton calling from the carrier in the Gulf.

"Jake?" he said, dropping into his desk chair.

"Morning sir."

"Morning," the President echoed. "I don't believe I heard the modifier I was hoping for—"

"Not applicable, sir," Boulton replied grimly. He and Lowell were in a secure compartment adjacent to the *Vinson*'s main communication's room. "Reconnaissance confirms Heron missile aboard *Kira*," the DCI went on.

"Damn—" Hilliard replied, taking a few seconds to digest it. "One?"

"One."

"Deployed for launch?"

"Negative. Missile in assembly, not launch, mode.

"Conclusion?"

"Destination Nicaragua."

"There's a Soviet missile base there and we missed it? Is that what you're telling me?"

"Affirmative. Potential exists."

"How? They take up baseball?!" Hilliard exploded.

"I don't know sir."

"Do they know that we know?"

"Negative. Cover was threatened but maintained."

"Good. Now we need verification. Something solid that Phil can present in Geneva. And I don't care what it takes to get it, Ferrets, SR-71s, clandestine recon, bribery, torture. Just get it fast."

"Flash priority, sir."

"Faster than that, Jake," the President said sharply. "The Kremlin's just turned up the heat." He swiveled to Keating and held out a hand.

Keating put Deschin's letter in it and made an expression to let the President know it concerned him.

"Give me a rundown on their minister of culture," the President asked, turning back to the phone.

"Aleksei Deschin—Politburo member since 1973, very close to Kaparpov, wields unusual power for non-strategic minister due to said relationship, war hero, educated in the West, shrewd, cunning, sharp as they come," Boulton recited, adding, "Evaluation is first hand. Subject served as DCI's key OSS/partisan contact in European Theater WWII."

"You think he's in line for the top job?"

"Negative. Per our evaluation, candidates are: Tikhonov, Dobrynin, and Yeletsev, who's a long shot."

"Front runners?"

"Tikhonov, now. Yeletsev later."

"Then why the hell is *Deschin* the one sending me cables urging that in memory of dear departed Dmitri, and out of respect for our mutual goal of disarmament, we accelerate the pace of the talks?!"

"Don't know, sir. His involvement creates heightened suspicion of duplicity."

"Great. This is very frustrating, Jake. The guy is pushing for an immediate blanket endorsement of the Pykonen Proposal. He's giving me exactly what I want and I can't take it because we don't have a fix on this damned Heron. We can't tread water forever, Jake."

"Agreed. Experience suggests Kremlin will media-leak Deschin's letter to create pressure."

"The question is, how do I stall without appearing to be placing obstacles in the way of disarmament? Without losing what I want?! They've got *us* on the 'qui vive,' when it should be the other way around! I mean—" He noticed Keating signaling him and paused. "Hold on a sec? Phil's waving at me like a matador." He covered the phone and glanced to Keating. "Shoot."

"I have an idea that'll buy us some time."

"Can't entrap another spy, Phil," the President warned. "We used that excuse last time. And we sure as hell can't clean house at the U.N. again."

Keating shook no. "None of the above, but I know it'll work."

"Hang onto it," Hilliard replied brightening, and turned back to the phone. "Jake? We'll carry the ball in Geneva. Nicaragua's all yours. Oh—please convey my admiration and thanks to those two brave men."

"To one, sir. Second was lost at sea. I'm sorry."

The President sagged. "So am I, Jake," he said solemnly. "Thanks." He hung up, stood and looked out the window taking a moment to collect himself, then turned to Keating.

"I hope you have a brainstorm for me, Phil."

"What am I bid for '*the* potential stumbling block to the smooth progression of the talks'?"

Hilliard brightened, sensing where he was headed. "The one with a slight German accent?"

Keating nodded and grinned.

Chapter Forty-four

The queue for Lenin's Tomb moved—as Muscovites say—"slower than the frozen Moskva."

Melanie had been inching forward for well over two hours, concerned that the Politburo members would be gone by the time she got inside. Finally, she walked between the two Red Army guards flanking the bronze doors at Sentry Post Number 1 and entered the vestibule. The line turned left and down a flight of granite steps that led to the feldspar-walled viewing chamber.

The queue entered the severe space from behind the catafalque, which was centered on a black marble platform where the official mourners were seated. The Premier's angular coffin lay open and tilted slightly to afford a better view of its occupant. The line circled six deep along a marble railing that ringed the platform.

At first, Melanie's view of the official group was obscured by the blankets of flowers that covered the base of the catafalque. Gradually her sight line moved around it, and one by one, the weighted faces came into view: Gromyko, impassive with button eyes; Tikhonov, austere and openly presumptuous; Dobrynin, a kindly grandfather's countenance; Yeletsev, affable, with a trace of impatience; Tvardovskiy, bellicose and clearly bored; Mrs. Kaparov; and then—Deschin.

Melanie's heart rate soared at the sight of him. The resemblance *was* strong, she thought; and he still had the pride and quiet intelligence she had seen in her mother's photograph. The line seemed to be moving much too fast now. Melanie kept hanging back, fighting to hold her place along the marble railing. Others in the line bumped and shoved her as they passed, their eyes riveted on the Politburo's hardened faces rather than the waxen countenance of their deceased Premier.

Pasha, who was a short distance behind, became concerned and left the queue.

Melanie was trying to catch Deschin's eye when she felt a hard poke atop her shoulder. She turned to see one of the Red Army guards towering above her.

"Move along, madam" he hissed in Russian, using several sharp jerks of his head for emphasis.

Melanie nodded that she'd comply, and stole a last glance at the official mourners. The guard's arrival had attracted some attention. Deschin was looking right at her. She locked her eyes onto his, and broke into a hopeful smile. It had been four days since she mailed the letter. Certainly, he'd received it, and would recognize her from the picture she included. She stood her ground against the guard's presence, waiting for Deschin to acknowledge her—a smile, a nod, a signal of some kind that would indicate he was reaching out—but it never came. There wasn't the slightest glimmer of acceptance in his eyes, only contempt for the disturbance she had caused.

The guard's fist tightened around her arm. He directed her out of the line forcefully, and ushered her aside to an alcove where Pasha was waiting.

"Why didn't you keep moving?" Pasha demanded as the guard moved off. He wore a black raincoat and the peaked cap; and his eyes were veiled by green-tinted prescription lenses. He spoke in Russian at low volume but with an intensity that frightened her.

"I'm sorry," Melanie said. "I don't understand."

"Passport," he said in English, condescendingly.

Melanie took it from her bag and handed it to him.

Pasha's eyes flicked from her face to the photo. Then he removed a black leather notebook from his coat.

"Oh, and my visa," she said, assuming he was KGB, and would relent on seeing the green seal.

"Your name and passport number are sufficient," Pasha replied, copying the information in bold strokes.

"Where are you staying?"

"Hotel Berlin."

Pasha noted it. "We don't tolerate public disturbances," he said. "Do you understand?"

"I'm sorry. I didn't realize that I had—"

"Do you understand?" he interrupted.

"Yes, I do."

He nodded crisply and returned her passport. "You're not a Soviet citizen, so I won't detain you, now. But this will be reported," Pasha threatened. "My superiors will decide if you should be arrested and charged with hooliganism. I suggest you avoid such behavior in the meantime." He directed her to a side door, pushed it open, and gestured she leave.

Melanie hurried into the narrow alley that was shrouded in late afternoon darkness. She followed it back to Red Square, frightened by Pasha's threat, and depressed over what had happened with Deschin. Maybe he wanted to acknowledge her, she thought, but couldn't, under the circumstances. Then again, maybe he *hadn't* gotten the letter, and assumed she was a troublesome Muscovite. Either way, he was her father, and his disdainful glare made her feel small and rejected.

Spring hadn't come yet to the barren plains three hundred miles north of Moscow. The temperature in the concrete cell had plunged along with the sun.

Andrew's fear had given way to a preoccupation with keeping warm. "When do they turn on the heat in this place?" he asked his bruised cellmate, who had introduced himself in English as Viktor, explaining he once taught languages in an elementary school.

"Wait," Viktor replied with a knowing smile, "we still have warmth from the lights. They're turned off exactly ten minutes after dinner, and then—" He was interrupted by the sound of the door being unlocked.

It was the pig-eyed guard. She threw two mattresses and two blankets into the cell, and slammed the door.

Viktor kicked the bedding across the cell in disgust. "They did this because you're here," he said. "They don't want you to go back to your country and tell of our barbaric jails."

"Incredible," Andrew muttered, amazed that they thought

he'd consider the threadbare blankets and thin, lumpy mattresses a humanitarian gesture.

"What are you doing here, anyway?" Viktor wondered as they arranged the bedding on the floor. "I thought Americans vacationed in Disneyland and Las Vegas."

"Business," Andrew replied with an amused smile. "I decided to stay and visit Leningrad. I hear it's really beautiful."

"Yes, yes, it is," Viktor said wistfully. "How did you end up in here?"

"They got me on a driving technicality. What about you?" he asked, stealing a glance at Viktor's bruises.

"I'm what they call a dissident."

"You mean you don't agree with the way the government's running things."

"No, no," Viktor replied, amused at the thought. "The entire population would be branded dissidents if that were the case. No, Andrew, the difference is, I want to do something about it. And that is where they draw the line. They can't allow organized opposition. You see," he went on, lowering his voice, "we have a network—we duplicate and distribute literature; we hide political criminals; we help people who want to leave." He removed his shattered glasses and rubbed the cut on his nose. "They wanted me to name refuseniks who are in our group—Jews who wish to emigrate and have been turned down," he added in explanation.

"Yes, I know—about them," Andrew said, catching himself in midsentence. He empathized with Viktor and was inclined to confide in him. He almost said "Yes, I know a refusenik in Leningrad." But he remembered his warning to Melanie, and it gave him pause. "For what it's worth," he went on, "your cause has a lot of support in the West."

"So I've heard," Viktor said in a subdued tone. He glanced at Andrew obliquely, deciding something. "I know I have no right to ask this, Andrew," he said uncomfortably, "but my family is in Leningrad, and my wife doesn't know I've been arrested. Perhaps you could get a message to her for me when you arrive?"

"Gee, I don't know," Andrew replied, taken by surprise. "I'm in enough hot water as it is."

"Just a phone call," Viktor pleaded. "I'll give you the location of a safe public box. You say, Viktor is in Novogorod

Prison, and hang up. That's all. My Lidiya's English is much better than mine," he added with husbandly pride.

Andrew thought about it for a moment. He heard the desperation in Viktor's voice, and felt guilty for hesitating. "Okay—If I ever get out of here."

"Don't worry," Viktor said. "Traffic violations aren't that serious. You will soon be—" He was interrupted by a metallic clunk as a guard slid back the hatch that covered the slot in the steel door.

Viktor leaped up and took the two bowls the guard pushed through. The soup was lukewarm at best; but the air was so cold that wisps of steam rose from the oily surface. Two chunks of bread came through the slot and bounced on the floor.

Andrew picked them up.

Viktor gave a bowl to Andrew, grabbed a piece of bread, and settled on the mattress scooping the soup into his eager mouth.

Andrew plopped opposite him, and stared at his bowl glumly, sickened at the odor of boiled cabbage. Of the few foods he disliked, boiled cabbage was the one he detested. It literally made him gag.

"Eat," Viktor said, gesturing to the lights to remind him. "It's hard to eat soup in the dark."

Andrew tried a spoonful and made a face.

Viktor chuckled. "*Now* you are in hot water."

Andrew avoided the bits of chopped cabbage, and sipped the broth slowly. Each spoonful made him shudder, and left grit on his teeth. Mercifully, he thought, the lights went out well before he could finish.

They sat in the darkness and talked into the night, finally falling asleep on the lumpy mattresses.

Andrew tossed and turned fitfully. It seemed as if he'd just dozed off when the lights went on and he heard the clang of the steel door.

The pig-eyed woman and another guard entered. They grabbed Viktor beneath his arms and pulled him to his feet. He had been sound asleep, and was startled and confused and resisted them. They slapped him awake, and dragged him out of the cell.

The door slammed loudly.

Andrew flinched at the sound. He sat on the mattress, stunned,

and huddled against the cold, watching his breath rising in front
of his face.

Valery Gorodin was in an office down the corridor. He stood
at a window that overlooked a barren field.

"I'm wasting my time," Viktor announced as he entered. His
voice had an edge that Andrew never heard. The vulnerability
was gone from his face, and he stood tall with military bearing.

The pig-eyed guard was right behind him. She helped him into
his police greatcoat to warm him, and handed him a mug of
steaming coffee.

"You're sure?" Gorodin asked.

"Positive. I tried every angle," Viktor replied disgusted.
"He's very cautious. He danced around any reference to dissidents, or refuseniks, no matter how I came at him."

"Then, we were right," Gorodin said thoughtfully. He had
assumed Andrew's contact would most likely be someone on the
dissatisfied fringes of Soviet society. It was always that way in
such cases.

"Definitely," Viktor said. "But he'll never divulge who. I see
no reason for me to spend another second in that meat locker
with him."

"Nor do I," Gorodin replied. "You think he'll make the
call?"

"Oh yes," he said, smiling. "He hesitated when I asked, and
felt quite guilty about it."

"Good," Gorodin said. "Then we'll simply resume our original plan." He looked to the pig-eyed guard, and said, "Release
him."

The hard-packed woman left the office and took Andrew from
his cell to the interrogation room. He had no idea why, until she
returned his shoulder bag, and said, "Pay your fine, and you're
free to go."

"Fine?"

"It covers the cost of food and lodging. One hundred dollars,
American."

Andrew winced, and gave her the cash.

She pocketed it—in a way which told him she would keep it—
and led him outside to the Zhiguli.

"This is a new day," she said. "Remember, no more than five hundred kilometers."

"Oh, don't worry," Andrew replied. "You made the point painfully clear."

He got behind the wheel, started the engine, and roared off, thinking about Mordechai Stvinov and the package of drawings, and getting the hell out of Russia as soon as possible.

But he drove cautiously, glancing often at the rearview mirror, and scrupulously observing the 60 km speed limit. The whomp of a helicopter rose above the sounds of the Zhiguli. Andrew had been driving over an hour, and thought he'd heard it several times before. A coincidence? Were they following him? Where was it headed? Unable to spot it, he rolled down the window, grasped the side-view mirror, and, tilting it at various angles, finally found the chopper directly overhead. He decided he would ditch the car when he got to Leningrad and travel by Metro as a precaution. The city had just appeared on the horizon when it started raining.

The slick road slowed the Zhiguli's progress, but soon it was moving north on Moskovskiy, the showcase boulevard of Peter the Great's grand dream; and in the misty rain, Andrew thought Leningrad resembled one.

He turned off Moskovskiy well before reaching the heart of the city. The rain had intensified by the time he found a place to park on Dobrisky, a crooked street behind the Mir Hotel. He put on a slicker, left the car, and walked the glistening streets to the phone box Viktor had designated on the corner of Ligovskiy.

The green kiosk was unoccupied.

Andrew glanced about cautiously before entering, then lifted the receiver, pushed two kopeks into the slot, and dialed.

"Allo, kto eta?" a woman's soft voice said.

"Viktor is in Novogorod Prison," Andrew said slowly, envisioning a young, vulnerable woman relieved to know her husband was at least alive. "He's doing okay." He hung up, wondering how families like Viktor's don't lose hope. He had no idea Viktor was KGB, and the number was an extension at local headquarters. Nor, despite his precaution, did Andrew see the two men in black raincoats and fedoras who had staked out the

phone box, and followed him through Victory Park to the Metro
station on Moskovskiy.

Andrew took the Red Line to the Nevskiy Prospekt station,
transferring to the Blue for Vasil'yevskiy Island, the large delta
at the mouth of the Neva which flows around it to the Gulf of
Finland. It was late afternoon when the train came through the
tunnel beneath the river and stopped at the station on Sredniy
Prospekt. Andrew climbed the steps to the street. The rain had
settled into a steady drizzle. He took the typed page from his
wallet and checked Mordechai Stvinov's address. Deyneka Street
was on the waterfront. He jammed his fists into the pockets of his
slicker and headed west on Sredniy.

Shops were closing, and the streets were desolate. There was
little activity around the warehouses and piers when he arrived.
An icy wind came off the water in noisy gusts that answered the
moan of boat horns.

Dusk was falling.

Andrew walked between fog-shrouded buildings, ripe with the
stench of urine and creosote, until he found Number 37. It was a
weathered three-story hulk, made of brick and corrugated steel.
He glanced at the entrance but kept walking in order to famil-
iarize himself with the building and surrounding area.

A few miles away, refusenik Mordechai Stvinov came out of
the Frunze Naval College on Liniya, where he worked as a math
tutor. Several years ago, he had given up his position as a maritime engineer with the Naval Ministry, distancing himself from
so called state secrets in the hope of eventually being allowed to
emigrate.

Mordechai went to a bicycle that leaned against the fence. It
was an old three-speed model, with heavy frame and thick tires.
He slipped a metal clip around his ankle to keep his trousers out
of the chain, and was unlocking the bike when a colleague approached.

"Why do you lock what no one in their right mind would
steal?" the fellow teased.

Mordechai chuckled, then rode off in the rain, heading west
along the Neva as he did every night on his way home. His
square, confident face had once been handsome; but now it was
heavily lined and sagged, and his eyes were watery, and his hair

had turned almost white, and he appeared older than his fifty-six years.

Twenty minutes later he was hauling the bike up the two flights of stairs to his flat, a dingy one-room affair with sleeping alcove and bath. Mordechai turned on the light and shut the door with a shoulder. The ceiling had leaked, and there was a small puddle on the floor. He leaned the bike against the wall and removed his raincoat, fetching a towel to mop up the water. That's when he noticed the sheet of paper that had been slipped beneath the door. It bore the damp imprint of the bicycle tire. Mordechai unfolded it. The repeatedly typed call to action told him the note was from Raina.

A sharp tapping on the window directed Mordechai's attention to a figure crouching on the fire escape in the darkness. Mordechai hurried to the rain-spattered window; but before opening it, he stared at Andrew, and put a finger to his mouth, warning him not to speak.

Andrew nodded he understood.

Mordechai let Andrew into the flat, then went directly to the kitchen table. A menorah that held a few burned-down candles stood on the chipped porcelain top. A tiny Israeli flag was stuck into one of the empty holders. Mordechai removed the utensil drawer, reached into the vacated space, and came out with a Magic Slate—a red-framed, gray letter-sized board covered with a clear plastic sheet. One writes with a wooden stylus on the sheet, which is then peeled up from the backing, to erase the words—instantly. Magic Slates are made for children, but in the Soviet Union they are used by those who know their apartments have been bugged, or might be raided, by the KGB.

Mordechai had more than one stylus.

"Who are you?" he wrote on the slate in Russian.

Andrew looked at it, shook his head from side to side, and wrote—"English?"

"Fine. Who are you?"

"Andrew Churcher. Theodor was my father."

Mordechai studied him for a moment, and nodded knowingly, then wrote—"What do you want?"

"Drawings of the tanker."

Mordechai's eyes widened apprehensively. He brusquely

peeled up the plastic sheet, clearing the slate. Then wrote—
"Again? Why?!!"

"KGB killed my father and took the others."

Mordechai became saddened, then concerned. "And Raina?"

"She's okay. Says hello. She said you could get the drawings
for me."

Mordechai considered the request for a moment, nodded resolutely, and wrote—"You have a car?"

Andrew nodded.

Mordechai wrote—"Tomorrow 5:15 A.M., exactly. Go to Service Station Number 3 on Novaya Drevnya. Ask for *Lev*. Tell
him your spare tire needs repair. He'll put the drawings under the
carpet in the trunk."

Andrew studied the information, then nodded, indicating he
had it memorized.

Mordechai peeled up the sheet slowly, listening to the chattering sound of the plastic and watching the words vanish, then
wrote—"Be careful. One mistake, and I'll never get out."

Andrew nodded solemnly, shook Mordechai's hand, and
mouthed, "Thank you." Then he zipped his slicker, went out the
window, and started down the fire escape.

Mordechai closed the window behind Andrew and returned to
the table. He concealed the Magic Slate, then sorted through the
contents of the utensil drawer. It held the usual assortment of
string, rubber bands, bottle caps, nails, and screws, loose among
a few hand tools. He pinched a large carpet tack between thumb
and forefinger and put it in the pocket of his raincoat.

Andrew came off the fire escape into an alley, and headed
toward the rainy waterfront streets.

Patient men with faces of stone were watching from hiding
places in the alley, atop the roofs, and on the piers, water drip-
ping from the brims of their fedoras.

Chapter Forty-five

Earlier that day, a U.S. Air Force 707 arrived at Geneva's Cointrin Airport at 11:05 A.M. Phil Keating bounded down the ramp to a waiting limousine, thinking about how he was going to stall the Russians.

Twenty minutes later, the stretched Lincoln—Stars and Stripes fluttering on either side of the distinctive grille—was speeding along Quai Mont Blanc on the western shore of Lake Geneva. It turned into the drive of the Beau Rivage Hotel, and stopped at the canopied entrance.

Gisela Pomerantz came from the lobby on the arm of a uniformed doorman, who escorted her to the car. She got in and the limousine pulled away, heading for United Nations Plaza.

"Sorry I wasn't here when you called," Pomerantz said as she settled next to Keating.

"No problem. Something important I wanted to cover in regard to our conversation the other evening."

"Indeed, we had several, Philip," she replied demurely. "So, I'm not sure how I should take that."

"As Germany's minister for strategic deployment," he replied forthrightly, taking a long drag on his cigarette before softening his tone, and adding, "though there's a part of me that wishes it could be otherwise."

"A part of me, too," she replied wistfully. "What's on your mind?"

"Your position on disarmament. You see, in light of recent developments, I've suggested to the President that a more forceful presentation of your policies would be in the best inter-

ests of the United States. And despite his earlier reservations,
I'm pleased to report, he was in full accord.''

Pomerantz looked at him like he'd gone south.

"Gisela," he went on, "I need to buy some time to close the
loop on this *Heron* thing. The problem is, the President can't
stall at this juncture without losing face, especially if it turns out
to be nothing.''

"But a hard-liner can.''

"Precisely. I hasten to add, this afternoon's session would be
a perfect time to unpack some of that baggage—''

"—And sprinkle a little hawk guano on the bargaining table,''
she said, understanding.

"A *little*," he said in a friendly warning. "I've worked out a
scenario I think you'll find acceptable.''

Pomerantz raised a brow and thought about it for a moment,
then broke into an intrigued smile.

Less than a mile away, a gray Mercedes 600 came down Avenue de la Paix, and drove through Ariana Park to the United
Nations Palace.

A horde of reporters and TV camera crews descended on the
Mercedes as it came to a stop at the entrance. Soviet Disarmament Negotiator Mikhail Pykonen got out, clearly pleased by
their presence. He knew what was on their minds, and he wanted
to talk about it.

"Is Moscow upset that Minister Deschin's letter to President
Hilliard was leaked to the press?''

"It was a private communiqué," he replied in Russian, an
aide translating. "My government assumed it would remain so.''

"Are you suggesting Washington is responsible?''

"I suggest you draw your own conclusions.''

"Why would *they* do so, when it puts them under additional
pressure?''

"It puts us all under pressure.''

"Have you received a response?''

"No.''

"When do you think one will be forthcoming?''

"I believe my American counterpart is more qualified to answer that than I," Pykonen replied, nodding to an approaching
limousine.

The heads and cameras turned to see the stretched Lincoln pulling to a stop. The correspondents ran toward it, leaving Pykonen and his group behind.

The wily Russian smiled and went inside.

Phil Keating scowled when he saw the faces and cameras peering through the windows of the limousine.

"Not a word," he said to Pomerantz as they stepped out of the limousine into a barrage of questions about Deschin's communiqué and President Hilliard's response.

"No comment," Keating said tersely. He repeated it several times and ushered Pomerantz through the crush of reporters into the United Nations Palace.

Inside, the delegates took their places at the long table beneath the crystal chandeliers.

Pykonen stood and held up a briefing paper which he'd distributed previously.

"Due to recent interludes, I'm sure you've had ample time to evaluate my government's proposal," he said. "On resumption, I officially confirm the Supreme Soviet's commitment to the points outlined herein, and to the spirit of our communiqué to President Hilliard. I eagerly await the President's response." He nodded to Keating and took his seat.

"I have a response for you, sir," Keating said, removing some papers from his attaché. "One which I'm sure you'll find in that same spirit. One which—"

"Pardon me, Mr. Keating," Pomerantz interrupted. "Though my government is in accord on objectives, I'm forced to remind the delegates that we differ strongly on how to achieve them. Chancellor Liebler is quite concerned that sudden withdrawal of the nuclear security blanket which has swaddled western Europe for so long might create a climate of mistrust. We believe a weaning, if you will, would better insure adherence to disarmament once achieved. To that end, the Republic of Germany proposes a five-part pullback. Phase one—a global limit of four hundred warheads be placed on intermediate range weapons systems."

Keating played along, squirming impatiently in his chair as she enumerated.

"One hundred per side deployed within range of Europe; the

remainder on home territory—one hundred on Soviet soil, a like number in the continental United States. Phase two—"

"—If I may, Minister Pomerantz," Pykonen interrupted. "I find your lack of faith disturbing and unfounded, and would like to know if the other delegates share it?"

"I have no objection to that," Pomerantz replied as she and Keating had planned. They knew what she would be advocating was sane policy, but they had no delusions Pykonen would accept it.

"Good," Pykonen said. "I suggest we vote on my government's proposal *now*, as a way of making that determination."

A favorable rumble rose from the delegates.

Keating anticipated the move. He would have done the same if their positions had been reversed. Now, if the rest of the hand played out as he expected, he was quite certain Pomerantz had just bought him a day.

"In that case, gentlemen," Pomerantz said, "I ask that the vote be held off until tomorrow. That will allow me to finish my presentation, thereby giving you a valuable basis of comparison."

"I'm not at all pleased at the prospect of a delay," Keating said, feigning he was upset.

"Nor am I, but it *is* a reasonable request," one of the delegates chimed in, going on to solicit agreement from the others.

"All right," Pykonen said wearily. "But I propose that we vote without discussion tomorrow, to avoid any further delays. Agreed?"

"Agreed," Pomerantz said.

"Agreed," Keating echoed grudgingly, supressing a smile.

Chapter Forty-six

It was 4:30 A.M. Monday, in Leningrad. The rain had stopped, but the fog still hung between the piers and warehouses. Mordechai Stvinov wheeled his bike from the vestibule of the run-down building where he lived. He pedaled to the corner and turned north on Sredniy.

When he was out of sight, three men came from the doorways and darkness where they'd been waiting. One fetched a Volga from an abandoned warehouse across the street. The others got in, and headlights out, the black sedan cruised slowly after the bicycle.

On leaving Mordechai's flat the prior evening, Andrew took the Metro back to Dobrisky, the secluded street in the southeastern quarter where he'd parked the Zhiguli. He slept uneasily in the backseat for about five hours. On waking, he walked to the Mir Hotel and had a cup of coffee in the snack bar. Then he returned to the car and headed for Service Station Number 3 on Novaya Drevnya Street.

Mordechai left Vasil'yevskiy Island, crossing the Tuchkov Bridge to the Kirov Islands, which make up the northwestern section of the city. He pedaled the length of Bolshoy Prospekt and onto the arched bridge at the end of Kirovskiy. He coasted down the far side to Novaya Drevnya, and was about two blocks from the service station, when he pulled the bike to the curb and dismounted. He reached into his pocket, then winced and withdrew his hand suddenly. The carpet tack he sought was sticking into the tip of his finger. He removed it, and sucked the dot of blood, then bent to the rear tire of the bicycle and pushed the

tack into the rubber. The air rushed from the puncture with a
rapid hiss.

Mordechai was crouching to the tire when the black Volga
cruised past behind him and turned right at the corner. He didn't
notice it. As soon as the tire was flat, he began walking the bike
along the curb.

Like all service stations in Russia, Leningrad Number 3 is
state-operated, and open round-the-clock. Things were quiet at
this hour, but drivers would soon be tanking up for the work-
week. Four attendants were readying the pumps. A fifth stood
beneath a hydraulic lift, draining the oil from an old Moskvitch.

Lev Abelson, a diminutive birdlike man of fifty, was the boss.
He was sitting at a desk in the office next to the service bays
reviewing repair orders. It was 5:02 A.M. and still dark when he
glanced out the window to see Mordechai walking the bike toward the office.

"Mordechai," Lev said as he came out the door. "The only
time you come to see me is when you have a flat." He crouched
to the bike and spun the rear tire until he found the tack, then
circled it with yellow chalk. He pulled it from the tread, caught
Mordechai's eye, and asked, "Same tire as last time, isn't it?"

"Yes," Mordechai replied, and holding Lev's look, added,
"and the seat's come loose again too. Maybe you can tighten it
for me while you're at it."

Lev nodded knowingly. "Sure. You want to wait?"

"I can't. I have to get to work." Mordechai said. "A friend
will pick it up soon. His car has a spare tire that needs to be
fixed."

"He can come anytime," Lev said with a little smile. "I'll
have it ready."

Mordechai waved and headed off.

Lev rolled the bike through the office into a back room where
auto parts were stored, and latched the door. He took a wrench
from a pocket in the leg of his coveralls, loosened the nut beneath the bicycle's seat, and started twisting and pulling upward
to remove it.

Mordechai was crossing Novaya Drevnya when he saw two
black Volgas and a police van come out of the darkness at high-
speed and converge on the service station. One of the Volgas

veered in his direction. Mordechai started to run, cutting between
two apartment buildings toward a footpath that paralleled the
river.

The Volga screeched to a stop. Three KGB men got out. Two
went after Mordechai. The third ran to the station, joining four
uniformed policemen who piled out of the van. They began
rounding up the attendants, using truncheons to subdue those
who protested.

Gorodin and another KGB agent got out of the second Volga,
and strode quickly toward the office.

In the storeroom, Lev had just removed the bicycle seat. The
end of a plastic bag—that had been twisted and wrapped with
clear tape, causing it to resemble the wick of a huge candle—
was sticking up out of the tubular frame. Lev grasped it, and
pulled slowly upward.

The plastic bag contained drawings of the tanker *VLCC Kira*—
the ones that delineated the modifications in the bow area. They
had been duplicated on 2.5 mil tracing mylar, tightly rolled,
wrapped in protective plastic, and slipped down into the section
of tubular frame beneath the seat. They'd been there for years.

Lev was pulling the long, thin cylinder of drawings from the
frame when Gorodin tried the knob, then kicked open the door to
the storeroom. Lev bolted for another door that led to the work
bays.

Gorodin lunged and got a handful of his coveralls. He spun
Lev around, and backhanded him a shot that sent him reeling
toward the KGB agent who was standing in the doorway. The
agent sidestepped, drove a fist into Lev's midsection, doubling
him over, then put a foot into his rump and booted him out the
door.

Gorodin crossed to the bike, pulled the roll of *Kira* drawings
from the frame, and smiled.

It was exactly 5:14 A.M. when the Zhiguli turned into Novaya
Drevnya and approached Service Station Number 3. Andrew saw
the attendants being herded into the police van by the uniformed
officers. He fought the impulse to hit the brakes and make a
screeching U-turn and, instead, drove past the service station in-
conspicuously.

The doors of the crowded Metro car were just closing as Mor-

dechai slipped between them. Despite his appearance, decades of
bike riding had kept him fit. He had sprinted along the river,
through a grove of trees, and down a staircase to the Metro station on Vyborgskaya, losing his KGB pursuers in the morning
rush hour crowds. But he had no doubt he'd be arrested before
the day was out. He knew he'd never be allowed to leave Russia
now, and would soon be suffering the frigid inhumanities of the
Gulag. He decided there was one thing he had to do before the
KGB tracked him down.

Andrew hadn't seen Mordechai, and didn't know he'd almost
been captured—how the drawings would get to the service station wasn't something they'd discussed. Andrew's first thought
was to warn Mordechai the KGB was onto him. He headed for
his flat in the Zhiguli.

About five minutes later, Gorodin and two of the KGB agents
left Service Station Number 3 for the same destination—a frustrating drive through Leningrad's interwoven maze of streets and
canals where traffic is funneled across countless bridges, and is
often snarled. It took Andrew an hour in the Zhiguli to make the
same trip that took Mordechai fifteen minutes on the Metro.

Andrew parked right in front of the waterfront building and
went in the main entrance. There was no need to climb fire es-
capes, and enter through windows now; the KGB knew everything. There was nothing to hide. Andrew dashed up the stairs,
ran down the corridor to Mordechai's flat, and rapped on the
door.

"Mordechai? Mordechai, you in there?"

He tried the knob. The door opened, and he entered the darkened flat, not closing it.

Light spilled into the sleeping alcove through the bathroom
door, which was slightly ajar.

"Mordechai?"

Andrew crossed the room and pushed through the door.

"Hey, Morde—" he bit off the sentence and looked away re-
pulsed. Mordechai was slumped in the bathtub. His left arm hung
over the side, hand resting on the floor, fingers splayed lifelessly
in a massive pool of blood. Andrew backed away and closed the
door. He was swallowing hard to keep from retching when he
heard footsteps coming down the corridor toward the flat. The

KGB hadn't wasted a minute, he thought. He started for the window on the far side of the room.

A shadow darted into the flat from the corridor.

Andrew realized he'd never make the window, and ducked behind the half open door.

A large man in a raincoat entered.

Andrew moved swiftly in the darkness, grasped the back of his neck, and spun him hard, face first, into the wall behind the door. The man bounced off the plaster. Andrew grasped his throat, and was about to bash a fist into his face when the lights came on.

Andrew flinched and pulled the punch, startled to discover he was face-to-face with McKendrick.

"Ed!" Andrew exclaimed.

"Drew!" McKendrick growled, tugging on Andrew's hand that was still clutching his throat.

"Are you all right?" Andrew asked, removing it and backing off a step.

McKendrick nodded, rubbing his neck.

"I'm sorry," Andrew went on. "I thought you were the KGB. I just had a—" Andrew let it trail off, suddenly struck by the fact that the lights had come on. He swung a curious glance to the fixture overhead, then to the switch next to the door behind him. His head snapped around, and he gasped, recoiling in shock at what he saw in the doorway.

"Hello, son," Theodor Churcher said with a weary smile. His left arm had been amputated below the elbow, and the sleeve of his coat hung limply and flat against his side. He looked gaunt and tired; but his eyes still sparkled, and he was very much alive.

Andrew was traumatized. In the last hour, his emotions had been battered and wrenched beyond words. He stared at his father, feeling ecstatic that he was alive and angered at the agony he'd been through unnecessarily. He had no thought of embracing him.

"God," Andrew finally rasped in a whisper. "What happened to you? How'd you get here?"

"Getting here was the easiest part," Churcher replied. "We flew into Helsinki, and trained in this morning. The rest is a little more complicated."

"I'll bet it is," Andrew said sharply, working to control the anger and hurt that had been building since Raina had confirmed his father's collaboration with the Soviets.

"What's that mean?" Churcher challenged.

"It means I know what you did," Andrew replied evenly. "And I want to know why?"

Churcher's face reddened at the remark.

"Hold on," McKendrick said, reaching out to calm him and prevent the confrontation from escalating. Then, shifting his look to Andrew, he asked, "Didn't you just come at me thinking I was KGB?"

"That's right," Andrew replied, realizing he'd been so stunned by his father's appearance he'd lost his edge. "We'll have to talk someplace else," he concluded in a commanding tone to signify he intended to pursue the matter. He led the way as they hurried from the flat, got into the Zhiguli, and drove off.

Moments later, Gorodin and the KGB agents arrived. Gorodin stared at Mordechai's body in the bathtub, and smiled. He had the *Kira* drawings, their source was dead, and SLOW BURN had been preserved. He went to KGB headquarters and called Deschin. When informed he wasn't available, Gorodin left a top secret message for immediate dispatch, then headed for the airport.

Andrew had driven several miles along the waterfront and pulled the Zhiguli into an abandoned pier. It was a vast structure of rotting timbers and rusting steel sheet. McKendrick remained at the car, keeping watch on the entrance, while father and son walked amidst the discarded packing crates and litter, Churcher telling of his confrontation with Deschin in the submarine, and explaining how he'd survived.

"You still didn't answer my question," Andrew replied when he'd finished.

"No time for that," Churcher said with finality, expecting his tone would dismiss Andrew, as it always had. "If we're going to beat these Russian sons of bitches, we've got to get our hands on that package of drawings, fast. Ed tells me you've been chasing it."

"That's right—" Andrew replied, fighting to overcome a life-

time of conditioning that was now prompting him to back away
from the matter of his father's treason.

"And—"

"The KGB showed up."

"Damn. What about Mordechai? I was counting on him to get
us another set."

"He's dead," Andrew said flatly. Then getting back to what
was on his mind, but no longer able to confront his father directly, he prodded, "The only way you'll beat the Russians now,
Dad, is by coming forward with the truth."

Churcher's eyes narrowed.

"What are you talking about?" he asked warily.

"Your deal with Aleksei Deschin. It doesn't take a genius to
figure out it's connected to what's going on in Geneva. But
you're the only one who knows the details."

"Right—on both counts," Churcher said. "The Russians
could come away with all the marbles. And I'm the only one
who knows how."

"Then, call Jake Boulton and fill him in."

"You and I have our wires crossed, boy. I'm not out to even
the score in Geneva. I'm out to settle one with Aleksei. He got
what he wanted, but *I* didn't. Like I said, I called him on it, and
he tried to kill me. Those drawings are the only way to tighten
the screws and force him to pay what he owes."

"The paintings—" Andrew said incredulously.

"Right," Churcher went on. "And once I have them, and his
people have things in Geneva right where they want them—" he
paused, and brightened savoring the thought "—*then*, I'll send
Jake the drawings to make Aleksei pay for *this*." He raised his
left arm and shook the stump angrily.

"But not otherwise."

"That's right."

Andrew couldn't believe that his father had no intention of
righting the wrong.

"It really bothers you, doesn't it?" Churcher asked.

"Yes. It bothers me a lot," Andrew replied, the feelings of
anger and betrayal intensifying, supplying the courage that had
deserted him earlier. He looked his father square in the eye and

asked, "How would *you* feel if you found out your father was a traitor?"

Churcher's eyes flared. "Don't you dare stand in judgment of me!" he exploded. His voice echoed in the empty structure as he whirled and began walking away.

"Why not?" Andrew challenged, pursuing him, no longer able to contain his outrage. "I don't hear you denying it! How could you do it? How?"

"You know how many nuclear weapons we have?" Churcher retorted. "And how many *they* have?"

"That's not the point!"

"Between us, we could blow this planet to bits a hundred times over," Churcher went on. "What the hell's another dozen or two?"

"Dad—You sold out your country!"

"Bull!" Churcher said, stung by the truth and trying to conceal it. "I don't have to take this! Who the hell do you think you are anyway?"

"I'm your *son*!" Andrew said, his voice trembling with emotion. "I believed in you. Defended you. Do you have any idea what it's like to look up to someone all your life, to try to emulate him, and then—"

"You did a lousy job," Churcher snapped cruelly.

"I did my *best*," Andrew replied. "And I'd always felt ashamed because I thought I'd failed. Now, I'm ashamed for trying. All these years you held yourself up as an example—Theodor Scoville Churcher: model citizen, champion of free enterprise, war hero."

"All true."

"All *lies*! You were working for the Russians!"

"I was working for myself!"

"It was wrong! Dead wrong, and you know it! Why don't you admit it?"

"Maybe it was," Churcher mumbled defensively.

"And do something about it?" Andrew continued, not hearing him.

"I said I was wrong, dammit!" Churcher shouted. "I shouldn't have done it!"

Andrew was taken back more by the admission than the volume. He studied Churcher's face as they glared at each other. Despite the anger, there was a pathetic blankness in his father's eyes now, and his skin had a gray, waxen pallor. The old coot *looked* old, Andrew thought, old and exhausted.

"Why?" Andrew asked softly after a long silence. "Why'd you do it?"

"That's a tough one," Churcher replied in a subdued voice. His stamina still hadn't returned, and the angry exchange left him weary. "To tell you the truth, I've never really thought about it much."

"Well, it's time you did."

Churcher nodded, accepting, almost welcoming, the sudden and dramatic change in their roles. "I wish I could say it was misplaced ideals or something equally honorable," he began. "But it comes down to greed, I guess. Greed and power. I got used to having my way, to getting what I wanted and believing that if Theodor Churcher wanted something, it was right. But I sure as hell never set out to hurt anyone." He paused, his face softening, voice taking on a sincere timbre as he added, "I sure never wanted to hurt you, son."

"But you did, Dad. You hurt a lot of people—me—Jake—Ed—Raina—"

"You know about her—" Churcher said flatly.

"Yes, she's given up a lot to help you."

"Those bastards have her?"

"Not as of two days ago. But it's only a matter of time after what happened this morning."

Churcher didn't reply, but Andrew could see the thought of it pained him deeply. It had never occurred to him that his father had fallen in love. He'd always assumed his pride wouldn't allow it.

"I'll make amends," Churcher said in an uncharacteristically contrite tone.

Andrew nodded thoughtfully. "Start with Geneva."

"I'm sorry son, but I can't do that," Churcher replied, his lips tightening in frustration. "I've worked too long and hard to spend the rest of my life in disgrace. I want to make up for what I've done, God knows I do," he went on, anguished. "I really do. You have to believe that. But I can't just come forward. I can't. You understand?''

Andrew considered it for a long moment, stealing a glance at the sleeve that hung limply at Churcher's side. His father had been a risk taker all his life, and had always gotten away with it. And if there'd been a price to be paid, somehow it had always been paid by others—but this time it had cost *him*.

"Okay," Andrew finally said, his tone indicative of his resolve. "We'll find another way."

Churcher nodded, relieved, and settled on a packing crate. "Ed?" he called out, waving McKendrick over.

"You two okay?" McKendrick asked as he hurried toward them from the Zhiguli.

"We worked it out," Churcher said softly.

"Time to get back to business," Andrew said.

McKendrick nodded in agreement, pleased that they'd made their peace. "What do you think the KGB will do with those drawings?"

"Deliver them right into Aleksei's hands," Churcher answered. "No doubt about it."

"Any idea where he might keep them?" Andrew asked.

Churcher nodded emphatically. "His dacha in Zhukova." He laughed ironically, and added, "Truth is, I know *exactly* where. We're remarkably alike."

"I'll get them," Andrew said decisively.

"Not so fast," Churcher snapped. "For openers, the place is alarmed, and guards are posted on the grounds whenever Aleksei's in residence. I can get you around the alarm; but to have even half a chance, you'd have to know when he won't be there."

"And make sure he doesn't suddenly show up," McKendrick added pointedly.

"I can do that," Andrew said thoughtfully. "I don't want to waste time talking about it. Where in the dacha?"

"Hold it, Drew," McKendrick said. "You've been covering for me long enough. It's time I—"

"No way," Andrew interrupted. "You're not a hundred percent yet; fifty, if you're lucky. I could've mopped this place with you, and you know it. I've picked up a few things in the last six weeks. *I'm* doing this."

In the past, Andrew would have looked to Churcher for confirmation. But it was McKendrick who did it now.

Churcher studied Andrew, deciding, then he nodded. He almost smiled.

Chapter Forty-seven

That same morning in Moscow, Aleksei Deschin and the other members of the Politburo, along with government and military officials and family members, all assembled on the grounds of the Kremlin prior to burial services for the deceased Premier.

A military honor guard led the cortège through the Nikol'skiye Gate into Red Square. The group proceeded to the section of the Kremlin Wall, west of the gate, where the remains of prominent Soviet officials are entombed. Here, they joined an assembly of international representatives who were seated in front of a platform that had been constructed at the base of the Wall.

A small square of red bricks had been removed. A bronze urn that contained the Premier's ashes stood in the opening, framed in musty blackness.

Deschin was moving toward the platform to deliver the eulogy, when a courier made his way through the throng and intercepted him. He handed the cultural minister a sealed official envelope. It contained the communiqué from Gorodin, which read:

THE SHIP HAS BEEN SALVAGED

Deschin smiled and whispered a brief instruction.

The courier hurried off.

Deschin bounded up the steps to the platform. There was a spring in his step now, a confidence that had been missing since Churcher first threatened to undermine SLOW BURN. Deschin went to the podium and began extolling Kaparov's contributions to mankind and the Soviet state.

The Kremlin-watchers in the assembly were surprised. They'd expected that Nikolai Tikhonov, the acknowledged front-runner, would deliver the eulogy. What they'd seen as a forgone conclusion was suddenly open to speculation. A buzz spread through the crowd.

When Deschin finished speaking, a granite slab—the name *DMITRI KAPAROV* written in gold dimensional Cyrillic letters across it—was set into the opening in the Kremlin Wall.

Then, as tradition dictates, a signal went out through all of Moscow. And for the next five minutes, sirens wailed, factory whistles tooted, and ship and train horns blew in tribute.

Deschin stood at the podium, listening. The deafening cacophony sent a chill through him, and filled him with a sense of destiny.

Gorodin strolled brightly through Leningrad's Rzhevka Airport. The task had been completed, and Andrew's movements were no longer of interest. Other things were on his mind now. Before boarding a flight to Moscow, he went to a long-distance booth in the telegraph office and made a call—a call he didn't want to make from a KGB phone.

Pasha was sitting in the lobby of the Hotel Berlin, reading *Izvestia*, the state newspaper, when he was summoned and went to the manager's office to take Gorodin's call.

"How is our guest getting along?" Gorodin asked.

"She's spending a lot of time in her room."

"I assume that means she hasn't yet seen any of our cultural activities?"

"Only from afar. There was a death in the family, and she attended the services. I made sure she couldn't extend her condolences personally."

"Good work, Pasha," Gorodin said enthusiastically. "Who knows, she may soon have the chance."

When Aeroflot SU-1078 arrived at Vnukovo, Gorodin was met by a driver who had instructions to take him to Deschin's apartment.

The cultural minister had gone there directly from the funeral services. He was in his study, planning the strategy he would use to succeed to the premiership. It had never been his ambition.

The cultural ministry wasn't a breeding ground for Soviet Premiers. But now that it was within his grasp, he really wanted it. The perfectly timed success of SLOW BURN and the need for continuity at the helm were undeniable. And he would use them to overpower the coalition of wizened oligarches on the Politburo who had been pushing for Tikhonov's ascendancy.

Deschin rose from his desk and went to the bay window. He was deep in thought when a black Chaika circling the Square caught his eye. The sedan turned into Proyezd Serova Street, and stopped directly beneath the window. Gorodin got out carrying a long cardboard mailing tube, and hurried into the building.

"Greetings, Valery!" Deschin said ebulliently as Gorodin entered the apartment.

"Greetings, Comrade Minister," Gorodin replied, handing him the mailing tube.

Deschin smiled, and slipped on his glasses. Then he unscrewed the cap from the tube and removed the drawings, ascertaining they were, indeed, of the *Kira*.

"And the source?" he asked.

"A refusenik," Gorodin replied. "He saw the error of his ways and saved the State the cost of prosecution and imprisonment."

Deschin beamed. "I knew I could count on you, Valery. The Service is fortunate to have a man of your caliber in its ranks."

It most certainly is! Gorodin thought, forcing a smile. He'd had his fill of praise. Twenty-five years of it. Twenty-five years of breaking his balls for—Well-done, Valery! And for most of them, he'd lived in Cuba, in that island armpit, and played nursemaid to SLOW BURN. Now, he'd saved it twice in a month's time; *twice* saved the Kremlin's key national security program, and again words—but this time he was ready.

"Ah, this is a great day for Russia, comrade," Deschin concluded.

"Yes, sir. And for you, as well," Gorodin replied.

"That remains to be seen," Deschin said, assuming Gorodin was referring to the premiership. "But I *was* selected to deliver the eulogy—a good sign. Despite the long and close relationship I had with the Premier, there'd been rumors the honor would go to Tikhonov."

"I'm pleased to hear it, sir; but I had something else in mind—a personal matter."

"Personal?" Deschin replied, intrigued.

"In a manner of speaking," Gorodin said slyly. He took Melanie's letter from his pocket, and handed it to Deschin. "I mean, I realize everything must be seen in the light of the current political climate."

Deschin immediately noticed that the envelope was addressed to him, bore uncancelled stamps, and had been opened. He was removing the contents when he recognized the WWII photograph—recognized himself hugging Sarah Winslow—and froze. His fingers were cold and unsteady as they slipped the four paper-clipped items fully out of the envelope. His eyes darted to Melanie's note. The closing prior to the signature made him shudder. His heart started racing, then his face flushed and he broke out in a sweat. He took a moment to collect himself, and pulled a sleeve across his forehead. Then he read the copy of Sarah's letter. When finished, he held Melanie's picture to the light, contemplating it. "She's here," he finally said. "I saw her."

"I know," Gorodin replied.

Deschin flicked him a wary look, then he swept his eyes in a circle from Gorodin, to Melanie's picture, to her note, to Sarah's letter and WWII photograph—making an assessment of all the factors in the equation as he calculated. Then, his eyes narrowed and held Gorodin's.

Gorodin returned the look unblinkingly; and in that moment, all was communicated. Gorodin didn't have to say he had copied the documents—which he had—nor did he have to ask for what he wanted, or make threats to obtain it. They were givens, and Deschin knew it.

You blackmailing son of a bitch! Deschin thought, the anger starting to boil. A Soviet Premier with American offspring? Lenin would turn over in his tomb! The Politburo would never knowingly make such a selection. Then it occurred to him that Gorodin could have taken the information to one of his adversaries—to Tvardovskiy—and he maintained his composure, and smiled at his good fortune.

"You know, Gorodin," he said, "few men possess the

qualities necessary to handle such a delicate matter as skillfully as you have.''

"Thank you, sir.''

Deschin put an arm over Gorodin's shoulders. "You're a bachelor, aren't you, Valkasha?" he said as he directed him across the room.

"Yes, I'm afraid, I just never found the right woman,'' Gorodin replied with a shrug.

Deschin lifted a framed photograph that stood on his desk, and handed it to Gorodin. It was a print of the WWII photograph Sarah Winslow had kept on her dresser. "Even when we do,'' Deschin said wistfully, "they sometimes slip away, taking everything that matters with them.''

Gorodin nodded with understanding. "You've served the motherland unselfishly, and with such distinction, for so long, sir," he said. "You could rightfully consider the whole of the Soviet people your family.''

"Perhaps. But a man's own flesh and blood—" Deschin paused reflectively, letting the sentence trail off. Then he patted Gorodin on the back, and added more brightly, "I have no doubt our people will be equally well served by *your* rise through the ranks.''

Gorodin smiled, his long sought membership in *nomenklatura* assured. "I'll make every effort to prove worthy of your sponsorship,'' he said.

"I've no doubt of it,'' Deschin said thoughtfully. He studied him for a moment and added, "You'll begin tonight—by bringing my daughter to Zhukova.''

Chapter Forty-eight

After leaving the abandoned pier, Andrew drove his father and McKendrick to Leningrad's Finlyandskiy Station to catch the late morning train back to Helsinki. En route, Churcher familiarized Andrew with the grounds and layout of Deschin's dacha and, with McKendrick's help, worked out precisely how he would gain entry. Before getting out of the Zhiguli, Churcher took a camera from his briefcase and gave it to Andrew.

It was a simple, seventy-nine-dollar 35 mm Olympus: compact, fully automatic, built-in flash. "This might come in handy," he said. "I smuggled the drawings out in plain sight last time," he went on, grinning at the recollection. "Rolled them up with the plans of a processor we were developing for the Mining Ministry, and carried them on the plane in my hand. But I wasn't planning on being that lucky twice."

"Thanks," Andrew said, taking the camera. It was slightly larger than a pack of cigarettes, and slipped neatly into his shirt pocket.

"Go get 'em, kid," McKendrick said. He mussed Andrew's hair, got out of the car, and went to the trunk to get their bags.

Churcher remained for a moment. There was a look of pride and acceptance in his eyes Andrew had never seen before.

"Good luck, son," he said softly. "I'm with you."

Andrew nodded. "Bye, Dad. I love you."

Churcher bit a lip, popped the door, and got out.

Andrew headed for Moscow.

Churcher and McKendrick boarded the Helsinki Express and settled into their compartment. The train was still in the station when Churcher said, "I'm going to the head." He walked to the end of the car, but continued past the lavatory, went down the steps to the platform, and hurried off. The train had pulled out by the time McKendrick went looking for him. It was racing along the main spur when he completed his search and realized Churcher had left the train.

It took Andrew almost nine hours to drive to Moscow. He parked on Zhandanova Street, a short distance from the Berlin, and went directly to Melanie's room.

The time was 8:39 P.M.

She was packing.

"What's going on?" Andrew asked, baffled. It was the last thing he'd expected, and it completely changed the thrust of his approach.

"I'm leaving."

"Why?"

"I found out I'm not wanted here."

"Your father won't see you?"

She nodded forlornly, and threw an armful of clothing into the soft travel bag on the bed.

Andrew winced. He just assumed Melanie had made contact with Deschin by now.

"He said that?" he asked.

"He didn't say anything. Not a word," Melanie said with evident bitterness. "Hold this, will you?" she asked. She handed him a plastic bag and started tossing toiletries into it.

"Maybe he didn't get your letter yet?"

"I thought about that, but it's been almost a week. And I haven't been out of this room for days, so I know I didn't miss his call. He got it, Andrew. I know he did. The woman at the Embassy was right. I'm an embarrassment to him." She forced an ironic laugh at the thought of her naiveté. "I was a fool to think he'd welcome me with open arms. I romanticized the whole thing. He probably slept with every nurse he could get his grubby paws on."

She tossed a bottle of shampoo into the plastic bag, did the twist-tie, and put it in her travel bag.

"Besides," she went on, "I'm running out of money, and I can't take anymore time from my job."

"Look, you've come this far, and—"

"Right, and I've got nothing to show for it," she interrupted. "I don't know where he lives. I don't even have a phone number." She shrugged, and turned to the dresser for a few last items.

Andrew clicked on the television.

Melanie's head snapped around in reaction as he turned up the volume and crossed the room toward her.

"*I* do," he whispered.

"You?" she asked, puzzled.

Andrew nodded a little apprehensively.

"You mean you've been watching me go crazy trying to contact him, and all along you knew how?" she asked indignantly.

"No. Now, calm down, okay?" he replied. "I got the information this morning from my father."

"I thought he was dead?"

"So did I. I'm as confused as you are, believe me."

"Sure," she said sarcastically, and resumed packing.

"Melanie, it's a dangerous situation. I didn't want to get you involved."

"Now you do—"

Andrew nodded. "To make a long story short, my father made a—a deal with the Russians. Something that could really hurt the United States."

"He was involved in espionage?"

"Good a word as any," he replied, trying to hide the shame he felt. "I've been trying to get my hands on some documents that can turn it around—and your father has them."

Melanie looked at him in disbelief.

"It's important, Melanie," Andrew went on fervently. "There's a lot at stake. People have put their lives on the line to help me."

"You're asking me to risk my life?"

"I'm asking you to take your father to dinner—to the ballet, anywhere. Keep him busy for an evening, so he and his KGB watchdogs won't get in my way."

"Andrew—I just told you he won't see me."

"He will once he hears your voice."

She shook no. "I still wouldn't help you."

"Why the hell not?!"

"I had a run-in with the KGB."

"You're kidding—"

"I wish I were. They threatened to arrest me. They still might," she replied, her voice cracking. "I can't take any chances. I'm afraid."

Andrew was suddenly hearing the snap and squeak of surgical rubber, and imagined Melanie being strip-searched by the pig-eyed policewoman, or more likely her pig-eyed brother. He shuddered at the thought. "I can't say I blame you," he said, softening his tone.

She smiled, and leveled a tender gaze at him. "I like you, Andrew. I might even love you," she said, thinking of the many times she'd sworn that she would never, ever again, utter those words to a man, and of her long-standing decision to avoid love affairs, to keep her emotions walled in, as a way of insuring she'd never get hurt again.

Andrew didn't react to the remark. He didn't know how. He couldn't remember the last time anyone had said they loved him.

"I'm not sure what made me say that," Melanie continued, amazed that having done so, having allowed the wall to crack, she was now letting it crumble. "I mean, we hardly even know each other, not to mention I've got fifteen years on you."

"Fourteen," Andrew said with a warm smile.

"I guess, if I'm honest with myself," Melanie went on, "it's because lately—I've had feelings that I haven't had in years." She said the last part slowly, cautiously, then paused, and shrugged vulnerably before adding, "But I don't want to end up in Siberia, and I don't want to die. I've gotten along without my father all these years. I'll manage somehow."

She planted a light kiss on his lips, swept the travel bag off the bed, and left the room.

Andrew let out a long breath, and sat down on the bed to collect his thoughts. His concentration was broken by applause from the television, where "Let's Go Girls!"—a popular Soviet game show—was in progress. Three zaftig women from a dairy collective had been competing in a milking contest, and the winner had just raised her pail in triumph.

Melanie checked out of the Berlin, and took a taxi to Sher-emetyevo Airport.

Andrew left Melanie's room, went to a street corner phone box, and called Deschin's dacha. There was no answer. He made a beeline for the Zhiguli.

A few minutes later, a Volga pulled up in front of the Hotel Berlin. Pasha got out, hurried inside, and discovered Melanie had checked out.

She was at Sheremetyvo, in the check in line for the late evening flight to London with a connection to JFK, thinking about her father, and Andrew, and having second thoughts about leaving, when she heard a voice.

"Miss Winslow—"

Melanie turned. A chill went through her when she saw Pasha approaching. She was going to be arrested by the KGB and thrown into one of those horrible prisons! And for what? She hadn't done anything! Lucinda Bartlett's words rang in her head: "Subject to their laws! Embassy could do little to help you!" She started backing away, terrified; then, panicking, she turned and ran through the terminal toward the street.

Pasha pursued her outside to the arrivals loop.

A black Volga roared forward and screeched to a stop next to her, blocking her way. The front passenger door popped open.

Pasha caught up with Melanie and bear-hugged her toward it. She was trying to knee him in the groin when Gorodin's hands came from within the car and pulled her inside. Melanie whirled blindly, pummeling him, struggling to get free. Gorodin parried the blows, got hold of her wrists, and held them tightly until she recognized him.

"Gorodin!" she exclaimed.

"Your father wants to see you," he said, relaxing his grip when she stopped struggling.

Pasha tossed her travel bag into the backseat and got in next to her.

Gorodin tromped on the accelerator.

The Volga lurched forward and roared into the night.

*   *   *

Andrew had the Zhiguli's gas pedal to the floor, heading down
the M2 highway for Zhukova village. The paved ribbon led to a
gravel road that snaked through the estate country southwest of
Moscow. A low stone wall told him he was nearing Deschin's
estate. He killed the headlights and engine, coasting for about a
quarter mile before pulling off the road into a grove of cottonwoods. The Zhiguli rolled to a stop behind a dense thicket of
brambles that concealed it.

He slipped out of the car, went to the trunk, and removed the
jack—bumper type with shoe that ratchets on a long, notched
square tube. The L-shaped tire iron that doubled as a ratchet handle was affixed to the tube. Next, he unclipped the shoulder strap
from the snap rings of his suitcase, and hooked one of the fas-
teners into each end of the tube, making a sling. After closing the
trunk, he put an arm through the makeshift sling and, carrying
the jack against his back like a rifle, hurried off in the darkness.
The wind blew in halfhearted gusts as he came to a rise that
overlooked Deschin's dacha.

The eighteenth-century czarist mansion was surrounded by cottonwoods, and sprawled across a swale in the rolling landscape.
A fieldstone and wood facade rose in tiers beneath a steeply
sloped snow roof that had deep overhangs and numerous dormers.

The ground level was comprised of two main wings: residential—dining room, library, and study—on the left; and main-
tainence—kitchen, servants' quarters, garages, and storage
facilities—on the right. Long corridors branched off from a two-
story entrance hall connecting them. Sleeping quarters were on a
second level that spanned the lower wings.

The windows were dark, and neither cars nor guards were visible as Andrew approached.

The way in—the way around the alarm system—was via the
roof. But as his father had warned, the overhangs and steep slope
made it inaccessible from the ground. Churcher had also told him
of the big trees, and now Andrew was hurrying toward a cottonwood off to the right side of the dacha.

The huge main trunk split into three smaller ones. Andrew
climbed up into the crotch, and shinnied up the trunk closest to

the dacha. One of the limbs branched off and extended well over the roof. Andrew straddled it for a moment, catching his breath, then he grasped it with both hands and humped forward toward the dacha. He paused to snap off some twigs that were in his way, and saw headlights through the trees in the distance.

Two cars were winding along the approach road.

Andrew froze as Deschin's Chaika and a KGB Volga drove through the entrance and stopped on a graveled parking area in front of the dacha.

Deschin got out carrying the mailing tube that contained the roll of *Kira* drawings. He and Uzykin were joined by the two KGB guards who were in the Volga. Deschin gave them brief instructions, then he and Uzykin went to the dacha. Deschin tapped out a code on the keypad next to the door, deactivating the alarm system, and they entered.

Andrew was straddling the limb, thinking fast—thinking that he'd continue to the roof, hide behind the dormers until morning, and make his move after Deschin and the guards left. He watched warily as one moved off across the grounds at an easy patrol pace. Then, his eyes darted to the other, who went to a stone fireplace at the rear of the house and began tossing in kindling from a woodpile next to it.

This was no time for a cookout, Andrew reasoned, and Deschin sure didn't come all the way out here to burn garbage. *Damn!* he thought as it dawned on him, *the son of a bitch is going to burn the drawings!*

There'd be no waiting till morning, now. Unarmed, and one against six, Andrew decided that stealth rather than direct confrontation was still his best chance, and he resumed his journey.

He was about halfway to the dacha when he reached a network of thick branches that blocked his way. He pulled a leg back over the limb, and turned sideways onto his stomach. Then, hands grasping the limb like a fat gymnastics bar, he eased over headfirst until he was hanging beneath it, about twenty-five feet above the ground, and began working his way hand over hand toward the roof. He'd traveled a short distance when he spotted the patrolling guard approaching on a course that would take him between the tree and the dacha—right beneath Andrew.

Andrew adjusted the position of his hands, and swung his legs up around the limb to lessen the strain on his arms and minimize his profile.

The movement dislodged a large piece of bark.

Andrew craned his neck, and watched the curved, jagged-edged square wafting toward the ground.

It was headed right for the guard, right for a three-point landing on his head. But a little gust of wind altered its course slightly. And it fell behind him—within a millimeter of grazing the back of his raincoat—as he strolled directly beneath Andrew.

It hit the ground with a little click.

The guard paused in midstride, cocked his head curiously, and turned around.

Andrew was hanging directly above him—*like a skewered pig at a Texas barbecue,* he thought, hoping it wasn't a precursor of things to come.

That's when the guard noticed the headlights of an approaching car and, instead of looking up, started walking toward the entrance gate.

Andrew sighed, relieved. He swung his legs down from the limb, and continued hand over hand toward the dacha. He was soon hanging above it, his feet about four feet from the roof. He had planned to just drop onto it. But the house was occupied now, and he didn't want to make a thud when he landed. He realized that the limb and up-sloping roof were at converging angles, which meant the distance between them would diminish as he moved outward. So, he kept going—the limb bending slightly under his weight, the roof rising toward him—and finally, the waffled tips of his Reeboks scraped against the slate surface below. He inched a little farther, and let go, landing silently in a crouch.

The car that had gotten the guard's attention pulled through the gate and crunched to a stop on the gravel next to the other vehicles.

Andrew had made his way to the center of the dacha's roof, behind two sharply peaked dormers that concealed him. His eyes widened in amazement when first Gorodin, and then Melanie, got out of the Volga, and were ushered into the dacha by the guard.

Pasha drove off in the Volga.

The guard resumed his rounds.

Andrew crawled around to the front of one of the dormers. Two small French windows were set into the recessed facade. He slipped the blade of a pocketknife between the overlapping frames. The latch had been painted over, and it took three tries before he broke the bond and it flicked open. Despite his father's assurances that only ground floor doors and windows were alarmed, Andrew opened these with apprehension, expecting to hear the piercing shriek at any moment. But his anxiety was unfounded.

Next, he unslung the jack and set it on the roof. It wasn't part of his plan to get into the dacha, but into a locked room inside it. Placed horizontally across the door at lock level, the jack would easily bow the jambs the one half to three quarters of an inch necessary to expose the deadbolt, allowing the door to be opened. But now that the house was occupied, there'd be no using the jack, not with its noisey ratchet; once inside, he'd have to improvise. Andrew left the jack behind, and climbed into the attic without incident.

Gorodin showed Melanie to a guest room on the second level and put her suitcase on the bed. She went to a mirror, took a brush from her purse, and began running it through her hair. En route from the airport, he had informed her of Deschin's stake in the current political scene, and she was thinking about that now, thinking about *her* father becoming the Soviet Premier.

"Ready?" Gorodin asked.

She straightened her clothing, and took a moment to compose herself. "Yes," she said nervously.

"Remember," Gorodin warned, "Pasha and I are your father's friends. We share his secret. But *officially,* you're a representative from an American dance company, meeting the minister to arrange a tour."

Melanie nodded, and followed Gorodin from the room.

The guard at the stone fireplace behind the house thought he had a fair-sized blaze going. But only the paper he had stuffed beneath the wood was burning, and it soon went out. He was trying to relight it when the patrolling guard arrived.

"Give me a hand with this," the inept fire-maker said. "The minister will be out here any minute."

"I doubt it," the other replied. He broke into a salacious grin, adding, "And so would you, comrade, if you'd seen what just arrived."

"Ah, he's starting a little fire of his own."

"Precisely. I can't imagine he'll be interested in yours until she leaves."

It was a natural conclusion. The state-supplied women were dispatched here as well as to the Moscow apartment. And the guards had seen many arrive.

Gorodin showed Melanie into a large study, shutting the big wooden doors behind him as he left.

The room was ringed with chestnut wainscoting, and covered in dark floral-patterned paper. Bulky thirties furniture, and heavy draperies, gave it the gloomy feeling of Deschin's Moscow apartment.

He was sitting in a big square armchair that swallowed him. A cigarette burned in his left hand. Smoke rose into the light that came from a reading lamp. The glow grazed the side of his face, leaving his features obscured, and sent a bold shadow across the floor in front of him.

Melanie remained where Gorodin had left her, and stood unmoving until Deschin broke the electrifying stillness.

"Sit down," he said in a strong voice, gesturing to a chair opposite his.

Melanie smiled demurely, and sat on the edge of the cushion. Her eyes hid behind the rise of her cheekbones, flicking nervous glances at him.

"I hope I didn't embarrass you the other day," she said awkwardly, in a dry voice.

Deschin neither reacted nor replied, staring at her impassively for a long moment. "You couldn't," he finally said. "I didn't know who you were."

"And I was so sure that you'd gotten my letter, and were rejecting me," she said with a nervous laugh.

"It came this afternoon," he said.

"Oh—"

"What do you want?"

"Nothing," she replied defensively, unnerved by his manner. "I don't *want* anything."

"Why did you come here?"

"I was curious about you. I wanted to know what you were like."

"Then, *that's* what you want."

"I guess so. Yes."

"Why now? Why at this time?"

"I didn't know you existed until about a month ago. I found out after my mother died."

Deschin didn't expect that, and stiffened.

Melanie saw it, and regained some of her confidence. "You know, Gorodin told me what's going on. I can't believe you think I came all this way to hurt you. Why are you being so hostile?"

"You—threaten me," he replied, surprised by her directness, which pleased him. "You always have."

Melanie blinked in astonishment.

"Yes, I knew," he said before she could ask. "I always thought this day would come."

How? she wondered. "My mother's letter was never delivered. It was sealed. I opened it."

"And so did Military Intelligence," he explained. "The war was almost over, and they knew our countries wouldn't be allies much longer. When they saw my code name on the envelope, they steamed it open to examine the contents, then delivered it unsealed—a subtle way of informing me I was no longer trusted."

"You read it, sealed it, and sent it back—"

Deschin nodded.

"Why?"

"To protect myself."

"You mean professionally?"

He took a long drag on his cigarette, and shook no. "Emotionally," he replied. "I was devastated when your mother decided to leave Italy. We'd been through so much together. It took me a year to get over her. When I read the letter, when I saw what we could've had—" he paused suppressing his bitterness. "It was a way of denying it. I couldn't allow myself any expectations." His chest heaved, and he stubbed out the cigarette and pulled himself from the chair.

Melanie felt saddened, but her eyes flickered with anxiety as he circled behind her. She wasn't sure what to expect until the light caught his face, and she saw that, despite it all, he was pleased she was there.

"Gorodin told me it's been a trying quest."

"Yes, it has."

"I hope I prove worthy of it," he said, holding out a hand. She took it, and he helped her to her feet. They were about to leave when Deschin glanced to the mailing tube that was leaning against his chair. He took it, and led the way from the study.

After climbing through the dormer, Andrew had crawled across the rafters in the unfinished attic to a ceiling hatch. He eased it aside and reached through the opening into the darkness, running his hand along the ceiling. His fingers found a light fixture and tugged on the pull chain. The bare bulb came on with a loud click that made him flinch. He peered down into a utility room, where a small patch of floor was visible amidst an assortment of tools and equipment, then eased down through the opening.

Melanie and Deschin had crossed the entry hall and were walking down one of the corridors toward the maintenance wing. Deschin detoured to an alcove where a door that opened onto the rear of the dacha was located, and peered outside. The fireplace was unattended. A few lazy flames were licking at the charred stone. He snapped his fingers several times, and the guard came running.

"What's the problem?" Deschin asked in Russian.

"We thought you'd—prefer to wait, sir," the guard replied, flicking a nervous look to Melanie.

"I asked you to build a fire, comrade. I expect it to be done. Notify me when it is."

The guard nodded stiffly and hurried off.

Deschin closed the door and shook his head in disgust. "Something I'd hope to have accomplished before you arrived," he said to Melanie as they moved off down the corridor.

In the utility room, Andrew was completing his descent, taking care not to dislodge anything that would make a noise. He had barely touched down when he heard footsteps in the corridor on the other side of the door. He stood on his toes, stretched to the light fixture, and unscrewed the bulb a few turns to shut it off.

The footsteps came closer and closer.

Andrew turned the knob gingerly and opened the door a crack.

Deschin and Melanie walked right past him and turned a corner at the far end of the corridor.

Andrew slipped out of the utility room and followed. He laid back and peered around the corner, watching as they continued to a heavy wooden door.

Deschin took keys from his pocket, unlocked the door and swung it open, gesturing to Melanie to enter first.

She stepped tentatively into the darkened space.

The glimmer of a pale moon came through a wire glass skylight, silhouetting what appeared to be an immense winged insect overhead.

Deschin followed, closing and bolting the door. "You said you wanted to know me—" he said, letting the sentence trail off as he turned on the lights.

The room exploded with brilliance and color.

Picasso's incendiary "Three Women" was directly opposite the entry. A huge Calder mobile hung beneath the skylight. Each wall displayed great works of art from the Hermitage and Pushkin: Cézanne, Gauguin, Matisse, Renoir, Monet, among them. Deschin's gallery was no match for Churcher's museum, but the contents would more than hold their own—these were original works.

Melanie was stunned, as Deschin had anticipated.

"Venture about," he said with a pleased smile. "I'll be right back."

Melanie nodded, her eyes darting from the Picasso to Cézanne's "Woman in Blue" on an adjacent wall.

Deschin went to a workroom within the gallery where paintings were stored and crated. He paused in the door and stole a glance at Melanie, watching her for a moment. A proud smile tugged at the corners of his mouth. Then he entered the room, put the mailing tube on a table, and went to a cabinet. The package Gorodin had stolen from Churcher's museum was on the top shelf. Deschin put it on the table next to the mailing tube, and returned to the gallery.

Andrew was in the corridor right outside the gallery now. He pulled some crumpled rubles from his jeans, and tore the corner off one of them. Next, he wet his thumb and forefinger with saliva, rolled the paper between them, and forced the tiny spitball into the keyhole in the gallery door, then hurried back down the corridor to the utility room.

Melanie was standing in front of a Degas when Deschin rejoined her. The tiny masterpiece was from the lyrical series of ballet dancers that the Impressionist had painted near the end of his life.

Deschin looked from the painting to Melanie's splayed stance, and smiled knowingly.

"My mother danced," he said.

Melanie turned to him, her face suddenly aglow.

"Oh—" she exclaimed in a fulfilled whisper. "I always knew it came from somewhere."

"Your grandmother's name was Tatiana. Tatiana Chinovya," he said, pleased at the effect of his remark.

"Where did she dance?"

"With the Bolshoi," he said proudly.

"My God—" Melanie said, awestruck.

"In the ensemble," he added, tempering his answer but not her reaction. "When I was a child," he went on reflectively, "I would slip backstage and watch her perform. I was always so fascinated, and felt such pride."

He paused, and touched Melanie's cheek with his fingertips.

"We both have her face; but you have her fine bones, and no doubt her talent. A man couldn't ask for more in a daughter. You're all I have, you know."

Melanie's face flushed with warmth.

"Was Sarah happy?" he asked somewhat suddenly.

"Yes, I think so."

"Good," he said, trying to sound detached.

Melanie sensed his wistfulness, despite it. "But I always had the feeling her life wasn't—complete," she went on for his sake.

Deschin felt his eyes getting misty.

"Your grandfather was in the military," he said brightly to get past the moment. "He cut quite a handsome figure in his uniform. I have pictures of him—and many of your grandmother dancing."

Her expression told him he didn't have to ask if she wanted to see them. He led the way from the gallery, turned off the lights, closed the door, and inserted the key into the lock. But it wouldn't turn. He removed it, checking that he had the right one.

As Andrew had planned, the key had pushed the spitball to the rear of the keyhole. The speck of paper was only a few millimeters thick, and the key appeared to be fully inserted despite the fact that it wasn't. Nevertheless, the offset was enough to keep the key's ridges from properly engaging the pin tumblers—just enough to prevent the lock from turning.

Deschin inserted the key again, with the same result. He shrugged, assuming something in the mechanism had broken, and headed off with Melanie.

Andrew heard them pass the utility room. He waited a few moments, then slipped into the corridor and entered the gallery.

Melanie and Deschin returned to the study. He went to a desk and pressed a button on the phone, then removed a photo album from the book shelves behind him, and brought it to Melanie. They settled side by side on a sofa and began looking through the pictures.

A few moments later, Uzykin came from his quarters in response to the buzz. He opened the door to the study, waiting until Deschin beckoned before entering.

"I couldn't lock the gallery," Deschin said, giving him his keys. "See what you can do with it."

Andrew had made his way to the gallery workroom and found the package and mailing tube on the table. Heart pounding, fingers shaking, he unscrewed the cap, slipped the drawings from the tube, and flattened them on the table. He was reaching to his pocket for the camera when the lights in the gallery came on. His head snapped around at the brightness. He hurried to the workroom door and peered into the gallery.

Uzykin had opened the door, stabbed the key into the lock, and was trying to turn it. He stood on the far side of the door, which opened inward and blocked his view of the gallery. He pushed the key in and out of the lock repeatedly, twisting and jiggling it to get it to turn—and then all of a sudden it did. His machinations had mashed the spitball against the metal back plate, mushrooming the paper out, around the tip of the key; thereby allowing him to push it all the way into the cylinder, and turn it.

Andrew heard it; heard the unmistakable rotation of the tumbler and thrust of the deadbolt. He realized he was about to be locked in and was starting to feel panicky when he heard the sound again, and then again.

Uzykin was turning the key back and forth repeatedly now, watching the deadbolt go in and out to make certain it was working properly.

Andrew took the package of drawings addressed to Boulton, slipped it into his waistband against the small of his back, and hurried into the gallery. He slid along the wall, timing his steps to the sound of the lock to cover any noise.

Uzykin stopped working the key.

Andrew froze a distance from the door. The Riffian warrior of Matisse's "Moroccan In Green" stared impassively over his shoulder. Uzykin was about to close the door, and lock it. Three fast strides put Andrew directly behind it. On the fourth, he smashed the sole of his shoe into the hardwood frame. It caught Uzykin square in the face with a loud thud. He let out a groan, and went sprawling across the floor.

Andrew scooted around the door, into the corridor.

Uzykin got to his feet and staggered after him.

Andrew was hurrying down the corridor in search of the alcove where the door that led to the rear patio was located, when he heard Uzykin shouting for help.

Deschin and Melanie were in the study, looking through the photo album, when they heard the sound and exchanged uncertain glances. The gallery was in the maintenance wing at the opposite end of the dacha, and the distance and heavy wooden doors on the study had muffled Uzykin's shout.

Gorodin, however, was in the kitchen getting something to eat. *He* heard it clearly, and headed for the corridor.

Andrew had almost reached the alcove when he heard Gorodin opening the kitchen door up ahead. He reversed direction, and bounded up a flight of stairs.

Gorodin had just entered the corridor when Uzykin stumbled around the corner. "The gallery!" he gasped. "Someone was in the gallery!"

Andrew was hurrying down a second-floor corridor, opening doors in search of Melanie's room. When he saw her travel bag on the bed he knew that he'd found it. He slipped inside, took the package from his waistband, and scribbled a message across the label beneath Boulton's address.

He figured his chances of getting out of the dacha with the package were fifty-fifty, but had no hope of getting out of the country with it. His father's score with Deschin would have to go unsettled. The game in Geneva, on the other hand, could still be won—if he could get the package to the U.S. Embassy. But the KGB would have every street and entrance blanketed with agents by the time he got there. He'd never get near the place, let alone inside. Melanie would have a far better chance.

He put the package of drawings into her travel bag, pushing it down beneath the clothes, then zipped it and left the room, hurrying down the corridor.

Gorodin realized Andrew had to have taken the stairs. "Stay here," he ordered, stationing Uzykin at the base of the staircase. The only way Andrew could get out of the dacha now was by going out a window onto the roof, and Gorodin would be outside waiting for him. He ran down the corridor toward the entry hall.

Curiosity had gotten the best of Deschin. He left Melanie in the study and was crossing the entry hall, when Gorodin arrived.

"Andrew Churcher," Gorodin said sharply as he hurried past him. And that's all he had to say. Deschin blanched and took off for the gallery.

Gorodin charged out the front door into the night, calling out for the two KGB guards. The one who had been working on the fire was coming to the door to inform Deschin he had it going. Gorodin almost ran right past him. "The roof!" he said. "Look for someone on the roof!"

Andrew had slipped out a window, and was crouching behind the dormers. He spotted them, scurried across the slate surface in the opposite direction to the edge, and made the long jump to the ground in the darkness. He landed with a loud, jarring thump.

Gorodin heard it and ran toward the sound.

Andrew was coming around the corner of the dacha to the front of the grounds. Gorodin and the guard were running right toward him. He stopped suddenly, feet skidding in the gravel, and reversed direction.

The patrolling guard had been at the opposite end of the grounds when Gorodin called out. He was heading for the front of the dacha when he saw Andrew running toward the rear. He pulled his gun and settled into a two-handed stance, tracking him.

Andrew charged down the gravel driveway, legs churning, arms pumping, lungs gasping for air. He glanced back to see Gorodin and the other guard coming around the corner of the dacha behind him. There was a blaze in the fireplace now. He yanked a piece of kindling from it as he ran past.

The patrolling guard squeezed off a shot. The round whistled past Andrew's head and shattered one of the stones in the fireplace.

Andrew whirled, on the run, and tossed the flaming stick in the direction of his pursuers. It pinwheeled through the air, and landed right on target—right on the long snowy drift of cottonwood pookh that had blown against the rocks which edged the drive. The volatile fuzz ignited right in front of Gorodin and the two guards in an explosive *whoosh*. They recoiled at the brilliant flash. It had the effect of a thousand strobes, so tightly constricting their pupils that they couldn't see, and went stumbling about in the dark.

Andrew dashed headlong between the cottonwoods, across the field, and over the rise to the Zhiguli. He jumped inside, chest still heaving, hand stabbing the key at the dash, wishing he had left it in the ignition. Finally, the engine roared to life, and the car exploded from the thicket.

"After him! Hurry! Hurry!" Gorodin shouted when he heard it. The two KGB guards searched the darkness for their Volga, and took off after the Zhiguli.

Gorodin ran back into the dacha, rejoining Deschin and Uzykin. "He got away!" he exclaimed.

"With the drawings!" Deschin said angrily as they dashed down the corridor toward the study.

Melanie had gone to the window in response to the commotion

outside. She whirled, startled, as the door blasted open, and they
hurried past her to the desk.

Gorodin and Deschin each grabbed a phone, and dialed frantically.

"Traffic police!" Gorodin barked in Russian. "Fugitive alert
to all units!" he went on when the connection was made. "Andrew Churcher. American. Driving black Zhiguli, plate number
MSK6254. Apprehend at all costs!"

Deschin was on the line with Tvardovskiy. "Yes, yes, the
drawings, Sergei! He got away with the drawings!"

"You didn't destroy them?" the KGB chief angrily replied.

"I was preparing to do just that when they were taken," Deschin shouted, realizing Tvardovskiy had him on the defensive,
positioning him to take the blame. "Internal security is your responsibility, Sergei, not mine," he countered in an ominous
tone. "SLOW BURN has been jeopardized because your people
let Andrew Churcher outsmart them."

"You're forgetting there's GRU involvement here."

"Indeed, there is." Deschin exploded. "There'd be no SLOW
BURN without GRU! Maybe we should turn over internal security to them, too."

Gorodin let out a relieved breath. He'd finished his call, and
was listening to Deschin, concerned he would hold him responsible.

"It's your problem, Sergei," Deschin went on. "Get it
solved." He hung up, took a moment to settle, and crossed to
Melanie.

"This is a regrettable turn of events," he said.

"There's no need to apologize," she replied, unnerved. She
hadn't been able to understand the phone conversations, but she
heard "Churcher" mentioned repeatedly amidst the Russian, and
heard the running and the gunshot. And she could see both men
were shaken. She knew what had happened. "I think I should
leave you two alone," she concluded.

"Stay a moment," Deschin said sharply. It was a command,
not a request.

Melanie was already leaning forward in the chair to stand. She
remained that way.

"Gorodin tells me that you made the acquaintance of a young

man named Andrew Churcher," Deschin said. "Have you seen much of him?"

"No. Just a few times, casually," she replied, thinking Deschin had suddenly reverted to the distant, wary person she'd encountered earlier.

"Three times since arriving in Moscow," Gorodin said. "The most recent being this evening on his return from Leningrad. The hall attendant at the Berlin noted the time was eight forty-two."

Melanie flicked him a glance, trying to appear annoyed rather than intimidated by the surveillance.

"What did he want?" Deschin asked.

"Nothing," she replied, feigning ignorance of all Andrew had told her. "I think he was going to suggest we have dinner, but I was packing when he arrived, and I left for the airport almost immediately."

"Did he say anything to you about what he was doing here?" Deschin asked.

"Yes, he said he was buying horses."

"Indeed, many of them. Perhaps, he introduced you to other friends or acquaintances in Moscow? People he might stay with, for example?"

"No, he didn't," she replied. "Why?"

"It's not your concern. It's a government matter. Unfortunately, I must deal with it."

Melanie nodded that she understood. "Good night," she said with a nervous smile. She touched his hand awkwardly, and walked toward the door, taking the photo album with her.

Deschin watched after her for a thoughtful moment, then gestured to Uzykin that he should accompany her.

He caught up with Melanie in the corridor, ushered her through the entry hall, and up the stairs. "Let me know if there's anything you need," he said as they approached the guest room.

"Thanks. I'm sure I'll be fine," Melanie replied as she entered and closed the door. The simple pine furniture and dormered ceiling gave the room a homey feeling she hadn't noticed earlier. She moved her travel bag aside and sat on the bed, absentmindedly turning the pages of the photo album. Her eyes saw the snapshots of her grandmother dancing with the Bolshoi, but her mind kept drifting to Andrew, to thoughts of him being hunted by the KGB.

Chapter Forty-nine

At about the same time the KGB was starting its manhunt for Andrew, President Hilliard sat with Jake Boulton in the Oval Office.

"Negative, sir," Boulton reported on CIA efforts to confirm the existence of the Soviet missile base in Nicaragua. "KH-11 sat-pix are negative. High altitude SR-71 Blackbird reconnaissance, as well as low-level runs by private pilots, same result."

"What about field agents?" Hilliard prodded. "We've sent enough people down there to double the population. Not one of them came up with anything?"

"Negative, again, sir."

"Goddammit, Jake," Hilliard exploded. It wasn't only the bad news that irked him but also that Boulton had a way of maintaining an emotional detachment which the President couldn't. "Phil is out of excuses, and out of tricks!" Hilliard went on. "And we're out of time! We either have something solid when the delegates reconvene, or we've lost it all!"

He spun his chair on its pedestal in an angry gesture, then took a moment to settle himself.

"When the hell was that tanker recommissioned?" he asked impatiently.

"Twenty-six July, seventy-three."

"And we've determined *unequivocally* that she's been making the same circuit ever since?"

"Affirmative."

"How many circuits per year?"

"Four max. Average of three would be—"

"—Well," the President interrupted, an edge of sarcasm in his

369

voice, "I guess we can assume the *Kira* hasn't been ferrying the same missile around in her bow for the last fifteen years."

"Agreed."

"So the *best* scenario is that there are at least forty of them out there somewhere," the President concluded, his voice starting to rise. "Forty Soviet *Herons* aimed right down our throats! And despite all the technology and personnel at your disposal, you can't tell me where the hell they are!"

"Affirmative."

"Christ!" the President exclaimed, disgusted. He whirled, strode from the oval office, and slammed the door behind him. He didn't have to ask Cathleen to call the garage.

A low sun streamed between the trees as the President walked Arlington's hallowed fields. He stood staring at Janet Hilliard's headstone, thinking he was failing her. The thing he wanted most was slipping away, and he felt powerless to stop it.

Chapter Fifty

It was early morning in Moscow. A three-car KGB caravan raced at high speed along the M2 highway towards Zhukova village. Tvardovskiy's Chaika was in the lead.

Melanie had fallen asleep in her clothes, and awoke after a few hours of fitful rest. The dacha was quiet, and the view from her window was much like the New Hampshire countryside. She undressed, showered, and put on some makeup. She was digging through her travel bag in search of fresh clothes when her hand came upon the sharp-edged package—the package of *Kira* drawings. And across the label Andrew had hastily scrawled:

U.S. EMBASSY *NO MATTER WHAT!*

She was standing there holding the package, shocked at the import of her discovery, when she heard cars roaring onto the grounds. She went to the window, pulled back the curtain slightly, and peered out.

Tvardovskiy's Chaika and two Volgas came to fast stops on the gravel below. Men in fedoras and black raincoats began piling out of them and slamming the doors. Uzykin came from the dacha and ardently greeted Tvardovskiy, who led the stony entourage inside.

The scene struck Melanie like something out of Nazi Germany—like the Gestapo tipped off to the whereabouts of a resistance organizer. They were there for her, she thought. They'd caught Andrew, and forced him to tell them what he'd done with the package.

She latched the door and began searching frantically for someplace to hide the package. Behind the dresser? No. They'd find it. And deny as she might, who'd believe her? The window. She could throw it out the window into the bushes. They'd think Andrew had ditched it if they found it there—but not if he'd told them she had it. She was darting back and forth across the room gripped by panic when it dawned on her that the dacha was still quiet. The KGB men weren't clambering up the stairs. Their fists weren't pounding on the door. If they knew she had the package, if they were there for her, they'd have broken it down and arrested her by now. She stared at the package for a long moment, listening, and thinking of a way to minimize the risks. She put the package on the dresser and picked at the corner of the incriminating label with a fingernail to remove it. But time had firmly affixed the adhesive, and the corner broke off in a little chip. She shuddered with dismay, her mind searching for a way to camouflage it.

Downstairs, Tvardovskiy and his KGB entourage had trooped into the study, joining Deschin and Gorodin.

"We have a hijacking in progress," Tvardovskiy announced. "I think it's Churcher."

"Why?" Deschin asked.

"The plane's destination was Estonia. You recall Madame Maiskaya?"

"His father's woman, of course."

"An Estonian. We picked her up at Yaroslavl Station after she gave Churcher her car, and have been interrogating her since. She insists she has no idea where he's headed, now."

"Out of the country. Where else?"

"Then why hijack a domestic flight?"

"Because it would be impossible to elude security at Sheremetyvo and board an international one, but he could get on a domestic flight at Vnukovo undetected and—"

"Yes, yes, and turn it into an international one," Tvardovskiy interjected, understanding.

Deschin was nodding gravely when the phone rang. Tvardovskiy blocked his hand and snatched up the receiver. It was the chief of air security.

"It's Churcher," the embarrassed fellow reported.

"You're sure?"

"Yes. His name's on the manifest, and the passport control ledger, as well."

"Destination?"

"The pilot radioed he's being forced at gunpoint to divert to Helsinki. We had every international flight covered. We never thought he would—"

"Yes, I know," Tvardovskiy interrupted angrily and, turning to the others, said, "It's definitely him."

Deschin leaned across the desk and turned on the speakerbox, so all could hear the conversation.

"Does the pilot still have his weapon?" Tvardovskiy asked.

"No, that was the first thing Churcher demanded."

"What about the air marshall?"

"He was found unconscious in an airport men's room. His weapon was taken."

Deschin burned Tvardovskiy with a look, reached out, and picked up the extension.

"How many passengers aboard?" Deschin asked.

"Seventy-nine, sir."

Deschin winced and let out a long breath. "That plane must be stopped," he said.

Melanie had dressed, and was now hurriedly cutting a rectangle out of the paper sack that they'd given her at the hotel concession when she bought the stationery. An Intourist symbol, which she reasoned would give the package of drawings the appearance of having been purchased there, was centered in the rectangle. She put a dab of nail polish behind each corner, and glued it over the existing label, covering Andrew's message as well as Boulton's name and address, then put the package in her travel bag, atop the clothes, unhidden. She slipped out of the room wondering how she could leave the dacha without raising suspicion.

She had gone down the stairs and was crossing the entry hall when she heard voices at the far end of the corridor. One of the doors to the study was partially open when she arrived. She peered in.

Tvardovskiy noticed her immediately, and flicked a penetrating stare in her direction, then sent Uzykin to close the door. Uzykin's approach alerted Gorodin to Melanie's presence. "I'll

handle her," he said. He stepped into the corridor, closing the
door behind him.

"What do you want?" he asked tensely.

"I feel in the way," she replied. "I mean, maybe I should go,
and come back when he has time to see me."

"That's up to Minister Deschin," he replied. "And he can't
be interrupted now."

"Why not? What's going on?"

He eyed her for a moment, deciding, then led her down the
corridor away from the door. "Your friend Churcher hijacked a
plane," he replied.

"Oh, my God."

"He's a fool. He'll never get away with it."

"What are they going to do?"

"Intercept and destroy," he replied coldly. "The decision was
just made."

Melanie recoiled, horrified. But the initial shock was nothing
compared to the chilling realization that followed—the extreme
action had been ordered because they believed Andrew had the
package. The package in her travel bag. The dilemma was tearing her apart. Every bone in her body was prompting her to
shout, "No! No, don't! Andrew doesn't have the package! I do!
I have it!" But she heard Andrew's words and saw what he'd
written, and she knew what he wanted, and didn't.

The hijacked Antonov-10 was a regularly scheduled flight
from Moscow to Tallinn, the capital of Estonia, a major seaport
on the Gulf of Finland. The turboprop had turned onto a new
heading for Helsinki, barely fifty miles across the gulf, when two
MiG-29 Fulcrums scrambled from Ptovshak Airbase on Hiiumaa
Island, seventy-five miles due west in the Baltic. It wasn't by
chance that the Fulcrums had been selected. The tactical fighter
was the newest and fastest in the Soviet arsenal, armed with six
A-10 medium-range air-to-air missiles—three heat-seeking, three
radar homing—on two pylons under each wing, and one AA-11
under each engine duct. Only one would be needed to blow the
Antonov out of the sky.

"Target is twenty miles from international waters," ground
control reported. "It can't be allowed to leave Soviet airspace.
Rapid closure mandatory!"

"Damn!" Tvardovskiy said in response. The call from the chief of air security had come through the *Vertushka*. The Kremlin operator had patched the line into the radio transmission between the Fulcrum and ground control, and the group in the study was listening on the speakerbox.

"Projecting intercept in two minutes," the pilot of the lead Fulcrum reported as he walled his throttles.

The afterburners on the Tumansky R-33D turbofans kicked in. The MiG rocketed forward at Mach 1.8, the rapid acceleration pinning the pilot to his couch. In exactly one minute, the Fulcrum had covered thirty of the seventy-five miles to the Antonov-10.

"I have the target on High Lark," the pilot reported, tracking the Antonov on his long distance radar. "Course two-seventy at fifty-five hundred. Distance to target forty-five."

In the next minute and twenty seconds, the MiG-29 had closed to within five miles.

"I have visual contact," the pilot reported. "Target is eighty degrees to starboard."

The group in Deschin's study smiled with relief.

"Target is five kilometers from international waters," ground control reported. "Engage immediately. Repeat, engage immediately."

The pilot reached to his console and flipped a row of switches. "Weapons systems on," he reported.

"Three point five to international waters," ground control prompted. "Fire when ready."

The MiG's radar maintained a continuously updated fix on the target. The pilot was watching the floating half circles on his fire control screen. They slowly moved together to form a glowing orange ring. A green dot suddenly popped on at its center.

"Missile systems aligned; Z.G indicator is lit, warheads locked on," he reported when the dot appeared.

"One point five to international waters," came the response in an urgent tone.

No one in the study moved.

"Fire dammit, fire," Deschin prompted in a tense whisper.

The pilot positioned his thumb over the yellow button in the center of his joystick, and pressed it.

One of the AA-10 missiles dropped from the Fulcrum's starboard pylon, came to life with a *whoosh,* and left an arrow-straight trail across the morning sky.

"Heat seeker launched," the pilot reported coolly as he throttled back, putting the Fulcrum into a sharp turn to avoid the debris from the upcoming explosion.

Ten seconds later the missile darted into one of the Antonov's port side turboprops, and exploded with a loud *whomp.* The plane went careening out of control across the sky until the fuel tanks blew. Then, it came apart like a smashed toy, and fell in a rain of bodies and debris into the Gulf of Finland.

"Target is destroyed," the pilot reported.

The group in the dacha erupted with a cheer.

Melanie and Gorodin heard it in the corridor. Her shoulders sagged at the knowledge Andrew had been killed. The emptiness she felt was quickly replaced by determination—nothing was going to stop her from getting that package to the Embassy.

The doors to the study swung open, giving rise to a congratulatory rumble. Deschin, Tvardovskiy, and the KGB group, carrying their hats and raincoats, trooped out in an ebullient mood.

Tvardovskiy spotted Melanie and Gorodin, and leaned to Uzykin. "Who is that woman?"

"Her name's Miss Winslow. She's with an American dance company."

Tvardovskiy glared at Deschin with alarm. "An American?" he asked in a sharp whisper.

"Yes, we've been discussing the possibility of—"

"She goes. *Now!*"

"She's here as my guest. *I'll* be the one who decides when she leaves."

"As you've so often reminded me," Tvardovskiy said pointedly, "internal security is my responsibility. And as far as I'm concerned, there shouldn't be an American in *Moscow,* let alone in the home of a Politburo member, until the premiership is decided. She goes."

It wasn't an accident that the KGB chief failed to mention "candidate," Deschin thought as he nodded in compliance. Forcing the issue would be dangerous. A tug of war over Melanie chanced revealing her identity.

Deschin turned from Tvardovskiy and approached her. "I'm sorry, Miss Winslow," he said with formality, "but circumstances are such that I'll have to postpone our exchange. I think it would be best if you left."

"I see," Melanie replied, following his lead, and hiding her relief at the sudden ease of it. Gorodin and Pasha would drop her at the hotel, and she'd be at the Embassy in no time. "I know everyone in the company will be disappointed," she went on. "They've been looking forward to dancing for your audiences."

"I said postponed, not cancelled," he replied, catching her eye. "We've started something here, and I feel very strongly about it. I'm sure we'll find a way to continue."

"I was hoping you'd say that," she said with a smile, pleased at the hidden meaning. "I'll do everything that I can to make certain we do."

Deschin nodded knowingly.

"Thanks for everything. You've been a most gracious host," she went on.

"Get Miss Winslow's bag," Deschin said to Uzykin.

"No," she said too sharply, at the thought of him finding the package. "I'll get it."

She was turning to go when Deschin took her arm, stopping her. "It's all right," he said, dispatching Uzykin with a nod. Melanie shuddered with concern as the KGB guard hurried off. Deschin was still holding her arm. He felt the tremor run through her, then saw her hands tighten nervously into little fists. It was an odd reaction, he thought, abrupt and out of context. Something was terribly wrong. He questioned her with a look. She blinked nervously, and averted her eyes. And in that instant, in that fleeting display of vulnerability, Melanie unknowingly confirmed what Deschin suspected—*she* had the package of drawings.

Melanie forced a smile, and quickly regained her composure. Uzykin wouldn't search her travel bag, she reasoned. Why would he suspect she had the package? It was blown up along with Andrew. She glanced back to Deschin, thinking, despite their intentions, she might never see him again. There were so many questions she didn't get to ask. So much left unsaid between them. She longed to embrace him and whisper, "Good-bye, Fa-

ther.'' It was tearing her apart that she couldn't. And after his
veiled remarks, she expected to see the same longing in his eyes;
but there was only distance now—a cold, ominous stare that told
her he knew, told her she'd given herself away. Her heart
pounded in her chest as she wondered what he'd do.

Deschin was doing the same. He had to find a way to get the
package without revealing Melanie had it. To do otherwise
would mean she would be caught spying red-handed, and
charged with espionage. There'd be no explaining it away. Tvardovskiy would be ruthless. At best, she'd be sent to a KGB
prison; at worst, she'd face a firing squad.

"Ah," Deschin exclaimed, as an idea struck him. "There's
something you should take with you Miss Winslow." He started
down the corridor ahead of them and, calling back, added, "I'll
meet you all outside."

She watched with trepidation as her father hurried off. Despite
all she'd been through to find him, she'd have given anything to
be out of there now, out of Russia.

Instead, the head of the KGB had just taken her arm, and was
ushering her down the corridor behind Deschin, the group of
agents in tow.

Deschin planned to intercept Uzykin, and search Melanie's
travel bag in private. But Uzykin was already crossing the entry
hall with it when Deschin entered from the corridor.

"Put that in my car," Tvardovskiy called out from behind
them as he approached.

Melanie's heart sank at the implication.

Uzykin nodded, continued through the entry hall, and out the
door with the bag.

Deschin couldn't possibly stop him. His mind searched frantically for an alternative plan, and found one. Instead of stopping
Melanie, he'd allow her to leave, and have Gorodin intercept her
after Tvardovskiy dropped her at her hotel and was long gone.

"Where is it you are staying?" Tvardovskiy asked in clumsy
English as they joined Deschin.

"The Berlin," Melanie replied.

"Ah, I know it well."

I'll bet, Melanie thought. "But I'd prefer to go to the US
Embassy first," she went on with as nonchalant an air as she

could muster. "I have to report that we're postponing the dance exchange."

Tvardovskiy nodded agreeably.

Deschin shuddered, his mind reeling. There'd be no way to stop her at the Embassy. He'd have to wait until they left to brief Gorodin, which would make it impossible for him to get to the Embassy before they did. And even if Gorodin tailed them closely, Melanie would be out of the Chaika and inside the Embassy gates before Gorodin ever arrived.

Tvardovskiy saw the distant look in Deschin's eyes. "Aleksei?" he said.

Deschin stared at him blankly.

"You were going to get something?"

"Oh, yes, of course," Deschin replied, coming out of it. He hurried off, forced to play out his charade, agonizing over the painful decision. His country stood on the brink of unchallenged nuclear superiority, of being in the position of ultimate power it had long sought but never enjoyed, a position of being able to actually make demands on the West. And Melanie stood in the way. The only way he could save it now was by sending his daughter to jail. If he didn't, SLOW BURN would be finished and his chance at the premiership along with it.

Tvardovskiy led the group out of the dacha. Uzykin had put the bag in the Chaika's trunk. The driver closed it as they approached, then opened the rear door of the car, and gestured Melanie to enter.

Melanie didn't know what Deschin was up to, but under the circumstances she'd just as soon get the hell out of there before he reappeared. She glanced over her shoulder, dreading his return, then moved quickly to get into the Chaika when she didn't see him. She had grasped the door frame, and had one foot on the sill when Deschin's voice rang out.

"Just a minute, Miss Winslow," he said sharply as he hurried out of the dacha.

Melanie froze, and turned slowly to face him.

He approached carrying a parcel, and handed it to her. His eyes locked onto hers for what seemed like an eternity before he flicked a little glance to the Chaika's trunk. "Good luck," he said.

She forced a smile, took a deep breath, and got into the car. Tvardovskiy joined her.

The black sedan roared off.

The other KGB vehicles followed.

"Well, it's done," Gorodin said, relieved.

Deschin tightened his lips in a thin smile and watched the line of cars wind through the trees until they were out of sight.

Chapter Fifty-one

President Hilliard returned to the White House from his visit to Arlington Cemetery in a gloomy depression. That evening, he picked at a light dinner while watching a Marx Brothers movie in the White House screening room. It gave his spirits a short-lived boost. Now, he was in the Oval Office, nursing a bourbon, pondering the arms control situation.

It was 1:46 A.M. when the DCI called.

"Hello, Jake," Hilliard said wearily. "What's up?"

"Mission accomplished, sir."

"Pardon me?" Hilliard replied cautiously.

"Station chief in Moscow reports full set of drawings on *VLCC Kira* in hand. Preliminary analysis identifies deployment site."

"Geezus!" Hilliard exclaimed, the hair on the back of his neck springing to life.

A half hour ago, at 9:17 A.M. Moscow time, a Marine guard at the US Embassy ushered Melanie into the CIA station chief's office with the package addressed to Boulton. The Chief notified the DCI immediately. He ordered that the package be pouched to Helsinki. The courier departed Moscow on Aeroflot INT-842 at 10:30 A.M., arriving at the Embassy just past noon. CIA personnel set up a digitized satellite transmission to Langley. By 6:32 A.M. EST, Boulton and the President were in the Oval Office staring at photocopies of the *Kira* drawings. The highly detailed plans revealed where and how the Soviet missiles were deployed.

"Theodor—you goddamn son of a bitch," Boulton said bitterly, almost to himself.

The President nodded in agreement. "Right under our noses all along," he said awestruck.

"Deployment site is nothing short of brilliant."

"Sure as hell explains why we couldn't find them. I owe you an apology, Jake."

The following afternoon at United Nations Palace in Geneva, Soviet negotiator Mikhail Pykonen took his seat at the long table, fully convinced that the threat to SLOW BURN had been ended once and for all.

"Gentleman," Keating began, "I'm pleased to inform you that I've been authorized to accept the Pykonen Proposal in full. However, before I take that action, I have one question for my Soviet counterpart. One which Germany's deputy minister first put to President Hilliard and myself months ago."

"Please," Pykonen replied graciously, concealing contempt for what he assumed would be another delay.

Keating nodded and gestured to Pomerantz.

"Whatever happened to the *Heron*, sir?" she asked.

"The *Heron*?" Pykonen replied, trying not to sound surprised.

"That's correct. Your SS-16A," Keating replied.

"I'm quite familiar with the nomenclature, Mr. Keating. The program was discontinued fifteen years ago, as you very well know."

"In other words, the system was never deployed."

"I'd say that would be a reasonable conclusion," Pykonen said, getting irritated. "Please, Mr. Keating, spare us the pain of further stalling tactics."

"I'm forced to agree with Minister Pykonen," another delegate replied."

"Yes," said a third. "Let's get on with it, Keating. Unless you can prove what you're inferring."

"Oh, I can," Keating replied, nodding to an aide. "But I'll let you be the judge."

The doors to the meeting room opened. A large-screen television was rolled in. The aide turned it on, then put a phone on the table next to Keating. He depressed the blinking button and lifted the receiver. "Whenever you're ready," he said.

All eyes turned to the television.

A sign that read—*138*—filled the screen.

"That transmission is coming via satellite—" Keating said with a dramatic pause.

The image started zooming back, revealing an offshore pumping station—Churchco 138. The camera was mounted in a helicopter that had been on the landing pad and was slowly lifting off.

"—*live* from the Gulf of Mexico," he resumed.

The image continued widening to include the *Kira.* The supertanker was tied up at a floating offshore wharf. Massive hoses snaked over her side like huge aortas, filling her compartments with crude.

"About fifteen years ago," Keating continued, "that supertanker, the *VLCC Kira,* was reoutfitted with a unique capability in Leningrad shipyards. And now, you're going to see it in action."

Captain Rublyov was on the *Kira*'s bridge. He saw the chopper circling, but thought nothing of it. They were always buzzing around the pumping stations. But he *didn't* see the team of U.S. Navy divers who were brought in by helicopter the night before. Nor had he seen them at the far end of the massive wharf, in scuba gear and wet suits, as they slipped into the water a short time earlier. Two underwater television cameras that can virtually see in the dark were mounted on their sea sleds.

The television screen appeared to go blank for a moment. A school of pogies swam into view. The image had switched from helicopter to undersea camera.

The divers advanced toward the *Kira* on their underwater sleds.

The section of hull below the water—gradually became visible on the television screen.

The delegates gathered around it intently.

Soon, a hairline of light split the undersea darkness and began to widen. The *Kira*'s bulbous bow had cracked open on its centerline, like the halves of a gigantic mussel shell. The one-hundred-foot long sections slowly hinged apart, exposing the lower missile assembly deck—the deck which Lieutenant Jon Lowell never saw.

The *Kira* had been taking on crude for days. But missile deployment couldn't commence until her holds were at least two thirds full to insure the hull was low enough in the water to be concealed when it opened.

The water rolled up into the massive bow cavity with a tumultuous gurgling, and engulfed a missile launching tube. A Soviet SS-16A *Heron* was sealed inside.

The tube was six feet in diameter and thirty feet long. The interior launch apparatus—though fitted with a self-contained steam generator and hi-band receiver for remote activation—was identical to those used on nuclear submarines. But the exterior had been substantially reinforced, and fitted with sharp-edged planes that spiraled around it from a pointed base, giving the launch tube the look of an undersea auger—which it was. It perched at the end of a hydraulic arm, like a gargantuan dentist's drill.

The hydraulic arm was gyro-gimbaled to hold its position in the sea while it moved to the precise commands of a motion-control computer. Like a long-necked sea monster, it lowered the augered launch tube from the bowels of the ship into the water. Then it began bending at the elbow, bringing it into a vertical position beneath the *Kira*'s hull. When fully extended, it had positioned the augered tube's drill point thirty feet above the floor of the Gulf.

In a control room in the *Kira*'s bow, technicians sat at instrument consoles monitoring the deployment. The chief missile technician evaluated the data, then pressed a button initiating phase two of the operation.

The hydraulic arm began telescoping downward in response. It stopped when the drill point pressed against the surface of the continental shelf eighty feet beneath the *Kira*'s hull.

Another signal started the augered tube turning slowly. The sharp blades began drilling a cylinder into the muddy sediment that, in this area, covers the Earth's basalt mantle to depths of a hundred feet. Powerful air jets in the drill point helped loosen the ooze. High velocity vacuums on the hydraulic arm sucked up the debris to prevent it from surfacing.

Since being reoutfitted, the *Kira* had taken on crude from thirty-six Churchco offshore pumping stations. And each time, it left a *Heron* behind in the muddy sea bottom. The high concentration of metal created by the storage tanks and docking facilities was responsible for the missile base being virtually impervious to detection. The multispectral scanners and thermal and infrared sensors in KH-11 satellites would have immediately detected a concentration of metal in open sea—where there had been none before; but couldn't detect a relatively minuscule addition to the high concentration already present at a drilling or pumping station—a concentration which tended to vary widely as tankers and support vessels arrived and departed, compounding the detection problem.

The delegates watched with growing astonishment as the augered launch tube gradually screwed its way into the sea bottom. When it was fully seated, the hydraulic arm disengaged, and began retracting into the *Kira*'s hull. The launch tube's watertight hatch that explodes open on missile-launch was concealed beneath a soft mound of silt.

The delegates were aghast.

Keating let the impact register, then said, "Should one of those hatches become exposed, and be noticed—by maintenance divers for, example—*this* covered it." He passed out copies of a Churchco memo which Boulton had procured. It was signed by Theodor Churcher, and authorized installation of underwater environmental control sensors that monitored seismic activity, and the chemical content of the seawater. The affixed specification sheet depicted a disc-shaped unit which looked exactly like a launch tube hatch.

"It's a hoax," Pykonen scoffed, gesturing to the television where the hull of the *Kira* could be seen slowly closing. "Totally lacking in credibility."

"I agree, it *is* very hard to believe," Keating replied. He exchanged smiles with Pomerantz, then leaning to the phone, said, "Quite a show, gentlemen. May we have verification now?"

Moments later, one of the Navy divers came into view. He swam toward the camera until his mask filled the television screen, then displayed a plastic-wrapped copy of the Communist party newspaper, *Pravda*.

"That's today's edition," Keating said to the delegates. He looked to Pykonen, adding, "President Hilliard thought you'd find his selection of newspapers especially appropriate under the circumstances." He didn't have to remind Pykonen that *Pravda* means truth.

Chapter Fifty-two

The front-page headline of the *International Herald Tribune* read:

SOVIET MISSILES IN GULF OF MEXICO

Beneath it was a series of underwater photographs, that had been released by the Pentagon, of the *VLCC Kira* deploying the *Heron*.

The Soviet delegation had stormed out of the talks in protest the previous afternoon. Pykonen immediately called Moscow to report the devastating news. But the Politburo was in session, debating the merits of various candidates for the premiership and it took him longer than anticipated to get through the *Vertushka*. He spent the evening on the phone with Gromyko and Dobrynin, working out the official Soviet position.

The arms control talks had been indefinitely suspended in the interim, and the following morning, Pykonen faced a swarm of reporters at Cointrin Airport, prior to his boarding a flight to Moscow.

"The Soviet Union officially and categorically denies the false accusations brought by the American delegation," Pykonen said through his interpreter.

"The evidence seems irrefutable, sir," one of the reporters prodded. "How do you account for it?"

The interpreter was still translating the question when Pykonen interrupted in English. "Soviet film experts are in agreement that state of the art special effects techniques and electronic trickery were used to create this underhanded deception," he replied angrily. "Be advised, my government has no doubt this is but another example of Washington involving Hollywood in foreign policy matters. Evidently, Mr. Keating, and those he represents, never believed that the Soviet Union would negotiate in good faith, and when suddenly faced with our sincerity and openness, they employed these purveyors of smut and violence to undermine the talks. We note this was accomplished with the assistance of the Republic of Germany, and we condemn this despicable attempt to embarrass our nation. It is most deplorable, especially at this time when the Soviet people are still mourning the tragic loss of a beloved leader.''

The Aeroflot Ilyushin 62M with Pykonen aboard had just taken off when the Politburo—stung by the loss of the nuclear superiority SLOW BURN had promised, and freed from the political constraints it had imposed—bypassed Aleksei Deschin and selected Nikolai Tikhonov as the new Premier.

A short time later, in another section of the terminal, Phil Keating entered a Lufthansa VIP lounge, carrying a bouquet of flowers.

"Good morning," he said, approaching Pomerantz, who was standing thoughtfully at one of the huge windows.

"Good morning, Philip. What beautiful flowers," she replied as she turned, and he set them in her arms.

"It's the least I can do," he replied. "We'd have never gotten onto the trail of the *Heron* if it weren't for you. You more than earned them."

"You never gave me the chance," she teased, eyeing him flirtatiously.

"I came close."

"Well, I haven't given up on you, Keating," she said spiritedly. "Though, we'll probably both be in rocking chairs by the time I pull it off."

"Don't knock it till you've tried it," Keating said with a grin. "I spent an entire weekend in a rocker once."

"And?" she asked intrigued.

"Beth got pregnant, and I spent a month in traction."

Pomerantz was laughing when the last call for her flight was announced. "That's me, Philip."

"We stung 'em pretty good, didn't we?" he said as he escorted her to the gate.

"Yes, but they always come back for more."

"I sure hope so."

"Oh, they will—and I'll be here."

"So will I."

"I have a wonderful antique rocker at home. I'll make sure I bring it along." She kissed his cheek, then turned and hurried down the boarding ramp.

All three network news programs opened with the story of Nikolai Tikhonov's ascendancy. President Hilliard leaned back in his chair thinking chances for an arms control agreement before the end of his term were nonexistent now. In light of the humiliating events in Geneva, the elderly Soviet Premier, and the older oligarches who advised him, would undoubtedly revert to cold war paranoia, and back away from disarmament. The President was in a morose mood when Boulton entered the Oval Office.

"Tikhonov—very unsteady at swearing in ceremonies," the DCI reported. "Advanced emphysema."

"Prognosis?" Hilliard asked in a hopeful tone.

"He'll be gone within a year."

"So will I," Hilliard said glumly, referring to his term. He was thinking a quick change in regimes might give him another chance for an arms control agreement.

"NATO wanted a draw," Boulton said encouragingly, seeing his disappointment. "You gave it to them."

"Not the one I wanted, Jake."

"Can't win them all, sir."

"I can try," the President said firmly.

There'd be no presidential library fund-raisers, no rush to publish memoirs after his term in office, he vowed. Not until the job was done. Not until nuclear disarmament was achieved. He'd be out of the White House, but he'd still be in the thick of it. The political wags on the Hill wouldn't have to wonder how private citizen Jim Hilliard was spending his time. Jennings would tell them on the evening news.

That afternoon, he went for a walk in Arlington. He placed

some fresh flowers at the base of his wife's headstone, and
straightened them just so.

"I'll be back," he said.

Lieutenant Jon Lowell was brought directly to CIA headquarters
at Langley for further debriefing. Boulton offered him a job during the course of it, and Lowell accepted. It wasn't a difficult
decision; flying ASW would never be the same without
Arnsbarger. Before leaving, Lowell requested a moment alone
with the DCI. Boulton knew what was on his mind. He'd been
thinking about it, too, and agreed when Lowell proposed it.

Cissy and her son were out back picking oranges when Lowell
arrived. Cissy rushed right into his arms, her eyes brimming with
tears. The kid kept a few steps distance, taking it all in with a
forlorn sadness.

"He died in the service of his country," Lowell said softly,
hugging her.

"I never believed he didn't," Cissy said, her face brightening.
"I miss him so much."

"So do I, Cissy," Lowell replied solemnly. "He gave his life
to save mine. They would have killed us both if he hadn't."

She leaned back from Lowell and stared at him for a moment,
the impact of his words registering. "He thought the world of
you, Jon."

"I'll never have another friend like him."

"You know," she began, her voice cracking with emotion,
"there's something about him just being gone like that, lost at
sea. It's so much harder to accept. I mean, every time the phone
rings I get this feeling that maybe, just maybe—" She paused,
choking up, a steady stream of tears rolling down her face.

"I know," Lowell said compassionately, running his hand
over her hair to calm her. "We talked that night. He told me he
was going to marry you," he went on, bending the truth for her
sake.

An appreciative smile brightened Cissy's sad face. She rubbed
some tears from her eyes, then looked to her son sympatheti-
cally, and put a hand on his shoulder. He lunged forward, wrapping his arms around her waist, and hugged her.

Lowell mussed his hair.

"How're you doing, tiger?"

The kid shrugged. Then, his face sort of peered out from behind Cissy's skirt and screwed up with a question, the way children's faces do before they ask them. "This mean he was a
hero?"

"Yes," Lowell replied softly, crouching down so that they
were eye to eye. "He was a hero."

Valery Gorodin's membership in *nomenklatura* was not to be.
Instead, he was assigned to Military Department 35576—the
GRU's spy school on Militia Street in Moscow. For several
weeks now, he'd been teaching the Soviet Union's best and
brightest what he knew how to do better than most—screw the
KGB. He and Pasha met at Lastochka for dinner once a week.

"How's it going?" Pasha asked.

"Boring. What makes you think this week would be any better
than last?"

"Well," Pasha replied in a tantalizing tone, "a GRU courier
handles many sensitive documents."

"And?"

"Tell me, does your first name end in *IE* or *Y*?"

"Very funny. *Y*, you know that. Why do you ask?"

"If my memory serves me correctly, I recall seeing a document this morning mentioning that the GRU rezident at our UN
Mission is being called back. It seems the poor fellow is unable
to cope with his KGB counterpart."

Gorodin leaned across the table, burning with curiosity. "You
saw the official list of candidates?"

"Of course not," Pasha replied, as if it was beneath him.
Then, eyes twinkling mischievously, he added, "I saw the official *recommendation*."

Aleksei Deschin's dream of becoming Premier ended with
SLOW BURN. He took comfort in the knowledge that it was
Tvardovskiy who drove Melanie to the U.S. Embassy that morning, and every time since then, whenever Deschin saw the KGB
chief, he smiled, savoring the irony of it.

Tvardovskiy had no inkling as to why, and always felt a per-plexing uneasiness.

A few weeks had passed when Tvardovskiy arrived at the Cultural Ministry to discuss security for an exhibition of works from the Hermitage and Pushkin museums, scheduled to tour the United States.

"Good morning, Sergei," Deschin said with the unnerving lit-tle smile.

"Aleksei," the KGB chief replied, checking his fly.

Deschin handed him a list of personnel who would travel with the exhibit, and required clearances.

Tvardovskiy perused it for a moment. "There don't seem to be any problems," he said, pausing briefly before adding, "I see you've decided to make the trip."

"Yes, the Metropolitan was adamant that I supervise the in-stallation," Deschin replied.

"Aghhh, New York is a horrid city."

"True," Deschin said philosophically, "but once you give life to something, Sergei—Well, you know how it is—" He splayed his hands, letting the sentence trail off.

In the weeks since she'd returned from Moscow, Melanie Winslow had gone back to the dance company and thrown her-self into choreographing routines with renewed vigor. Indeed, the parcel Deschin had given her contained the old photo album, and the snapshots of her grandmother dancing were the source of Melanie's inspiration.

It was a warm Saturday afternoon as she got out of a taxi in front of her building. Gramercy Park was alive with children and nannies pushing carriages. A few joggers were running laps out-side the fence.

Melanie had spent the morning at the theater and the afternoon at Bloomingdale's. She entered her lobby carrying a shopping bag, and paused to check for mail. There were a few pieces in her box. She shuffled through them and came upon a folded note.

Her heart pounded at the handwritten message.

She dashed from the building, crossing the street toward the gate at the north end of the Park. Her eyes searched for him in the spaces between the cast iron pickets as she ran. Her hand was shaking, and she could hardly get the key into the lock. She swung the gate open and, not taking the time to close it, dashed down the gravel path. He was talking to a scruffy six-year-old when she saw him. She froze in her tracks. Then she let out a joyful cry, and started running toward him.

Andrew heard the shout, and turned just as she ran into his arms. They clung to each other with crushing force. Finally, Melanie leaned back, staring at his face, as if making sure she hadn't accosted a stranger.

"It was my father," Andrew replied to the question in her eyes. "He's the one who hijacked that plane." Andrew took a deep breath, reflecting on the day he'd returned to Houston and discovered his father wasn't at Chappell Hill, as he'd expected. When McKendrick told him about Churcher leaving the train, Andrew pieced it together.

"I'm real sorry, Drew," McKendrick had said.

"Me, too," Andrew replied sadly. "But it's fitting, in its way. He would have been devastated by the disgrace—" He let the sentence trail off, and lifted a shoulder in a halfhearted shrug.

"He paid his debt, son," McKendrick said spiritedly, and, forcing past it, added, "now, as he'd say, let's get to business. Churchco's got eleven companies, seventy-two thousand employees, and no boss. You think you're up to it?"

Andrew thought for a moment and nodded. "Yes, I am," he said with a quiet determination that confirmed it. "But there's someone I have to see first."

"Ahhh," McKendrick said knowingly. "You slipped into one of those flesh-crazed madonnas after all."

Andrew smiled shyly, and shook no.

"A special one?"

"That's what I'm thinking," Andrew replied.

Melanie stood in the park, hugging the breath out of him now. "I still can't believe it," she said, tears running down her cheeks.

"Neither can I," Andrew replied. "I mean, I wouldn't be here if it wasn't for my father. He really outsmarted them," Andrew went on with a reflective smile. "He knew the Russians were certain they'd killed him, and would assume I had hijacked that plane.''

"How'd you get out of the country?''

"I drove to Helsinki. Once they thought I was dead, they stopped looking for me. Funny,'' he went on reflectively, "the last thing my father said to me was, 'Good luck, son. I'm with you.' I didn't know what he meant at the time, but now I—'' Andrew paused and shrugged, his eyes filling at the recollection. "You know,'' he resumed, trying to maintain his composure, "he wasn't the type who could let his emotions show. I mean, I don't think he ever said—ever said that he loved me. But—'' Andrew bit a lip and gently leaned his forehead against hers as the feelings welled up from deep inside.

Melanie kissed his cheek and embraced him comfortingly.

They stood in silence for a long moment, the sun dropping behind the buildings, sending long shadows across the grass.

"But he did,'' Andrew finally whispered.

"So do I,'' she said softly.